Everyone is talk ~~T0015043~~ **ll**

"When it comes to sexy rodeo cowboys, look no further than talented author Kari Lynn Dell."
— B.J. Daniels, *New York Times* bestselling author

"An extraordinarily gifted writer."
— Karen Templeton, three-time RITA Award–winning author, for *Reckless in Texas*

"Real ranchers. Real rodeo. Real romance."
— Laura Drake, RITA Award–winning author, for *Reckless in Texas*

"Look out, world! There's a new cowboy in town."
— Carolyn Brown, *New York Times* bestselling author, for *Tangled in Texas*

"Great characters, great story, and authentic right down to the bone."
— Joanne Kennedy for *Reckless in Texas*

"Dell's writing is notable, and her rodeo setting is fascinating, with characters that leap off the page and an intriguing series of actions, conflicts, and backstory elements that keep the plot moving... A sexy, engaging romance set in the captivating world of rodeo."
— *Kirkus Reviews* for *Reckless in Texas*

Also by Kari Lynn Dell

Last Chance Rodeo

Texas Rodeo
Reckless in Texas
Tangled in Texas
Tougher in Texas
Fearless in Texas
Mistletoe in Texas
Relentless in Texas

TANGLED
in TEXAS

KARI LYNN DELL

Published by Sourcebooks Casablanca, an imprint of Sourcebooks
P.O. Box 4410, Naperville, Illinois 60567-4410
(630) 961-3900
sourcebooks.com

Originally published in 2017 in the United States of America
by Sourcebooks Casablanca, an imprint of Sourcebooks

Printed and bound in the United States of America.
OPM 10 9 8 7 6 5 4 3 2 1

A special shout-out to Dr. J. Pat Evans and Don Andrews, ATC, who began what would become rodeo's Justin Sports Medicine Program. And also to my friend and mentor, Dr. Tom Weeks, and to Dr. Pepper Murray, whose name I borrowed as a placeholder for the hundreds of doctors, physical therapists, massage therapists, and athletic trainers who dedicate their time and expertise to caring for the most stubborn and independent of athletes—professional cowboys.
—Kari Lynn Dell

In memory of Kari Lynn Dell; your books will always bring us joy.

Chapter 1

DELON SANCHEZ WOKE UP PISSED OFF AT THE WORLD. No different from every other morning in the past four months. But for Delon—proud owner of the fan-voted *Best Smile in Pro Rodeo*—it was like being trapped inside someone else's skin. And that guy was turning out to be an asshole.

He made a fist and beat on his pillow, as if he could pound the dreams out of it. Those stupid, pointless dreams where he hadn't been hurt right at the end of the best rodeo season of his life and didn't feel his shot at a world title disintegrate along with the ligaments in his knee. The dreams where he went on to the National Finals Rodeo and walked away with the gold buckle, heavy and warm and so damn real he could still feel the shape of it when he woke up.

Empty-handed.

He jammed his fist into the pillow again. His subconscious was a cruel bastard and a whiner on top of it. An injury yanked the trapdoor out from under some cowboy's gold buckle dream every year. That was rodeo. Hell, that was life. Delon was no special flower that fate had singled out to trample.

He flopped onto his back. A spider sneered at him from the corner of the ceiling, lounging on its web. He was tempted to reach down, grab a boot, and fling it. The way his luck was running, he'd just miss, and it'd bounce off and blacken his eye. He stuffed his hands behind his head with a gloomy sigh. They should have drawn a chalk outline in the arena where he'd fallen, because the man who'd climbed down into the bucking chute that night was nowhere to be found.

He'd disappeared in the thirty-two seconds from the nod of his head to the moment of impact.

Thirty-two seconds.

He'd timed it on the video out of morbid curiosity. Less than a minute before the paramedics jammed a tube down his throat and reinflated the lung that'd been punctured when the horse trampled him, wiping out his knee and busting two ribs.

In that short time, his entire world had disintegrated.

Either that or it had been an illusion all along. But that was his fault. He'd let himself want too much, dream too big. Other people could reach up, grab the world by the throat, and make demands. Every time Delon tried, he got kicked in the teeth.

Whiner.

He flipped the spider the bird, kicked off the blankets, and got up. Time to dress for another of the increasingly frustrating therapy sessions that only emphasized his lack of progress. He had plateaued, his therapist kept saying, trying to make it sound like a temporary setback. And now she'd gotten married and run off—to Missouri, of all the damn places, as if there were no good men left in Texas—forcing him to absorb yet another in a barrage of unwelcome changes.

But hey, maybe this new therapist had the magic touch that would give him back his life. Or at least his career.

He slipped down the back stairs, escaping his apartment above the shop at Sanchez Trucking without seeing a soul, but had to stop at the Kwicky Mart for gas. With only two thousand people in Earnest, Texas, the face at the next pump was bound to be familiar.

And it would have to be Hank. At nineteen, the kid was a worse gossip than the old men down at the Corral Café. He hopped out of the family ranch pickup, so nimble Delon wanted to kick him. "Hey, Delon. How's the knee feelin'?"

"Fine." Delon turned his back, hunching his shoulders against the bitter January breeze as he jammed the gas nozzle into the tank of what his big brother jeeringly called his mom car. Well, screw Gil. If the elder Sanchez had paid more attention to safety ratings, he wouldn't have thrown away the brilliant, God-given talent most cowboys—including Delon—could only dream of.

Hank lounged against the side of his dad's one-ton dually while it guzzled four-dollar diesel like sweet tea. "Looks like it's gettin' pretty serious between Violet and Joe. Think they'll get married?"

Delon made a noncommittal noise and mashed

harder on the gas nozzle. Short answer? Nope. Joe Cassidy would be gone when the shine wore off, back to Oregon. Bad enough he'd leave Violet in pieces, but there'd be one brokenhearted little boy too. *Delon's* boy. Until now, Delon had just shrugged and laughed at Violet's dating disasters. She couldn't seem to help herself, so he might as well just let her get it out of her system—but she'd never brought her disasters home to their son before.

Beni worshiped Joe. So did every bull rider in the pro ranks—for good reason. As a bullfighter, Joe's job was to save them from getting stomped, and he was damn good at it. Playing the hero made him hugely popular with the buckle bunnies, and it was no secret that Joe had accepted plenty of what the rodeo groupies offered. So no. Delon didn't think Joe was the marrying kind.

A red Grand Am whipped around the corner, and the little blond Didsworth girl—Mary Kate?—distracted Hank with a smile and a finger wave. He returned it with a cocky grin. "I hear she's got a thing for bullfighters."

"Don't they all?" Delon muttered.

Even Violet. And she should know better, being a stock contractor's daughter. What was it with women, lusting after men dumb enough to throw their bodies in front of large, pissed-off farm animals? Sure, it was exciting, but the long-term career prospects were not great. *Said the guy who got a knee reconstruction for his twenty-ninth birthday.*

The girl parked down the block, climbed out of her

car, and made sure Hank and Delon were watching as she sashayed into the drugstore.

Hank gave a low whistle. "I gotta get me a piece of that."

"She's a human being, not an apple pie," Delon snapped. "And she's still in high school."

"Old enough to know what she wants." Hank turned his smirk on Delon. "And you should talk. Like you've never gone stupid for a hot blond."

Tori. The memory slammed into Delon. Another of those times he'd made a grab for something *way* out of his reach. And fallen hard. "That was a long time ago," he said stiffly.

"But you were seein' her for, what—five, six months?" Because of course there were no secrets in Earnest, and on the rare occasions that the past died, it was buried in a very shallow grave. Hank shot him a sly grin. "You never brought her around, not even to meet Miz Iris. Sounds like a booty call to me."

Delon had to choke down his fury for fear of sparking the gasoline fumes. Besides—damn it to hell—he couldn't argue.

"Can't blame you. I seen pictures." Hank made a show of wiping his brow with his sleeve. "She was *smokin'*. Melanie and Violet and Shawnee called her Cowgirl Barbie."

Tori might've looked perfect, but she was definitely not made of plastic. Delon would know. He'd examined every inch of her on multiple occasions. Had planned on doing it a whole lot more, until he'd called her that one last time.

We're sorry, the number you have reached is no longer in service...

"Too bad she wasn't the one you knocked up. Senator Patterson's daughter? Beni would be like royalty around here."

Delon slammed the nozzle back onto the pump and wheeled around, biting off a curse when pain stabbed through his busted knee. "Honest to shit, Hank, why someone hasn't strangled you yet is beyond me."

Hank gazed back in wide-eyed bafflement. "Why? What did I say?"

Only the gas pump between them stopped Delon from running the little bastard down as he drove away. He reached over to the passenger's seat, grabbed a Snickers bar, and ripped it open with his teeth, but even the blast of sugar and chocolate couldn't ward off the memories. Tori, with her long blond hair sliding like expensive satin between his grease-stained fingers and eyes as blue as her blood. Whose family spread was a Texas legend, the owners reigning as kings and queens of the Panhandle for well over a century.

Tori, who'd disappeared without so much as a *Kiss my ass, cowboy, we're through.* And *stayed* gone.

He'd been stupid enough to be surprised, even after seeing how being a rich girl's whim had worked out for his brother. Tori and Krista were stamped from the same cookie cutter, sugar-frosted temptation with glittery sprinkles on top. How could a man stop at one bite? Especially Delon, with his sweet tooth. But all he and Tori had in common was mutual lust and the fact that his father trucked loads of cattle, while Richard Patterson served on the United States Senate subcommittee with oversight of the Federal Motor Carrier Safety Administration. The Sanchezes' idea of a big night out was prime rib with all the fixin's at the Lone Steer Saloon. The Pattersons had dined at the White House on multiple occasions during the last Republican presidency.

Yeah, Delon had had a real chance there.

Sometimes he wondered if he'd been following in his brother's footsteps for so long that he couldn't help himself. Little League shortstop—check. Defensive back and punt returner on the Earnest High School football team—check. Bareback rider—check. High class, heart-breaking blond—check.

Illegitimate son—yep, check that one too.

Except Delon had done his brother one better for a change. The mother of his son was—or had been, pre-Joe—one of his best friends. Having a baby with Violet had made Delon a permanent part of the Jacobs clan, who had folded him in like he was blood-born. But Gil *had* knocked up the rich blond, and now he waged an endless war against her powerful family to be a significant part of his son's life. At least Delon didn't have to drive clear to Oklahoma to see Beni. He just had to share him with goddamn Joe Cassidy.

Delon crammed the rest of the Snickers into his mouth and punched up the playlist he'd labeled *The Hard Stuff*. The bass notes vibrated clear down into his gonads, and he thumped his fist against the steering wheel in time to the beat. He might drive a mom car, but he'd match the custom stereo system against any teenager cruising Forty-Fifth in Amarillo.

When he pulled into the parking lot at the clinic, Delon sat for a moment to delay the upcoming appointment. His new physical therapist was probably competent as hell. Panhandle Orthopedics & Rehabilitation was the best in the region—they wouldn't hire anything less. But he was so damn tired of rolling with the punches—of taking the crumbs he was given and pretending he was satisfied.

Don't kick up a fuss now, Delon. Your mother can't come visit if you're gonna throw such a fit when she leaves.

He scowled, drop-kicking that memory into the distant past as he climbed out of the car. On the worst days along the rodeo trail—beat-up, exhausted, and homesick—he'd always been able to paste on a happy face. He was the guy who could work the crowd, the sponsors, the rodeo committees, trading on the face God had given him to the tune of as much sponsorship money as some of the world champions. Now he could barely manage a smile for the receptionist.

Beth, a faded redhead with tired eyes who didn't have much luck hiding her prematurely gray roots or the hard miles that had put them there, smiled back.

She clicked a few times with her computer mouse. "Got you checked in, Delon."

"Thanks. Can I go ahead and warm up?"

She shook her head. "Tori said she wanted to do a full evaluation first thing. She'll be right out."

His heart smacked into his ribs at the name. Then he blew out a dry laugh. Geezus. He'd really let Hank get into his head. Yeah, his—no, scratch that—*the* Tori he'd known had been studying physical therapy. But a Patterson wouldn't work at a general orthopedic clinic. She'd be at a highfalutin research hospital, developing new techniques for treating Parkinson's disease, or at one of those exclusive joints in Houston or Dallas that treated pro football and basketball players.

Besides, even his luck wasn't *that* bad.

Then the waiting room door opened. A woman stood there—tallish, slender, and almost plain, wearing khakis and a white Panhandle Sports Medicine polo shirt. Her shoulder-length hair was the color of caramel. She was probably wearing makeup, but it was the kind a man never noticed. No jewelry. No glitter. No frosting of any kind on *this* Tori.

Then the voice that had whispered through his memories for almost seven years said, "Hello, Delon."

The floor tilted under his feet. He knew he was gawking, but he couldn't stop himself. She didn't smile. Didn't…anything. Her face was as blank as if they'd never shared more than a cup of coffee. She gestured toward the open door, cool as spring water. "Come on in."

She turned to lead the way without checking to see if he followed. Delon squeezed his eyes shut, taking a moment to steady himself. Here he'd been thinking his life couldn't get much more screwed up than it already was.

That'd teach him.

Chapter 2

DELON WAS STILL GORGEOUS. WHICH, OF COURSE, Tori had known. He'd been one of the top bareback riders in the country for years, and fans and sponsors alike swooned over that face, that body, and that way he had of making every person feel like he'd been waiting all day just to smile at them alone.

He wasn't smiling now.

Tori led him through the open gym space immediately adjacent to the waiting room, past patients sweating on stationary bikes, grunting painfully through sets on the weight equipment and stretches on the mat tables. She pointed Delon down the hall toward one of the four private treatment rooms. He walked with the distinctive, slightly duck-footed gait of a bareback rider who'd spent a lifetime turning his toes out to spur bucking horses. From behind, the view was spectacular, despite loose-fitting nylon warm-up pants and a plain navy blue T-shirt. His body was denser, the way men got as they matured. The changes only made him more attractive. More…there.

She'd never seen him in workout clothes. Hell, she'd

barely seen him in clothes at all, back in the day. Most of the time they'd spent together had involved the opposite of dressing for the occasion. She poked at the memory, the way her dentist poked her cheek to see if she was numb enough for him to start drilling. *Can you feel that? No? Great. We can go ahead then.*

Ah, the blessed numbness. It had settled around her like thick cotton batting, layer after layer, down the long highway between here and the Wyoming border. By the time she'd crossed into the Panhandle, she hadn't felt anything but the most basic biological urges. Eat. Drink. Pee. Sleep...well, she was working on that one.

Everything else was muted. Grief. Guilt. The gossamer thread of anger that wound through it all. She was aware of their presence, but from a safe distance. An induced coma of the heart, so it could finally rest and heal.

If anyone could penetrate her cocoon, it should have been Delon, but she had looked him straight in the eye and there was...not exactly nothing. But what she felt now was an echo from far in the murky past. Which meant her concerns about whether she could effectively function as his therapist were ungrounded, at least from her perspective. From Delon's...hard to tell, since he had yet to say a word. He hesitated at the treatment room door, as if unsure about being trapped in the confined space with her.

"Climb up on the table," she said. "I want to take some measurements."

He didn't budge. "It's all in my chart."

"I reviewed Margo's notes, but I prefer to form my own opinions." When he still didn't move, she added, "You won't be charged for the evaluation, since it's solely for my benefit."

She held her breath as he stood for a few beats, possibly debating whether to turn around, stomp back to reception, and demand to be assigned a different therapist. Being fired by a star patient wasn't quite the impression she wanted to make on her first day. Damn Pepper for insisting that she take over Delon's rehab when she transferred here, but she'd rather hang herself with a cheap rope than explain to her mentor why she shouldn't take the case.

Delon finally moved over to the table. But rather than sit on it, he braced his butt against the edge and faced her, arms and ankles crossed. The pose made all kinds of muscles jump up and beg for attention. A woman would have to be a whole lot more than numb not to notice.

"So you're back from…"

"Cheyenne," she said, filling in the blank.

He blinked. "Wyoming?"

Was there any other? Probably, but only one that mattered. "Yes. I did my outpatient clinical rotation at Pepper's place, and he hired me when I graduated."

"Pepper *Burke*?"

"Yes." Surgeon to the stars of rodeo. The man who'd performed Delon's surgery, also in Cheyenne, where

Tori had made damn sure their paths hadn't crossed. "I've worked for him since I graduated."

She watched the wheels turn behind Delon's dark eyes, connections snapping into place. Cowboys traveled from all over the United States and Canada to be treated by Pepper and his staff. "Tough place to get hired on."

"Yes." She gestured toward the table. "If you're satisfied with my credentials…"

He blinked again, then squinted as if he was seeing double, trying to line up his memory of college Tori with the woman who stood in front of him. She could have told him not to bother. She'd shed that girl, layer by superficial layer, until there was barely enough left to recognize in the mirror.

Whatever Delon saw, it convinced him to slide onto the treatment table. She started with girth measurements—calf, knee, thigh—to compare the muscle mass of his injured leg to the uninjured side. As she slid the tape around his thigh, she felt him tense. Glancing up, her gaze caught his, and for an instant, she saw it all in his eyes. The memories. The heat.

Her pulse skipped ever so slightly, echoing the hitch in his breath. Her emotions might be too anesthetized to react to his proximity, but her body remembered, and with great fondness. A trained response. No more significant than Pavlov's drooling dogs.

"Lie flat," she ordered and picked up his leg.

Halfway through the series of tests, she knew Pepper's

concern was justified. If anything, Delon's injured leg was slightly stronger than the other, testament to how hard he'd worked at his rehab. Four months post surgery, though, he should have had full range of motion. Instead, when she bent the knee, she felt as if she hit a brick wall a few degrees past ninety. She increased the pressure to see how he'd react.

"That's it," he said through gritted teeth.

Well, crap. "How does it feel when I push on it?"

"Like my kneecap is going to explode."

Double crap. She sucked in one corner of her bottom lip and chewed on it as she considered their options.

"Is there any chance it's going to get better?" His voice was quiet, but tension vibrated from every muscle in his body—for good reason. He was asking if his career might be over. It wasn't a question she could, or should, answer.

She stepped back and folded her arms. "I'll give Pepper a call. He'll want new X-rays, possibly an MRI—"

"What will an MRI tell him?" His gaze came up to meet hers, flat, black, daring her to be anything less than honest.

"Whether you've developed an abnormal amount of scar tissue, either inside the joint or in the capsule."

"And if I have?"

"He can go in arthroscopically and clean up inside the joint." But from what she'd felt, she doubted that was the case.

"What about the capsule?"

She kept her eyes on him, steady, unflinching. "You had a contact injury with a lot of trauma. The capsule may have thickened and scarred in response, or adhesions may have formed between folds. There are ways to address the adhesions."

"But not the other kind."

"No. And there are limits to how much we can improve it with therapy. You'll have to learn to live with a deficit."

That would mean a shorter spur stroke with his left compared to his right leg, in an event where symmetry was a huge part of the score. How many points would the lag cost him per ride? Five? Ten? Enough to end his career as he knew it.

"Worst-case scenario, we can get you to at least eighty percent of normal. Then we can look at your biomechanics, make adjustments—"

He gave a sharp, impatient shake of his head. "The judges aren't stupid. They'll notice if I try to fake it."

She didn't argue. After the thousands of hours he'd spent training his body to work in a very precise groove, telling Delon he had to change his riding style was no different from informing a pitcher they couldn't stay in the major leagues unless they changed their arm angle or a golfer that they had to retool their swing.

The tight, angry set to Delon's shoulders suggested it might be a while before he would consider trying. Well, he was in luck. He'd landed a physical therapist who knew all about adapting to loss. One of these days, she might even get around to finding *her* new style.

Delon sat up abruptly and swung his legs off the table, forcing her to step aside. She pulled out a business card and scribbled a number on the back.

"For today, stick with your regular exercise program. Between now and your next appointment, I'll decide what changes we need to make. If you want to go ahead with the X-rays and MRI, let Beth know on your way out, and she'll make the arrangements." She handed him the card. "That's my direct line if you have any other questions."

He turned the card over and studied the front for a long moment. Then he looked at her, his face a wooden mask. "What does your husband think of living in Texas?"

"I wouldn't know."

His fist curled around the card. "Sorry. Divorced?"

"Dead," she said and walked out the door before he could join the legions who'd expressed their heartfelt sympathy when they didn't know fuck all about Willy except what they'd heard on the evening news.

Chapter 3

DEAD.

There were less brutal ways to say it. *Widowed. Passed away. I lost my husband last…*year, summer, whatever. But Tori had deliberately picked that flat, ugly word and said it with her eyes empty. Abandoned. Set in a face Delon barely recognized. Leaner, harder, her cheeks hollowed out like a person who'd been ill. Or heartsick.

She was Tori but not Tori. He realized now how much of her former beauty had been manufactured. Hair bleach, push-up bras—even the intense sky blue of her eyes must've been colored contact lenses. Now her eyes were more gray than blue. The color of mist. Or ghosts.

He slammed the heel of his hand on his car's center console. He wanted to rage. He deserved it, goddammit. His fury had built, coal by glowing coal, the entire time she'd examined him like nothing more than a specimen under a microscope. No explanation for her disappearance. No apology. Then she'd looked at him with that cool, blank expression and said yeah, his knee was probably fucked. He wanted to curse her for confirming his worst fears.

For waltzing off to Wyoming and getting married and never looking back. Cheyenne, for hell's sake. All the times he'd competed there in the past six years…

You might have to learn to live with a deficit.

Live? Sure. He could *live* just fine with a bad knee. But ride? When she'd said those words, a fresh wash of panic had spilled into the vat of old hurt and humiliation, and he'd been two seconds away from exploding. And then she'd stolen his thunder.

Dead. Dead, dead, dead.

As he pulled through the gates of Sanchez Trucking, the wind kicked up dust from beneath his tires and sent it whirling across the gravel lot, spinning and skittering like his thoughts. He parked, turned off the car, and just sat there, trying to breathe. The yellow steel shop was two stories tall at the peak to accommodate semis, trailers, and the chain hoists that dangled from steel beams above and wide enough for three pull-through repair bays. The far right side housed office space at the front and a one-bedroom apartment upstairs. Home sweet home.

People asked why he didn't get a house, more space, but they had an entire shop for Beni to run tame under the watchful eyes of the mechanics. Beni loved the trucks and hanging around with the drivers. Besides, Delon was gone—used to be gone, he corrected himself bitterly—more often than he was home. And now…

until he figured out what was next, he might as well save some cash and stay where he could still pretend to be a real part of Sanchez Trucking.

The front door banged open, and one of the drivers stomped out, strode over to an idling pickup, slammed into the cab, and roared away, spewing an angry rooster tail of gravel and dust. That couldn't be good. And if there was smoke at Sanchez Trucking, ten to one Delon knew who'd started the fire.

He slung his gym bag over his shoulder and walked through an open bay door, past an engine they'd pulled the day before for a total overhaul, and into a dusty, wood-paneled hallway, the concrete floor tracked with grime.

Their secretary barely spared him a glance as she bustled around the beat-up reception desk, collecting stacks of trip sheets, delivery receipts, bills of lading, and invoices. Scanning and cloud backup be damned, Merle Sanchez insisted they keep paper copies of everything. The computer system did allow Miz Nordquist to run their office from home, though, rather than "that stinking shop." Given that she had the face and disposition of a thundercloud, no one objected.

"What's wrong with Jerry?" Delon asked.

She jerked her head toward his dad's office, at the front of the building. "Your brother."

Bingo. Delon found his dad slouched behind the desk, elbow on the armrest of the big leather chair and chin in hand, expression grim. Gil stood at the window, a narrow slice of darkness through the square of sunlight.

"What's up?" Delon asked.

His dad blew out a weary sigh. "Jerry got an offer from an oil company up in the Bakken."

"North Dakota?" Delon shivered. Closest he'd ever come to freezing his ass off was in Valley City in March. "Must've been one hell of an offer. When's he done?"

"Now," Gil snapped.

Delon jerked around in surprise. "He's due to load out for Duluth tomorrow night."

Silence. Delon looked from his dad to Gil and cursed. "You cut him loose and left us hanging?"

Gil slapped his hand against the window hard enough to make the pane vibrate. "I've been bustin' my ass, working the loads so he could get home more since that new kid was born, and this is how he repays us."

"So you booted him out the door?" Delon let out a growl of impatience. "For Christ's sake, Gil. He's a good operator and he's HAZMAT certified."

Gil wheeled around to glare at Delon. "He quit. I just accelerated the process."

"He won't stick in the oil patch," Delon argued. "Just long enough to get a jump on paying for that new truck, then he'll be out of that frozen hellhole, headed south."

"And I'm supposed to welcome him with open arms?"

"Guys like him are hard to find—"

"The kind who takes advantage of you, then spits in your face?"

Their dad straightened, cutting his hand through the air to signal *Enough!* Lord knew, he'd had plenty of opportunities to use it over the years. "We need to figure out who's gonna take his load. What do we have for a truck?"

Delon stared at his dad in disbelief. He wasn't even going to try to salvage the situation? "The white Peterbilt is ready to go."

"Then we just need a driver. I'm hauling hay to Quanah 'til the end of the week."

"I can get Miz Nordquist to cover dispatch and take it myself." Gil scowled. "It'll cost me."

Mostly in beer for all the drivers and mechanics who had to deal with the woman in person. Delon let it hang for a minute, debating whether to let Gil off the hook he'd buried in his own ass, but it came down to doing what was best for the business. And a chance to get out of town, even if it was to Duluth. After ten years of criss-crossing the country on the rodeo trail, he was going stir-crazy in Earnest.

"I'll take it."

"What about Beni?" his dad asked.

"Violet asked to keep him a couple of extra days. Joe's gonna be here."

Another silence. Someone else's family might ask how he felt about that, but the Sanchez men didn't discuss feelings unless they involved the latest idiotic mandate from the Department of Transportation. Building up this business from a single worn-out cattle hauler hadn't left Merle Sanchez much time for the touchy-feely crap. He'd kept his boys fed, clothed, and mostly out of trouble. The rest they'd had to figure out on their own.

What did Merle think when he looked at the sons who wore the Sanchez name so much more easily than he did, with his ginger hair and freckled skin? Did he search for some piece of himself in them or curse the dark skin and hair of the woman who'd deserted him? Lord knew, he would never say.

"You sure your knee is up to it?" he asked Delon.

"I'll stop and walk out the kinks when I need to."

"Works for me." But Merle looked to Gil for confirmation, as if he had the final say.

"The paperwork's at the front desk," Gil said, starting for the door. "I've gotta go make some calls, find someone to take Jerry's HAZMAT loads until I can get a permanent replacement."

The hitch in his gait was more pronounced than usual as he walked out, pausing at the front desk to grab a folder before he disappeared into his lair. On the door that slapped shut behind him, an engraved plate said *The Dispatcher*. Below it, one of the drivers had taped up a handwritten paper sign that declared *Enter at your own risk.*

"You're welcome," Delon muttered.

His dad gave him a wry smile. "We do appreciate the help."

We. As if there was a "them," separate from him. And he'd let it happen. As he'd built a name and a fan base, the demands for autograph sessions and sponsor appearances had increased, eating into the time between rodeos. At home, he'd spent every available moment with Beni, as often as not at the Jacobs ranch with Violet and her family. Meanwhile, his brother had slithered into the position at Sanchez Trucking that Delon had always assumed would be waiting for him. Gil, who'd once said he'd rather have his balls cut off than be chained to a desk. Which left Delon...what?

"I can talk to Jerry," he offered. "Smooth things over before he leaves."

Merle shook his head. "Your brother is right. We did everything we could to keep him. When—or if—he comes back, we can't make it easy for him. Otherwise, he'll just use us again and take off soon as he gets a better offer."

Hell. Delon couldn't argue with that logic.

Merle shifted in his chair, visibly switching gears. "What did you think of the new therapist?"

"She's...different." Which was the truth. Tori was nowhere near the same girl he used to know.

"Is that good or bad?"

Odds were it didn't matter. Delon fought to keep the cold punch of misery from showing on his face. If the joint capsule was scarred beyond repair, the best therapist in the universe wouldn't be able to fix what ailed his knee. Whether he could stand to see Tori twice a week until they admitted defeat...

"I haven't decided yet," he said. And that was the honest truth too.

Chapter 4

TORI WALKED INTO THE RECEPTION AREA AND caught Beth with her chin in her hand, mooning out the window as Delon walked by. She angled a curious look at Tori.

"You know him?"

"Used to." Tori jotted a reminder on a home exercise sheet for the patient she'd seen after turning Delon over to a PT aide to run through his exercises in the gym, then finish off with his knee packed in ice for twenty minutes. "We had sex for a few months, when he had time between rodeos."

Beth's jaw dropped a notch. "So y'all, um, dated."

"No. Just sex." Tori held out the sheet. "Could you make two copies of this?"

"Sure." Beth took the paper but didn't move, paralyzed by an acute case of excess information.

Tori grimaced apologetically. "Sorry. Lately, anything that pops into my head seems to fall right out of my mouth."

Or, more likely, after months of knowing every one of her words, every smile, and every tear would be weighed, measured, and judged against an impossible standard, her filters had burned out.

Beth laughed, then tilted her head toward where Delon was climbing into his car. "So…"

"Everything you could imagine."

Beth fluttered a hand over her heart. "Well, that'll improve my fantasy life."

"Glad I could help," Tori said and went to take a shot at persuading Mrs. Swisher to pack away her precious hand-tied rag rugs before she tripped and broke her other hip.

At five o'clock, she let out the breath she'd been holding for eight hours and climbed in her car for the forty-five-minute drive to Dumas. A whole day down and no one had jumped up, pointed, and shouted, "I know you!"

The fact that her new place was only ten miles from Delon's hometown of Earnest had given her some pause. First she showed up as his therapist, then in his neighborhood. He might think she was stalking him. He could think again. She had been wooed and won by twenty acres fully fenced, with an indoor arena and without the ridiculous price tag attached to anything closer to Amarillo.

Her mouth twisted as she glanced ahead and behind at the stream of evening commuters trickling north out of Amarillo. Bored. Distracted. Tired. Impatient. Only she was thrilled by the sheer mundanity of being just one more working stiff. For now anyway. She wasn't naive or optimistic enough to believe her paper-thin cover would hold forever, but she would count every dull, anonymous day as a blessing.

She'd learned to take the lack of attention for granted in Wyoming. She had never been a celebrity on par with the Bush twins or Chelsea Clinton, who would be stalked by the media even if they moved to the cloud forest of Ecuador. Though her father's name and face were familiar to anyone who ladled up political news with every meal, he hadn't reached the level of national fame that brought his family under constant scrutiny—unless they did something to attract it.

Except in the Panhandle. Here, just being a Patterson was enough. Or in Tori's case, too much.

The road dipped to cross the Canadian River bridge, then continued up the other side and on toward Dumas. As Tori's gaze wandered over the winter-brown prairie rippling beyond the carved bluffs of the breaks, she felt the familiar tug deep in her gut. *Home*, the land whispered. All she wanted was a piece of it where she could exist like any normal human being.

In other words, the impossible.

Her last attempt at being a regular Panhandle gal had been a complete failure. She'd been so proud of herself, defying her mother, dropping out of medical school, and coming home to pursue a degree in physical therapy at the college in Canyon. While she was at it, why not go whole hog and become a cowgirl? Unlike the horse shows—where she'd dominated in the junior ranks—no one could claim her success as a roper was due entirely to her name and the impeccably trained and bred Patterson horses.

Of course, that had been assuming she'd have some success.

She'd been a terrible roper. Everything about it was contrary to the style of riding her previous trainers had ingrained into her mind and her muscles. The girls on the rodeo team pitied, resented, and—in a few notable cases—openly mocked her. In the face of their contempt, she became intensely self-conscious, which made her roping even worse.

Tori wasn't good at failure. She was even worse at admitting defeat. So she'd clung stubbornly to the fringes of the rodeo crowd, sitting at a table near their default territory in the student union, trying to insinuate herself into the group. A few welcomed her with the bright, fawning smiles a Patterson learned to recognize in the cradle. Others were unbearably polite. She almost preferred the outright hostility. If nothing else, it had prepared her—as much as anything could—for the aftermath of Willy's death.

And now here she was, back at the beginning. Or some version of it. She let her thoughts unspool like the ribbon of asphalt that took her north. Naturally, her mind headed straight for Delon and another January, seven years earlier.

She shouldn't have gone to the party. She'd dithered until almost eleven o'clock that New Year's Eve. Stupid, to go by herself. She'd never even been a party person, for the same reason that she didn't date much. She'd watched too many of her prep-school classmates be victimized by an asshole looking for his fifteen minutes of internet fame. Only on rare occasions, with boys who were equally protective of their privacy for similar reasons, had she allowed herself to cut loose a little or let one of those dates extend past her front door.

But this party was right there in her apartment complex. She could hear the music and the shouts, see cowboys and girls wandering in and out. Maybe tonight, when they were laughing, relaxed, a little drunk, they'd give her a chance.

Of course she did it all wrong. Or right, to those who expected her to show up looking like a spoiled, clueless princess. Thousand-dollar hand-stitched boots. Chunky turquoise jewelry. A floaty little silk dress with a top that tied at the neck and middle but left her back naked down to her sterling silver concho belt.

She'd realized her mistake as soon as she saw the other ropers lounging against a wall. Naturally it would be Shawnee, Violet, and Melanie—the rock-solid core of the rodeo team. Violet was the daughter of Jacobs Livestock, even worked the arena as a pickup rider. Melanie was sixth-generation Panhandle ranch stock, and Shawnee's dad had been a world champion team roper. They wore fancier versions of their usual jeans with colorful blouses. Their jewelry and makeup were as party perfect as Tori's, though probably not as expensive, and Shawnee had used some kind of product to transform her wild mop of brown hair into less unruly curls. But unlike Tori, they were still Amazons of the arena, still looked like they could kick ass.

And they despised her.

Tori had hesitated, looked around for anyone else to talk to, but these were mostly pro circuit cowboys. Older. Harder. A little scary when they were at this advanced stage of inebriation. She worked her way, keeping her exposed back to the wall, to the corner where the three amigos stood sipping beer.

"Uh, hi." Tori tried a smile. "Crowded in here."

Shawnee looked her up and down, then smirked. "Hot damn, if it ain't Cowgirl Barbie. You got Cowboy Ken waitin' outside in the pink convertible, or are you lookin' to git yerself a man who's actually got something in his shorts?"

Everyone in the immediate area burst out laughing. Tori's face went beet-red. She stammered something about finding a beer and dove into the crowd to escape. Bad move. The apartment was so packed she could barely squeeze between bodies. More than one hand strayed across private parts of her anatomy. A sob of panic bubbled in her throat as the mass of human flesh pinned her in place. She squirmed, trying in vain to make forward progress.

A beefy arm snaked around her hips and a pelvis ground against her butt. The man's breath was hot against her bare shoulder. "You keep rubbing that fine ass of yours up against me, darlin', I'll scratch that itch between your legs."

She drove her elbow into his gut, exactly as her father's bodyguard had taught her. He grunted and fell backward, setting off a domino effect. Tori dove through the space he'd vacated, tripped over a tangle of feet, and tumbled face-first onto the love seat. The cowboy sitting there threw up his hands to catch her around the rib cage. She grabbed his shoulders and found herself nose to nose with rodeo's answer to Zorro, minus the mask. Black shirt. Black hat. Black hair. Chiseled jaw and cheekbones. And those eyes. Were they truly black too, or was that just the shadow from his hat brim?

He grinned and her heart actually skipped a beat. "Just droppin' in, or were you plannin' to stay awhile?"

"Sorry. I'll just…" She tried to push herself upright, but the wave of stumbling bodies had bounced off the opposite wall and sloshed back in their direction.

"Hold on." The man in black lifted her off her feet, turned her sideways, and plopped her down on one of his muscular thighs, leaving his hands on her waist. "Your knee was fixin' to do permanent damage."

Her face went a few degrees hotter as she realized her skirt had flared out to drape over his leg, leaving her bare butt in direct contact with the starched denim of his jeans. Teach her to wear a thong. "I, uh… sorry. Again."

"No harm, no foul." He craned his neck to examine her back. "You're coming undone."

Sure enough, she was on the verge of flashing the entire room. She reached up and behind, shoving her boobs under his nose, but her fingers fumbled the satin strings tangled in her waist-length hair.

"Here. Let me." He scooped her hair aside and reached around her, his shirt pulling snug across the powerful bulge of muscle in his shoulders and arms. His fingers brushed her bare spine as he moved to the lower tie, and sensation exploded at every point of contact, a thousand individual fires flaring to life.

"There." He gave the strings a firm tug. "I double-tied the bows, just to be safe."

"Thanks, um..."

"Delon." One arm tightened around her as he stuck the other out to fend off a drunk who toppled in their direction. "And you are?"

"Tori." She hesitated, then added, "Patterson."

"Nice to meet you," Delon said without a blink.

Hallelujah. One person in the room who didn't give a damn about her family. He certainly didn't have to tell her his last name. In early December, Delon Sanchez had competed at his first National Finals Rodeo, leaving with a pocketful of cash and predictions that he'd be the next Panhandle boy to bring home a world championship. As an alumnus of the rodeo team—he'd graduated with a two-year associate degree in business the spring before Tori arrived—he had been the hottest topic of conversation at school for weeks.

Especially among the rodeo groupies who lingered,

like Tori, around the edges of the real cowboy crowd. These girls hunted cowboys the way earlier generations of Patterson men had once stalked lions and water buffalo on the African plains, before it became a hot-button issue. A world champion was the ultimate prize, but nabbing a top fifteen contender earned serious points. A man who looked like Delon must've always been a target, but now, as a local boy done good, he'd become the equivalent of bagging a snow leopard.

And, from what Tori had overheard, almost as elusive.

But he didn't look skittish as he cocked his head, studying her. "We definitely haven't met."

"Um, no. And I should get off," she said, then blushed harder. "Of you, I mean. I was just, um, leaving."

"Don't go on my account." Delon blessed her with another of those heart-tripping smiles, then shifted his gaze to the impenetrable wall of humanity between them and the door. "You're not getting outta here right now anyway."

Not with her clothes and her dignity intact. As if to prove the point, a whoop went up and a shirt came flying out of the middle of the throng, followed by a bra, then a woman was hoisted above the crowd, her boobs bouncing as she pumped her arms to the music. The walls of the room vibrated with cheers of approval. Tori dropped her gaze, unaccountably embarrassed. God, she was such a sheltered twit.

"The boys are getting out of hand." Delon squeezed her waist, his hand warm through the thin silk of her dress, and gave her a look that set off another explosion, deeper, more centrally located. "You'd better stick with me."

Another drunk swayed dangerously close, nearly clocking Tori in the ear with his elbow. Delon shoved him away and pulled her deeper into the couch, until her hip was snug against his. She had to drape her arm across the back of the cushions, her fingers grazing his shoulder. Close up, he smelled like distilled manhood. Clean sweat, some woodsy kind of soap, and—she inhaled deeply and frowned— a hint of diesel exhaust and grease? Of course. Sanchez Trucking. She'd seen their sponsor signs at the college rodeos.

Dear Lord. What was she doing, snuggled up close enough to sniff a complete stranger? But she felt infinitely safer with him than pitting herself against the crowd. And somehow, despite the fact that his arm was now wrapped around her waist, his touch felt respectful. His body, like hers, held a certain kind of tension, as if unaccustomed to casual intimacy.

And he was trying very hard—if not entirely successfully—not to look down her dress.

"Hey, Delon! Happy birthday, dude!" a big, burly guy yelled, sticking out a hand.

As Delon leaned forward to shake it, his chest rubbed up against Tori's nipple, hard, hot muscle sliding across thin silk in a caress so intimate she flushed from head to toe. *Note to self: next time, wear some damn underwear.*

"It's your birthday?" she asked.

"Yep." He gave her a pulse-thumping grin. "Looks like I got the best present ever."

She smiled back, letting her body melt against him as she sank into a haze of arousal, the conversation flowing past in a blur as one person after another stopped to chat or shake Delon's hand. Their curious glances couldn't penetrate her bubble, and their names evaporated in the heat waves rising off her skin as every move generated more friction between their bodies.

The moves were becoming more intentional, on both their parts. His palm caressed her back and molded her against him, hip to shoulder. She let her hand fall onto his shoulder to feel the flex of his deltoid each time he reached up to shake a hand. Incredible that she had enough brain function to remember the names of the muscles. *Flexor carpi radialus, brachioradialus, extensor carpi radialus longus*…all clearly defined in forearms exposed by the sleeves he'd rolled up to his elbows.

Imagine what the rest of him would look like naked.

When she shuddered, Delon tilted his head to look into her eyes. "You okay?"

"Yes. Fine." Assuming she didn't spontaneously combust right there on his lap.

Then someone yelled, "Hey, assholes, it's almost midnight. Grab a girl and get ready to plant a big sloppy one on her."

Delon's hand skimmed up to the nape of her neck as the crowd chanted, "…five, four, three, two…"

At one, his mouth touched hers. There was an

instant of hesitation, then the kiss went hot, deep, no time wasted on polite preliminaries. She dove into the heat and he took her even deeper, into a dark swirl of lust that obliterated everything else in the room.

Delon pulled away, looking equally dazed. He blinked his gaze back into focus. "You ready to get out of here?"

She gulped, then nodded. He lifted her to her feet and stood with ease. He snugged his arm around her hips. "Stay close."

He plowed through the crowd, clapping shoulders and shaking hands as they went, leaving a trail of smiles in his wake. *Interesting.* Delon had forcibly relocated at least a dozen people and made them like it. Not one saw the dogged intent under that smile.

Her father would have been impressed.

Tori tensed at the sight of Violet Jacobs leaning in the entryway, the arm of a wide-bodied steer wrestler curled around her shoulders. Her eyebrows rose when she saw Delon.

"You're still here?" Then her gaze landed on Tori. Her eyes narrowed and her mouth went tight. "Got a new friend, I see."

Delon pulled her forward a step. "This is Tori."

Tori and Violet stared at each other for a long beat, then Violet shifted her attention back to Delon. "Y'all still comin' to dinner tomorrow?"

"Like we'd skip Miz Iris's cookin'," Delon said. "Who all's gonna be there?"

"Just family."

"See you then," he said.

Outside, the cold night air hit Tori's bare skin like ice water and she shivered. Delon wrapped his arm around her shoulders, pulling her into the heat of his body.

"You and Violet are related?" she asked.

He shrugged. "Same as. Early on, my dad hauled stock for Jacobs Livestock. My brother and I were underfoot at their rodeos from the time we could walk, and later Miz Iris watched us when Dad had long hauls."

"What about your mother?"

"She's gone," he said tersely, his cheerful mask slipping for an instant. He paused, frowned, and slapped his pockets. "Crap. I forgot. I don't have the keys. Did you drive?"

"No." She hesitated, heart pounding. How could she even consider trusting this man? But she did. She couldn't even say why, beyond what she knew of his reputation. There was just something…

Before she could talk herself out of it, she pointed across the parking lot. "I live over there."

He took a moment to decide. A moment just long enough to convince her she'd made the right decision. Then he smiled, slow and sweet, and drawled, "Well, all right, then. Lead the way."

All these years later, she still hadn't decided whether it had been a stupid decision…or a very, very good one.

Tori swore and slammed on the brakes, nearly missing her turn. Thank God there'd been no one behind her. She hadn't lived at this place long enough to operate on autopilot while her mind was off on a stroll. A quarter mile down the dirt road, as she turned into her driveway, her phone rang. Glancing at the caller ID, she cursed.

Then she parked the car, took a deep, bracing breath, and said, "Hello, Mother."

Chapter 5

TORI WAS NOT AFRAID OF HER MOTHER. EXACTLY. Call it healthy and well-justified caution. Claire Briggs-Patterson was a world-class neurosurgeon, accustomed to performing marathon procedures on only the most complex cases. Her concentration was unbreakable, her tenacity and attention to minuscule details the stuff of legend. Fabulous traits if you were her patient. Not so much if you were her daughter.

Especially the daughter who wasn't toeing the family line.

"I'm at a symposium in Chicago," Claire said, skipping over the niceties like *Are you settling in at your new house?* and *Did your first day on the job go well?* These were not what Claire considered to be pressing topics of conversation. "I spoke to one of the directors of the Northwestern University Prosthetics-Orthotics Center. With the overwhelming demand for advanced prosthetics from the Veterans Administration, they are desperate for doctoral candidates with practical experience. He is extremely interested in hearing from you."

Tori swallowed a sigh. "I already have a job."

Her mother was too smart to dismiss her career outright. Instead, she said, "I know, darling. But the research they're doing at Northwestern is changing the lives of soldiers who've lost limbs. Your contributions would affect thousands of amputees."

Tori thumped her head against the steering wheel to shatter the beguiling images forming in her mind. Laboratories full of sleek, state-of-the-art equipment. Fellow researchers—brilliant, intense, and dedicated to the betterment of mankind. Proud, smiling men and women, returned to the ranks of productive society, their joyful families clustered around them.

"I'm emailing you an article on the work they did with one of the Boston Marathon bombing victims. So inspiring." Claire's voice was pure silk, but her sales pitch was rough as a cat's tongue across the surface of Tori's conscience.

All those people you could be helping if you weren't so selfish.

This was what made her mother dangerous. Claire wouldn't push. Wouldn't nag. She would simply keep searching out opportunities and waving them under her daughter's nose until she found the one that tempted Tori beyond reason.

Tori examined her armor, piece by piece, to be certain there were no gaps before she answered, "I haven't even settled in here yet. And I hate Chicago."

A long, weighted pause, designed to give Tori ample time to consider how petulant and self-centered she sounded. Then a barely audible but distinctly reproachful sigh. "Well, I'm sure eventually you'll be ready to move on. I'll just keep my eyes open."

Translation: *Expect to hear from me again.*

Tori could have told her not to bother. Could have insisted that she loved her work. She liked to think her current patients were equally deserving of her best efforts—Delon flashed into her head, but she chased him out—and there were hundreds of aspiring researchers who would jump at the chances Claire offered her.

It would have been a waste of breath. "I'm doing fine, Mother. And I appreciate the call, but I need to get to my chores."

"I suppose you're still roping." She said it like another mother might say *I suppose you're still mainlining heroin.*

"Yes. Good night, Mother."

She pulled the phone away from her ear, disconnecting almost before Claire's distant "Good night, Victoria."

Tori scrubbed the back of her hand over her forehead, wiping away imaginary sweat. One more bullet dodged. Then she grinned, picturing her mother's face if she could see what Tori was looking at right now.

Directly in front of her sat what might be the ugliest house in the Texas Panhandle. But hey, ugly was cheap, especially located beside a graveyard for old farm equipment. And the squatty, cinder-block structure probably had a better than average chance of surviving a tornado. But even if a twister did wipe the thing clean off the face of the earth, it would double her property value.

The lone occupant of her pasture came at a trot, greeting her with low, snuffling nickers. She'd be flattered, but it wasn't like she had any competition for Fudge's affection. She stepped out of the car, inhaled, and blew out a long, deep breath. The only sound was the occasional car humming past on the highway beyond the field full of deceased tractors. No supposedly well-meaning strangers to ask how she was *really* doing, their concern like tiny needles, probing for untapped reserves of pain to siphon off for their own incomprehensible purposes. No sanctimonious prigs to enlighten her about how a woman in her position should behave.

And Willy's family—she adored them, but there were so many of them, and their grief was so huge it drowned her. They seemed compelled to keep it fresh, scraping at the wound as if the sight of blood somehow kept Willy close.

Tori understood. God knew, she did, but she had bled out months ago, and now every tribute, every memorial, every bittersweet memory dragged up at Sunday dinner was like a knife on bone. She had to escape or be crushed by the weight of their collective suffering.

So she'd come home. Yippee.

She loved the soil and sky of the Panhandle, with its endless horizons and jagged canyons. She'd fallen for Cheyenne in part because the arid landscape felt familiar. So did the people—ranchers, ropers, salt of the earth types. The kind Tori had always wanted, and failed, to be accepted by here in the Panhandle.

Tori hitched the long strap of her messenger bag over her shoulder and leaned against the corral fence to rub the narrow white strip on Fudge's face. He did not enjoy alone time. Fudge was the equine equivalent of a junior high girl—if he had his way, he wouldn't even take a leak by himself. Tori dumped her bag on the hood of her car and went into the barn to fetch hay and toss it in Fudge's manger. He wandered in through the open gate at the end of his run to bang one hoof on the wooden fence, impatient for the scoop of sweet feed she dumped in his bucket.

She gave his forehead one last rub, then switched off the light, retrieved her bag, and headed up the narrow, uneven sidewalk to what she'd begun to think of as her bunker. A fortress where she could go to ground when being human and reasonably functional got to be too much.

There was a package on her doorstep. She picked it up—heavy for its size—and examined the return address. Elizabeth? What could her older sister possibly be sending her? It wasn't even time for their regularly scheduled ninety-day phone call, which Tori was pretty sure was slotted into Elizabeth's electronic calendar, somewhere between *Publish groundbreaking scholarly article* and *Cure cancer*.

Tori gave the package an experimental shake and got a metallic rattle. Huh. She tucked it under her arm to punch in the security code on the system her father had insisted she install, just like in every other house she'd occupied—except for the one she'd shared with Willy. Not even the senator could persuade Willy Hancock that he wasn't capable of defending his own home. And his wife.

Inside, Tori flipped on the light in the galley kitchen, just off the entryway. The low-watt bulb and yellowed glass globe didn't provide the best illumination, but given Tori's current lack of interest in decor and house-keeping, dim lighting was the place's most attractive feature. She dropped her bag on the dingy linoleum and set the package on the cheap Formica countertop. Fishing a steak knife out of a drawer, she cut the packing tape and lifted out the bubble-wrapped bundle.

And stared, baffled, at an armadillo that appeared to be constructed of rusty bike parts. He wore doll-sized boots and a miniature cowboy hat. A horseshoe formed his arms, and a twisted wire was made to look like a rope, the loop frozen midswing. When Tori set him down—it had to be male with that grotesque, leering grin and a tiny metal cigarette sticking out of the corner of his mouth—he rocked onto his back.

Dear God. It was even uglier than her house. Tori clapped a hand over her mouth to stifle a laugh, which seemed rude even if Elizabeth couldn't see her. With six years' difference in age and an even bigger gap in inter-ests, they'd never been incredibly close, but seriously? This was what her sister considered to be her style?

She rummaged around in the box and found a single, folded piece of notepaper with the logo of a medical supply company at the top.

Thought you could use some company in the new house. Love, Elizabeth

Company? She glanced at its lewd smile and laughed outright. Yeah, that thing would be a real comfort to her. Tori examined the creature from every angle and concluded that it was intended to be a wine bottle holder. She didn't even drink wine.

Shaking her head, she pulled out her phone and spent five minutes composing a tactfully worded text.

Got your housewarming gift. Thank you. It's one of a kind.

Or so she hoped. She set the phone aside, stripped off her jacket, and tossed it in the recliner. Too bad Elizabeth hadn't sent a coatrack instead. After two weeks in the house, Tori had still only unpacked the bare minimum. Clothes. Dishes. A couple boxes of personal stuff. The rest was all stacked in the spare bedroom, awaiting that magical day when she would suddenly give a shit.

The buzz of her phone, loud against the hard countertop, made her jump. Elizabeth already?

Stopped for a dinner break before finishing up a late shift at the lab, she wrote, rightly assuming that Tori would wonder what had possessed her sister to respond in less than twenty-four hours. Pratimi dragged me to a flea market in Napa last weekend. We laughed so hard when we saw that armadillo, she said I had to send it to you. You need a reason to smile at least once a day.

Tori's throat clenched around a hard, aching lump. Her answering words were blurred by a well of tears. Leave it to Elizabeth. Just when you thought she was completely oblivious. And bless Pratimi—who, in deference to their father's position as a political conservative, was referred to only as Elizabeth's roommate or coworker—for occasionally forcing Elizabeth to take a moment to interact with segments of humanity that weren't seen through a microscope.

He's perfect, Tori typed.

He's hideous, Elizabeth replied. But you can probably teach him to drink beer.

Tori gave a soggy laugh. Maybe, if it's a longneck.

They signed off, Tori feeling warmer than she had in days. She swiped at her eyes as she walked down the hall and into her bedroom. Stripping off her work clothes, she tossed them onto the lone piece of furniture, a plastic patio chair beside the closet. Her sweatpants were in the tangle of semi-clean laundry on the floor. She pulled them on along with one of Willy's flannel shirts, big enough to hang almost to her knees, and wandered to the bathroom to scrub off what remained of her makeup. Back in the living room, she grabbed the remote from beside the television and looked at the photo on the top shelf of the entertainment center.

"Hey, babe. Whatcha in the mood for tonight?"

Willy didn't answer. Which was good. When her dead husband's picture started talking back, she'd have to drop a wad on either a shrink or a ghostbuster. Besides, his spirit had no reason to follow her to Texas. They had no unresolved issues. It'd taken most of a year, but she wasn't furious with him anymore. Well, not as often. Or as furious. She kissed her fingertips, pressed them to his face, then settled into the nest of blankets on the couch to stare at the television until exhaustion or boredom put her to sleep, hopefully not to dream.

Not that she had nightmares. Her dreams were wonderful. It just hurt too damn much to wake up.

But tonight…as she flicked through the channels, it wasn't the well-worn memories of Willy that haunted her. Seeing Delon had breathed stuttering life into what had once been her fantasy. A job at one of the top therapy clinics in Amarillo. A house and acreage somewhere between the city and Earnest. Horses. An arena. And now, she'd made it come true. Almost.

All that was missing was the dark-eyed cowboy who, back then, could have turned it from a dream into a home.

Chapter 6

DELON HAD PICKED UP HIS LOAD AND WAS ROLLING across Nebraska by Friday afternoon, right on schedule. But if the dashboard computer beeped at him one more time, he swore he'd pull over on the side of the highway and take a tire iron to the damn thing. Was that all Gil had to do, sit in the office and pepper him with messages and calls? Yes, for hell's sake, Delon knew there was snow in the forecast. He had an FM radio, a smartphone, and a clue.

His cell phone buzzed, amplified by the stereo speakers. Delon punched a button on the steering wheel to answer. "What?"

"I uploaded a map into your GPS unit," Gil said. "When you get to Duluth, turn off one exit before you think you should. It's a roundabout way, but there's road construction on the shorter route and…"

Blah, blah, blah. He'd forgotten Gil was the world's worst backseat driver, and now, with his high-tech dispatch system, he could do it by remote. Delon tuned him out, keeping a wary eye on a silver BMW that'd been dogging his tail for the last twenty miles.

"You got that?" Gil asked.

"Sure thing, boss," Delon drawled.

Gil was silent for a beat, then said, "Fuel's cheapest at the next stop down the road. They've also got a decent café and good showers. Might as well hit both, as long as you've got the time."

"Got a preference whether I piss standing up or sitting down?"

Another pause. Then, "No, but as long as you've got the tools handy, you can go ahead and fuck yourself, Poster Boy."

The phone clicked off, and George Strait came back on the radio, still trying to peddle that piece of "Ocean Front Property," while Delon muttered curses his brother couldn't hear. Delon hated that nickname, which was why Gil had tagged him with it the moment he'd done a series of ads for a western-wear company. That was Gil. Always the smart-ass. The words hadn't changed much since they were kids, constantly heckling each other. But back then, the insults were delivered with a laugh and received the same way. Now...

Delon couldn't remember the last time they'd laughed together. Before the hellish night everything got flipped upside down and torn apart along with Gil and his goddamn motorcycle. Riding bucking horses like a wild-ass crazy man hadn't been enough of an adrenaline rush for Gil. He'd had to go faster and harder, until he finally skidded over the edge.

Delon had been bitten by the rodeo bug, but Gil was

consumed. Delon would've been content to just hit the Texas circuit rodeos. Gil had to have the world. Like everything else, little brother went along for the ride. Delon had figured he'd have his fun, a few years of living the rodeo dream before he settled into his predestined spot at Sanchez Trucking. Except Gil had trashed his own future, so he took Delon's instead.

Delon rubbed his aching knee. He was tempted to motor past Gil's designated truck stop out of spite, but he needed an ice pack and that shower, and he'd almost polished off his family-size bag of peanut M&Ms. Besides, butting heads with Gil wouldn't show his dad he could be an asset above and beyond cranking wrenches in the shop or picking up an occasional load.

The phone rang again. Delon punched the button and snapped, "What, did you forget to specify that I should fuck myself doggie style?"

Silence. Then a quiet clearing of the throat that was distinctly female. "Did I catch you at a bad time?"

Too late, he checked the caller ID. *Panhandle Orthopedics.* "Uh, Beth?"

"Tori."

He winced. "Sorry. My brother—" Then he remembered. "Oh, hell. It's Friday. I forgot to cancel my appointment."

"Yes. Beth said you've never missed, and you didn't make arrangements for the X-ray or MRI. After our discussion about your knee, I wondered…"

Not wondered. Worried. He could hear it in her voice.

Tori was concerned about him. No doubt it was on a purely professional level, but hey. As far as he knew, it was the first time Tori had ever been bothered by his absence, so he'd go ahead and call that a win, if a pretty poor one.

"I'm fine. Didn't toss myself off a cliff or anything."

"I didn't think…" Tori trailed off, then cleared her throat again. "Actually, I wondered if you'd decided to switch to a different clinic."

Ah. So her concern wasn't only for him. "It just occurred to you that this might be awkward?"

"Of course not. I tried to tell Pepper, but I couldn't exactly *tell* him, so he insisted…"

In other words, his surgeon had personally assigned Tori to his case. It should've been all Delon needed to hear, but the nasty snake coiled in his gut itched to lash out. He bit his tongue and let off the accelerator as a seventies-vintage grain truck merged onto the interstate in front of him, a rooster tail of dust hanging above the county road to the south. The local farmers would be glad to see some moisture, even if the truckers weren't so crazy about the forecast.

"I understand if you'd prefer not to work with me," Tori said stiffly.

"Well, now, that depends." He let a touch of sarcasm leak into his drawl. "Will I show up for therapy someday and find you gone? No word, no warning?"

Her voice went from cool to downright frosty. "You mean the way you always let me know whether you planned to drop by again?"

Damn. She had him there. And instead of scoring a point, he'd just given her a clue how much her leaving had bothered him. He rolled up on the grain truck, eased into the left lane to pass, then started to swing back into the driving lane when a horn blasted. He yanked the wheel to the left just in time to avoid running the Beemer into the ditch. Twenty miles of riding his bumper and the dipshit had to cut between him and the grain truck to pass on the right, dead center of Delon's blind spot.

"You stupid son of a bitch!"

"*Excuse* me?"

"Not you." Delon laid on his horn. Beemer guy flipped him the bird. Delon returned it in kind, muttering, "Same to you, asshole."

The silence on the phone was so complete he thought Tori had hung up. Then she asked, "Where are you?"

"Just south of Omaha. Last-minute trip. That's why I forgot to call about my appointment before I left."

"For Nebraska."

"Minnesota. My brother lost his temper and we lost a driver, so I'm on my way to Duluth."

"In a semi?"

There was an odd note in her voice that set his back up. "Yeah. Why? You got something against truck drivers?"

"No. The trucking industry is vital to our national economy." She quoted as if from one of her dad's press releases, which pissed him off a little more, but her voice was almost wistful. "It seems…interesting."

Delon snorted. "Then you've never driven across Kansas."

"It can't be any worse than eastern Wyoming."

Good point. "You like road trips?"

"Yeah." It came out on a sigh. "Willy and I traveled all over to team ropings, but since…well, I stayed pretty close to home the last year or so."

So much information in those few words. Her husband had been gone for over a year. And he'd been a roper. Victoria Patterson, of *the* Texas Pattersons, had married a damn Wyoming twine twirler. *Willy Hancock. Cheyenne.* Something niggled in Delon's brain, as if he'd seen or heard the name during Frontier Days and should remember.

"Do you still rope?" he asked, instead of the far less tactful questions buzzing in his head.

"Yes. Quite a bit better than I used to." She gave a quiet snort. "But I guess you wouldn't know."

Because he'd never seen her swing a rope, let alone compete. They'd preferred indoor activities when he was in town. But he'd heard, via Violet. Yeah, Tori rode well enough. She should, after all the private lessons and years of scooping up awards on her family's blue-blooded, professionally trained show horses. But roping? Not a clue.

She cleared her throat again. "So…you're planning to come in on Tuesday?"

He hadn't decided—until now. Even if her interest was only professional, she'd cared enough to worry and to call, and she was the only person who knew what he might be facing and wasn't afraid to be straight with him. Besides, Pepper *had* handpicked her, which meant she was the best.

Above all, he refused to admit it bothered him to see her. "I'll be there, unless the snow in South Dakota is worse than they're predicting."

"Okay." Her tone lightened a shade as if in relief. "Drive safe."

Her parting words triggered an avalanche of memories. She'd said the very same thing every time he'd dragged himself away from her and out the door to the next rodeo. And every time, it had been all he could do not to make a U-turn before he hit the city limits.

He shook the last three M&Ms out of the bag and ground the peanuts between his teeth, staring out at miles and miles of almost nothing. He was facing at least three days on the road, with nothing to occupy his mind but worries, regrets…and wondering what his life might be like right now if he had let himself turn around.

Chapter 7

AFTER WORK ON FRIDAY, TORI EXERCISED FUDGE IN the indoor arena, sharpened her own skills by roping the plastic, steer-shaped dummy, then lingered beside Fudge's stall after she'd put him up, leaning on the wood planks and listening to his rhythmic munching. She didn't want to go inside. Not yet. Talking to Delon, picturing him out on the open road, had put an itch under her skin. She was well aware that a trucker's life wasn't as cool as it seemed, but the thought of packing up and rolling clear across the country...

To Duluth. She rubbed a shiver from her arms. Definitely over-romanticizing. Tori frowned, mentally replaying her telephone conversation with Delon. She felt as if they'd resolved something. She just wasn't sure what. He clearly wasn't thrilled by her presence. Why should he be? What they'd had might not have been an epic love affair, but it had left a mark. Literally, on a couple of occasions. Rug burn. Ouch.

Funny how she could recall with perfect clarity the way her jeans had chafed on her raw knees and yet feel only a vague shadow of the aching and yearning she'd been sure would be the death of her. Showed what she'd known about pain.

She sighed, pushed away from the stall, then paused at the barn door to watch a car crawl down the gravel lane. A lost soul about to discover they'd turned onto a dead-end road—a nice metaphor for her own life. To her surprise, the car turned into her driveway. Only her family knew where she lived. Her mother was still in Chicago. Her sister was either holed up in her lab at Stanford or sharing takeout with Pratimi in their cozy, Spanish-style condo in Palo Alto. And her father...

The silver Lincoln whispered to a stop, and Robert Patterson's lean frame unfolded from behind the wheel. Alone. He had half a dozen minions who were retained solely for the purpose of herding him directly from meeting to legislative session to press conference with no detours. He hadn't made a surprise appearance since her third birthday, and she only remembered that because she'd seen the pictures. Her pulse thumped and the too-familiar bile of terror rose in her throat. Had something happened to her mother? Elizabeth? But no, his body language and expression were too relaxed for bad news. She tucked away the knee-jerk fear and studied him as he surveyed the house with its ratty scrap of lawn and spindly shrubs. He didn't look down his elegant Patterson nose. Despite everything, he had very few pretenses, which made him wildly popular with the working class.

It saddened Tori to see the lines scoring his face, the gleam of silver in his blond hair. That damn job was making him an old man before his time. And if his supporters had their way, it would only get worse.

She stepped out of the barn. "Hey, Daddy. This is a surprise."

"Tori!" His smile was immediate and genuine. "What are you doing out here in the dark?"

"Just finishing up the chores." She made a show of peering into the empty car. "You're alone? What did you do, chew through your leash?"

He blinked at her unaccustomed bluntness, then smiled again with a twinkle of mischief. "Climbed out the bathroom window during the debate about whether to order Mexican or barbecue for dinner. I've been in meetings all day in Amarillo, and at the rate that we're running in circles, we're going to be at it until morning."

"Seriously?"

"Which part?"

She laughed. "What did I do to rate a jail break?"

"I wanted to see your place." He rested one palm on the roof of the car, letting his eyes take another tour that ended where she stood. "And I wanted to see you. I've barely said hello since you've been home."

She heard the guilt, also familiar, and answered with the usual shrug. "You're busy."

"That's a piss-poor excuse."

Okay. Wow. That kind of ruthless honestly was new. "It's okay—"

"No, it's not." He drummed his fingers on the car roof, his jaw set. "I've missed too much. I should've known your husband better, Tori. Should've at least been able to come to his funeral."

"I appreciate that you didn't." As much as she'd yearned to have him there, the publicity had been crazy enough as it was.

He angled his head in acknowledgment. "Still, I should've managed more than a couple of flyby visits in all the time you were married. I'm not going to make that mistake again, now that you're here."

"Okay." Because really, what else could she say? "Do you want to come in?"

"I'd love to, but sooner or later, those people will stop yelling at each other long enough to notice I'm not there. If I don't dawdle, I can use the Very Important Call excuse. Top secret, matter of national security, blah, blah. But I did bring you something." He opened the rear door of the car with a flourish to reveal…a pet carrier? Oh, hell. He'd brought her a damn puppy.

"Uh, wow. I appreciate the thought, Daddy, but I really can't—" A low yowl cut her off, a sound that vibrated with raw fury. Tori angled her head, squinting. "What have you got in there?"

"A cat," he declared proudly.

Oh Lord. That was even worse. "I'm not really a cat person, Daddy."

"I know. That's why I got this cat."

"Uh…okay. And this cat would be what kind, exactly?" She started to reach out a hand toward the carrier.

He caught her wrist. "Don't do that!"

She jerked back.

"It's a barn cat," he said. "A stray, probably feral. The guy at the animal shelter said it'd be best not to try to touch her. She's, um, very aggressive."

The yowl sounded again, raising the hair on the back of Tori's neck. "You brought me a deranged cat?"

He laughed, but his smile faded to dubious concern as he gazed at the crate. "Your grandfather firmly believed the only good cats are the kind that don't want a damn thing to do with people."

"That would explain why I'm not a cat person," she said, recalling the hostile, skittish cats that had stalked their barns.

He reached in the car and hoisted the carrier at arm's length. Claws flashed through one of the slats. "She's spayed and she's had all her shots."

Including the tranquilizer dart to put her under so they could stuff her in that box, Tori assumed. She could see only a hunched shape the size of a large raccoon and the baleful gleam of yellow eyes.

"She's just agitated from being carted around," her dad said. "I'm sure she'll settle right down. Keep a bowl of cat food up in your hayloft, and you'll hardly even know she's here."

His voice echoed with the sound of best-laid plans and all the disaster inherent, but what could she do? Tori followed along as he carried the hissing package to the barn door, set it down inside, and flicked open the latch. For an instant, nothing moved. Then the door slammed back and a streak of some nondescript color shot out and disappeared into the darkness, startling a snort out of Fudge.

"Well, that was easy enough." Her dad closed up the crate, carried it back to the car, and handed her a twenty-pound bag of cat food. While she stood cradling it in her arms, he reached out to stroke her hair. "Call me if you need anything—a chore boy, company, somebody to fix a parking ticket. I'll make the time, no matter what."

"Okay." Sure. When hell froze over, she'd drag him away from matters of dire national concern to hold her poor little hand. She shifted the bag to one arm so she could hug him with the other. "Thanks."

"You're welcome." He hesitated, taking another long look around her dingy yard. "Tori...I don't mean to pry, but have you tried...moving on? Seeing someone new?"

No. But the tawny, dark-haired image of someone "old" flashed much too quickly and easily into her mind. She shook her head. "It was too complicated in Cheyenne."

"Are you ready?"

"I don't know," she said truthfully. "I suppose it would depend on the man."

And dammit, no, she didn't mean one specific man.

He gave a single, thoughtful nod, then squeezed her shoulders. "Have a good night, sweetheart."

If so, it would be the first in a year and a half. And now, on top of the ghosts of husbands and boyfriends past, she would have the company of the vague certainty that her father had decided to *help*.

Lord save her.

Chapter 8

DELON WASN'T QUITE SURE WHAT TO EXPECT WHEN he walked into the physical therapy clinic for his Tuesday morning appointment. Tori had been so incessantly on his mind, the memories so vivid, it was a shock all over again to see this new, muted version of her.

This time, she did smile, even if it was quick and impersonal.

The receptionist, on the other hand, had been smirking behind her coffee cup since he stepped through the door. What the hell? It would have been obvious at his first appointment that he and Tori had known each other before, but the gleam in Beth's eyes made him feel vaguely indecent. Surely Tori wouldn't have yakked to a coworker about just how *well* they'd known each other.

Would she?

"What did you tell her?" he demanded the moment he and Tori were alone in the treatment room.

She didn't look up from poking at her tablet. "Tell who?" she asked absently.

"Beth. She was looking at me like…well, you know."

Tori's hand paused over the touch screen. Then she

closed her eyes and breathed out what looked like a very bad word. "That would be my fault."

He goggled at her. "You *told* her?"

"Not intentionally." She clasped the tablet in both hands and pressed it to her midsection like a school-girl, chin tucked. "Lately, things just…pop out." Her eyebrows pleated. "I wonder if it's possible to develop a form of post-traumatic Tourette's Syndrome."

"Tour…*what?*"

She opened her eyes, her gaze apologetic but so direct he would've taken a step back if his butt hadn't already been pressed against the side of the table. "I'm sorry. It was incredibly unprofessional. And chauvinis-tic, now that I think about it. I made the unconscious assumption that you, as a male, wouldn't be embar-rassed by having your sexual exploits discussed."

Geezus. Who talked like that? It was like having a conversation with an encyclopedia. "What trauma?" he asked.

She blinked. "Excuse me?"

"You said post-traumatic something or other. What trauma?"

"Oh." Her lashes dropped and she angled her head away to stare at a spot on the floor. A breath pushed her shoulders up, then let them fall. "My husband's death was very…sudden and attracted a lot of attention. Willy knew so many people, and all the others…" Her mouth twisted into a bitter, distant relative of a smile. "It was amazing, how many of them felt it was their God-given duty to advise me on the proper way to grieve my husband. And point out what was improper, of course."

Willy Hancock. Again, the name rang a distant bell. Someone important, well known in Cheyenne, she'd said. The kind of man a Patterson would marry. A big-time sponsor whose hand Delon had shaken during a publicity gig at Frontier Days? Maybe one of the local dignitaries—politicians and community leaders— introduced during the opening ceremonies while Delon stood on the back of the chutes, bouncing in place, mentally and physically gearing up to climb onto the bucking horse in the chute below him.

"I don't mean to make excuses, but I suppose I do owe you an explanation." Tori ran a finger along the edge of the tablet, still contemplating the pattern on the carpet. "For nineteen months after he died, I had to be so careful with every word. Every expression. Not just what I said but who I talked to or smiled at in case someone got the wrong impression. Women hustled their men away from me like I was so desperate I might try to eat them alive. It was insane. I was on the verge of coming undone, and it wasn't going to be pretty. His family is already suffering enough...so I left."

"And came here."

"Where else?" She shrugged. "They would be devastated if they thought I was running away from them. But coming home...well, that's different. Acceptable." Her mouth twisted again, and her eyes glinted as her gaze came up to meet his. "But somewhere between here and Wyoming, I seem to have run out of fucks to give. As you've probably noticed."

"I'm getting the drift," he said.

"No doubt." She drew back her shoulders, her mouth set. "You have every reason to request a different therapist. And grounds to file a privacy complaint. I won't dispute either."

God. She sounded like a damn lawyer now. But underneath all the fancy talk, he caught a glimpse of scar tissue, still vulnerable and painful to the touch. She was as fucked up as he was. Possibly worse. Instead of firing her, he had a ridiculous urge to gather her up, pet her hair, and tell her it would all be okay.

As if he had any idea.

"What if I don't change therapists?" he asked.

She blinked again. "You still want to be my patient, after…everything?"

"Is there someone here who'd do a better job?"

Her eyes went cool, her jaw firm. "No."

"Then switching would be stupid, wouldn't it?"

She stared at him for a long moment. Then she gave a brisk nod and lifted the tablet. "In that case, let's talk about the changes I want to make in your exercise program." Then she paused and flicked him a lightning-fast grin that made his heart bump in surprise. "I also promise to refrain from bragging about getting to see you naked."

And there he was, goggling again.

Two hours later, Delon parked in front of Violet's house. Used to be he wouldn't have thought twice about walking into her single-wide trailer and helping himself to a cup of coffee and one of her mother's fresh-baked cookies. Today, if he'd dared, he would've sat outside, honked his horn, and waited for Beni to come to him.

He climbed out of the car, his knee stiff from the chill. Dark clouds hung low and spit a few snowflakes, the weather trying hard to be miserable and doing a damn fine job. His muscles twinged from Tori's brutal workout. Until she got her hands on him, he'd thought he was in pretty good shape. They had to bring his entire musculoskeletal system into balance, she'd declared. Hips, core, shoulders, even his neck—she'd pinpointed every weakness, then tackled them one by one. He suspected that by morning, it would hurt to lift an eyebrow.

The front door flew open before he could raise his fist to knock. Delon braced himself for a tackle-hug from Beni, but it was Violet who stood there, face flushed, dark hair mussed up like she'd been wrestling.

More like *wrasslin'*, as Gil called it.

Violet tugged her shirt straight, trying not to be obvious about it. "Delon! You're early."

"You said you wanted to leave for the airport at noon." He looked over her shoulder at the clock, which read eleven thirty. "Is Beni all packed and ready?"

"Yes. I sent him…I mean, he went over to Mom's for a bit. She's making cupcakes." In other words, she got rid of the kid so she could give Joe a proper send-off. Violet combed her fingers through her hair and gave a nervous laugh. "I'll, um, go grab his stuff."

She left him standing in the open door and hustled to Beni's bedroom.

Joe Cassidy sauntered out of Violet's bedroom, the tails of his faded denim shirt hanging loose over his jeans. He flashed a cautious smile. "Hey, Delon."

"Joe." The muscles in Delon's neck and shoulders went tight, his voice stiff. He and Joe eyed each other, wary on Joe's part, hostile on Delon's.

This was his place, dammit. The Jacobs ranch had been his second home as long as Delon could remember, but since Beni came along, it had become the hard rock center of his world and Violet his touchstone. For the past six years, they'd shared everything except a bed, a mutual decision to avoid complicating their situation. He'd always believed that someday, some way, the time would be right and they would both be ready to take that final step.

Until Joe showed up.

Joe rocked onto his heels, unsettled by the silence. "Any idea when you're gonna be ready to get on some horses?"

"No."

Joe's eyes narrowed a fraction at the blunt response. "No sense rushing it."

"So my therapist says." It gave Delon a weird tingle of pleasure, knowing Violet would freak when she heard about Tori. Another of those petty victories he'd decided to savor, especially after this morning.

Bragging. His mind slammed up against the thought again and splattered a few more brain cells. All this time, he'd thought of himself as her dirty little secret, and Tori considered him worth bragging about? How was he supposed to...

Violet came bustling out of Beni's room, her arms loaded with his duffel, a jacket, a handheld video game, and a backpack for preschool. Hell. How was Beni almost six years old already? Next thing Delon knew, he'd be fumbling through explanations about girls and sex. Then again, Beni probably already knew more than enough from hanging around the shop and behind the bucking chutes at his grandpa Steve's rodeos.

Violet shot a glance at Joe, then bounced it over to Delon, measuring the tension in the room. Her mouth tightened as she dumped her load on Delon. "Thanks for letting him stay a couple extra days."

"No problem."

"I'll call Mom, have her send Beni over."

"I'll go get him."

"Okay. Thanks." She folded her arms tight across her chest, shivering in the cold blast of air from the door. "I'll see you Friday, then."

"We'll be here."

And that was that. No coffee. Damn sure no sugar.

Delon hobbled down the steps and across the lawn to toss Beni's stuff in the back seat of his car. When he glanced back at the house, he saw them through the window, Violet's head on Joe's shoulder. Joe stroked a hand over her hair and pressed a kiss to her forehead, a gesture somehow more intimate than if Delon had seen them naked.

He slammed his door, wheeled the car around, and drove the twenty yards to park across the driveway, in front of the big white frame house where Violet had grown up. Rapping once on the door, he let himself in. Iris Jacobs would've smacked him upside the head for waiting to be invited into her kitchen. His nose twitched at the mingled scents of vanilla cupcakes, pot roast, home-baked bread, and fresh coffee. Only two men sat at the table with steaming mugs, but they qualified as a roomful. Steve Jacobs and his nephew Cole both pushed the six-and-a-half-foot mark, solid as hundred-year-old California redwoods.

Iris smiled at him—round, soft, a half-pint version of Violet in thirty years. "Close that door and leave the cold outside."

"Daddy!" Beni hopped down off a stool and bounded over to throw his arms around Delon's waist, smearing cupcake batter on the front of his jacket.

Delon ruffled his inky black hair, amazed all over again at the miracle that was his son. Delon's spitting image but a little too much like his uncle Gil for comfort. All out, all the time.

Beni pulled away to frown up at him. "How come I can't go to the airport with Joe and Mommy?"

"They need some alone time," Iris said, saving Delon the trouble of answering.

"Why?" Beni demanded. "Mommy and Daddy never have alone time."

"Uh…" Stymied, Delon looked to Iris, who moved her mouth but didn't make any words. Steve and Cole showed no inclination to jump in. Real helpful, those two. "Mommy and I are just friends."

Beni opened his mouth, but Iris cut him off at the pass. "Joe and your mommy are a different kind of friends. And besides, haven't you missed your daddy?"

Beni shrugged. "He's here all the time now. And he doesn't do fun stuff like Joe."

The dismissal was an arrow straight through Delon's heart. "We'll go swimming tomorrow at the indoor pool in Dumas."

"But I want to go to the airport today," Beni whined.

"You can't," Cole said. "So hush, or I'll eat your cupcakes."

"Nuh-uh!"

Cole reached over, grabbed a cupcake off the cooling rack, and stuck the whole thing in his mouth.

"No fair!" Beni protested, but he hushed, knowing it wasn't an idle threat. Cole would consider a dozen cupcakes a light snack.

"Come help me clean up the last of the batter." Iris set the bowl and a spatula in front of Beni's stool—another punch of nostalgia to Delon's heart. How many times had he hovered in this kitchen, hoping for a chance to lick the bowl? Hell, he was tempted to fight Beni for it now.

Iris poured a cup of coffee and set it on the table. "Sit yourself down. You look tired. And sore. I suppose this weather's got your knee acting up."

"Yes, ma'am," Delon said, to all of the above.

"I'll set you a plate," Iris said, reaching into the cupboard.

Delon was sorely tempted—a man didn't turn down Miz Iris's food without a second thought—but picturing Joe and Violet together right across the road spoiled his appetite. "No, thanks. I stopped by the Smoke Shack earlier."

Miz Iris could smell a lie from a mile off. Her mouth folded into a disapproving line. Then her expression turned sympathetic, and that was worse. "Well, you'll need something for dinner. I'll make you up some sandwiches to take along."

"Do I have to go?" Beni whined. "There's nothing to do at the shop."

"You have all the same games as you have here," Iris scolded.

Of course Beni dragged his feet about leaving the ranch. His pony was here, the dogs and cats, his grandmother's bottomless cookie jar. Time with his dad wasn't a novelty anymore. It was stupid to take it to heart, but Delon's heart hadn't been in a real common-sense kind of mood lately. He left his coffee untouched and bundled his reluctant child into coat, boots, and gloves.

When Iris handed him the bag of food, she held on for a beat, nailing him with one of those looks. "Don't be a stranger, you hear?"

"Yes, ma'am." But his gaze dropped away from hers. How could he promise that when he'd been a stranger for months, even to himself?

Chapter 9

JANUARY IN THE PANHANDLE WAS A FICKLE BITCH. Early in the week, the temperature had climbed into the sixties. Today, Tori tugged the zipper of her canvas jacket higher and pulled the hood of her sweatshirt up over her baseball cap to ward off the needle-sharp wind, her chest a mess of tangled-up emotions. There was nothing she'd rather do on a Saturday afternoon than go to a team roping—unless that roping was in Childress, Texas. Then she might prefer jogging naked in a winter breeze. It couldn't make her feel more exposed than walking into this arena. An outsider. A stranger. Until that inevitable moment when someone realized who she was, and then they would *think* they knew her and that would be worse.

But she couldn't just quit roping. Not after all the time and work she'd put into it and Willy had put into her. She also couldn't leave Fudge standing around, a good horse wasted. She tightened his cinches, then squared her shoulders, shrugging off the weight of curious gazes from ropers who read the lettering emblazoned on the side of her pickup. *Willy Hancock. Wyoming Team Roping Classic. Champion Heeler.*

Then they looked at Tori and wondered, *Who the hell are you?*

Excellent question. In Cheyenne, she was a Hancock, a name synonymous with team roping. They trained the best horses and took home more than their share of the prize money. As Willy's wife, Tori had been smack-dab in the middle of the crowd by default. Now it was just her again, but Willy had given her skills, and he'd given her Fudge. What she didn't have was practice. Team roping, by definition, was not a solitary pursuit. She had an arena, and once they were delivered tomorrow, she would have steers. All of which were wasted without a partner. Yet another reason she had to bite the bullet and get to know the locals.

She walked the gauntlet of trucks and trailers parked in rows out behind the indoor arena. Eye contact. Smile. Nod. Try to look friendly instead of the *keep your distance* face she'd perfected by the end of her father's first term in office. When she passed through the door and into the arena, her blood stirred at the sight of well-groomed dirt, the musty scent of dust and horses, the relaxed chatter and chuckle of ropers. Nothing else gave her that same shimmer of excitement, anticipation. Even Fudge felt it, tugging at the reins. Or he was eyeing that dandy little strawberry roan mare tied to the fence. Knowing his penchant for love at first sight, she tied him beside a homely sorrel that pinned his ears when Fudge tried to nuzzle up.

In the office, the secretary took her name without a flicker of recognition. "Head or heels?"

"Header. Put me in three times." She'd chosen this roping because it was a draw pot. All she had to do was tell them she preferred to rope the horns and they'd draw three partners to rope heels for her. Tori handed over her entry fees and went back to her horse, dug out her best rope, and climbed aboard to join the parade of ropers circling the arena. On the second lap, she heard a big, bawdy laugh that made her jerk Fudge up short and look around for the source.

Shawnee Pickett. Shit. She *would* have to be here.

Tori gritted her teeth and kicked Fudge into a lope. He moved out smooth and easy, pushing into the bit more than usual due to the long layoff. She wrapped her fingers around her rope, tracing the hard twist of nylon with her fingers. She'd earned her place in the arena. One person couldn't take it away.

"All right, listen up!" the announcer declared.

She began to recite team numbers and names. The roping was a three header, meaning Tori could rope up to four steers with each partner, but only if they made qualified runs. A miss meant she was out with that partner. If she and her heelers caught every steer, she'd get to make nine runs. A bad day would mean three *no times* and she was done.

She'd drawn up as team number thirty-two with someone named Randy and team sixty-eight with John somebody. The announcer droned on and on, down through the list, until finally, "Team number one hundred and six, Tori Hancock and Shawnee Pickett."

No way. Tori slammed her fist on her saddle horn. Like this wasn't hard enough, she had to draw up with Shawnee? Tori eased through the crowd of ropers congregated on the left side of the arena, out of the way of the roping box, until she was only a few horses away from her nemesis. Shawnee looked exactly the same. Heavyset body, round face, wild mop of dark brown curls yanked back into a bushy ponytail. But, Tori had to admit, her makeup was perfect as always, and today her sweatshirt was a vivid pink with *Rope Like a Girl* stamped on the front.

In fact, if you hadn't experienced her personality, you might actually say she was attractive.

"Team number thirty-two, Tori and Randy, you're up!" the announcer repeated loudly.

Oh crap. Her heeler was already sitting in front of the chute, waiting. Tori built a hasty loop, her face burning as necks craned to see the idiot who was holding up the action.

"Sorry," she mumbled, hustling Fudge into the heading box.

Her heeler gave her an encouraging smile as he settled his horse in the right-hand box. Tori put Fudge's butt in the corner of the left-hand box, cocked her arm back, and nodded. Too soon. She wasn't set, and Fudge's first powerful stride slid her to the back of the saddle. She compensated by leaning out but that only got her shoulders too far forward, so when she let go of the loop, it plopped onto the back of the steer's head, limp as cold spaghetti.

Tori reined up and muttered another, "Sorry."

Her heeler shrugged, as if to say *It happens*.

Not to her. Not very often. She might not be the fastest roper, but she was consistent. She planted Fudge at the back of the mob of ropers, yanking on the reins when he nosed the butt of the horse in front of him and nearly got kicked in the teeth. *Okay. Deep breath. Relax.* But she tensed again when Shawnee rode into the heeling box, said something to her header, then laughed, like she was so good she didn't have to bother to concentrate.

Her header caught the steer sharp around the horns. As he wrapped his rope around the saddle horn and took the steer left, Shawnee's buckskin zipped right in behind, giving her a perfect throw. Her loop floated in under the steer's belly and scooped both hind feet cleanly out of the dirt. She whipped a dally around the saddle horn, the header pivoted his horse to face up as the ropes came tight, and the judge's flag snapped down.

"Six point nine seconds," the announcer said to a smattering of applause. "That's fast time so far. Next up…"

Shawnee accepted hand slaps as she rode through the crowd, straight to where Tori was sitting. Tori stiffened, but Shawnee's gaze skipped over her without pause as she swung the buckskin around and parked in front of Fudge. And of course Fudge reached out to sniff the horse's butt.

Tori yanked on the reins. "Stop it!"

Fudge gave another half-hearted tug, then dropped his head to sulk.

Shawnee was too busy running her mouth to notice. "Hey, Lou, you buy any steers yet?"

"Nah. Too expensive. Been practicing on the dummy."

Shawnee slapped her coiled rope onto the saddle horn. "Same as everybody. Can't find a soul within an hour of Amarillo who's ropin' real steers."

Tori eased Fudge away to the front of the pack where she didn't have to look at or hear Shawnee. More deep breaths. By the time the announcer called her name again, she had herself straight. Ready.

Her heeler was an older guy, potbellied, a bright red wild rag tied around his neck. "Watch this steer. He'll stall and drop his head as you run up on him."

Tori threw him a grateful smile for the tip. This time when she nodded, she was ready and got up and over Fudge's neck the way she should. As predicted, the steer heard them coming and threw on the brakes. Tori checked up, but Fudge ignored her, nearly passing the steer. She hauled back on the reins, and he bounced hard on his fronts, jacking her into the swells of her saddle as she threw her rope. The loop spun around the steer's right horn and off.

"My horse is a little fresh," she said to her heeler by way of apology.

He just smiled, tucking away the loop he hadn't had a chance to throw. Tori coiled her rope and steered Fudge into an empty space back in the corner where she could give herself a couple of mental head slaps in preparation for her next run. She would *not* let Shawnee screw with her. *Never again. Beginning now.* When the announcer called their names, Tori didn't even glance at Shawnee as they rode into the boxes.

"Got us a good one, Blondie. You turn him, I'll clean up the rest."

Blondie? Seriously? Who said that to a partner who was about to nod for stock? Tori rode forward, then back, resetting both Fudge and her brain. *Okay. Clear.* She tightened up the reins and waited for the steer to look straight out the front of the gate. Then she nodded.

They got a perfect start, Fudge's nose on the steer's hip three strides out of the gate. Tori's eyes were focused on the steer's horns, but she heard Shawnee's buckskin coming up hard on her right. Tori took two more swings, just to be sure, then threw. The loop felt as if it stuck to her hand. Like a wild pitch, it sailed high, arcing a foot above the steer's head. Tori dropped her chin, wheeled around, and headed back to the corner, rope dragging behind. She hadn't thrown a loop that bad in *years*. Her eyes burned with humiliation as she rode Fudge to where she'd left her rope bag and swung off.

And damned if Shawnee didn't follow her. "Hey, don't I know you?"

Tori shrugged, coiling her rope in quick jerks.

"I could swear..." Shawnee snapped her fingers. "Barbie! I'll be damned. Should've recognized you by that loop you just threw."

Tori's chin snapped up and she glared across Fudge's

back. "Were you born an asshole, or is it something you have to work at?"

Shawnee blinked. Then she folded her arms and leaned on the saddle horn, raising her eyebrows. "Somebody's gone and got 'em some teeth. Where ya been, Barbie?"

"None of your business." Tori grabbed Fudge's reins to make her escape.

Running away again, Princess? The mocking voice in her head sounded a whole lot more like her own than Shawnee's.

She stopped. Dammit. She would not let Shawnee—or her own lack of confidence—ruin one of the few things she had left that gave her real pleasure. As clichéd as it might sound, the best way to beat 'em truly was to join 'em, and Shawnee had unwittingly extended an invitation.

Tori turned around. "If you want to rope real steers, call me this week at Panhandle Orthopedics. I'll give you directions to my place."

Shawnee's jaw dropped. "Are you serious?"

"Do I look like I'm joking?"

"Uh, no."

"Then I'll talk to you next week."

As they strode through the door and outside, away from the other horses, Fudge gave a sorrowful whinny.

"I hear ya, buddy," Tori said.

But unlike Fudge, she didn't look back.

Shawnee didn't call until Wednesday, and then—thank the saints—she only left a voicemail. "If you meant what you said about roping some steers, I'm free on Friday evening. Let me know where and what time."

Tori replied with a text. Her address and Seven o'clock.

Friday afternoon, Tori strolled into reception to find Beth, one of the other therapists, and two patients—all female—huddled around the narrow slot of a window that opened from the waiting room into the therapy gym.

"What are we watching?" she asked, pushing onto her tiptoes to peer over their heads.

Oh. My. She'd started Delon's appointment with a quick exam to see how his knee had tolerated the new exercise regimen, and finding no increase in pain or swelling, she had sent him off to the gym with an aide to supervise today's workout. Finished, he had his heel propped high on the weight rack, fingers wrapped around his foot, damn near doing the splits. The position pulled his sweatpants snug across his thighs and butt. Then he pivoted his upper body to reach down for his ankle, and his audience gave a collective sigh.

Tori's mind jumped back to the first time she'd witnessed his impressive flexibility. Her palms tingled with the memory of curving around that perfect butt and…

She shook out her hands but couldn't look away. *Seriously unprofessional, Tori.* But she'd challenge anyone who appreciated the male form to wrap their fingers around one of those hard, muscled thighs and not notice exactly how much man was attached to it.

"He goes through the exact same routine every time," the other therapist said, a note of awe in her voice as he swung upright and stretched both arms behind him, his gray Aggies T-shirt molding to his chest and shoulders. "It's like a dance."

Choreographed to whatever beat came through the buds stuffed in his ears, loud enough to render him oblivious to his audience.

"Maybe we should tuck dollar bills in his waistband," Tori suggested dryly.

The other women broke into shocked giggles, then scattered as Delon straightened and turned toward the window. Tori sidestepped the herd and went out to interrupt Delon and ruin everyone's fun. She waved at him to follow her from the gym back to one of the treatment rooms where they could speak privately, trying to ignore her body's little hum of interest as he brushed past her in the doorway.

Her phone buzzed as he settled onto the treatment table. She pulled it out, checked the number, and gave an apologetic grimace. "Mind if I take this?"

"Go ahead."

If only the mechanic on the other end was so obliging. "Next Wednesday's the soonest we can fit you in."

"I can't rope with a tractor stalled in the middle of my arena. I'll pay extra for someone to come today."

"No can do. Want me to put you on the schedule for next week?"

"I'll make a few more calls and let you know." Tori sighed, frustrated, as she hung up. She'd already tried half the repair shops in the Panhandle. No one was interested in working overtime on a Friday. On the bright side, she now had a valid reason to call Shawnee and cancel their practice session. She turned her attention back to Delon. "Sorry. Now, we need to talk about your MRI—"

"What kind?"

She blinked. "Of MRI?"

"Tractor," he said.

"Uh, red. Old."

"Make? Model? Gas or diesel engine?"

She scrunched her face, trying to recall what the real estate agent had called it. "An International B-something, burns gas, came with the place. It's been running kind of rough. Last night, it died and wouldn't start again."

"How big is it?"

"This tall." Tori held up a hand, palm down.

Delon gave a slow, thoughtful nod. "I can get it fixed."

She stared at him for a couple of beats, comprehension slow to dawn. "Oh. I never thought...your shop does tractors?"

"Not usually, but that's a simple engine. Won't be cheap to get it done today, though."

"Whatever. I just want to get this over with."

His eyebrows rose. "This?"

"Long story." She pulled out one of her cards to

scribble her address and cell phone number on the back. "Tell the mechanic that the tractor's in the indoor arena. I won't be home until around six."

He tucked the card in the pocket of his T-shirt. "Is it okay if I start working out on my spur board at home?"

She had to take a moment to picture what he had in mind. "Stationary or the kind that bucks and spins?"

"Stationary."

She considered the potential for injury—virtually none at this point in his recovery—and nodded. "That's fine. What about the MRI?"

"I'd rather hold off until I see how the spur board goes."

In other words, he had to see what his knee could do. Or couldn't. And that was for the best. For now, she would focus on preparing Delon's body to accommodate his new limitations. But before they could really move forward, he had to accept that he was never going be the same. Then he might be ready to let her try to make him better, even if "better" also meant "different."

"Go for it," she said, handing him a pair of ice packs. "You can report back at your Tuesday appointment, and we'll decide about the MRI."

He headed back to the gym to kick back on one of the mat tables to ice his knee, and she retreated to her office, where she pecked through endless screens to enter notes on the computer. Stupid software. She finally clicked Done and hustled out to grab her next patient. As she reached the waiting room door, it opened and a man stuck his head in to glance around the gym. Around fifty, she guessed, longish ginger hair and eighties sideburns—shades of Kris Kristofferson back when he was seriously hot.

"Hey," he said to Delon. "I was hoping to catch you before you left."

Delon hesitated a beat too long, during which the man caught sight of Tori. His smile was easy and open. "Oh. Hi. You must be the new therapist."

"That's me," Tori said, watching Delon for a clue.

He wiped his expression blank. "Tori, this is my dad, Merle Sanchez. Dad, this is Tori."

Merle strode forward, the smile broadening as he stuck out his hand. "Good to meet you."

Tori could only stare at him, mute, as he pumped her hand. This was Delon's father? But he was so...

"Whatcha doin' in Amarillo, Dad?" Delon asked.

"I delivered that old Mack we sold to Soderstroms and figured I could catch a ride home with you."

"Sure. I'm done here." Delon grabbed his gym towel and swung his feet to the floor, much too eager to make himself—and his father—scarce. "I'll see you Tuesday, Tori."

"Wait...*Tori*?" The combination of Delon's obvious discomfort and hearing her name again lit a spark of recognition. Merle Sanchez's eyes widened as his gaze jumped from Delon to her. "Are you the same Tori who was, um—"

"Yes. Nice to meet you." She cut a swift glance at his son. "Finally."

Then she dragged her next patient out of the waiting room and left Delon to do the explaining.

Chapter 10

Tori's phone rang as she settled at her desk after ushering out her last patient of the morning. She looked at the number, her eyebrows climbing. Twice in a week?

"Hey, Daddy. I hope you're not calling to say you found a stray wolf for me to adopt."

"Why would I...oh! The cat." He sounded vaguely nervous, which made all her defensive antennae snap to attention. "No more pets. I, um, wondered if you were busy next Friday night."

Oh, hell. Whatever he wanted, it couldn't be good if he sounded that uncertain. "Depends. What am I going to get roped into?"

"The Buckaroo Ball. I agreed to be one of the hosts, but I need a date."

Tori squelched a groan. The Buckaroo Ball was one of the biggest fundraisers of the year, an excuse for the Panhandle's most well-to-do to dress up, pay exorbitant prices for mediocre prime rib, and bid obscene amounts of money in the charity auction.

And gawk at what the local gossip columns had

called "the mysterious Miss—or should that be *missing*—Patterson."

"I'm sorry, Daddy, but I'd rather stay out of the public eye."

"I know, sugar, but I have a plan. We won't mention your married name, and I'll tell everyone you're visiting from out of town. Which is true, since you live in Dumas. If you go all out with the hair and makeup and glitter, no one from work will even recognize a picture in the paper." He paused a beat, then added, "I'd love to spend an evening with you. And it *does* benefit the Cowboy Crisis Fund."

Damn him for being almost as ruthless as her mother at exploiting her weaknesses. The crisis fund helped cowboys with medical expenses when their insurance fell short or was nonexistent. A number of her patients in Wyoming had been beneficiaries, which was the only way they could afford therapy. It was one cause she was honor bound to support.

She blew out a silent, resigned sigh. "What time?"

"I'll pick you up at seven at the town house."

"Have the housekeeper ship up all the formal dresses I left in the closet at the ranch, and it's a date." He might guilt her into attending the ball. He could not force her to go shopping.

"Thanks, sugar. Love you."

"Love you too, Daddy."

Tori scowled at her phone for a moment, then pushed it aside, tapping a finger on Delon's file, open on her tablet. According to the clinic's records, Delon still lived above the shop at Sanchez Trucking. More telling, instead of a wife or significant other, he'd listed his dad as his emergency contact. But Tori knew for a fact that Delon also had a son. She'd seen the kid propped on his daddy's hip during a televised interview at the National Finals a couple of years ago. But who was the mother? Better question, *where* was the mother? Not in Delon's medical file, that much she knew.

Which was none of her business. Unless Delon broached the subject, she had no excuse to go poking around in his private affairs, but his professional life was out there for the world to see, and it was time she took a closer look.

She unwrapped the deli sandwich she'd brought for lunch and popped the top on a Dr. Pepper before pulling up an internet browser and typing in *Delon Sanchez* and *bareback riding*. She would start by studying his normal riding style, then move on to other successful bareback riders, looking for ways to adjust Delon's mechanics to compensate for the limited motion in his knee. The search results scrolled onto her screen, and she jacked forward in her chair. At the top of the list, with over twenty thousand hits, was a video titled *Delon Sanchez bad wreck*.

She hadn't thought to look for footage of his injury. Tori's lungs tightened as she clicked the Play button. The image was grainy, filmed at night on a cell phone camera with limited zoom capabilities, but she could see that the arena glistened under the lights, a lake of standing water pocked with mud.

A gate swung open and the horse vaulted out, bucking high and hard, straight across the arena, water spraying from under his platter feet. Delon matched him jump for jump, spurs rolling clear up to the rigging, then snapping back to the horse's neck before its front feet hit the ground. His upper body was tight, no wild flopping, no head bouncing off the horse's rump. Precision. Control. Delon's trademark. Until it all came undone.

The bronc threw on the brakes at the fence, and its hind legs skidded, then splayed, the momentum carrying its hindquarters up under its body. For an instant, the horse hung there, nearly vertical. Tori sucked in a breath, sure it would flip onto its back and crush Delon. Then it toppled onto its side, splashing down like a breaching whale. When it scrambled up, Delon was still aboard, both hands clamped on the stiff handhold, but the rigging had slipped sideways.

The horse bolted around the end of the arena with the pickup riders in hot pursuit. The rigging kept slipping, dropping Delon's body closer to the pounding hooves with each stride. Tori's hand curled, her fingers digging into the plastic armrest of her chair as the bucking horse thundered toward the fence with Delon hanging out on the side, his head dangerously exposed to the steel posts. The pickup man kicked hard, his horse straining to squeeze into the gap and push the bronc away from the fence. When Delon's hand came loose from the rigging, he fell directly in the oncoming horse's path.

Tori flinched as the big brown gelding slammed into and over Delon. The pickup horse stumbled and went to its knees, sending the rider hurtling over its head. God only knew how the horse avoided crashing down on top of him. For an instant, there was utter silence. Then chaos, as cowboys and medics came running from every direction. Even though she knew the outcome, Tori held her breath as they clustered around Delon, easing him upright with no weight on his left leg.

She gasped when she saw him crumple, and the medics sprang into frantic motion. Delon had stopped breathing. Only for a few moments, until the EMTs intubated him and inflated his punctured lung, but still. Even though Pepper had told her, she hadn't truly comprehended...he'd stopped *breathing*. She was suddenly intensely aware of how that must feel. The panic. The helpless terror.

She took a deep breath, appreciating how the oxygen flowed into her lungs on command. Then she frowned and tapped Pause. *Wait just a damn minute.* While she'd been focused on Delon, one of the bullfighters had sprinted to the aid of the fallen pickup man. That bullfighter was Joe Cassidy; everybody in rodeo knew him. And the pickup man who'd run Delon down—

The pickup man wasn't a *man* at all. It was Violet Jacobs.

Chapter 11

DELON BRACED HIMSELF FOR AN INTERROGATION ON the drive back to Earnest, but his dad only said, "So that's Tori."

"Yep."

Merle nodded. "Well, if she's like the rest of her family, she's good at her job."

"Seems to be."

And that was the sum total of the conversation.

Back at the shop, Delon walked straight to his bedroom closet and pulled out the gear bag he hadn't touched since the night of the wreck. When he dragged the zipper open, the smell hit him—dust, rosin, leather, and the sweet antiseptic scent of the benzoin used to stiffen his glove. Aromas meant to be accompanied by banging chutes, the snorts of bucking horses, the strains of the national anthem. What Beni called the "bareback riders get ready" song because they were nearly always the first event of the rodeo.

His riding glove could stand up on its own, like medieval armor formed to fit his hand. Traces of mud were still visible in the seams of the chaps folded at the bottom of the bag, but someone had taken the time to clean up his gear and stow it properly while he was flat on his back in the hospital. He slid his hand into the glove and flexed his fingers, feeling the bite of hardened leather. For the first time since he was thirteen, there were no calluses to protect his palm.

He really had gone soft.

He pulled the glove on and worked his hand into the stiff rawhide handle of the rigging. His blood rose instantly at the creak of rosin. For a moment, he fought the urge. He should wait until he was sure he was alone. Then he hissed a curse. He was in the mood to kick the shit out of something, and no one would pay any attention to him in the old, walled-off section of the shop.

He shoved his feet into a pair of boots, caught up the cinch with the hand that wasn't still stuck in the rigging, and headed out the back door. The flick of a switch lit a single row of fluorescent lights below. His mind reeled back over hundreds of hours, thousands upon thousands of spur strokes, and two half-grown boys with big dreams. His rodeo career had started here. Not in an arena but this grimy, ill-lit corner of their father's shop.

The contraption that sat in the middle of the cramped space looked like a poor attempt to build a wooden doghouse—six feet long, wide at the bottom, with short straight sides and a top that slanted to a platform slightly wider than his butt. The front narrowed and sloped away from the body, forming the approximate shape of a horse's neck and shoulders if it had its head down, bucking. They'd padded the seat and shoulders with foam and carpet remnants, then worn it to shreds with the pound and scrape of boot heels.

Later they'd designed a fancier model with a pretty decent bucking motion using an electric motor and a flywheel off a junker truck, but once they'd mastered real live horses, it had been relegated to one of the sheds out back. This old board was all they needed to stay sharp and hone their personal styles: Gil flung back, his head slamming off the horse's rump, his spur strokes free and wild. And Delon, shoulders cocked forward, his body tight and controlled, each stroke precise.

Bareback riding was the X-games event of rodeo, the best rides straddling the razor-thin line between going big and crashing. The harder the horse bucked, the bigger the score. The cowboy was rewarded for opening up and taking chances, unless he teetered over that line and lost control. The judges wanted to see long, flashy spur strokes, but you'd better stay centered and your boot heels had better be planted in the horse's neck before its front feet hit the ground on the next jump or they'd dock points.

Delon damn near always beat the horse to the ground, his spur strokes dead even and snappy. Consistency was Delon's hole card, but Gil was the one people had lined the fences to watch. Electric, unpredictable, but always worth the price of admission.

Shaking off the memories, Delon checked the CD in the battered boom box on its shelf above the workbench.

Guns N' Roses. Perfect. His heart pounded to the beat as Axel howled the opening bars of "Welcome to the Jungle" through the forty-amp speakers Delon had wired into every corner of the room. He pulled his hand free and strapped his rigging onto the board, then propped one heel on the seat and reached for his ankle, his muscles only offering a mild protest as he touched his cheek to his knee. His body responded to the familiar routine, his brain kicking off a slide show of all the times and all the places he'd warmed up this way—from the Cow Palace in San Francisco to the coliseum on the boardwalk in Atlantic City, from Calgary to Houston, and hundreds of other rodeos in between.

On this last Friday night in January, he should be in Fort Worth or Rapid City, South Dakota, standing on the back of chutes inhaling the perfume of dirt and horse shit and rosin, the chute boss yelling that he'd be coming out of number six so get his rigging strapped on. Cowboys and contractors would be jostling past, thumping him on the back and yelling, "Go get 'im." Then he'd be climbing over the back of a chute to ease down on a horse's warm, hard back while it snorted and showed him the whites of its eyes.

He was nowhere close to ready to be done with that life. The admission tore something loose inside his chest and set his heart thudding like a hammer strike against his sternum. He clenched one end of a leather lace between his teeth and wrapped the other around his wrist to tie his glove on. Then he slung a leg over the spur board, worked his hand back into the rigging, and scooted his hips up into position. Free arm cocked up and back, he nodded his head.

His feet lashed out, thudding solid against the wood. He jerked his knees up, heels dragging against the worn carpet. The right one clicked the edge of the rigging. The left came up a foot short. He cursed and spurred again. And again. And again. With each stroke, the rhythm got more ragged as his right leg outpaced his left. Sweat slicked his forehead, and his knee burned as he focused every ounce of his will on making it work.

It wouldn't.

He dropped his feet and bowed over the rigging, his breath a harsh rasp, his eyes and throat burning as all the fear and pain and frustration of the past months flooded through him.

"Looks like shit," Gil said.

Delon jerked upright, searching the shadows until he found his brother's lean form lounging against the open door to the office hallway, a Coke bottle in hand. Humiliation balled up into fury. "Did I ask your opinion?"

"It's your lucky day. You get a freebie." Gil tipped the neck of his bottle toward the spur board. "Is that the best you can do?"

"Yes." Delon yanked his hand out of the rigging and swung off the spur board, gritting his teeth against the bright arc of pain when his left foot hit the ground.

"Is it gonna get any better?"

"I don't know." Delon tossed his glove into his bag, then turned to fumble with the buckle of the cinch, work the leather latigo free, and fold it in precise loops through the D-ring.

"When will you?"

Delon secured the latigo, then rolled up the cinch on the opposite side of the rigging. "Pepper wants to do another MRI to see if there's scar tissue or something he can scrape out. He might be able to get more of the motion back."

"But probably not all."

"No." Delon shoved the rigging in his bag and zipped it shut.

"Be easier if you rode right-handed. Frees up your left leg."

Delon gave a derisive snort. "We both know how well that went."

"You might be a little more coordinated than when you were fourteen."

Delon shook his head. If swapping hands was the only way to compensate for his knee, he was screwed.

"What are you gonna do if doesn't get better?" Gil asked.

"Hell if I know." Delon grabbed the rigging bag and thumped it down on top of the spur board, turning to sneer at his brother. "Got any suggestions, boss man?"

Gil gave him a steady, dark stare. "You could pry that stick out of your ass. Life fucks with people. Deal with it, Delon."

They weren't just talking about bucking horses anymore. Delon wanted to lash out, ask Gil who made him the expert, but he already knew. Fate. Bad luck. Bad decisions. They'd all ganged up to teach Gil a whole shitload of lessons. And Delon was still following his lead, despite every vow to the contrary.

Delon turned away to shut off the boom box. "I can't force my knee to bend."

"No, but you could let your hips do more of the work. Rear back and open up a little."

Of course. Gil's mantra. *For fuck's sake, D, have a little fun. You ride like someone's holding a gun to your head.*

"That's not my style."

"No. It was mine." Gil's mouth twisted into a mockery of what used to be his smile. He straightened and tossed his bottle into a metal trash can with a resounding crash. "God knows, turning out like me is a fate worse than death."

Delon couldn't lie. Couldn't force out the truth. For years, he'd wanted nothing more desperately than to be just like his big brother. Sometimes, in the dead of the night when he couldn't hide from himself, he still did. He stood in the light and watched Gil disappear into the darkness, his footsteps an uneven tap and scrape on the concrete. The sound tore at a scar deep inside Delon's soul. One that had never healed over completely and probably never would.

Delon would've preferred to avoid Gil indefinitely, but he had to go into the office to get the keys to the service pickup. Gil popped his head out of the dispatcher's office as Delon slipped them off a hook.

"Where are you going?"

"I gotta run over to Dumas, take a look at a tractor."

"Doing house calls now, are we?" Gil drawled with a lift of his eyebrow that made it an insult.

"Fuck you, Gil."

"Save it for the customer." Gil folded his arms and smirked. "Especially if it's who I assume it is. Dad told me about your new therapist. Funny you didn't see fit to mention her name."

"It's no big deal." But guilty heat seeped under Delon's skin. On the surface, Tori was—well, had been—so much like Gil's ex that being with her had felt like something else he'd stolen from his brother. *Look what else I've got that you can't have anymore.*

But he couldn't see anything in Gil's expression beyond the usual sharp glint of sarcasm. "Uh-huh. That'd be why you're hustling over to console the grieving widow on a Friday night."

Delon stiffened. "What do you know about Tori?"

"As much as the internet had to tell me. That husband of hers was big news."

Delon swore under his breath. "You ever heard of respecting a person's privacy?"

Gil shrugged. "Fine. If you don't want to know what happened to Willy Hancock, no skin off my ass."

Willy Hancock. Cheyenne. Delon frowned, talking more to himself than Gil. "I remember something…"

"Step into my office and I'll show you."

Delon hesitated. Gil was probably screwing with him. Then again…

The computer made a sound like a ringing phone, and Gil disappeared into his office. The mouse clicked, then springs creaked on Gil's chair before he spoke in a teasing voice Delon hadn't heard in a very long time. "Hey, sugar. Now there's a sight for sore eyes on a lonely Friday night."

A woman giggled, sounding almost as if she was in the room. One more thing the Sanchez boys had in common—a love of high-quality sound systems. "You're wastin' that charm on me, Gil Sanchez," she said. "I can't be bribed."

"You sure? I got good stuff."

"Yeah? Like what? You gonna send your hottie of a brother to pick up the next load I give you?"

Delon clenched his hand around the pickup keys but couldn't make himself leave.

Gil's laugh had an evil ring to it. "You bet. He's still on the disabled list, but he can drive."

"When's he gonna be able to ride again?"

The hesitation was barely noticeable. "Not sure. Do we have a deal? I got a driver sittin' dead in the water an hour down the road from you, lookin' for a back haul. And I'll send you Delon just to keep him from pacing around here, makin' us all nuts. With three hundred loads a day out of that warehouse, you must have something you can give my driver in the next day or two."

"Hmmm."

Delon eased over to peek around the doorframe. Gil's oversize double monitors spanned the far wall of the cramped space. The one on the left shuffled between sections of highway maps, with red arrows to indicate the progress of Sanchez trucks, courtesy of the new GPS system. On the right screen, Delon saw a woman poking at computer keys, her face and hair done to perfection—if the Farrah Fawcett look was still the ultimate in style.

When had Gil turned into a borderline computer geek? He'd come to work full-time after his accident by force, not choice, and he hadn't been happy about it. Or anything else, for that matter. Days had passed when he hadn't bothered to show up at all. Everyone understood he was skating on treacherously thin ice, but no one knew how to pull him to safety.

Somewhere along the line, he'd found his way back. Now this little office was the heart of Sanchez Trucking, and it seemed as if the whole company moved to the accelerated beat of Gil's pulse. Or the thrum of his guitar, which he'd settled onto his lap. He picked at it while he waited for a reply. In a bigger company, someone other than the dispatcher would schedule the loads, but they hadn't reached that threshold or found anyone Gil would trust for more than the long weekends he spent in Oklahoma with his son. As far as

Delon could tell, work and Quint were the sum total of Gil's existence.

The woman on-screen tapped some more, mumbling to herself. "Reefer. Reefer. Flatbed. Hmm…I have a load of personal hygiene products—baby wipes and stuff—that's due to load at ten tomorrow morning, headed to Albuquerque. The trucking company already called to say their driver will be late. They've been makin' a habit of that. Wouldn't hurt to give 'em a wake-up call."

Gil struck a triumphant chord on his guitar. "I'll have our guy there no later than nine. And as soon as you find another load for me, I'll send Delon out for a visit."

She giggled again, then promised to email Gil the paperwork before signing off. Gil leaned back and strummed—*bah-bah-bah-bum-bah*—the triumphant opening chords of "Dueling Banjos."

Delon glared at him. "You just whored me out for a load of asswipes."

"Seemed appropriate, considering your attitude lately." When Delon didn't bother with a comeback, Gil tipped his head, continuing to idly strum the guitar while studying his brother. "Since you're here, I assume you want to know how Willy Hancock died."

Delon shrugged. Gil leaned forward and clicked a tab in his browser. The web page for a Cheyenne newspaper popped up. Delon stepped closer.

"Jesus Christ," he whispered, staring at the photo of a mangled pickup below the headline.

Cheyenne Cowboy
Sacrifices Life to Save Children

Local roper and rancher Willy Hancock died on Thursday after intentionally driving his pickup into the path of a car that was speeding toward a group of kindergarten students in a school crosswalk. The car struck the driver's door at forty miles an hour, killing Hancock instantly. Police confirmed that the driver of the car was reading a text message...

"It made national news," Gil said, dead serious now.

"I remember." *Willy Hancock. Cheyenne.* Of course. "They did a big tribute during Frontier Days, introduced his family, had the kids and their parents there. I had no idea…" That Tori was one of the solemn crowd on the stage in front of the grandstand. He shook his head. "I had no idea he was married to a Patterson. Why didn't we hear anything?"

Gil clicked again and a photo popped up. Tori, graveside, in a black dress and a wide-brimmed black hat, her eyes dull with pain in a face so pale she was almost transparent. Delon felt as if a truck engine settled on his chest, crushing his lungs.

Gil skimmed a finger under the people clustered around Tori. "See anyone you recognize?"

Delon leaned in, squinting. Tori was flanked by an older couple who were clearly not the Pattersons. The man was big and barrel-chested, the woman a nonde-script blur. None of the other faces around them were familiar either. "Her parents weren't there?"

"Nope. Not a single mention of her daddy."

Easy enough to guess why. "The press would've gone nuts if they'd known where she came from."

"They went nuts anyway—at least in Wyoming. It made a minor splash at the national level, but the report-ers were so caught up in the *Hero Saves Children* angle, they didn't bother to look at his wife other than the usual quotes from the devastated widow—along with all fifty or so of his closest relatives." Gil rolled his eyes. "The Hancocks breed like damn rabbits. She just dis-appeared into the mob. Besides, Patterson is a common name. Why would anyone connect a cowboy's wife in Wyoming to the man who'd just been named the chair of Senate Appropriations?"

Delon stepped back and braced his hand against the doorframe to catch his balance. He looked at Tori's stricken face, and his throat closed up. He cleared it twice before he could speak. "Who was he?"

Gil raised his eyebrows, questioning.

"Her husband. His family. Who was he?"

"What it said in the newspaper. Rancher. Roper. Horse trainer. Big family, but not big bucks." Gil shrugged. "Just a guy."

An ordinary guy. No better than any other mother trucker. And Tori had married him anyway. The real-ization hit Delon hard, shattering a certainty so deep inside, he felt like every other part of him would come undone. It wasn't fair, dammit. Willy Hancock was from Wyoming. He didn't know any better, so he'd just gone for it, the way Delon had done that first night. Before reality, that coldhearted bitch, had slapped some sense into him. Except it turned out reality wasn't exactly what he thought, and some other guy who didn't know a Patterson from a regular girl got the prize.

Gil clicked to close the browser and swiveled his chair to bend his head over the guitar, plucking out an unfamiliar but catchy melody. Probably something he'd written himself. Another unexpected side of Gil that had emerged in the last few years. "Turn in an invoice for any parts you take tonight so I can adjust the inventory. I assume your services are on the house."

He gave the word *services* an insulting twist that snapped Delon's spine straight. "I'll leave the bill on your desk, boss man."

"Whatever, bro."

Delon stomped upstairs, wincing as his knee complained about the unaccustomed workout. He grabbed an ice pack and a Coke on the way past the refrigerator. Twenty minutes later, he pulled on work boots and a jacket, stuffed a pair of grease-stained gloves into his pocket, and headed out his back door. Halfway open, it stuck, blocked by a paper bag. Delon glanced around, saw no one in the shop, and bent to pick it up.

A weird pang ricocheted around inside his chest as he pulled out a battered bareback rigging with the initials *G.A.S.* branded into the leather. Delon choked on a raw-edged laugh. Gil used to like to brag that even his initials were flammable. Delon skimmed his fingers over the rawhide handhold, reversed from his own because Gil rode right-handed. Even in that, they were polar opposites. He hesitated, then slid his bare hand into the rigging and tightened his fingers.

The backward grip felt off-balance and wrong, and holding it felt like violating a rodeo commandment. *Thou shalt not mess with another man's equipment.* Ten years ago, Gil would've punched him for even touching the thing.

Delon put the rigging in the bag, folded the top tightly closed, and stowed it in the back corner of his closet, next to his own. These days, it wasn't any use to either of them.

Chapter 12

TORI RUSHED HOME FROM WORK ON FRIDAY EVENING to find a white service pickup parked in front of the barn, *Sanchez Trucking* lettered on the door. Delon had come through with a mechanic. When she stepped out of the car, Fudge cantered in from the pasture, trailing a stream of low, desperate nickers.

She paused at the fence to scratch under his jaw. "Oh, come on. You have the roping steers for company now."

He did something that looked very much like an eye roll.

"Shawnee's coming tonight, so we get to rope. That'll be fun, right?"

Fudge snuffled grimy snot onto the front of her jacket in response, which pretty much summed up how Tori felt about it too. She rested her forehead on his and closed her eyes, absorbing the musky scent of horse, the silken prickle of his hair against her skin. God, what she'd give to just curl up in her blanket nest on the couch...

An unearthly screech sent Fudge wheeling away, snorting in alarm. There was a shouted curse, followed by a series of thuds from inside the barn. Heart thumping, Tori jogged across the yard, cut around the back corner of the barn, and slammed into a hard male body.

He stumbled backward. "Ouch! Shit!"

"Delon?" She shook her head, dazed by the collision. "What were you doing in my barn?"

His hair stuck up in tufts on one side, and his jeans were unbuttoned, gaping open. One earbud dangled loose. He cast a baleful glare at the barn. "I went in there to take a leak, and something jumped me."

Oh, hell. Tori reached inside the door and flicked on the light. Sure enough, a pair of malevolent eyes gleamed from under the hay manger.

"What is wrong with you?" Tori demanded.

The cat curled a paw and gave it an insolent lick.

"What is it?" Delon asked.

She switched off the light. "A cat."

"Like...a bobcat?"

"Like Garfield," she said. "Only with homicidal tendencies."

Delon brows lowered. "And you own this thing because..."

"Pest control." She let her gaze slide down to his waist. "You might want to close up shop."

He muttered another curse and wheeled around. As he bowed his head to zip and button, she saw the punctures on the side of his neck. Damn and double damn. The hellcat had drawn blood. She stepped close, lifting her hand just as Delon turned around. They came face-to-face, nose-to-nose. Surprise made her suck in a breath—and a lungful of warm, healthy man. Clean and spicy with a chaser of engine grease, a combination so uniquely Delon it made her head spin.

She should have stepped back. Instead, she touched his neck, feeling the sharp rap of his heartbeat under her fingers. "You're bleeding."

"It smarts."

He raised his hand to cover hers. For a long moment, they stood, locked in place, as tension revved like an engine from a low hum to a scream. She'd had her hands on him dozens of times at the clinic while she put him through his paces. Why should this be so different? But she felt the matching catch in his pulse, saw the heat build in his eyes. They were so close and so alone, in this alley between the barn and the arena where no one could see. One step and Delon could have her pressed up against the wall, the way he'd done the night he showed up fresh off a win at San Antonio, so fired up they barely got the front door closed...

She jerked her hand free and stepped back. He stared at her for a beat, his rumpled hair falling over his forehead, those amazing eyes dark in a way they hadn't been back then. Full of shadows and storms—and desire. Current or remembered? Best not to wonder.

"Why are you here?" she asked.

"Fixing your tractor, remember?"

She gave an impatient shake of her head. "You said you'd send a mechanic."

"I did." He spread his hands to say *Here I am*, and the gleam in his eyes sharpened, as if he sensed how her body clenched at the view. "As long as you're here, you can give me a hand."

Her mind slipped again, into the quicksand of memories. Oh, she'd given him a hand, all right. And a mouth. And… She ground her teeth, irritated. Damn him, invading her space this way. She wouldn't have accepted the offer if she'd known he planned to do it himself.

He paused at the door to the arena and glanced over his shoulder as he tucked the earbuds into his pocket. "Coming?"

Not lately, her body whispered. *But if you've got a few minutes…*

Tori growled under her breath but had to follow him. Inside the arena, the tractor hood was open, its innards exposed, a toolbox and a portable battery charger on the ground next to it.

Tori lingered by the door. "What's wrong with it?"

"Nothing some basic maintenance won't fix," he said, shooting her an accusing glare.

She returned it in kind. She'd only owned the thing for a month—it wasn't her fault if the previous owners had neglected it. "Can you get it running tonight?"

"I said I would." He wiggled his fingers. "I'm almost done working my magic."

Her breath hitched at a new explosion of memories. She knew what those hands could do. Could feel the soft rasp of calluses against her skin as his palms slid over her…

For God's sake, *stop*! She resisted the urge to stomp her foot in annoyance. What had happened to her little cocoon? One touch, one steamy look from him, and the damn thing just up and disintegrated, leaving her as trembly as a newborn colt and just as clueless. Letting those eyes and that body get to her again was beyond stupid.

"Here." His voice became abrupt, his expression shuttered as he handed her one end of an extension cord. "Plug this in. I don't know where the outlet is."

She did, then planted herself safely on the opposite side of the tractor as Delon popped rubber, cup-shaped connectors onto the spark plugs. "So…this is your place," he said.

"Yep." Though he hadn't phrased it as a question, there were half a dozen embedded in the casual statement. She ignored all of them.

"Why Dumas?"

"Property is cheaper out here."

He worked in expectant silence for a few beats. When she didn't further enlighten him, he shot her a glance over the tractor. "Did your family disown you?"

"No." If only it was that simple to become a non-Patterson.

Delon popped the last spark plug connector into place, then straightened. "Then why not live at the ranch?"

"It costs too much." A price wrung out of her soul,

drop by drop, in guilt and failed obligations. *With great fortune comes great responsibility.* The Patterson creed. She alone had walked away. Call her selfish, but she'd let the rest of her family bear the burden of moral duty to mankind and country. She'd vowed to avoid being extraordinary at all costs. So far, so good.

"Live in our house, play by our rules?" Delon bent to adjust the settings on the battery charger. The view did not suck. He glanced over his shoulder. "You said your mother was upset that you dropped out of medical school."

Tori dragged her attention back to the conversation. "Is."

"Excuse me?"

"*Is* upset. My mother's ambitions for me don't have an expiration date."

Delon shot her a baffled look. "She still wants you to go back to medical school after all this time?"

"At this point, she'd settle for a PhD." Tori shrugged. "If one angle doesn't work, she tries another and another until one day, you find yourself doing what she wants."

"Doesn't she care what *you* want? If you're happy?"

Tori gave a dry laugh. "She deals in survival rates. Functional capacity. Measurable outcomes. Happiness cannot be calculated so is therefore irrelevant."

Delon shook his head. "That's messed up."

"That's my mother. Relentless. But not evil. That's what makes her scary. She truly believes she's doing the right thing. She's convinced that someday, I'll wake up and regret that I didn't take advantage of my opportunities to have a bigger impact."

And she might be right, at least about the impact part. Tori helped one patient at a time. Her mother's technical advances and her sister's research could benefit thousands. But Tori couldn't imagine regretting her chosen path. She liked digging into each individual case, watching her patients improve, day by day, reveling in every small victory.

Now if she could just find a way to count Delon among those victories.

"What about your mother?" Tori asked. Tit for tat and all. "You said she was gone."

Delon gave the battery one last swipe before tossing the rag on top of the tractor engine. "She lives on the Navajo reservation."

In Arizona? Or New Mexico? Both, maybe. Tori's brain sifted and shuffled images—Delon so dark, his dad so fair…

Delon jumped to the conclusion for her. "My grandfather took his stepfather's name. We have no Hispanic blood."

"Oh. That must be weird, people assuming…" That he was different from what they expected from his last name? Huh. Sounded vaguely familiar. "How long has she been gone?"

He rummaged in his toolbox for a plastic, cylinder-shaped gizmo and screwed it down over the nearest battery terminal, twisting it back and forth to scrub the metal post clean. "Her father had a stroke when I was four. Her mother already had severe diabetes. They couldn't live alone, so she went home."

Her father. Her mother. Not *my grandparents.* A telling distinction.

"Did she try to take you with her?"

He shook his head. "They lived way out on the mesa. No electricity. No running water. We would have had to go to a boarding school. She thought we were better off here."

"Did she come back to visit?"

He paused, then said, "At first."

"It didn't go well?"

"It was fine, until she had to go." He reattached the battery cable and tightened the bolt with a quick jerk of the wrench. "Every time she left, I threw screaming fits, my brother would yell that he hated everyone, and Dad would sit up all night for a week staring at the television." He hitched rigid shoulders. "The visits got further apart, until finally it was just phone calls on birthdays and holidays and a week with my mother in the summer."

God. It sounded like an extended version of hell. "Your dad hasn't remarried?"

"They aren't divorced. Never got around to it, I guess."

"Oh. That's..." Sad. Her heart ached, imagining a child trying to understand his mother's repeated abandonments. "It's hard to picture you throwing tantrums."

"It never did me any good." The corner of his lip curled. "I get a lot further being the nice one."

He twisted *nice* into an insult, and the depth of his bitterness set Tori back on her heels. Whatever had scraped him this raw was fairly recent. His anger was ragged, an uncomfortable fit, as if he hadn't had time to grow into it. Probably just about four months.

"I watched the video of your wreck. Violet ran you down."

His hands stilled for an instant. "It wasn't her fault."

"I suppose she did the best she could, given the situation." But agreeing didn't take the acid out of Tori's voice. "Still part of the family, I take it?"

Delon stared at her for a long, charged moment. Then his eyes narrowed. "You don't like Violet?"

"Violet never liked me. None of her crowd did, from the moment I walked on campus."

He fiddled with the cables so long she thought he wouldn't respond. "Do you know Krista Barron?"

Tori blinked at the unexpected tangent. "Her daddy and mine were elected to the Senate the same year, and we went to the same private school in DC."

But Krista was three years older than Tori and very…adventurous, so they'd never been more than casual acquaintances. Odd that Tori turned out to be the true rebel. Nowadays, Krista Barron-Tate was the very proper wife of an up-and-coming Oklahoma politician. "What's Krista got to do with me?"

"Besides being a rich, sexy blond? She bailed on law school to come slumming in the Panhandle."

"She's from Oklahoma. I was born and raised here." With the exception of those excruciating prep school years in DC, separated from the land, the sky, and especially her horses.

Delon only shrugged. "Krista hooked up with one of the local boys for a few months. She got pregnant. He wanted to marry her, but the Barrons weren't having some no-account cowboy for a son-in-law. They tried to cut him out of the kid's life. He wouldn't let go, and the custody battle got ugly. So when you showed up…"

They all saw another spoiled brat, looking to sow some wild oats and wreak havoc. "This cowboy…is he a friend of yours?"

"Nah." Delon gave a hard laugh. "Just my brother."

And *pow*! The light bulb finally turned on. She tucked her arms tightly around her waist to contain the slow roll of her stomach. God, she'd been such a fool. "You had no idea who I was the night we met."

"No."

Shit and damn. When she'd dropped Delon off that next morning, Tori had been so sure he would call her before the end of the day. Maybe pop by before he left town for the first rodeo run of the season. She'd waited. And waited. While he'd gone to the Jacobs ranch for New Year's dinner, where goddamn Violet had poured poison in his ear. And Delon had soaked it up, because wasn't a woman just like her already making his brother's life hell? Of course, he'd listened. The miracle was that he'd ever come near her again.

Well, at least now Tori understood exactly why Violet's attitude toward her had gone from amused contempt to palpable animosity after that New Year's Eve.

He hopped up onto the tractor, pulled out the choke knob, and turned the key. The engine groaned, coughed, then sputtered to life. He adjusted the throttle until the tractor settled into a steady roar. "There you go," he yelled over the racket. "Let it run for at least ten minutes before you turn it off."

He climbed down and unclipped the charger cables. She coiled up the extension cord as he gathered his tools.

She followed him, pausing at the arena gate to hand him the cord. "Thanks. For coming out on a Friday night and all."

"I'll send you a bill."

As he stepped out the door into the darkness, she said, "Hey, Delon?"

He looked back, eyes wary. "Yeah?"

"If it makes you feel any better, I never thought you were all that nice."

He stared at her for a long moment, then gave another of those hard smiles. "You didn't really know who I was either."

Chapter 13

WELL, THAT WENT JUST FUCKING GREAT. DELON slammed the door of his apartment behind him and tossed his coat onto a couch worn threadbare around the edges. Nothing better than digging up ancient family bones and chewing them over. What was it about this stripped-down, brutally honest Tori that made him feel obliged to respond in kind?

His boots thudded, first one, then the other, against the wall as he kicked them off, then stalked out to the kitchen and fished a bag of mini Snickers from the back of one of the cabinets, where he'd hidden them from Beni. Empty. He balled up the plastic and fired it at the trash can. It bounced off the wall and ricocheted onto the tile floor. Dammit. He'd polished off the last of the bag in his car on the way to Tori's, and the clerks at the Kwicky Mart were starting to make smart-ass comments about his chocolate habit. He could drive back over to Dumas, he supposed, but he wasn't quite that pathetic. Yet.

So now what? He turned a slow circle to examine his hearth and home. Nothing to do here. Everything else might be a mess, but his apartment was in perfect order. Breakfast and lunch dishes stacked in the drying rack, Beni's toys stowed away in a big wooden box in the corner, books and DVDs lined up neatly on the shelves of the entertainment center. He'd vacuumed and dusted the previous weekend—he'd even taken down the photos from the wall to polish the glass.

Six months ago, the gallery on the wall had illustrated his life. Pictures of Beni as a toddler grinning from beneath the brim of Delon's too-big hat. On his pony, with Delon on one side and Cole Jacobs on the other, all of them proud as punch. A group shot from Thanksgiving two years ago, the whole mob gathered around Miz Iris's overloaded table. And one of Beni as a baby, cradled in Violet's arms, with Delon smiling proudly beside them. The perfect family.

Delon snorted out a breath. The perfect idiot, more like. He'd wanted that life, that security, so badly for Beni. A normal family with all the usual parts. His son would never waste letters to Santa begging for his mother to show up at Christmas. Beni wouldn't be the center of battles over every holiday and long weekend like Gil's son. Delon wanted better for his kid. He'd thought Violet wanted the same. They'd grow into it as they aged, he'd imagined, from friendship to love. He should've known better. Violet had always been a sucker for the renegades. Guys like Joe Cassidy. Gil. Not Delon.

If it makes you feel any better, I never thought you were all that nice.

He and Tori had had sparks—the whole damn fireworks show—but she didn't know the real him. The boring one. She only knew the cocky bastard he'd pretended to be when he was with her. His gaze moved across the rest of the pictures. Action shots of him at San Antonio, Pendleton, the National Finals. Even Cheyenne. The photographer had snapped that photo as the horse launched out of the chute, the spectators in the infield grandstand clearly visible.

Had Tori been one of them? He stepped close, squinted, and examined the faces row by row but didn't find hers. Had she watched him ride? Cheered just a little? Or had she made a point of being elsewhere during the bareback riding? He lifted his hand to the claw marks on his neck. Felt the cool touch of her fingers. Saw the pop of awareness in her eyes. Yeah, she remembered, but it was buried deep, inside a woman he didn't recognize any more than he recognized himself these days.

Dredging up those old feelings was a straight shot to disaster, with the hurt and resentment lying coiled in the middle of it all, waiting to lash out and bite them. And still, his body hummed from brushing up against hers out there behind the barn. The featherlight touch of her fingertips.

His gaze ranged over the pictures on his wall. His past. It seemed as if that was all he could see anymore. Once upon a time, he'd had a clear vision of where he was headed. Then Fate had reached down, crumpled his road map into a ball, and tossed it in the trash. Without the family he'd built with Violet and Beni, without the rodeos, with no solid position at Sanchez Trucking beyond mechanic and part-time truck driver...

He flopped down on the couch and let his head fall back, eyes closed. Who would have dreamed, on that New Year's Eve seven years ago when anything had seemed possible, that his life would come to this?

If he hadn't been on such a high, he might have questioned his luck when Tori landed in his lap, but it was his birthday and he'd had a couple of beers and a whole night of back slaps and handshakes to loosen him up. For the first time, he felt like his own man. Not Gil Sanchez's little brother. Not another wannabe. He looked into the eyes of people he'd known most of his life and saw respect. Admiration. More than a touch of envy.

He saw his reflection, and it said, *You are for real, Delon Sanchez.* So when heaven dropped into his arms, he scooped it up without a second thought.

He'd fended off plenty of groupies along the rodeo trail and had learned to suspect the motives of any strange woman who got too close too fast, but the instant he touched Tori, he knew she was different. She looked like sunlight and smelled like the shady corner of a flower garden where he could play Adam to her Eve.

It had taken some coaxing before she relaxed against him. She seemed both fascinated and nervous, like a tourist at the petting zoo. *And here we have a genuine American cowboy. Watch yourself, now. They've been known to bite, especially tender young things...*

The kiss at midnight had damn near vaporized him. He had to get her out of there. Where, he had no idea, but he wanted her alone. Then she completely blew his mind by pointing across the parking lot. "I live right over there."

He stared at her, stunned. She couldn't mean...she wasn't offering...was she? The way she was looking at him, her eyes wide with equal parts nerves, defiance, and desire...

His mind blanked out with lust, and he heard his voice saying, "Well, all right, then. Lead the way."

Even though he knew he should say thanks a million—make that ten million—but no. He'd spent a lifetime trailing along, learning from his brother's mistakes. This was the first time in months he'd been tempted to even bend his own rules, let alone break them, and since he wouldn't trust any condom that'd been stuffed in his wallet for weeks, he didn't bother to carry them. But...

So there wasn't any sex in their immediate future—that didn't mean he had to stop touching her.

Her apartment was a carbon copy of the one they'd just left—living room separated from the kitchen by an island, two bedrooms and a bath down the hall—but all resemblance ended there. Delon had been in places that screamed money. This one whispered. The couch was real suede, the tall coffee shop-style table and chairs some kind of hardwood with a marble top. A pricey-looking area rug covered most of the generic tan carpet. Everything was pure quality, including its owner.

Out of your league, a voice hissed in his ear.

He jammed his hands into the front pockets of his jeans. "Nice place."

"Thanks. I'm going to go, um…" She gestured down the hall. "Are you hungry? We could order a pizza or something."

"Sure. I can do that." Food. Good excuse to hang around. Talk. Keep his hands busy. Delon pulled a cell phone out of his shirt pocket. "Got any preferences?"

"No green pepper or fruit."

And definitely no onions or roasted garlic. He fully intended to get another taste of her, even if it was only a nibble instead of the full-meal deal.

She disappeared into the bathroom. He dialed the pizza place and wandered the living room as he placed his order. The watercolor print over the fireplace was a Buck Taylor, one of Delon's favorites. Then he looked closer and realized—holy shit—it wasn't a print. He was looking at the original.

The girl on the phone said, "New Year's Eve, it's gonna be at least an hour for delivery."

"That's okay." He could think of all kinds of ways to kill time. Like kissing Tori and touching her…and then strolling outside to dive into the unheated pool before he burst into flames.

His whole body vibrated with desire, a motor revved to the red line. He set his cowboy hat brim up on the table, then rolled his shoulders and arched his back to work out the kinks. His body—yeah, the muscles too—was stiff. He bent, touched his toes, and felt the tug in his hamstrings. Out of habit, he kicked his heel onto the back of one of the chairs and reached up to grab his ankle, pulling his chest to his knee. He held the stretch for a count of twenty, then rotated his upper body to the side and bent at the waist to press his palms to the ground on either side of his toes. Another count of twenty, then he kicked his foot off the chair, swung it down, and popped upright to find Tori staring at him.

"Excellent...flexibility," she said.

"Five years of gymnastics."

Her face lit up like a schoolkid who knew the right answer. "Like Ty Murray."

"Yep."

The Texas native had rocked the rodeo world, winning seven all-around world titles. When he'd claimed gymnastics played a big part in his success, every aspiring cowkid in the country had begged his parents to join. Merle Sanchez had said no, he didn't have time to run them to lessons, but once again, Iris Jacobs had saved the day, offering to take them instead.

He brushed his hand across the top of the chair in case he'd smudged it. "I was stove up from being stuck on that couch for so long."

Her eyebrows rose. "What can you do when you're loose?"

"Wouldn't you like to know?" He laughed when her face went red, even as a part of him was thinking, *Who is this guy, flirting and teasing?* Just this once, he wasn't going to overanalyze. Wouldn't worry about tomorrow. For one night, he could just do and be what he wanted.

Tori pressed her palms to flushed cheeks. "I am the Queen of Inappropriate tonight."

"You seem fine to me." More than fine. Exceptional. He strolled over and looped his arms around her waist, pulling her close. The heat flared up all over again as she melted into him. "But I might have to kiss you again to be sure."

He didn't think it could get any hotter, but *whoa*. All of her was nestled up nice and snug against all of him, and now their hands had room to roam. He could've spent hours letting her hair flow like satin over his hands as they memorized the curve of her back—down, then up, then down again. The calluses on his riding hand scraped against her bare skin and she shivered.

She caught his hand and pulled it up to where she could inspect it. The skim of her thumb across the line of calluses at the base of his fingers was like a lick of fire. "From riding?"

"Yes."

She brushed a kiss over the calluses, then followed up with a flick of her tongue in the center of his palm.

He groaned, burying his face in her hair, his breath hot and fast against her neck, his heart beating a hole in his chest. "So much for not jumping you the minute we walked in the door."

"Actually, you didn't. It's been at least six minutes."

He gave a pained laugh. "So what are we gonna do with the other fifty-four before the pizza gets here?"

Her hands smoothed over his back, from his shoulders to his belt. "This works for me."

"Me too, but I'm not sure how much more I can take." He hesitated, then blew out a pained sigh. "I didn't come prepared for this, you know?"

There was an excruciating pause while he waited for her to shove him away.

"I am," she blurted. "Prepared, I mean."

Shit. Now he was gonna have to say, *Sorry, it's not like I don't trust you when you say you're on the pill or whatever, but it still ain't gonna happen unless I'm covered too. Literally.* He eased back. "I'm kind of paranoid because of…well, anyway, without condoms, it's too risky. For both of us."

Another pause while she stared at him as if trying to figure out if he was for real. Then she smiled. "I agree. So does my mother. That's why she makes sure my medicine cabinet is always stocked."

Delon's jaw dropped. "Your…mother?"

"She's very concerned that I'm going to throw away my future on…uh, well, you know."

A guy like you. That voice again, as if he was still some nobody from a nothing little town. But he wasn't, dammit. He was Delon Sanchez, National Finals bareback rider.

"Wait right here," he said.

He found the condoms right where she said, in the medicine cabinet. Three different sizes, two brands of each. All unopened, he noted. Geezus. Her mother really did believe in covering every possibility. He grabbed a box, tore it open, pulled out a packet, and started to shove it in his pocket, then thought better. If a man was gonna be prepared, might as well go the whole nine yards. He unbuckled and unzipped his jeans, breathing a sigh of relief. Then he rolled the condom on, yanked his shirttails out, and left them hanging loose as he walked back into the living room.

Tori had moved to one of the heavy wrought-iron stools at the breakfast bar and kicked off her boots. That little nothing of a skirt had ridden up on her thighs, showing off a mile of heart-stopping legs. When she saw him, her bare toes curled. God. She was killing him.

He stepped close and boxed her in, a hand braced on either side of her. "We've only got forty-nine minutes 'til the pizza guy knocks on the door."

Her eyelashes fluttered down and her voice went husky. "I heard bareback riders only need eight seconds."

He laughed, and then he kissed her again, and what little restraint they'd had was gone in a flash of pure flame. He devoured her mouth while his fingers went straight to the ties on her dress, top, then middle. The silk slid down to her waist. He covered her with his hands, all that warm, creamy flesh, and drew a moan from deep in her throat when his calluses scraped across her nipple. Ah. So she liked that, did she? Slowly, deliberately, he grazed his palm over her breast, and she groaned again, arching into his touch. She tugged at the buttons on his shirt, pushed it aside, and it was his turn to groan as her fingernails scraped lightly over his shoulders, chest, nipples, then lower.

He peeled one hand off her breast and moved to her thigh. Satin skin, firm, toned flesh. She curled her calf around the back of his leg as he stroked higher and higher, and then…his heart stuttered. He leaned back and pushed her skirt up so he could see what he'd just felt, and his heart *ka-whomped* again. A pink lace thong. Dear sweet Jesus.

She arched an eyebrow. "You like?"

"Oh baby." He slipped his fingers under the narrow elastic at her hip, then followed the curve of it down and in and muttered a curse when he found her as hot and ready as he was. She rocked into his touch, moaning as she pushed her hands under his belt and shoved his jeans down. She gasped, her hips jerking as his fingers slid deep into the center of all that slick heat.

"Oh God…" She breathed it like a prayer and went for his throat, using her teeth to scrape every nerve to a fever pitch.

He hooked both thumbs in her thong and dragged it past her knees. While she lifted her leg to push it the rest of the way off with her foot, he shoved his briefs down. Air shuddered out of her lungs when he cupped her butt in his hands and pulled her against him, flesh to aching flesh. She reached, stroked, and hissed her approval when she found the condom already in place.

And then he was lifting her, driving hard inside her. Screw finesse. His want was too huge, the heat and silken clench of her around him too intense. He couldn't breathe. Couldn't think. Couldn't do anything but take and take and take some more as she wrapped her legs around him and pulled him in deeper. The friction and pressure built and spiraled until all it took was the stroke of his thumb to send her flying. He drove into her three, four, five more times, then arched, stiffened, his groan low and gut-deep as he exploded into her.

He collapsed against her, shoulders heaving.

"Oh. Wow." She was panting, her neck damp with sweat against his cheek.

He gulped in air. "No shit."

She rested her forehead on his collarbone as they waited for the earth to stop rocking. "That was...fast."

"Eight seconds, remember?"

She laughed, breathless. "Not sure I remember my name right now. But that was definitely..."

Insane. And for once in his life, he didn't give one solitary damn. He raised his head and grinned into her dazed, flushed face. "We still have thirty-three minutes before the pizza gets here. Wanna go again?"

And again. And one more time, in the shower late the next morning. By the time he stumbled out of Tori's car at Sanchez Trucking, everyone else was long gone, already seated around Miz Iris's dinner table, no doubt. He tried to rehearse excuses as he drove to the Jacobs ranch in a haze of infatuation, lust, and rubber-kneed exhaustion, but it was Violet, not her mother, who met him at the door and corralled him in the mud room, out of earshot.

"What the actual fuck, Delon? You couldn't even answer your phone?"

He pushed away the hand she'd planted on his chest. "It was turned off."

"And luckily, I had a pretty good idea why, or our parents would really be going nuts."

Oh, hell. "You didn't tell them—"

"Are you kidding? Like I'm gonna tell them where you spent the night. Honest to hell. Tori *Patterson*?"

Delon's foggy brain caught on a single word. One he'd barely registered the night before. "Wait. Patterson? Like…*the* Pattersons?"

Violet gave a disbelieving laugh. "Seriously? You didn't know?"

"Why would I expect her—" Jesus Christ, she was a *Patterson*? "What was she doing at that party?"

"She's going to college here. Trying to rodeo. How have you not heard?"

Delon shook his head, shock blasting away his euphoria. "I've been on the road. And distracted."

"Obviously." Violet folded her arms and glared at him. "I don't suppose you have any idea where your brother is?"

"No. Why?"

"He was supposed to be back from Oklahoma City yesterday. He never showed. Your daddy was so worried he called Krista. She said they'd had a huge fight. Something about her taking Quint to France for three months. Now he's MIA and not answering his phone."

The shock crystallized to ice in his gut. The way Gil had been since the accident, who knew where he was… or what he might have done. Delon cursed, soft but with feeling. That selfish, entitled bitch—

"Yeah," Violet said. "And now you're gettin' all sweet on her clone. Like I said, Delon, what…the…fuck?"

He blinked at her as his memories of the past twelve hours shifted, like someone had turned the kaleidoscope a half turn and the whole picture changed. Everything he'd thought he'd known about Tori. Everything he'd felt. Thought she felt too. Real? Or just a trick of the light?

The door behind him opened, admitting a rush of cold air and his brother. Gil was haggard, unshaven, his eyes slightly unfocused and dilated. Using his cane, so his hip must be killing him.

Alive, though. Reasonably whole. For now.

"What's up?" he asked, his speech not slurred but fuzzy around the edges.

Delon stared at him for a long, painful moment, this twisted shadow of what had once been his brother. His heart settled into the pit of his stomach. "Nothing," he said.

He kept it that way, no matter how his body screamed at him to just call Tori already. A day. A week. Every time he reached for the phone, he conjured up that tortured image of Gil and pulled back. By the second week, he knew it was too late. If he called now, after leaving her hanging, she'd tell him to go to hell.

And just to stomp out that one stubborn ember of hope, when he got back into town at the end of that first three-week winter rodeo run, he did call, bracing himself for the worst.

But she'd said yes. And yes again the next time. And the next. How the hell could he stay away from her if the answer was always yes?

Yes, he could pop by, even though he hadn't called until he was an hour out of town. Yes, he could come in at two in the morning when he'd driven straight down after the rodeo in Guymon so he could have a few extra hours with her. Yes, yes, *oh* yes.

Right up until the day she didn't answer at all.

He slammed his fist into the couch cushion. *Idiot.* Through all the night's prodding and prying and true confessions, he'd failed to ask the single most important question.

Why?

Chapter 14

TORI HAD JUST FINISHED SADDLING HER HORSE, still chewing over what the hell Delon meant with that crack about how she didn't know him, when an ancient pickup roared into her driveway. Shawnee's rig was straight out of an old cowboy cartoon—rusty, dented, what paint was left faded to an indefinable shade of green. The equally decrepit stock trailer had plywood wired onto the wooden slats on the sides to give the horse some protection from the elements and a rope tied around the end gate to hold it shut.

The pickup engine died with a sputter and a cough. Shawnee stepped out of the cab, planted her hands on her hips, and gave Tori's front yard a long once-over. "I love what you've done with the place."

"My curb appeal dropped ten points when you parked that thing in the driveway," Tori shot back.

Shawnee shrugged. "It's not the rig that counts, it's what you're haulin.'"

For which Tori had no answer because Willy had always said the same thing. She jerked a thumb toward the arena. "I'm going to gather the steers. Come on back when you're ready."

"I'm so ready I could damn near wet myself," Shawnee drawled. "Lead the way, Princess."

Tori opened her mouth, then snapped it shut when Fudge whinnied right in her ear. She tugged on the reins when he craned his neck to gaze longingly at Shawnee's trailer. "Don't go getting attached," she hissed. "They are not our friends."

Behind them, Shawnee hacked out a laugh.

Neither spoke as they warmed up, the rapidly cooling air inside the arena still except for the sound of muffled hoofbeats and creaking leather as they readied ropes, pulled on gloves, and tightened cinches. Shawnee rode into the heeling box on the right side, grabbed a lever to open the rear gate, and pushed the first steer into the chute.

Tori built a loop and tucked it under her arm, willing away the tension in her muscles. "I need to take my time on the first few, make sure my horse is working right."

"Whatever."

Tori backed Fudge into the box. Shawnee did the same with her buckskin, her right thumb on the electric release button for the chute. Tori scraped up her scattered thoughts, rolled them into a ball, and chucked it over her shoulder. The game was the same no matter who was sitting over there in the heeling box. *Rope the steer, turn the steer. Keep it simple.* Isn't that what Willy had told her a hundred times?

Don't miss, don't miss, don't miss...

She squashed the desperate little whisper and focused on her target at the base of the steer's horns. She nodded her head.

The gate banged open and Fudge launched from the corner, smooth as silk. She rode him into perfect position, then kept him there while she took two more swings and threw, acutely aware of Shawnee on the other side of the steer. The loop curled around the right horn but above the left. Tori let it lie and the rope dropped down and over the steer's nose. She ripped the slack out and the loop came snug. Half a head. Sloppy but legal. She wrapped the end of her rope around the saddle horn and went left.

Shawnee's horse swooped in behind, her loop curling around the steer's hind legs almost before he'd completed the turn, scooping up both feet. As she dallied, Fudge swung around to face the steer stretched between them.

"How was that?" Tori asked, then winced, because she sounded like a rookie who'd just turned her first steer. "Uh, the handle, I mean. How do you like them turned?"

Shawnee released her rope with a wide, leering grin. "Just like sex. Hard and fast and don't worry about the rope burns."

Which made Tori think of Delon, and damned if she didn't blush from head to toe, but in some weird way, the crude joke snapped the shimmering line of tension between her shoulder blades. She roped a dozen steers without a miss, her loop more sure with every throw.

Shawnee snatched at least one rear foot out of the dirt every time and two on the majority.

Tori retrieved her rope and released the last steer from the stripping chute, then chased the herd up the return alley. As Shawnee pushed them on into the chute, Tori patted Fudge on the neck, waiting. For applause, she realized with disgust. "Wow, you've really improved!" or "Way to go!" Even "Hot damn, Princess. Who knew you could actually rope?"

Shawnee said nothing. Just loaded a steer into the chute, got on her horse, and backed in the box, ready for more. Well, fine. Silence was good. From Shawnee, silence was a miracle. Tori ran Fudge up on the next steer, took a couple of extra swings, then roped the horns clean before taking the steer left and looking back to watch her heeler. Shawnee wasn't there.

Alarmed, Tori released her dallies and let the steer go. She wheeled Fudge around and saw Shawnee parked ten strides in front of the roping chute. "What's wrong?"

Shawnee fisted her hand around her loop and propped it on her hip. "You are aware that this is a timed event?"

"Yes."

"So what the fuck are you doing clear down there when you had a perfectly good throw right here?"

Tori felt herself flush. "I just wanted to be sure—"

"How sure do you have to be? Geezus, woman. I've been on shorter cattle drives." Shawnee stepped off and used the heel of her boot to scrape a line across the arena, twenty yards from the front of the chute. "Me and Roy go this far. You rope 'em after that, you're on your own."

Tori's teeth snapped together with an audible click. "Fine."

"Fine," Shawnee echoed and got back on her horse.

Except it wasn't. On the first steer, Tori took three swings and drilled her loop square into the back of his neck. The next loop spun around the right horn and off. And the next floated like a Frisbee over the steer's head.

Tori cursed and pulled up, coiling her rope in quick jerks. Why was she pushing so hard? Hadn't Willy taught her consistency was more important than speed? "I can't do this."

"You can't do it *yet*."

Tori set her jaw. "Willy always said if I turned every steer, I'd be in the money more often than not."

"That's real sweet." Shawnee's smile was as condescending as the words. "But Roy and I don't practice to win the little checks. If you're gonna rope with me, you gotta turn 'em for first place."

Tori stared at her, stunned at the utter gall. As if Shawnee was doing her a *favor* by showing up to use her arena and rope her steers. "Then maybe you should practice with someone else."

"Your choice." Shawnee dropped her loop, coiled up her rope, and turned to ride away. "If you don't figure you've got the *cojones*..."

It was such a juvenile dare Tori laughed outright.

"You're shitting me, right? You actually think that's gonna work?"

"Don't know. Don't care. I don't waste time doing things half-assed." Shawnee swung off her horse and picked up her rope bag, clearly serious about leaving.

Tori rode up and jabbed a finger at the line Shawnee had drawn in the dirt. "You'd rather watch me miss every steer right there than turn them down the arena and let you throw your rope?"

"Yep."

"That's...stupid."

Shawnee whipped around, suddenly fierce. "No, Princess, it's called trying. Pushing yourself. Getting better every day instead of just going through the motions. Your hunka burnin' love taught you how to rope pretty good. Now, if you'll quit being such a wuss, I'll teach you how to compete."

Tori stared at her, mind completely blown. First Delon, now this. It was just too damn much. She closed her eyes, dropped her chin to her chest, and took a long, deep breath. Then another. *Just tell her to fuck off and die.* But the words wouldn't come. Deep inside, that knot of rock-hard stubbornness refused to let her back down.

"Whatever," she said. "I can jump out and throw my rope in the dirt all night."

Shawnee grinned. "Now, there's a positive attitude. Get yer skinny ass in the box—we'll see if you can miss ten in a row."

When they finally turned the steers out for the night and uncinched their horses, Tori was exhausted, mentally and physically.

"So you know how I said earlier that I could pee my pants?" Shawnee asked. "I really mean it now."

Tori blinked at her, uncomprehending.

"You do have indoor plumbing, right? I mean, from the looks of that house…" Shawnee waved a hand in the direction of the concrete bunker.

Oh. Shit. She wanted to go inside. Where no one else had set foot since the day the moving company had dropped off her furniture.

"Uh, sure," Tori said and led the way across the yard.

Opening the front door felt like ripping off a scab. As they passed through the narrow foyer and into the living room, she felt Shawnee's gaze like a physical thing, reaching out and touching, leaving fingerprints in the dust on the cluttered coffee table, leafing through the magazines scattered on the floor, smudging the glass on the pair of photographs beside the television.

Tori made a jerky motion. "End of the hall, second door on the left."

"Thanks."

Tori veered into the kitchen and yanked open the refrigerator door. The shelves were jammed with the moldering remains of well-intentioned trips to the grocery store, real meals that never came to pass.

Somewhere in there... She rummaged around, pushing aside a bag of desiccated carrots, wrinkling her nose at a tub full of something that had gone green and fuzzy, and grabbed two Dr Peppers before any of the science experiments could rear up and go for her throat. She had a can in each hand when Shawnee emerged from the bathroom.

"Drink?" Tori asked, holding out a can to lure Shawnee back to the vicinity of the front door, the better to shove her out.

"No, thanks." Shawnee paused, her attention drawn to the pictures beside the television.

Tori set one can down with a clunk, then popped the top on the other. Anything to keep her hands busy so she didn't rush over and snatch the pictures from under Shawnee's nose—an action shot of her and Willy roping and another of the two of them grinning like fools as they were presented with trophy buckles, the first they'd won as a team.

"This your husband?" Shawnee asked.

"Yes."

Shawnee stuffed her hands into the pockets of her faded jean jacket. "I hate to be the one to point it out, Princess, but you married yourself a big ol' fat boy."

"Willy was not fat! He was just..." Loud and proud and big enough to be her entire world. "You couldn't squeeze Willy into any smaller package."

"That's what my mama says about me." Shawnee straightened. "You don't have a bed."

"No room in the moving van."

Which was a flat-out lie. She'd brought only the bare essentials, bits and pieces of their life that she couldn't let go. She had no need for a king-size bed without Willy to fill the vast empty space.

Shawnee blew out a gusty breath and turned to face Tori. "Okay, look, I suck at pussyfooting around. So I'm just gonna say—I googled you and your husband. I know how he died. Hell, I remember when it happened. I was at a ropin' up in Colorado, and all the Wyoming guys were talkin' about it."

Emotions rippled through Tori—shock, grief, the ever-present thread of anger because *Damn you, Willy, for leaving me like this.* But when she opened her mouth, what came out was "You google?"

"Yeah, I know how to run a computer. I can even spell most of the big words all by myself." Shawnee rolled her eyes. "This is the kind of snotty shit that made you real hard to like back in college."

"*I* was hard to like? You—" Tori jabbed a finger at Shawnee, then cursed as Dr Pepper sloshed onto the faded linoleum. "You told the rodeo coach it'd be a fucking miracle if he ever made a roper out of me. While I was sitting *right there.*"

Shawnee shrugged, unapologetic. "You waltzed in and treated our practices like they were a roping clinic, taking time away from girls who'd been working for that spot for years, and the coach fell all over you because your daddy might write the school a fat check."

"I was just—" So used to her family name greasing the rails she hadn't even realized it was happening. She scowled down at her soda can, thumbing the tab hard enough to snap it off. "I didn't think... You could've said something."

"I did."

"Not that kind of something!"

Shawnee made a *What can I say?* face. "Bitch is my default mode. When are we ropin' again?"

"Saturday afternoon?" Tori heard herself say.

"Can't. There's a big Wrangler roping in Childress this weekend."

Where Shawnee would have partners who could turn steers all day in the six-second hole. Unlike Tori. But that could change.

"Tuesday, then," she said.

"That'll work."

They walked outside, Tori trailing along behind and stopping to hover awkwardly in the middle of the driveway as Shawnee loaded her horse. Inside the barn, Fudge whinnied, shrill and high. The buckskin nickered in response, as if Fudge had earned that much respect. Shawnee slammed the back gate of the trailer, tied it shut with the chunk of rope, and ambled to the pickup. She paused, then puffed out her cheeks and let the air hiss between her teeth.

"Look, this is none of my business..."

"Like that ever stopped you."

Shawnee snorted, acknowledging the point. "Maybe

you being back, living right down the road from Delon, has nothing to do with him, but just in case..." She propped one hand on top of the door and leveled an accusing stare at Tori. "Delon is a good guy, and you really fucked him up last time. Don't do that again."

She climbed in her pickup and rattled away, leaving Tori to stare after her, open-mouthed.

Chapter 15

TORI DIDN'T EVEN HAVE TO ASK HOW DELON'S SESsion on the spur board had gone. First thing Monday morning, he called to say that yes, he did want to go ahead with the MRI. Beth worked her magic to get him an appointment with radiology on Tuesday morning and get the results to Tori by the time they were wrapping up his therapy that afternoon. Tori summarized the report, then pulled up the images and scrolled through them, hitting the high points as he sat silent, stone-faced. This, the same man who had once tied her to the showerhead with a pair of bandanas and…

She squeezed her eyes shut, glad she was facing the computer so he couldn't see her face until she'd scrubbed it blank. *Scrub. Crap.* Not the best choice of words. The memories had been blindsiding her left and right since that moment at her place when he'd touched her, looked at her *that way*. And then Shawnee had to go and make that crack about how her leaving had messed him up. As though he'd actually cared. Like she'd hurt him. But if those same memories were torturing him as well, he was doing a stellar job of hiding it.

"So what does all that mean?" he asked, tilting his head toward the MRI images.

"Short answer? There doesn't appear to be anything that could be addressed surgically."

"Pepper can't fix it." Delon's fingers curled around his knee, knuckles whitening.

"Not with a scalpel. There's another option."

"Which is?"

"Manipulation under anesthesia." She faced him, keeping her gaze steady and professional. "We can't tell by the MRI, but if adhesions between the folds of the joint capsule are the problem, they have to be broken. He could knock you out and force it to bend."

Delon winced. She didn't blame him. It wasn't a pleasant procedure to contemplate, even if he would be unconscious at the time.

"Will it work?" he asked.

"I can't say—"

He made an impatient noise. "You've done all your tests, felt it with your own hands. Do you think he can free it up?"

She hesitated, then said, "You'll gain some motion. I would be surprised if it restored the full range."

His jaw tightened a notch. "What's the downside?"

"You'll be sore afterward."

"I'm sore now. Not much to lose." He stood, his face still impassive. "Tell Pepper I want to give it a try. I'll grab my own ice packs."

When he was gone, Tori leaned against the wall and

massaged her aching forehead. Damn, damn, *damn.* Why couldn't there have been a bone spur or a handy chunk of misplaced cartilage that could be plucked out. *Voilà!* Not that she'd expected it to be that easy. She sighed and went to tell Beth to set up the appointment with Pepper. A boy of about five was perched on the reception desk, chattering excitedly as he pointed to a handheld computer game.

"And then you press this button and the ship shoots fireballs and *BOOM!* That's the end of the sea monster."

"Cool," Beth said.

"Wanna give it a try?" the boy asked.

Beth glanced over and saw Tori in the doorway. "Not right now, kiddo. Gotta get back to work."

"Let me guess," Tori said. "*Guardians of the Sea?*"

The boy's head whipped around, and Tori nearly gasped out loud. Dear Lord. It was Delon in miniature. The abstract awareness of a child was a damn sight different from the reality flashing his daddy's grin at her.

"You know about video games?"

Tori couldn't help but smile back despite a weird twinge in her chest. "I had…um, have…eleven nieces and nephews."

"This is Beni." Beth's eyes were as bright as the boy's, measuring Tori's reaction. "He's been keeping me company while his dad has therapy."

"I'm Tori. Your dad's therapist. Do you come along often?"

"Nah. I'm not so good at not bothering anyone."

Beni cast a guilty glance at the chair in the waiting room where he'd abandoned his jacket and a backpack. A bag of microwave popcorn was tipped on its side on the floor, a few kernels spilling out around a Coke can. "Mommy had to pick Joe up at the airport and his flight got delayed, so Daddy had to bring me."

Tori moved closer and held out a hand. "Can I see?"

Beni passed over the video game, and she studied the screen, then clicked a couple of buttons. "Want me to show you something awesome?"

"Sure!"

He scooted over, his shoulder pressing against her arm as he peered at the screen, the cowlick on the top of his head tickling her cheek. Shyness was definitely not an issue. Tori breathed in the scent of popcorn and the same manly soap his dad used, along with the familiar hint of grease and diesel fuel.

She ignored another twinge and pointed at the screen. "See this lever? Pull it."

Beni guided a character over and did as she instructed. A box opened with a choice of power-ups. "Whoa. Cool. I never saw that before."

"It doesn't appear until you have enough tokens. Now you can choose fireproof armor for your ship or add ice bombs to your arsenal."

He pinched his chin between thumb and forefinger, giving it serious consideration. "What would you do?"

Armor, of course. She left the ice bombs to her mother.

"Either is great," she said. "When you get another

two hundred tokens, you can come back and get the other one."

Beni pondered for another moment, then clicked. "If I have ice bombs, I can win tokens faster, so it won't be long before I can get armor too."

Impressive logic. Willy's nephews would've chosen based on which made the loudest noise. "How old are you, Beni?"

"I'm gonna be six. My birthday is Saturday. Wanna come to my party?"

Tori's gut splintered as if hit square with one of those ice bombs. She was pretty good at math, and six years plus nine months added up to *Tori, you total fool.* Beni Sanchez had been conceived more than a month before she'd stopped sleeping with his father.

"Are you okay?" Beni asked. "You look funny."

Behind him, Beth was eyeing her with equal concern, her curiosity dialed up to ten.

"I…um, yes. I just thought you were younger."

Beni made a sour face. "'Cuz I'm little. And I'm not in school, because I was a preemie so Mommy said they shouldn't rush me."

"I see." Premature? That might explain… "Do you know what preemie means?"

"Grandma says I didn't wanna wait my turn, just like always. My birthday was s'posed to be in March." His eyes narrowed, turning shrewd. "I think I should get to have two birthdays, but Mommy said no, I only got born once and she should know 'cuz she was there."

March. So Delon hadn't knocked up some other girl while he was popping by Tori's place for the occasional roll in the hay. Just immediately after she left, which only made her feel slightly better. And puzzled, because no matter how rushed or wild the sex, Delon had always been careful to the extreme when it came to condoms. Knowing his brother's story, she understood why.

The door to the waiting room swung open, and a couple walked in. The woman was tall, strong, both muscular and curvy with brown hair that just brushed her shoulders. Tori should have recognized her immediately, but she had no reason to expect to see that face here. When it clicked, it was like the cocking of a gun's hammer, sending Tori's defense mechanisms into red alert.

Violet Jacobs. The man held the door for her, the hand he curved around her waist blatantly possessive. Tori had only an instant to register that he was also familiar before Beni stuffed the video game into her hands and vaulted off the counter to fly across the room.

"Joe!" He grabbed the man's arm and tugged. "I've been waiting and waiting to show you the new trick I can do on my trampoline. Can we go now?"

"As soon as we talk to your daddy." Violet ran a practiced eye around the room, taking stock of the belongings Beni had scattered. "And you gather up your stuff. Where's your game?"

Beni waved toward Tori. "Over there. Joe, when we get home, can we—"

Beni's voice was drowned by a roar in Tori's ears,

the whoosh and crackle of a fireball that started in her gut and billowed upward to consume her entire being. Violet *fucking* Jacobs. Beni's mother. Delon's so-called friend, girl most likely to have warned him away from Tori—for his own good, of course—and then, apparently, jumped him the minute she was out of the way.

Violet stepped forward, extending her hand with a polite smile. "Hi, I'm Violet. You must be—"

"That's Tori," Beni cut in. "She's Daddy's new therapist and she kicks a—I mean butt—at *Guardians of the Sea.*"

"I know your mother," Tori said, spitting the words out like red-hot tacks.

Violet froze, her hand wavering in midair. Then her eyes widened and her arm dropped to her side. "Tori *Patterson?*"

"Yes." Her voice hissed like a tongue of flame.

They stared at each other, the air buzzing with tension. Beth put one hand on the phone, as if to call for help in the event of a brawl, and even Beni had gone still, those sharp, dark eyes bouncing from one grown-up to another. Joe's shoulders tensed as he rocked onto his toes, ready to defend against a threat. Which was ridiculous. She had nothing on Violet. But her name meant something to Joe. And why did Violet look like she'd been whacked upside the head with a two-by-four?

Joe hooked an arm around Violet's waist and pulled her back, his smile cautious as he slid into her place.

"Joe Cassidy," he said, offering the handshake Violet hadn't been able to complete.

Tori shoved the video game into his outstretched hand instead, the flames licking her throat, her cheeks. Her voice, though, was ice cold.

"We've met, but I doubt you remember. My husband, Willy, was on rodeo committee at Cheyenne. We hauled you and Wyatt back to your hotel from the beer garden one night." Tori sharpened her mouth into a razor-edged smile. "Much to the disappointment of the rest of the crowd, but Willy was afraid you would bring down the whole tent, doing that stripper routine with the poles."

Joe shot a chagrined look at Violet. "Uh, yeah. That was right after Wyatt's wife left him." His expression went sober, his voice rough with sincere regret. "Aw, shit. You're...you were Willy Hancock's wife. I'm sorry. He was a great guy."

"Yeah. He was."

Tori had to work to take in air. After weeks of emptiness, her chest couldn't expand to accommodate all the emotions flying around inside her. Silence fell again, stretched so thin by the tension in the small waiting area it felt as if the air might pop like a balloon if anyone dropped a word into it.

"Daddy!" Beni exclaimed. "Look! Joe's here!"

Tori jerked her head around to find Delon standing behind her in the open doorway to Beth's office. His gaze was fixed on his son, the way Beni clung to Joe's side, and for an instant, there was something raw and vulnerable in his eyes. Then he blinked, and his stony mask slid into place. His gaze moved to Violet. Her shock had faded, but she couldn't hide her dismay at the sight of Tori and Delon in such close proximity.

Violet attempted a smile. "We, um, thought we'd swing by here to pick Beni up. Save some time."

Before Delon could reply, Tori fixed Violet with a long, deliberate stare, then let it slip down to Beni as she poured sugar into her drawl. "And Lord knows, you don't waste any time."

As she sidestepped Delon to leave, she fired him a look designed to skewer him straight through the guts. His eyes flinched away. Dammit. She couldn't believe he had…with Violet…and…and…

She stomped back to her office and slammed into her chair. She'd been right on the money. Delon Sanchez wasn't a nice guy *at all*.

Chapter 16

DELON WATCHED BENI SKIP AHEAD, HANGING ON JOE, chattering about all the things they could do together like jumping on Beni's new trampoline, and could Joe teach him how to do that cool trick with the soccer ball? All the things Beni used to do with his daddy. Delon should be grateful this thing between Violet and Joe was temporary. Gil had suffered through nine years on the sidelines of his son's life. No wonder he was such a moody bastard.

Violet stalked along beside him, her cheeks slapped red with anger and embarrassment. "Nice of you to mention that Tori's back."

"What do you care?" The question was insolent, on the verge of rude. Hurt flashed across her face before temper shoved it aside. Delon had an instant to feel like a real prick before she lashed back at him.

"Oh hell, I don't know, Delon. Maybe because if you'd said something, I wouldn't have felt like a total ass in there."

And she would've been prepared to defend herself. Or maybe not. The Tori of old would never have slammed Violet that way.

He shrugged with exaggerated nonchalance. "If old girlfriends are a problem, it must be really awkward to go places with Joe."

Fuck you, Delon.

The unspoken words hovered in the air between them for a taut, brittle moment before Violet pulled them back with a deep, aggravated breath. She swatted a hand toward the red brick wall of the physical therapy clinic. "That is not just an old girlfriend. Don't try to pretend you don't give a shit that she's back, after I watched you moon over her for months after she left."

Months when Violet was pregnant with Beni and Delon thought she was too distracted to notice he was hemorrhaging from a chest wound. "You should've been thrilled. You were the one who told me to stay away, that she'd be nothing but trouble."

"So you thought it would be better if you just dropped by and screwed her once in a while?" Violet gave a savage, tooth-filled smile when he flinched. "Who were you ashamed of, Delon? Us or her? I assume that's why you never brought her around."

"What for? Target practice? Like you and Shawnee and the rest didn't get enough shots in at school."

Violet's mouth opened, then closed, and he could see the shame painted on her face. "You're right. We were assholes, and there was no excuse for the way we treated her. I'm surprised you never said anything."

"Would it have made a difference?" If anything, he'd guessed it would make things worse for Tori, an outsider poaching on their territory. Or he'd been too much of a chickenshit to let them see how much he cared. Another Sanchez, making a stone fool of himself over a woman who was clearly going places he would never belong. Something dark and corrosive squirmed in his gut, made him feel sick. Of himself. Joe. Violet. A past he couldn't undo, a future he couldn't grasp.

"I can't speak for the others, but it would have mattered to me," Violet said.

"Whatever. It's old news." He unlocked the car, grabbed Beni's overnight bag, and tossed it to Violet. "Next time, do me a favor and keep your advice to yourself."

She snorted, loud and derisive. "Like you did?"

"I've never commented on your love life."

"Bullshit." She jabbed a finger into his chest hard enough to make him flinch away. "You sat right there at my kitchen table and told me that I'd be best to steer clear because Joe was a womanizing hound dog."

Yes, he had. And he still wouldn't say *was*.

"And you obviously paid zero attention." He resisted the urge to rub what was sure to be a bruise on his sternum. Violet knew her own strength and wasn't afraid to use it.

"Exactly." She jabbed again, but Delon dodged out of range. "I heard you, but I listened to my heart, and I have no regrets. So instead of blaming everybody else for ruining your great romance, maybe you should figure out why you were so ready to let us."

They stared at each other for a long, heated moment, broken by the plaintive sound of Beni's voice from across the parking lot. "Mommy? Why are you and Daddy fighting?"

"It's nothing." Violet gave Delon one last quelling look before turning away. "Daddy's just tired and cranky because his knee hurts."

"Are you sure?"

Beni leaned into Joe's leg, his eyes wide with worry. Joe put a hand on his shoulder, holding the other out to take Violet's as she joined them. A cozy little triangle that left no room for Delon.

"Yeah. I'm sure." Violet fired another disgusted look at Delon, then injected a heavy dose of cheer into her voice. "What are we having for lunch?"

"Pizza!" Beni exclaimed and clambered into his mother's Cadillac, the argument already forgotten.

He didn't even wave goodbye.

Tori was still steaming when she got home from work that night. The latest email from her mother hadn't helped. Tori had replied with a slightly less polite than usual *thanks but no thanks*, then hit Delete without looking at the attached pictures of gleeful children— victims of traumatic brain injuries—who'd benefited from treatment at the esteemed institute, which was just dying to offer Tori a fellowship. In Los Angeles, for

God's sake. She'd rather move to Tibet. At least they had horses.

She jammed a baseball cap onto her head and boots onto her feet, grabbed a jacket, and slammed out the door, headed for the barn. She was almost glad Shawnee was coming to rope. She was in dire need of a sparring partner to work off the residual fury from her face-off with Violet, and Delon wasn't around to kick.

She booted a rock instead, sending it skittering into the scruff of dead grass alongside the house as she strode into the barn and flipped on the lights. Fudge blinked from where he lounged in the wood shavings in his stall, the devil cat curled in a ball on his back.

Tori made a derisive noise. "Really? You're that desperate?"

Fudge gazed back at her, unrepentant. The cat opened its eyes to malevolent slits and glared at her as it unwound, stretched, then vaulted off the horse's back to scrabble up a post and disappear into the hayloft.

She fetched a halter, shaking her head. "You're pathetic."

Fudge vaulted to his feet with a grunt and shook, his body an equine earthquake that sent wood chips flying. Tori picked a few remainders out of his mane, slid the halter on, and led him out to the hitching rail. At the sight and sound of Shawnee's decrepit pickup rattling to a stop in her driveway, Tori's anger roared back to life. Shawnee barely got both feet on the ground before Tori was in her face.

"You didn't tell me Violet is Beni's mother."

"It never came up." Then comprehension struck and Shawnee tilted back on her heels with a wicked gleam in her eyes. "You saw her? Where?"

"At the clinic. She and Joe stopped by to pick up Beni—who was apparently conceived about five minutes after I left town."

"More like a week." Shawnee's eyes took on an evil glint. "So let me get this straight. You, Delon, Violet, and Joe, all face-to-face. And Violet without a clue you'd be there."

"You forgot Beni."

Shawnee slapped her thigh. "Son of a bitch! And I missed it."

"I thought you and Violet were friends."

She shrugged. "I don't do the besties for life thing. She went pro rodeo with Jacobs Livestock. I stick to the team ropings. And I don't live up here in the sticks. Since college, the only time we see each other is when someone we both know gets married." Shawnee gave a gleeful laugh. "I bet she damn near shit a brick when she saw you."

Why? Tori was the one who'd been temporary. Violet had been a part of Delon's life forever. And would be forevermore, with Beni between them.

"How long were they together?" Tori asked.

"A couple of hours."

"*What?*"

"That's about how long it took them to sober up and dive for their clothes."

Tori stared at her, aghast. "She told you all the details?"

"Didn't have to." Shawnee flashed another evil grin. "Everybody in a hundred-mile radius of Earnest, Texas, knows exactly what night she got knocked up."

"How?"

"There must've been a hundred witnesses, and it was a shocker when they hooked up. Delon was at the Lone Steer drowning his sorrows. Violet, being a good friend, thought she should help him. She never could hold her booze, and he's not much better. Talk about a pair of sloppy drunks."

"How sloppy?" That might explain why, when Delon was so careful…

"Put it this way—there oughta be a warning label on condoms." Shawnee made a graphic, fumbling motion with her hands. "Do not attempt to operate when shit-faced."

"Do I want to know why Delon was out getting drunk?" *Please tell me it's not what I think it is.*

"He'd just got back in town and figured out you'd hightailed it without so much as a *go to hell.*" Shawnee gave her a wide, toothy grin. "Congratulations, Princess. You're the reason they have a kid."

Chapter 17

SCREW THE TIE. DELON FLUNG IT ON THE PASSENGER seat of his car, where it landed on a large bag of chocolate stars. *Share size,* the bag declared. Well, screw that too. He fished out half a dozen and popped them in his mouth. He didn't have anyone to share with except Beni, and too much sugar was bad for a kid's teeth.

He inhaled another half dozen chocolates as he rewound the argument with Violet. He should've called to smooth things over. He hadn't. Couldn't. It was like a gnarly, foul-mouthed troll had taken up residence in his head. Delon knew he was behaving badly, but there didn't seem to be a damn thing he could do about it. Every time he saw Joe, he vowed to be civil—friendly was asking too damn much—and every time, that stinking troll crawled out of his hidey-hole and drop-kicked Delon's good intentions into the next county.

At least Violet and Joe wouldn't be at the Buckaroo Ball. Not that the organizers hadn't tried to rope the great Joe Cassidy into making an appearance, but Violet knew better than to risk a public display of the lack of affection between him and Delon. Plus she would've had to trust Joe not to drop an f-bomb in the middle of dinner. She'd manufactured some excuse about Joe not being able to make a commitment due to his schedule.

There was no escape for Delon. Everybody knew he was sitting on his ass in Earnest, recuperating. They would prop him up in front of the crowd as the local rodeo hero who'd almost won it all, and he'd try not to snarl as he dodged the same questions over and over. *How's the rehab going? When will you be back on the road? Plenty of time for a late run at qualifying for the National Finals, right?*

All for a good cause, he reminded himself and shook the last crumbs out of the candy bag. Then he plastered on his meet-the-fans smile and prepared to take one for the Cowboy Crisis Fund team. He'd barely set foot inside the lobby when a short, round woman in orange swooped down on him.

"Delon! So good to see you." She looked him up and down with a gleam in her eye that went slightly beyond hospitality. "Mmm-mmm. I can't imagine what the single girls in this town are thinking, letting you wander around loose."

She latched onto his arm to drag him toward the ballroom, a huge necklace shaped like a sterling silver pistol bouncing in the deep cleft between her breasts and smaller versions bobbing at her ears—her concession to the western theme. As they walked, she leaned in to pat his arm and coo, "You're not even limping. Why, I bet you'll be spurring those broncos again in no time."

And so it begins. He made a noise that she took as agreement and let her haul him through the crowd, pausing every dozen steps to greet partygoers and make introductions. He arrived at the head table, his mind buzzing with unfamiliar faces and high-dollar perfume. His escort stopped short, frowning. All the seats were occupied except three near the center.

"Well now, that's odd. I arranged the place cards myself, and I had you down there." She waved a hand toward one end, where a heavyset man with aggressive eyebrows was ranting in the ear of the woman next to him while she stroked her butter knife as if debating whether to use it on him or herself. She spotted Delon's escort and fired a glare hot enough to melt the barrels on the sterling silver pistols.

"Oh my." The woman's grip on Delon's arm loosened. "If you'll just excuse me for a minute, there seems to be some confusion—"

"My fault," a voice said behind them, smooth and baritone.

"Senator Patterson!" She spun around. "We are so thrilled you could join us tonight! And your lovely daughter too!"

Delon's gaze snapped to the woman who stood slightly behind the senator. He had to blink twice to bring her into focus. *Tori?*

No. He was looking at Victoria Patterson, not the woman who was his therapist. She'd gone heavy with the makeup, darkened her eyes and reddened her mouth, and her hair was pulled up into a smooth twist on the back of her head, held in place by something that left a shimmering row of diamonds visible. More diamonds dangled from her ears and in glittering trios from a silver choker around her neck. Even the contacts were back, making her eyes glow an unearthly blue. She offered him a cool smile, her posture erect, her chin angled just so, as if balancing an invisible crown on her head. Suddenly, she was kick-in-the-guts beautiful again, in the high-class way that screamed *So far out of your league, cowboy.*

The senator captured one of the woman's fluttering hands and held it in both of his, paralyzing her with a smile. "I apologize. I had one of the servers switch the place cards. Victoria and Delon are old friends, and I knew they'd appreciate the chance to catch up while she's in town."

Tori's head jerked, her eyes widening for an instant before she pulled her ice princess mask back into place. Delon tried to do the same but the air had solidified into chunks that stuck sideways in his windpipe. They exchanged a quick, questioning look.

Did you tell him?

Tori gave a slight shake of her head.

Delon had a horrifying vision of a secret surveillance camera planted in Tori's apartment. Dear sweet God. That one afternoon alone, with the fudge cake and whipped cream...

A sliver of sanity worked its way through his

buzzing panic. No politician with a lick of sense—
which, granted, left out a sizable number—would want
video of his daughter's private affairs floating around.
Richard Patterson was not stupid. Besides, if he'd had
any idea what had gone on in that apartment, Delon
would've disappeared years ago, his mangled body
dumped in a canyon on the Patterson ranch for the coyotes to snack on. He definitely wouldn't be invited to
join them for dinner.

The poor woman had no choice. She dodged the
flaming skewers tossed at her by the woman at the end
of the table and escorted the three of them to their
seats. Tori avoided meeting Delon's eyes as he held her
chair, her dress and silvery lace shawl requiring her full
attention as she sat.

When they were arranged to her satisfaction, she
leaned sideways and muttered, "What are you up to,
Daddy?"

He disengaged from conversation with the man on
his left and smiled first at Tori, then Delon, his blue
eyes clear as a summer sky. "I'm saving you from that
battle-ax in the purple dress and Delon from the wind-
bag next to her. With any luck, they'll murder each
other before the end of dinner and neither of them will
ever darken the door of my office again."

Another wealthy constituent approached the front
of the table, hijacking Richard's attention. He greeted
her with that same guileless smile. "Joan! Good to see
you. You know my daughter, of course, and her friend

Delon Sanchez. What have you done with that husband of yours?"

And so it went, the senator holding court as his minions lined up to pay their respects, so smoothly polite it took Delon a good ten minutes to realize that Richard Patterson had created a force field of cordiality around his daughter. No one was given an opportunity to engage her in conversation. Questions about her whereabouts over the past years were deftly redirected. Neither her husband nor her married name were mentioned. And the senator accomplished it all with such warmth and charm the curious walked away unaware that they'd been ruthlessly thwarted.

Delon tilted his head close to Tori's ear to avoid being overheard. Her perfume tickled his nose—something tart with a hint of lemon, nothing like the sultry stuff she'd worn before. But still his body tightened, recognizing the warm scent of her skin beneath it.

"How is he not president by now?" he asked.

Tori's mouth flattened. "I'm sure they'll corner him eventually."

"But you're not in favor."

She wrapped the fringe of her shawl around one slender forefinger. "I have no desire to watch my father age twenty years in his first term. And being a first daughter is not appealing."

Of course it wouldn't be. Not if she wanted to continue her current career, which she seemed to love. But the president's daughter treating patients in a public facility? The security issues alone would make it impossible.

"How does your sister feel about it?" he asked.

"Elizabeth is ambivalent. She doesn't deal with the public, and it would mean an inside track to funding for her research."

"Which is?"

"Currently? Inserting pieces of DNA into immune cells to teach them to attack and kill cancer."

Delon blinked. "Wow."

"Yep."

"Is she married?"

"No. But she has a partner, a computer programmer who is possibly even more brilliant. I suppose they might get married someday, if Pratimi can haul her out of the lab long enough and my father's handlers decide a gay marriage in the family would help him gain ground with the independent voters."

Delon studied her expression, looking for any sign that she was joking. There was none. "Isn't that sort of…cold?"

Tori shrugged one lace-covered shoulder. "We Pattersons prefer to call it practical. Somebody has to save the world. Without people like my father to woo donors and my mother and sister to devote every waking hour to their chosen fields, children in this country would still be dying of the measles. My father would make a very good president."

"But it would suck for you."

"Yes."

"You could do something to scandalize the voters and ruin his chances."

She lifted an eyebrow. Her eyes glowed like arctic ice against the pale gold of her skin. "Are you offering to help?"

Their gazes caught and held. Heat flared between them like a flash of summer lightning, the resulting thunder rumbling through every fiber of Delon's body. A flush rose in Tori's cheeks.

"Well, that was stupid." She pasted a smile on her face and turned to greet the latest of her father's worshipers, leaving Delon to stew in his own simmering juices. When she eventually looked back at him, her face was once again calm and composed. Her gaze drifted down to the open collar of his shirt, and he wondered if she could see his pulse pounding.

"No tie," she said. "Wardrobe malfunction or fashion statement?"

"Both. I hate them, and I don't know how to make them work. Is it still black tie without the tie, or is that a violation of the rules?"

"Beats me. If the fashion police are on patrol, I'm in big trouble."

He gave himself the luxury of examining her. The swept-up hair exposed the back of her neck, where he knew she was especially sensitive. Bare shoulders played a game of peekaboo beneath the lace shawl, making him want to pull it aside, preferably with his teeth.

"You look fine to me." The understatement of the decade.

"I had a small problem with my shoes." With one of those wicked *dare-you* smiles that had always ended with him wondering if they might actually kill themselves this time, she lifted her skirt. "I forgot I needed some."

Delon burst out laughing. Underneath all her glitz and glamour, Tori was wearing scuffed cowboy boots.

Chapter 18

THAT LAUGH. TORI'S WHOLE BODY WENT HOT JUST from the echo. Delon Sanchez laughing was enough to smoke a girl's thong—assuming she still owned one. That little lack had turned out to be troublesome, since her stupid dress didn't allow for anything else. Going commando in this stuffed-shirt crowd had seemed mildly amusing until Delon showed up and filled her head with thoughts of what could be done given ten minutes and an empty back room. Tori pressed her hands to her flushed cheeks and blew out a long, heated sigh. If she didn't vacate this bathroom stall soon, rumors would be flying that she was doing something illegal in here, and if she looked as glassy-eyed as she felt, she'd confirm their suspicions.

She stepped out and immediately regretted her decision. The battle-ax in purple was at the sinks, making an elaborate show of freshening her lipstick. The click of the tube of lipstick snapping shut sounded like the cocking of a pistol. Potential gossip in sight. *Ready, aim, fire!*

"Victoria. Darling." The woman laid a manicured

claw on her arm. "What *have* you been doing with yourself?"

"Oh, you know. This and that. Keeping busy."

"And you're living in…" She trailed off, waiting for Tori to fill in the blank.

She shifted away to bend over the sink and crank the tap. "Farfromyou, America," she said, too fast and quiet for the woman to make out.

The purple people-eater stared at her for a beat, not quite ballsy enough to ask Tori to speak up. Finally she said, "Well, you look wonderful. The climate there must agree with you."

"Yes. It's so much like being here at home, some days I can barely tell the difference." Tori punched the button on the hand dryer, the roar drowning out conversation and leaving the human eggplant no excuse to linger.

Damn, this brilliant plan of her father's might just work. But wow, did she need a drink. An hour of sitting next to Delon, trying to ignore the hum of awareness between them, had drained her dry.

She had, as Shawnee said, really fucked him up, if only indirectly. The knowledge had snuffed out her anger at him for the scene at the clinic. All this time, Tori had assumed Delon had been, at most, disappointed when he found her gone. Maybe a little annoyed that she hadn't kissed him goodbye. But he'd been upset enough to get roaring drunk and make a mistake that had changed his entire life. Considering it had resulted in Beni, she wondered if Delon cursed her or thanked her.

With a quick sidestep, she angled through the crowd toward the closest bar. She should make boots a permanent fashion statement. For the first time in history, her feet didn't hurt at one of these dress-up things, and she could move fast enough to dodge most of the vultures. And it had made her father smile through whatever was drawing those tight lines around his mouth.

Her father...honestly, she appreciated his concern, but what was he thinking, putting her and Delon side by side, on display at the head table? Delon had handled it, though. He was used to the spotlight, and the boy who'd thrown temper tantrums had learned all too well how to play nice. Tonight, his public face was plastered on thick, glossy and impenetrable.

Tori slithered around a cluster of men debating what kind of quarterback Romo might've been if Landry were still coaching—dear sweet Jesus, it'd been damn near thirty years since the man stood on the sidelines, let it *go*—and arrived at the bar a few paces ahead of Delon. He'd been waylaid by two elderly women decked to the nines in rhinestones, fringed leather skirts, and white hats. The Goodacre sisters liked to go the full Dale Evans whenever the situation warranted. They also had hands like a two-headed octopus and were old enough to get away with it.

Tori couldn't blame them for wanting to get Delon in their clutches. Dinner over, he'd retrieved his cowboy hat. Combined with the white shirt, black jacket, and those dark eyes, it sent her tumbling down a rabbit hole of memories. He smiled, nodded, and tried to ease away from the sisters, but they clung like horn flies. As he freed his arm from one, the other clamped a bony hand on his butt. To his credit, he barely flinched, but his smile was getting tight around the edges.

"Give me two Shiner Bocks," Tori told the bartender. When he handed her the bottles, she caught Delon's eye and held one of them up.

He grabbed at the invitation like a drowning man, gesturing in her direction and dodging greedy fingers as he—wisely—backed away. He plucked the bottle from Tori's hand and chugged down a third of it, then whooshed out a breath.

"I always thought the Let 'er Buck Room at Pendleton was the worst for getting mauled, but those two make it look like a junior high dance." He watched her take a swig from her own bottle. "Beer doesn't really match your outfit."

"Does so." She lifted her hem and stuck one boot out as proof. "Besides, I never could develop a taste for wine. Or whiskey. But if you don't like Shiner, I'm not sure we can be friends."

He studied her for a beat, then took another long pull off his beer before lowering it to meet her gaze, his expression complicated. "Is that what we are? Friends?"

"Do you have a better definition?"

He thought about that for another excruciating moment. "I guess not."

She breathed out a sigh that should have been relief

but tasted uncomfortably like disappointment. As if she'd wanted more. How stupid was that? Anything else—well. Even if she had been ready to get involved— especially with someone who was permanently tied to the Panhandle—she couldn't imagine how she would fit with this older version of Delon. He was so contained. His emotions so carefully shielded. Exactly the opposite of Willy. Plus, there was Violet. According to Shawnee, Delon had all but lived at her place, pre-Joe Cassidy. And he was Beni's father. He had serious responsibilities. No longer the kind of man to spend the better part of a weekend wearing nothing but a cocky grin.

Damn, she missed that grin. A cold ache settled around her heart. She missed laughing. The unbridled, joyful kind that left you giddy and breathless, as if your soul was doing loop-de-loops in a clear blue sky. The first thing she'd fallen in love with was Willy's big, booming laugh, how easily he shared it. But he hadn't been the one to teach her to let go and fly.

Odd that she'd forgotten how much she and Delon had laughed together, like a pair of kids giggling in their secret clubhouse. And that, she realized with a start, was why she'd never pushed him for more. Even if her demands didn't scare him away, she'd feared reality would ruin their fun. So many times, she'd felt as if he was teetering on the edge, a step away from saying the words that would have changed everything, only to pull back.

And she'd never nudged him. Never risked popping their shiny bubble and letting the world inside. She'd chosen the euphoria of stolen hours over something more substantial, and when her heart refused to be satisfied, she'd kept her feelings bottled up until they congealed into resentment.

She'd set a deadline without ever giving him a clue that the clock was ticking down. *If he doesn't do something, say something, before I have to leave for my clinical rotation…*

Of course he'd failed. He'd never even known there was a test. And now life had stomped the laughter out of both of them.

"Tori?" he said, and she had to blink to bring this older, serious face into focus even though she'd been staring at him.

"I'm sorry," she blurted, but of course he didn't know she was apologizing for so much more than her rudeness. She pulled her gaze away, down to the bottle in her hand. "This is why they don't drag me to these social things much. I can only hold the pose for so long, and then…"

She was babbling. And he was looking at her as if he also wondered whether she'd snorted something while she was in the ladies' room.

"Never mind," she said. "Can we just—"

She had no idea how she might have finished the sentence, because a man stepped between them. Tall. Blond. Gorgeous. And built. His face was familiar. A person she knew in passing, but from where? He wasn't exactly forgettable, which meant she must have met him in circumstances very different from these.

"Delon," he said with a nod and the kind of smile only a certain class of people had reason to learn, mockery wrapped in such impeccable manners you might not even realize you'd been insulted.

Delon knew. His body went rigid, his eyes hardening to obsidian. "Wyatt."

Ah. Yes. Wyatt Darrington. Bullfighter extraordinaire, rebel spawn of an East Coast dynasty that would sneer at upstart ruralites like the Pattersons, whose serious money had only been made since the turn of the nineteenth century.

More to the point, Wyatt was Joe Cassidy's best friend. He turned a laser-sharp gaze on her. "Tori. It's good to see you again, though I wish the circumstances were different."

She assumed it was a reference to Willy and not the Buckaroo Ball, since Wyatt was apparently attending of his own free will. From what she'd seen and heard, Wyatt rarely felt compelled to do anything that didn't serve his needs. Which led to the question—

"What brings you all the way from Oregon to our little soiree?"

"I flew Joe down to visit Violet, but they had plans for the evening." The slight emphasis on *plans* was deliberate. Salt, meet Delon's wounds. His animosity toward Joe had been obvious, even in that brief encounter at the clinic. And there had been that moment, when he watched his son pour affection on his mother's new man...

His face darkened a shade as Wyatt blatantly ignored him, choosing to run a desultory gaze around the ballroom before saying, "I make a point of supporting the Cowboy Crisis Fund whenever possible."

"And you just happened to have a tuxedo along." Tori slathered on the Texas socialite drawl, insincerity dripping from every long, lazy vowel. "Aren't we the lucky ones?"

His eyes narrowed and she felt herself measured, assessed, her usefulness calculated. Then he smiled and she was reminded of a shark, gliding graceful and silent beneath the surface of eyes the color of a Caribbean sea. Out on the floor, the band brought the obligatory rendition of "Cotton-Eyed Joe" to a thrumming crescendo, then launched into "Waltz Across Texas."

Wyatt held out a hand. "Dance?"

"So sorry." She stepped around him, looped her arm through Delon's, and smiled a toothy smile of her own. "This one's spoken for."

She had to tug on Delon's arm to uproot him. He took two steps and stopped. For an instant, Tori thought he was going to refuse to dance with her.

Then he waved the Goodacre sisters over. "I hate to run off and leave you lovely ladies. Have you met Wyatt Darrington? He was voted Bullfighter of the Year last season."

Tori and Delon were both smirking when they reached the dance floor. And, Tori realized, still holding their beers. Lovely. But if it was good enough for John Travolta and Debra Winger...

Delon swung her into his arms. Despite his firm lead, she shuffled and nearly tripped. Her feet were still set to Willy's boisterous rhythm, and she kept overstepping Delon's more precise pace. They did a disjointed push-pull halfway around the floor before he paused by the head table to set down his beer, then take hers from her hand.

"Maybe that will help."

As he gathered her close, his hand slipped beneath the loose drape of her shawl and found bare skin. His fingers were cold from the bottle, and she shivered. She rested her hand on his shoulder, felt the flex of muscle, and her mind obliged by providing detailed, graphic images of all the times she'd gripped those very excellent, very naked shoulders, his skin gleaming with a sweat she'd helped him work up.

She stumbled again, hoping he mistook her flushed face for embarrassment. "Sorry. My fault. You're doing fine. It's just been a while."

"Seven years." His smile was part sympathy, part encouragement, part…something. When she blinked at him, he added, "Since we've danced. Together, I mean."

"I've never danced with you."

This time, the stumble was his fault, as he completely missed a step. "Of course you have. We…you and I…"

She shook her head.

"Never?" He stared at her, incredulous, as he spun her around the far corner of the floor.

Heat pooled in her abdomen as their thighs brushed,

Tori all too aware that she was wearing nothing beneath the flimsy fabric of her dress. "If you, ah, remember, we didn't go out much."

"I remember." And for a few beats, those memories swirled hot in his eyes. Then he shook them off. "I can't believe we didn't...are you sure?"

"Very."

"Oh." His gaze pulled away from hers to fix on a point somewhere over her shoulder as they glided and spun reasonably smoothly through the mob of dancers. A terse line dug between his brows. "We should have."

She could only shrug. The movement dislodged her shawl, and it slithered down to hook at her elbows, leaving her shoulders bare. They danced in silence through the chorus of the song, their bodies moving more easily together but still not entirely in sync. Who would've guessed their first dance would be so awkward when sex between them had been so natural, so...

"Why don't you like him?" Delon asked, fracturing a particularly vivid memory.

"Who?"

"Wyatt. You practically frosted his balls."

"He was being a prick."

Delon blinked, surprised either by her assessment or her language. "He was hitting on you."

"Only to piss you off."

Though she hadn't figured out what he had to gain by it. And she knew his kind. Hell, every man in her family was his kind, even her father when it suited him. Wyatt had something to gain or he wouldn't have sought out Delon, the one person in this massive ballroom who did not want to see him. Or was Tori his target? No. He'd asked her to dance to needle Delon. But why?

"He never used to be," Delon said, frowning. "A prick, I mean. When I saw him at the rodeos."

"Have you done something to irritate him?"

"Not that I…" Then he trailed off, and his hand tightened on her waist. "After my appointment on Tuesday, Violet and I argued. I imagine Joe told him."

And Wyatt was getting even by being rude? No, that was too simple. She glanced toward the bar. Wyatt was leaning against it, with a Goodacre sister on each side. One had a diamond-crusted claw on his chest. He snagged the other's hand as it wandered south of his belt, looking totally unperturbed as he caught Tori's gaze and raised a glass of something expensive on the rocks in a gesture that was the smug equivalent of a V for victory.

Son of a bitch.

Tori tripped over Delon's foot and nearly sent both of them headfirst onto the nearest table. Thank God for her boots. If she'd been wearing heels, she'd be face down in the centerpiece.

"You okay?" Delon asked, his hands gripping her shoulders as they regained their balance.

"Yes. I'm just…" Furious. At Wyatt. At herself, for letting that bastard manipulate her so easily—straight into Delon's arms, where she could distract him from making trouble for Violet and Joe. Right on cue, the band segued into a slow, dreamy number and the lights dimmed.

"This might be more our speed." Delon's hands slid down her arms, the brush of them setting fire to nerve endings she'd begun to think had died with Willy. His voice went low, a hint of the old mischief flirting with the corners of his mouth. "Wanna go again?"

Her body went hot, an inferno fed by all those memories piled one upon the other, each more flammable than the next. Oh yeah, she wanted. Many, many things, beginning with flipping Wyatt the bird and dancing until she and Delon found that magical rhythm they'd once had. She wanted, for one night, to be held. To be warm again. But this was not the place to let her reincarnated hormones have their way. And this was not the man. Too many ghosts of mistakes past were dancing along.

"We're one slow dance away from having our picture front and center on the society page," she said. "I don't think that would be good for either of us."

His hands dropped away, the warmth leaching out of his eyes as the walls closed in behind them. Impulsively, she reached up to skim her thumb over the clean angle of his cheekbone. "You're right, though. We should have done this sooner."

He caught her wrist, his grip like an iron bracelet, loose but unbreakable. "Why did you leave without telling me?"

They were attracting attention. Tori could feel the

curious gazes, hear the whispered innuendo. But he deserved an answer. "I was hoping you'd try to find me."

"*Find* you?" Emotions flickered over his face. Shock, confusion, a hint of irritation. "How was I supposed to do that?"

"You could have called my house."

"The Patterson ranch."

His voice held the same note of gross disbelief as if she'd suggested he dial up the White House and ask to speak to the First Lady. He glanced across the dance floor to where her father gleamed in the midst of his supplicants like a king holding court. Suddenly, Tori saw the separation between his world and hers through Delon's eyes. Not the shallow, albeit rocky ravine she had considered an inconvenience. To him, it was a chasm. Bottomless. Impassable. Finally, emphatically, she understood. For Delon, making that call was unthinkable.

"It was a test." His hand dropped away from her arm. In disgust?

"I was stupid and immature." Her long-held conviction disintegrated as she grasped the full consequences of her bitter, childish actions. For Delon. Herself. Even Violet. "I am truly sorry for that."

He stared at her for a long moment. Then he smiled, the curl of his lips so sharp it was like a hook sinking into her heart. "But you're not sorry you left."

"No." She let her gaze circle the glittering crowd, then come back to meet his. "This place decided who

I was before I was ever born. Boxed me up all nice and neat. There was no room to find the person I wanted to be."

"Willy Hancock's wife."

"Among other things. And you became Beni's father, so we both won."

"Is that what this feels like to you?" he asked. Then he turned and walked away.

Tori stood alone on the dance floor for several moments too long, staring at the spot where he'd been. Then she lifted her hand in an empty toast.

Here's to the shortest friendship on record.

Chapter 19

TORI WOKE TO THE SMELL OF COFFEE. SHOVING HER hair out of her face, she dragged herself into an upright position on the huge sectional sofa where she'd ended up after thrashing around for a miserable hour in the guest room. Her father smiled at her across a kitchen island slightly larger than Hawaii.

"I'm sorry, I didn't see you there. Did I wake you?"

She rolled her shoulders and yawned. "It's okay. I need to get home to feed my critters."

Not technically true, though Fudge would consider himself horribly abused if he didn't get his morning grain. She'd put out extra hay in the feeder and there was plenty of grass in the pasture. If the cat ran short on food, it could hunt up a mouse or drag down a passing jogger. Her dad strolled over and handed her a cup of coffee, then settled onto the opposite L of the couch with his own mug. They sipped, watching through floor-to-ceiling windows as the streets below slowly came to life. Three blocks away, a refrigerated truck pulled in behind a restaurant. Tori watched the driver angle his trailer up to a loading dock with the ease of long practice. That could be a Sanchez truck. Possibly even Delon.

"So," she said. "About last night…"

He held up a mollifying hand. "I know. I overstepped. I wanted to get you out of that house, see a little of your old sparkle. Delon just happened to be handy."

"You knew about us. Before."

"I knew about all your friends. For safety purposes."

And she'd known about his security measures. They'd had an unspoken agreement. She wouldn't fuss about the surveillance as long as it wasn't obvious. Now she wanted to squirm. How much had those invisible eyes seen and reported back to her father?

"About Delon…please don't."

He gave her a long, piercing look. When she didn't offer any further explanation, he nodded. They lapsed into silence. Her father crossed one leg over the other, tilting his dangling foot to examine the polished leather shoe. Tori lifted her cup and took a sip to hide her expression from her father's too-perceptive gaze. Ready or not, her emotions had busted out of their cocoon. It remained to be seen whether they'd be butterflies—or wasps. Her father shifted, planting both feet on the floor and leaning forward to rest his elbows on his knees, his serious discussion pose. The back of her neck tightened in alarm.

"Daddy?" she asked tentatively. "Are you okay? You know…physically?"

"What? Oh yes. I'm fine. Fit as a fiddle." He stared into his mug for a few beats, then drew a long, deep breath. "I guess I just have to blurt it out…I'm going to ask your mother for a divorce. And this time, I'm not taking no for an answer."

Tori goggled at him. Divorce. Her parents. *This* time? "You've asked her before?"

"Three…no, wait, four times. The first didn't really count. I was angry and I'd had too much to drink."

"And this was when?"

He circled the top of the cup with his thumb. "You were ten."

"You've been trying to divorce her for *nineteen years*?"

"Not continuously." He gave a helpless shrug. "You know your mother. She starts explaining why it's a bad idea, and she's so damn reasonable…by the time she's done, you feel ridiculous and irresponsible and end up apologizing for being selfish."

Yep. That was her mother. "If you've been that unhappy…"

He waved off her concern with a weary hand. "She was right. I had to think of you and your sister. And my career. Early on, a divorce would've been a disaster."

"You're up for re-election next year." And two years after that was the presidential election. She could hear her mother now: the calm, maddeningly rational explanations lined with thinly concealed threats. Claire had invested too much into positioning him for the presidency. He would *not* be allowed to do it without her.

His knuckles whitened as he gripped the coffee cup. "I'm pulling my hat out of the ring."

"Oh." *Oh shit.* As a midlife crisis went, this was a doozy. One that would send the political pundits into a nationwide frenzy.

He snuck a glance at her from beneath lowered eyelashes. Testing. Uncertain. Did he want her to talk him into it or out?

"You're sure about this?" she asked, careful to keep her voice neutral.

"Politics was never my first choice." His head came up and the resolve in his voice hardened. "I wanted to stay home and run the ranch, but I did as I was expected. Did it pretty damn well, if I say so myself. I've given the public thirty-five years of my life. Now it's my turn."

All right, then. No second thoughts there. "Have you told Elizabeth?"

"Not yet." He flashed a crooked grin. "I started with you, because I knew you'd understand."

"I…would?"

"You stand up to your mother. To all the family pressure." He shook his head in wonder. "I was in awe when you left medical school. And then the move to Wyoming. When you up and married Willy…" He grinned, clearly enjoying the memory. "I had the cardiologist on speed-dial the day I passed that news along. When you and I talked on the phone, the happiness just poured out of you. And then I'd hang up and go back to my day full of people who have a use for me, but no one who really cares. No one who lights me up that way."

"Oh, Daddy."

His face went grim. "When Willy died, it was a wake-up call. I can't stand thinking I might never feel the kind of love you felt for him."

Tears welled up in her eyes. For Willy. For her father. They would have enjoyed each other so much if they'd had a chance. "So I'm the bad influence."

His smile was so full of pride and hope she could barely stand to look at him. "I prefer to call you my inspiration."

"Awesome."

Maybe she could inspire him to keep her part in his rebellion between the two of them. But it wouldn't matter. Her mother would guess. For a woman who spent a large part of her days literally inside other people's heads, she missed nothing that went on in her family, and to say she would not be pleased was a gross understatement. And it was a sentiment that would be shared by a majority of the residents of Texas and an entire political party. It might be time to start scoping out jobs in another state. Or territory. Puerto Rico sounded lovely all of a sudden. Better yet, Brazil. They did a lot of team roping there. How many thousands of dollars would it cost to have Fudge flown to South America?

"When?" she asked.

"I had my lawyer file the paperwork yesterday."

Well. Hell. They were really doing this, then. Tori gave it until Monday, Tuesday at the outside, before the information leaked to the press and the media went wild.

He was staring into his coffee cup again. "She's flying in from her conference in Belgium this evening. I fly out for DC in the morning. I'm going to tell her before I leave."

Dump it on her and run, in other words. Tori set down her cup and moved over to sit beside her father and loop an arm around his waist, pressing her cheek to his shoulder. "Before things get too crazy, I want you to know I am proud of you."

"You too, sugar." He wrapped an arm around her and squeezed. "You too."

Chapter 20

IF MEASURED IN PURE, EAR-SPLITTING VOLUME, Beni's birthday party was a huge success. The five squealing, splashing boys raised enough ruckus in the indoor pool to disguise the fact that the guest of honor's parents weren't speaking to each other.

Violet was still fuming, and Delon still couldn't bring himself to apologize. He could have joined the boys in the pool, but he was in no mood to splash around with Joe. Plus his knee was throbbing in time to the beat of his heart thanks to standing around that damn ballroom, smiling and nodding, and keeping the width of the dance floor between himself and Tori at all times.

A goddamn test. His jaw clenched again, remembering her apology. *I was stupid.* Yeah, well, she wasn't the only one. She'd tested him and he'd failed. Spectacularly. In nearly six months of screwing around, he'd never even taken her dancing. Geezus. What a complete shitheel.

And even with the guilt churning in his gut, he couldn't forget the feel of her bare, silky skin under his palm as they danced. The sweet-tart smell of her. How she'd touched his cheek with that look in her eyes he couldn't decipher.

Those damn cowboy boots and how, when she'd stumbled and his hand had slid down over her hip, he'd felt nothing underneath that dress. And then he remembered how she'd been wearing a dress and cowboy boots and not much else the night he'd met her...

Delon slouched deeper into the chair he'd parked beside Violet's cousin Cole, who had been enlisted to act as a pack mule for the ton and a half of food Iris had whipped up. Cole was perfect company for Delon's murky state of mind—he rarely spoke when he was in a crowd larger than two and then only under duress. On the other hand, he was a massive reminder that things could be a whole lot worse. As a teenager, he'd lost his entire family in a car wreck, which only made Delon feel ungrateful. At least *his* brother was alive.

Luckily Iris Jacobs chattered enough to make up for all the rest of them, a little brown hen bustling here and there, making certain everyone got their fill of birthday cake and punch and four kinds of cookies and good heavens, could they believe Beni was already six?

Her chirpy comments were like needles in Delon's ears.

Finally, thank the stars, Violet called a halt and started dragging soggy, protesting boys out of the pool.

Beni latched his arms around Joe's neck. "Throw me one more time. *Please.*"

"Just once." Joe cupped his hands under Beni's foot, counted *one, two, three* and launched the boy into the air. A trick Delon had taught Beni. Their trick. Beni's squeal of delight was the last straw.

Delon shoved to his feet. "If y'all don't mind, I'm gonna skip dinner. Got a set of head gaskets to replace back in the shop."

"It can't wait?" Violet asked, doing a piss-poor job of hiding her relief.

Iris gave him a look that was more eagle than hen. "That's too bad. Carry this cooler to the car for me on your way out, would you?"

"Cole can get—" Violet began.

Iris cut her dead with a single glance.

"I'll just go check on the cake," Violet said and made herself scarce.

Cole, as usual, said nothing.

Delon hefted the cooler and followed Iris out of the hotel. She opened the trunk of the car and stood aside while Delon stowed the cooler, but when he would've stepped back, her hand clamped on his arm. For such a soft woman, her grip was like steel. So was her gaze.

"You know we think of you as one of our family, Delon."

"Yes, ma'am. And I appreciate it."

Her scrutiny was so intense it felt as if she could see clear to the marrow of his bones. "Life can throw a person some tough curves. This family of ours has had to deal with more than most. Losing Cole's parents and his brother. Gil's accident." She paused, waiting until he met her gaze. "Beni."

Delon felt heat stain his cheeks. "I…uh…"

"Don't get me wrong," she cut in. "That boy is the light of our lives. But when you and Violet came to us, told us she was pregnant…it was a tough pill to swallow. Especially for her father. A person gets their heart set on what's best for their child, and that was not what we wanted for Violet. But it was done and we had to make a choice: risk driving our daughter away or adjust our expectations. We chose to adjust, and we're all the better for it."

"Yes, ma'am," he mumbled.

Iris waved a hand toward the windows of the water park. Inside, Violet handed Joe a piece of birthday cake, trading it for a quick kiss. "That's another curve none of us expected, but so far, it's been a blessing too." She turned that steely gaze on him again. "This is our family now, Delon. We want you to be a part of it. It's your turn to decide."

She planted a kiss on his cheek, then stepped back. "Don't think about it too long. I miss my boys."

———

Delon barely refrained from burning rubber out of the parking lot. He had been told, hadn't he? By Violet, by Gil, and now Iris. He was outvoted, outnumbered, and out on his ass unless he swallowed that bitter pill and learned to play nice.

Well, fuck nice. He'd tried being what everybody

wanted. He'd tried screaming his head off. Either way, he was never the chosen one. Had Beni even noticed he wasn't at the Pizza Palace? He'd tried so hard for so long, and what did he have to show for it? A bum knee. A shitty little apartment with a bird's-eye view of the business he'd let his brother steal. A mediocre rodeo career. Give it a few years, people would hear his name and say, "Delon Sanchez… didn't he used to ride bucking horses or something?"

He meant to drive straight back to the shop—there really was a dismantled engine waiting for new head gaskets—but a few miles out of Earnest, his car turned off the road and parked itself in front of the Lone Steer Saloon. He stared at the sign, the namesake neon steer with a star on its forehead. Christ. Of all the places. Even his subconscious was taking potshots at him.

There was already a scattering of vehicles in the parking lot at five o'clock on a Saturday, mostly ranch pickups, locals stopping for a cold one or an early dinner. The scent of prime rib seeped into the car, but Delon's mouth didn't water. The day had stomped his appetite into the dirt. But he could sure use some liquid reinforcement. He got out, pushed open the heavy wood door of the Lone Steer, and walked into the very bar where he'd landed the last time woman trouble left him wanting to throat-punch the world.

The first beer slid down fast enough to make the bartender raise his eyebrows when Delon waved for a refill. He sipped the second one, staring morosely at the scars on the top of the old wooden bar. So Joe had Iris's blessing. Easy to see why. Besides being able to step in as a bullfighter, Joe knew bucking stock. Even Cole liked him, and Cole made a new friend approximately once a decade. After fifteen years of working for one of the biggest contractors in the Pacific Northwest, Joe could produce a rodeo from the ground up.

Unlike Delon. Sure, he'd lent a hand now and then, but he'd never had the slightest urge to be a true part of the business. After all, he had Sanchez Trucking waiting for him when his rodeo career was done.

He gave a sour laugh and sneered at the fool in the mirror behind the bar.

He felt rather than saw someone approaching. Maybe if he kept his head down, ignored them, they'd go away. No such luck. He caught the faint but unmistakable scent of chlorine as the newcomer slid onto the stool next to him. Fuck.

"I thought you were going out for pizza," Delon said without looking up.

"I sent Cole in my place," Joe said.

"Well, that'll double the tab."

Joe did something that was almost a laugh. Delon lapsed into stubborn silence.

"Didn't expect to find you here." Joe waved at the bartender, who was pulling a round of drafts for a group at the other end of the bar. "Lucky I happened to check out the parking lot as I drove by."

Yep. That was definitely how Delon felt. Lucky. A few more moments of dense silence passed.

Joe blew out a long breath. "Look, Delon, I know it's been rough. Fucking up a knee is bad enough without knowing it might've cost you a world championship. And you and Violet had a pretty smooth arrangement until I came along and butted in, so I don't expect us to be best buddies, but for Beni's sake, it would be good if we could at least fake it."

A reasonable request. Sounded like something the old Delon might have said. The nice guy, always nodding and smiling and getting along. Too bad *that* Delon was nowhere to be found tonight. He took a long, deliberate swallow of his beer.

When Delon didn't respond, Joe blew out another breath with a hiss of frustration around the edges. "Beni doesn't miss a thing. Kids never do. And it's the shits being caught in the middle when your parents can't get along."

"You'd know, seein's how your mother changes husbands more often than most people change their sheets." Delon angled Joe an insolent look. "I suppose that's why your dad doesn't have much to do with you. He got tired of tryin' to figure out who he was supposed to get along with this week."

Joe went still, temper sizzling in his green eyes. Then he was off the stool and on his feet with the blinding quickness that made him an outstanding bullfighter. The bartender froze like he didn't know whether to set Joe's beer down or just back away slowly.

"Violet was right. You're too busy feeling sorry for

yourself to give a shit about anyone else." Joe slapped a five-dollar bill on the bar. "And for the record, I don't see much of my dad because he preferred to sulk instead of accepting that my mother would rather be married to damn near anyone but him. You should be able to relate."

Joe stalked away with swift, effortless strides. Delon just watched him go. Even if he could catch him, what would he say? *You are absolutely correct. I am a sorry son of a bitch, and Violet and Beni don't need me now that they have you, and that's probably not your fault, but hold still so I can punch you to make myself feel better.* He muttered a curse and drained his glass.

The bartender slid Joe's abandoned beer over in front of him. "Might as well drink this one too. Sounds like you need it."

Delon considered telling the bartender where he could shove his sympathy, but he could use the beer to cleanse his wounds. Christ. Just once, he'd like to walk away from an argument feeling like the winner. *Hard to do when you're the one being a prick.* He took a big gulp of the fresh beer, but it didn't drown that righteous little voice. He fished out a twenty and slapped it on the bar. "Bring me a shot of tequila."

The bartender eyed the row of beer glasses and held out his hand. "Car keys first."

Delon bristled, then shrugged off the irritation. He had nowhere to be, no one expecting him, and it was early. He could drink until he fell off his stool and still have time to sleep it off in a corner behind the band-stand before closing time. He dug out his keys and slapped them on the bar.

The bartender pocketed them. "Cuervo?"

"Whatever."

"Salt and lime?"

"No." If he was gonna pay for this—and he would—he might as well start suffering now.

The bartender poured a shot and plunked it down. Delon twisted the glass between his fingers, took a deep breath, and tossed it down his throat. As he breathed through the burn, he saw the bartender pick up the phone, dial a number, then glance in Delon's direction as he cupped a hand around the receiver so the conversation wouldn't be overheard.

Great. The gossip mill was already in motion. Delon took another swallow of beer, feeling it hit the bottom of his stomach and dance a jitterbug with the tequila and all the crap he'd eaten at the birthday party. He should probably order a sandwich. Something solid. Instead, he picked up the shot glass and motioned to the bartender for a refill.

After the second shot, the voice inside his head began to slur its words. One more and he might shut that bastard up completely. He was vaguely aware that the tables and stools were beginning to fill and some-one had plugged a few bucks into the old-fashioned jukebox. He slouched over his beer, letting the noise wash over and around him, catching only a stray word here or there.

"...fucking Mexicans."

Delon lifted his head and squinted into the bar back mirror. A man and a woman sat at the table directly behind him. She was a Texas cliché—big hair, tight blouse, enough mascara to tar a roof. He was a wiry little jackass, narrow between the eyes, with the sun-baked, greasy look of an oil field roughneck. He was glaring at Delon.

"Goddamn wetbacks," the jackass said, loud enough to be sure he was heard. "First thing they do is sign up for welfare so they can sit on their ass and be worthless drunks."

Delon took one more sip from his beer. Then he carefully swiveled his stool around to face Jackass and his sweetheart. "Redskin," he declared, putting some effort into making the syllables distinct.

Jackass blinked, shot the woman a confused look, then shifted his stare back to Delon. "What?"

"Redskin. Chief. Injun." Delon rattled off a list of racial slurs. "I'm Navajo. Not Mexican. If you're gonna be an ignorant fucking racist, at least try to do it right."

The chair screeched, then clattered over backward as Jackass leapt to his feet. Delon was already standing, all the rage and pain of the past months finally finding a target. They met halfway. Delon dodged a wild swing and put his weight into an uppercut, his fist connecting with Jackass's jaw hard enough to shoot fire clear up to his shoulder. Jackass stumbled back a few steps, shaking his head. Delon was peripherally aware of the uproar around them—scrambling bodies, clattering chairs, and shouts of alarm and excitement. *Bar fight!*

"Squash that little prick, Delon!" someone yelled, and a few others cheered.

He backstepped, knees bent and fists cocked, into the clear space at the edge of the dance floor. Jackass shadowed him, weaving and feinting in what he must have thought was true boxer style. The tequila had slowed Delon's reflexes, and he was a little slow ducking the next punch. Hot pain burst in his ear when it connected.

Son of a bitch! Delon drove his fist into Jackass's gut, doubling him over, but before Delon could finish him off with another uppercut, he dove forward, his shoulder catching Delon in the chest. Delon staggered, fighting for balance, but momentum and the booze won. They went down in a heap, his bad knee buckling under their combined weight. Something popped, with a searing pain that felt like he'd been shot. He swore loud enough to make old ladies in the dining room blush, then landed a roundhouse punch square in Jackass's ear.

Abruptly, the weight was lifted off him. The bartender had Jackass by the collar and was dragging him away, through the avid circle of spectators that had gathered to watch the show. Delon stayed where he was, flat on his back on the grungy bar floor. Shit. *Shit.* He closed his eyes and gritted his teeth as he slowly, *slowly* straightened his leg. Other than the red-hot pokers jammed under his kneecap, it felt just dandy.

"Well, that was brilliant, little brother."

Delon opened his eyes.

Gil stood over him, his expression somewhere between disgust and amusement. He reached down a hand. "Come on. Let's wring you out and see what's left of your knee."

Chapter 21

"THE BARTENDER CALLED YOU," DELON SAID.

"He remembered the last time you strolled in here and started guzzling tequila." Gil raised his eyebrows. "At least this time you just knocked somebody down instead of knocking them up."

Delon flipped Gil the bird. Even that small motion hurt. Everything hurt. His knee. His hand, where it had smashed into Jackass's face. The ear that'd been boxed. His entire skull, as the buzz wore off and his brain cells began to scream in protest. Even his gut ached, knotted in disgrace and self-loathing.

Sulking. Drinking. Fighting. On his son's birthday. Father of the Year, right there.

He propped his elbow on the table and cupped a hand over his eyes to block the dim light that filtered through the open door. Gil and the bartender had hauled him back to the empty banquet room, dumped him in one chair and propped his bum leg up on two others, then packed it in ice bags. That ache, at least, was beginning to lose its teeth as the cold knocked the edge off. People in the crowd had declared they'd heard his knee pop. That couldn't be good. God. He'd have to show it to Tori and tell her what he'd done. As if he didn't feel quite stupid enough already.

A shadow fell across the door, the bartender carrying in a plate and a mug. He set them in front of Delon. "Prime rib sandwich and coffee. Ought to soak up some of the booze."

At the smell of roasted meat, Delon's stomach did a complicated shuck and jive. While he breathed through the nausea, the bartender disappeared, leaving them in the semidarkness. They sat in silence for several minutes, Gil lounging in a chair opposite him sipping coffee while Delon tore off a small chunk of the sandwich and forced himself to chew and swallow. The second bite went down a little easier. The third he followed with a swig of coffee. Out in the bar, the rumble of voices grew steadily louder as the weekend crowd began to gather. Someone cranked the volume on the jukebox. Saturday night, revving up. All Delon wanted was to pass out— for a week. Or two.

He glanced at his brother and caught the tail end of a smirk. "Glad you're having fun," Delon muttered.

"Nah. I was just thinking…this is the first time I've ever been the one pickin' up the pieces instead of being the wreck."

"Nice change?"

"I can't decide." Gil cocked his head, giving it serious thought. "Damn sure less painful, but not near as interesting."

"You always did figure the thrill was worth the spill."

"Better than dying of boredom."

"Yeah?" Delon took another sip of the bitter black coffee. "Getting a lot of thrills these days?"

Gil gave an insolent tip of his coffee cup. "Looks to me like we're sittin' at the same table, little bro. No woman, no rodeos, and a kid we see every other week. How's that safe and sensible route working for you?"

Not worth a shit. Normally he'd rather roll naked in barbed wire than confide in his brother, but in the half light, Gil's features were blurred, making him seem almost approachable. That combined with the alcohol sloshing around in Delon's system loosened his tongue. "Right now? Not one damn thing is working."

"I noticed." Gil set his mug on the table and shaped the curve of the handle with his thumb. "Nobody ever warns you how it's gonna suck when your kid falls in love with his mama's new man."

Delon's heart stumbled. That wasn't…he hadn't…

"You're supposed to be happy," Gil went on, his face stripped down to nothing but edges and shadows. "Don't you want what's best for your son? A stable home, his mother married to a decent man who's crazy about him? But what you really want to say is *fuck that. I'm* his dad. My kid doesn't need some other son of a bitch in his life. No matter how many times you tell yourself you shouldn't feel that way…"

Delon sat paralyzed. Exposed. As if Gil had plucked the words out of his soul and dumped them on the table, rotten and stinking. He couldn't deny it because Gil knew. He *knew*.

"What did you do?" Delon asked.

"Punched a few things. Wrote a lot of lousy songs about evil-hearted women." Gil hesitated, then added, "Took a lot of pills. I don't recommend that route. It's a bitch to quit when you finally pull your head out of your ass."

Delon stared at him. "You were—"

"I am," Gil said flatly. "An opiate addict. Turns out if you fuck yourself up bad enough, you can talk all kinds of doctors into giving you pain meds."

Geezus. *Geezus.* How had he not known? "I'm sorry. I should have..."

"Nothing you could've done, D. I wouldn't let you."

He blew out a long, defeated breath. "I don't know how to make anything better."

"You could start by not making it worse," Gil said with a pointed look toward Delon's knee. He leaned back, took a sip of his coffee, then shrugged. "Acting jealous because your kid is happy just makes you the asshole. For me, it was better to let 'em think Krista broke my heart. But that doesn't work in your case."

"Why not?"

Gil shot him a look of patent disbelief. "Violet? Come on. We've gone to their family reunions. Tell me you didn't wake up and feel like you accidentally slept with your cousin."

"It wasn't that bad," Delon muttered.

"It sure as hell wasn't good, or you would've done it again. What made you think the two of you could ever be a couple?" Then Gil slouched onto an elbow and sneered. "What am I saying? You're the kid who believed in the tooth fairy until you were damn near in high school."

Delon hunched lower in his chair, face hot. "You kept hiding money under my pillow."

"I was waiting to see how long you'd keep falling for it."

Bullshit. Delon knew the real truth—Gil had looked out for him because that was what big brothers did. In return, Delon followed wherever Gil led. Gil wanted to ride bucking horses? Then Delon would too. They'd take on the rodeo world together, Gil with a splash and Delon cruising along quietly in his wake. The Sanchez boys would be to bareback riding what the Etbauer brothers had been to saddle bronc riding. Until Gil wrecked it all. Words balled up in Delon's throat, a solid mass that threatened to choke him. All the things he'd wanted to say for all these years. Now he had the chance and it was too little, too late.

"I tried to talk to you, help you, after your accident." It came out more like an accusation than an apology, prickly with anger and sorrow and guilt.

"I didn't want help. I wanted to wallow." Gil shifted in his chair and rubbed his thigh, the corner of his mouth quirking. "It's the Sanchez way."

The laugh caught Delon by surprise—a dry, rusty

sound that scratched on the way out. "You, me, Dad. What the fuck is wrong with us?"

Gil nodded toward the open door. "Ask her. She's the therapist."

The bottom dropped out of Delon's already hollow stomach.

"Sorry. I can only tell you what the fuck is wrong with your knee," Tori said. "Your head is someone else's department."

Since it was too late to crawl under the table, Delon shot a filthy glare at his brother across it.

Gil responded with a careless shrug. "I figured she owed you a house call."

"Not really," Tori said. "I already paid my bill, and I have to say, your night and weekend rates are highway robbery."

She flipped on the light. Delon winced, cupping his hand over his eyes again. Oh yeah. The buzz was definitely fading. He spread his fingers a crack to watch Tori shuck her brown canvas work coat. She'd yanked her hair through the hole at the back of her baseball cap, and her Cactus Ropes sweatshirt had a hole in the front pocket. Her jeans were streaked with dust, and a single cotton roping glove was tucked in the right front pocket, as if she'd come straight from the arena.

Delon's mind felt like it was folding in half, trying to reconcile this casually profane creature with the vision in diamonds and silk from the night before, until he glanced down at her feet. She wore the same scuffed boots. The sight of them steadied him, like a familiar landmark in a strange city.

"Well, let's see it." She unwrapped the bar towel that held the melting bags of ice in place and dumped the soggy mess on the table in front of Gil. "Take care of those, would you?"

"Yes, ma'am." He tossed in a mocking salute but didn't move.

She ignored him, a pucker of concentration between her brows as she probed Delon's knee. He sucked in a breath when her fingers hit an especially tender spot near his kneecap.

"Is that the worst?" she asked.

"So far."

Her mouth pushed into a frown as she continued her inspection. "It'd be better if you weren't wearing jeans."

"Isn't it always?" Gil drawled.

Tori smirked. "Generally, yes."

Gil raised sardonic eyebrows at Delon over Tori's bent head. She intercepted the look and reflected it right back at him. "Got something you want to say?"

"You surprised me. I was expecting a Patterson, not a roper."

"Thank you," she said and went back to poking at Delon's knee.

Delon stared at the button on the top of her cap, thunderstruck. That was it. The difference he'd been trying to put his finger on. The hair, the makeup, the clothes—those were just superficial. The change in

Tori was fundamental, all the way to her core, and Gil had nailed it in one. Tori had become what Violet's dad would call a hand. Not a wannabe with her Cowgirl Barbie boots and matching Barbie horse. She was a true roper. An athlete, her body tuned for competition. And a damned fine body it was.

She gripped his thigh and his calf and bent his knee slightly. "Relax."

"Say that when you're not about to hurt me." He closed his eyes, took a deep breath, and made a concerted effort to let the muscles go loose. Tori steadied his thigh and pulled up on his calf, testing the ligament. The joint held tight. She repositioned the leg, massaged his thigh and calf with her fingers, then tried again. Still no slack that Delon could feel.

She slid her hand down to his ankle. "I'm going to try bending it. Tell me when to stop."

Delon nodded, eyes still shut, teeth gritted as she eased his heel toward his butt. The pain wasn't as bad as he'd expected, but something felt weird. Sort of loose. Then the same old pressure began to build, the steel band clamping around his knee. "Stop."

She did, but instead of straightening his leg, she said, "Look."

At first he didn't see what she meant. Then he blinked, stared, and blinked again. His heel was at least six inches closer to his butt than it had been since the surgery. "What's wrong with it?"

"More like what's right. You just cost Pepper a few

grand in fees." Tori released his leg and straightened, hands on hips. "It appears you've done a banner job of busting up the scar tissue all by yourself. Too bad you were awake to feel it."

"He didn't tear anything else?" Gil asked.

"Not that I can tell."

Without comment, Gil heaved to his feet, scooped up the towels and ice packs, and left.

Tori's gaze measured his uneven, hitching gait. "Hip?"

"Yeah. Motorcycle accident. Crushed the left side of his pelvis." Delon hesitated, then added, "It happened the night Krista broke it off with him."

Tori stiffened. "Well, I'll just go now—"

"You're not like her." He grabbed the sleeve of her sweatshirt so she couldn't walk away. "Even Gil said so, when he called you a roper."

Her chin dropped and she was silent for the space of a few breaths. Then she looked up and smiled, a rare, unguarded thing. "Thank you."

He let her go and settled his hand on his knee, his head spinning from more than the aftereffects of the tequila. "So that's it? I get drunk and fall on my ass and it's all better?"

"No. But at least now we have a fighting chance."

Tori shoved her hands into the pocket of her sweatshirt, lean and strong and determined. Delon pictured her in that blue dress, her arms and shoulders all sleek, bare muscle. What would she feel like against him now, with so much of her younger, softer self stripped away…

His body pulsed with a different kind of ache, even through the booze and the pain. He suddenly wished Gil would disappear so he could ask her to stay awhile. For what? He sure as hell didn't need another drink, and he was in no shape to stroll out to the dining room for dinner.

He rubbed a hand roughly over his knee, the stab of pain a reminder of why she was here. Professional interest only. "Sorry to drag you out on a Saturday night. Looks like you were busy."

"Shawnee came out to rope this afternoon. I was just putting my horse away when Gil called."

Delon shook his head, confused. "You still hate Violet, but you and Shawnee are friends now?"

"No. We just practice together. It's the team roping version of a booty call—in, out, no strings."

Like Delon, in other words. Shame twisted his stomach into a queasy knot.

Tori hesitated, then added, "And Shawnee only picked on me. Violet messed with *us*."

She gave the word an emphasis that made it important. Made *him* important, if only in the past tense.

We should have done this sooner, she'd said.

Was it just the booze, or did *this* mean more than dancing? Things like talking, being honest, asking for what they really wanted? But just like with his brother, anything he could say now was much too little and far too late, so he settled for, "Thanks again."

"You're welcome."

She studied him for a few beats, as if she wanted to ask the obvious questions, then said, "Come in first thing Monday morning. And ice the crap out of your knee until then. It's gonna be sore."

She didn't say good night, just turned and walked away. Delon let his head fall back and closed his eyes, floundering in a slough of desire, misery, and guarded optimism. Instead of totally wrecked, his knee was better. But how much? Enough?

At least now we've got a fighting chance, she'd said. But she hadn't said that the odds were in their favor.

Footsteps approached and then paused, too quick and light to be Gil. "Delon?"

His eyes popped open. Tori stood in the door.

"What's wrong?" he asked.

"I'm not sure. Miscommunication?"

"I don't understand."

"Your brother. He's gone." She glanced over her shoulder and then back again, her expression part baffled, part suspicious. "He took your keys and told the bartender I was driving you home."

Chapter 22

TORI HELPED DELON INTO HER CAR AND SHUT THE door behind him. He was a wreck, his hair sticking up, his shirt yanked out on one side and flopping over his belt. He slumped into the seat and immediately closed his eyes.

She climbed behind the wheel and started the car. "How long since your last drink?"

"An hour, give or take."

"How much did you have?"

"Three beers, two shots of tequila."

He remembered and could still count. That ruled out a serious concussion. "I assume you have ibuprofen at home?"

"Yeah."

The shop looked cleaner and classier than she remembered. The eaves and windows were trimmed with red, and a huge logo had been painted on the expanse of blank front wall—the silhouette of a bare-back rider in red and black, with *Sanchez Trucking, Inc.* circled around it. Neatly pruned shrubs lined the sidewalk on either side of the door marked

Office. Sheesh. Even a shop had better landscaping than her place.

"How do you get up to your apartment?" she asked.

"The stairs are around the side."

She stepped out of the car and was engulfed in Delon's signature cologne—grease and diesel exhaust. Even though she'd loved Willy, truly and deeply, one tiny corner of her heart had always twitched at that scent. She'd hated how it still affected her, but there it was, so all she could do was make damn sure her path didn't cross Delon's when he was competing at Cheyenne and avoid truck stops whenever possible.

And if her brain kept hopscotching between the new Delon and Willy and the old Delon, she'd be the one falling off barstools before long.

She hunched her shoulders against the chilly breeze and walked around to the side of the building. The staircase was metal, narrow, and steep. No way would she let Delon go up those alone. She went back to find him maneuvering his leg out of the car. He hissed in pain when his toe caught on the doorframe. She stepped closer and offered a hand. His fingers were warm and strong as always, but the clasp of his palm against hers felt different.

The calluses were gone. Those hard ridges on the fingers and palm of his riding hand that had been such a raspy, delicious contrast to her most sensitive spots. The nape of her neck. The inside of her thigh. Her nipples. She remembered how he'd smiled when he realized what it did to her—a dangerous smile full of wicked promises.

She let go so abruptly he lost his balance and had to grab the open car door to keep from toppling backward.

"Oops," she said. "Slipped."

And fell face-first into another hormonal bog. Damn. She really had to get ahold of herself before she went totally bonkers and tried to get ahold of Delon instead. That would be bad. Because he was her patient—and he was her past. They were both, to paraphrase his words, fucked up. Two broken halves couldn't make a functional whole. Could they?

"I can make it from here," he said.

She stepped back but fell in beside him as he limped around the side of the shop. "Those stairs are treacherous."

"I've had a lot of practice. I'll be fine."

"I doubt you were half tanked before. So rather than stand back and watch you roll ass over teakettle down a flight of stairs, I'll just follow you on up." His expression went mutinous, his bottom lip poking out, and she laughed outright. "Wow. I bet that's exactly what Beni looks like when he doesn't get his way."

His scowl dissolved into a weary sigh. "It's been a long day."

"Tell me about it." Beginning with her father's divorce bomb, but she wasn't thinking about that now.

Delon grasped the stair rail and stepped up with his good leg, then brought his sore leg level. Tori let him get two steps above her, then put her hand on the railing behind his, her upper body canted forward so she had leverage if he started to sway. Her position put his butt directly in her line of sight. Dear Lord, that was one nice butt. She yanked her gaze away, to a trio of trucks parked in a row alongside the shop, the chrome and polished paint of the tractors gleaming under the security lights.

A familiar fascination tugged at her sleeve. Big rigs had a sexy mystique, like modern day stagecoaches, the drivers perched high and proud, all that horsepower at their command. She'd had fantasies about Delon dragging her into one of those sleepers. Carrying her off to crisscross the country, just the two of them on an endless road trip, town after town of strangers who didn't know or care who her father was. She gazed at the nearest black one, as streamlined as a stealth fighter. *Climb on in,* it whispered. *I'll take you anywhere you want to go.*

Her head rammed into Delon's elbow as he stopped on the landing. When she stumbled, he grabbed the back of her coat and hauled her upright as easily as if she were Beni's size.

"Good thing you came along to keep me safe," he deadpanned, then raised his eyebrows. "Were you staring at my trucks?"

At first, she thought he said *butt,* and her face went hot before she realized he'd caught her checking out the semis. "They're pretty."

"Pretty." He spat the word out in disgust. "Next thing, you'll call them *cute.*"

She drew herself up, offended. "*Cute* is not in my vocabulary."

"But you do have a thing for trucks."

"I don't—"

"It's okay. Lots of girls do." His smile was sly, his eyes gleaming with something wild and dangerous.

She suddenly realized they were face-to-face on the landing, their bodies touching, if you didn't count the five layers of clothes between them. His hand was still on her shoulder, and his fingers tightened fractionally, as if he would pull her even closer. Her heart sprouted legs and launched into a frantic gallop. Oh God. What if he kissed her? She wasn't ready for that. Was she? If he leaned in and put his mouth on hers, would she shove him away or devour him?

He stepped back as far as the small space allowed. "I smell like a brewery."

Uh-huh. Now that she remembered to inhale, she had to admit his breath was a little, um, strong. "Got your keys?"

"My brother stole them, remember?"

Ah, yes. Gil Sanchez. She could absolutely see why he'd been irresistible to young, rebellious Krista Barron. The man wore trouble like the spiked collar on a junk-yard dog. "And he lives where?"

Delon pointed to a powder-blue manufactured home set far back in a corner of the huge truck yard, with an actual white picket fence, a swing set, and a basketball hoop above the garage, as if someone had deliberately set out to meet every clichéd definition of middle class respectability.

"Who is he trying to fool?"

"Krista's family and their pack of lawyers."

Oh. Well. *Bite my tongue.* "So the fence is ironic."

"That would be the polite word for it."

The windows of the house were dark, no car parked outside. "He must have slithered off to some satanic ritual."

Delon snorted. "You think my brother is in cahoots with the devil?"

"Are you sure he's not?"

Delon laughed, just a single *ha*, but it brought a hint of the old sparkle into his eyes. "There have been rumors, but it's mostly the church ladies, and they don't approve of anyone."

"Where there's smoke…" She looked around the landing. No place to hide a spare key. "How are we getting in?"

He reached over and opened the door. "This is Earnest."

And his father had no reason to insist on state-of-the-art security. Obviously, Delon could handle it from here, but she was curious, so she followed him in. It was exactly what you'd expect of a bachelor pad over a garage: a second-, possibly thirdhand couch, a shiny new entertainment center with a huge flat-screen television, and an oversize beanbag chair. The kitchen was a cramped nook to the right of the front door, with appliances straight from a seventies flashback. Through two other open doors, she glimpsed a bathroom slightly larger than her closet and a bedroom that couldn't hold more than the one double bed. There wasn't a toy or a spare sock cluttering up the place.

"Where do you put your kid?" she asked.

Delon glanced around. "Most of his stuff is at Violet's. He spends more time there since I'm—well, I was—on the road so much."

The explanation made perfect sense, but it was so backward—the all-American boy living in a man cave while his brother, the Lord of Darkness, ruled his own little island of suburbia. But then, until Joe, this had apparently been only a pit stop for Delon. His real home base had been at the Jacobs ranch. And now...?

Delon shifted on his feet, running a hand over his rumpled hair. "I need a shower."

Which was her cue to make a graceful exit. Too bad she didn't possess much grace, and the idea of driving through the pitch-black night to spend the rest of the evening in her empty house held so very little appeal. "I should stay, just in case. Bathrooms are the number one place for falls."

"I can manage a shower on my own."

"I wasn't offering to join you." The instant the words left her mouth, heat flashed over her skin. Oh, the things they'd done in her shower... She glanced around, desperate to distract both of them. "I can make you a sandwich or something while you get cleaned up."

He stared at her for a long moment, his expression a complicated mix of X-rated memories and *what the hell?* Then he shrugged. "Knock yourself out."

"Okay. And you..." She tried for her stern therapist voice. "Don't knock yourself out."

He grinned. A real one that reached all the way to his eyes, chasing the shadows away for an instant. "Yes, ma'am."

While he limped into the bedroom and rifled through drawers, she tossed her jacket on the couch and wandered over to the window in the far wall. It looked down into the shop, a bird's-eye view of what appeared to be a mad jumble of equipment and pieces of trucks dimly lit by safety lights over the doors. As her eyes adjusted, she began to see order in the chaos. Tools lined up on benches or hung on pegboards. Floors swept clean. Neatness appeared to be a Sanchez family creed.

Delon reappeared with a ball of clothes tucked under his arm.

"Nice view," she said.

Delon's expression went cool again, as if she'd offended him. "I like it."

"That wasn't sarcasm," she clarified. "It must be awesome to stand here and watch everything that's happening in the shop when it's busy."

"Yeah." He squinted, as if he couldn't figure out what she was up to. Good luck with that, since she didn't have a clue either. He gestured toward the bathroom. "I'll be in there."

"Leave the door unlocked." When his squint deep-ened, she added, "In case you do keel over. I'd hate to have to kick it down."

Amusement crept into his eyes again. "Could you?"

"Damn straight." She flexed one arm. "I'm a lot tougher than I used to be."

"I noticed," he said with a look that went right through her three layers of clothes. Then he limped into the bathroom and closed the door. The lock didn't click behind him.

Chapter 23

TORI WAS IN HIS APARTMENT. COOKING FOR HIM. Delon smelled the bacon as soon as he turned off the shower. Why hadn't she booted him out at the foot of the stairs and hightailed it home? Damned if he could guess. The handful of ibuprofen he'd swallowed hadn't kicked in yet, and as usual, the hangover was jabbing hot pokers into his brain before he even sobered up. This was why he hadn't been shit-faced in at least five years. He pulled on a white Dodge Trucks T-shirt over black nylon sweatpants. His knee hadn't swelled much yet, just a slight puffiness around the kneecap. Putting weight on it didn't hurt much as long as he took it slow, and it didn't feel like it would give way when he took a step, but it was starting to stiffen up.

When he limped out into the living room, Tori was pouring batter into his waffle maker. She flipped it over, then reached into the freezer, pulled out a cold pack, and pointed at the couch. "Sit."

"Why are you doing this?" he asked, too fried to beat around the bush.

She paused. "The waffles and bacon or the ice pack?"

"Either. Both."

She sucked in one corner of her bottom lip, the way she did on the rare occasions that she seemed uncertain. "I needed a distraction. Otherwise I would've spent the night looking for job opportunities in Brazil and trying to decide whether it was easier to get my horse there on a plane or a boat."

He blinked. "Brazil?"

"Well, they don't have rodeos in Puerto Rico. Do they?"

He gave his muddled head a shake. "You just moved home. Why are you job hunting?"

"Oh, you know." She waved a hand in a vague circle. "My mother. The media. It's going to be hell. Brazil probably isn't far enough."

Delon tried to think what was farther. Australia? He glanced around the room. No empty bottles in sight, so if she'd been in his beer, she'd hidden the evidence. "Toss me some bread crumbs, would ya? You lost me at Puerto Rico."

"What?" She blinked as if coming out of a fog, then closed her eyes and grimaced. "Sorry. It's that thing with the screwed-up filters again. Oh! The bacon."

She tossed the cold pack to Delon and hustled over to pull the pan off the stove, fish out half a dozen strips with swift, expert movements, and dump them onto a paper towel–lined plate. Apparently, Willy Hancock had been a bacon kind of guy. She'd never cooked anything but a Pop-Tart for Delon before.

He sank onto the couch, propped his leg up on a

pillow, and molded the cold pack around his knee. "So you're fleeing the country because…"

"My father filed for divorce yesterday." She checked the waffle and cast a glance over her shoulder. "Cool waffle maker, by the way—just like they have at hotels, at the continental breakfast bars. Willy loved those. I kept meaning to buy one but…" She trailed off, shrugged. "You know."

Yeah. He knew. But his brain had stalled back at *my father filed for divorce*. "Your parents are splitting up?"

"They haven't actually been together since…well, hell, I don't remember. Maybe before I started kindergarten?" She grabbed another bowl and beat the contents viciously with a whisk, then dumped eggs into a pan on the stove. "He does his thing, she does hers, and they only meet up for publicity purposes. Which is why she's going to be really, really furious."

"Divorce isn't a good career move?"

"Exactly." Tori pointed the whisk at him, then cursed when egg dripped on the floor. "Sorry. I've been wearing my brain down to nothing trying to imagine how she's going to block him this time."

"*This* time?"

"Yeah, that sorta blew my mind too." She grabbed a paper towel and crouched to wipe up the spilled egg. "I'm betting she'll play the stand-by-your-man card. Work up some tears at a press conference, blame herself for not being there for him, make a few vague references to other women." Tori froze midswipe and pressed a knuckle to her mouth. "Oh, hell. I never asked if there were other women. There must have been. He sure hasn't been getting any at home."

Delon had no idea what to say, so he just waited and watched, like a rubbernecker at a car wreck. Geezus. Senator Patterson. Potential presidential candidate. Divorced. Possibly sleeping around. This shit was gonna hit and splatter all over Texas. Hell, the whole country.

Tori jumped up and tossed the towel on the counter, then went back to the stove to turn the eggs. Having her in his kitchen cooking for him was surreal—in a dangerously good way. She doused the eggs with salt and pepper and gave them a violent stir. A chunk of half-cooked egg flew out, bounced off her chest, and plopped onto the floor.

"Dammit! I'm not usually a total disaster in the kitchen. I'm just—" She raised both hands and waggled them in the air to demonstrate her frazzled state of mind. "And it's stupid. I'm twenty-eight years old, and I've always known they weren't exactly a love match."

"They're still your parents." And divorce still sucked, no matter how old you were.

"They could destroy him," Tori said. "My mother. The media. The voters. All because he wants to have a normal life, with someone who wants *him*. Not Senator Patterson. Not the CEO of Patterson, Incorporated."

"Why did he marry her?"

"Because she decided he should." She gave a low, contemptuous laugh. "And she was—is—beautiful, which pretty much sealed the deal back when he was twenty-two and easily distracted by a nice rack." She moved over to check the waffle maker. "How many do you want?"

None, but he had to eat more than those few bites of prime rib sandwich or the ibuprofen would chew a hole in his stomach. "One's fine."

"Are you sure?" She picked up the bowl, tilting it for his inspection. "I made too much batter."

"That's fine, I—"

She plunked the bowl down and whipped around to face him. "Are you in love with her?"

"Your *mother*?"

"What? No! I meant Violet," she said, exasperated, as if that was who they'd been talking about all along.

"No." The answer popped out so easily, he had to look away in embarrassment, remembering how Gil had mocked his self-delusion. "Not the way you mean. Violet and I were...close. Comfortable, you know? Plus, Violet's parents are right there, and I wanted that for Beni. Everybody together. A regular family."

Tori fished out a crispy brown waffle, her jaw working as if she was chewing on words she was trying not to spit out.

"You think I was stupid." *Join the big fucking club*, he thought.

"No." She spread the waffle with butter and placed eggs and bacon alongside. "I just wonder..."

"What?"

She turned to fix him with a penetrating gaze. "Are you sure it was only for Beni?"

"Of course. Why else?"

She kept looking at him that way, like she could see every strand of the dark tangle of hurt and jealousy inside him. He ducked his head. "Beni deserves a family."

"So do you," she said and handed him his home-cooked breakfast.

He felt as if she'd stripped him naked, and not in a good way. She gave him time to recover, returning to the kitchen for silverware and syrup, which she handed over before stepping back and folding her arms.

"Look, I know I said that your head isn't my problem, but that's not true. We can't separate physical and mental well-being. In order to restore an athlete to their pre-injury level of performance, we have to address both." She'd switched on her therapist voice, cool and formal. "People underestimate the emotional repercussions of a major injury. You haven't just lost the ability to ride. You've been removed from your team—in your case, the circuit. Your friends call now and then, maybe stop by when they're passing through, but it's awkward. A form of survivor's guilt."

And he knew that particular brand of guilt better than anyone. He got another dose every time he looked at Gil.

Tori shifted, keeping a careful eye on his expression, waiting for him to tell her what she could do with her psychobabble. He just bent his head over his plate, too tired and bruised to pick another fight.

When he remained silent, she continued. "On top of all that, your family situation has undergone some fairly dramatic changes since Joe came along. It would be more of a shock if you weren't a mess."

"Well, that's a relief." He sawed a chunk off his waffle and stabbed it with his fork. "Is there a pill I can take for this?"

"Several, but they only delay the inevitable."

Her eyes emptied out for a second, as if she'd retreated to a place he couldn't follow. Had she tried the pharmaceutical route after Willy died? His gut twisted at the memory of Gil's confession. Opiate addict. Son of a bitch.

Tori refocused on him. "Every person experiences loss differently, but there are common stages." She held up a hand, ticking points off her fingers. "First, denial and isolation. This can't be happening to me. If I don't admit it, don't talk about it, it won't be real."

The Sanchez way, Gil had called it. Yeah, he had that one down.

"I think we can safely say you've reached the anger stage." Tori gave his knee a pointed look, tapping her second finger, then moved on to the third and fourth. "Bargaining and depression come next, not necessarily in that order. Bargaining doesn't last long. You figure out pretty fast there's nothing you can promise that will fix what's unfixable. But the anger keeps flaring up when you least expect it. And then…" She jerked a shoulder. "When you let go of the anger…well, sadness is the only thing left. Which is why it's easier to be pissed."

She wasn't just talking about him anymore. He swallowed twice to get a lump of waffle past the knot in his throat. "There must be something after depression."

"Acceptance. Or so I've heard." She whipped around and strode to the kitchen, gathering pots and pans and dumping them into the sink with a clatter.

He picked up a piece of bacon. Like the waffle, it was done to a perfect crisp.

"If you can reach that stage, you'll be able to straighten things out with Violet." She grabbed a bottle of dish soap and squirted it liberally over the dishes. "And you should. Family is important. I never had that kind of normal until I married Willy."

"And it wasn't possible to stay with his family after he died?"

She shook her head. "I couldn't play the part anymore."

"Which part?"

"Tragic widow, keeper of the eternal torch." She turned on the faucet and stared at the water as it streamed into the sink. "People love a hero. So much they start to think he belongs to them. Honestly, I'm not sure whether the sympathizers or the haters were worse."

"Haters?" Delon stared at her in disbelief. "For what?"

"Smiling. Laughing. Wearing a shirt that's too bright or too tight or not buttoned up to my chin. And the men…" She shook her head. "If one more sleazy prick had offered to help *ease my pain*, I would've bit something besides my tongue."

Delon stared down at the bacon, eggs, and waffle. What the hell was wrong with people? "What he did was incredible."

"It was a reflex." She cranked off the faucet and faced him, leaning her hips against the sink with her hands braced on either side. "Don't get me wrong. I'm amazed he saw what was coming and reacted so quickly, but it's not like he threw himself on a grenade. Willy never thought he could die. He was driving a one-ton, four-door dually, and the other guy was in a compact car. If the jackass hadn't looked up at the last instant and tried to swerve, he would've plowed into the rear fender instead of the driver's door. And even then…" Her breath fractured. "God, I bet Willy was pissed. If they'd let me write his epitaph, it would've said, 'Seriously? A fucking Subaru?'"

The laugh burst out before Delon could stop it. He clamped his mouth shut, aghast.

"Don't." Tori gave a quick shake of her head. "I've had enough of proper and respectful, especially when it comes to a man who was anything but. I need to be able to say what I think. Laugh a little and be pissed off a little and give Fate the middle finger instead of worshiping at the altar of Willy Hancock, loving husband and son and savior of children."

Her gaze met his, her emotions so raw it was all

he could do not to flinch. Despite all that had come before, she had never been this naked in front of him. The moment stretched unbearably thin, until it felt as if something inside him might rip wide open if he didn't look away.

"Do you really want to move to Brazil?" he asked, trying to sound like it didn't matter one way or the other where she went.

"No. Just someplace where there isn't all of...this." She made a gesture that wrapped her father's situation up in a nice little bow. Then she sighed. "Those first years in Cheyenne were so amazing. People actually saw *me*. Not the money. Not my daddy's politics. Just me."

"That's all most of them have seen here since you've been back," Delon argued.

"For now. But it won't last. A few people are already starting to put the pieces together. Next thing you know, they'll be tweeting my grocery list and debating on the state of my health and my love life based on how much toilet paper I buy."

Okay. Yes. That would suck. "Then what?"

"I'll stick it out as long as I can, for the sake of my job. Then I suppose I'll find some other place where nobody knows me or gives a damn about the Pattersons." She tucked her chin and studied her toes. "I hear the Pacific Northwest is a great place for ropers. And Montana is so overrun with movie stars buying up their pieces of the Big Sky, I'd be chump change."

In other words, anywhere but here.

Tori turned back to the waffle iron. "If you're sure you don't want another one, I'll put this away."

"Are you hungry?" he asked. Not to stall her. Exactly. She had done all the work, it was only polite to offer her a bite.

"I'll grab something on the way home."

"Eat. I owe you that much." When she started to shake her head, he added, "It'll just go to waste otherwise."

She hesitated so long he was sure she'd say no. When she did speak, it was as if the words were pulled out against her will. "That bacon does smell awfully good."

"Tastes even better." He waved a strip like a bone in front of a dog, then crunched it between his teeth.

She gave him an eye roll. "If you're gonna be that way…"

While she laid more strips of bacon in the frying pan and poured another dollop of batter into the waffle iron, he wolfed down the rest of his bacon and dug into the waffle. With each bite, the queasiness in his stomach settled and his headache eased.

Tori loaded her plate and came into the living room, pausing when she realized her seating options were limited to the beanbag chair or the slice of couch Delon's legs didn't occupy. She chose the beanbag, sinking down to sit cross-legged. Silence descended, cut only by the scratch of silverware on plates.

Delon grabbed the television remote and scrolled through the channel guide. "See anything you want to watch?"

"There." She pointed with her fork.

He squinted at the selections. A shoot-'em-up spy thriller, a comedy, one of those drama-slash-romance flicks where one of the main characters invariably died, or a cartoon. Please God, not the comedy. He'd watched the first half hour while he was stuck in the hospital and wasn't sure his IQ had recovered yet. "Which one?"

"At the bottom." She wriggled her butt, settling deeper into the beanbag. "The penguins kick ass."

So Beni said. Delon damn near knew the words by heart, but he could watch it again. They finished their meal without speaking, the silence a relief, as if they had both hit an emotional wall and needed a time-out. When their plates were clean, he maneuvered to his feet.

"I can—" she began.

"Got it." He tucked the gel pack under his arm and collected the plates.

"The kitchen—"

"Can wait until morning." He dumped the dishes in the sink, flipped off the overhead light in the living room, and fetched a pair of fleece throws from the bedroom. His had a bucking horse on it, a Father's Day gift from Beni. The one he tossed her had a cartoon platypus. "Might as well get comfortable."

Again, she looked as if she might argue. Then she nestled into the beanbag and pulled the throw over her. "Thanks."

They sat in the dark, staring at the television and

taking comfort from the presence of another human being. A fellow refugee from reality, if only for a few hours. Crazy, to get even this close when she seemed dead set on leaving again, but as long as he knew, as long he didn't let himself dream, he was safe, wasn't he?

He woke to someone jostling his pillow. He forced his eyes open and found Tori leaning over him, trying to tug her coat from the arm of the couch, under his head.

"What time is it?" he mumbled, twisting around to look out the window. Pitch-dark.

"After midnight. We both slept awhile."

She gave the jacket another tug, but it was pinned under his shoulder. He was warm and relaxed, still half asleep. Before his mind could fully engage, he reached up and caught her wrist. She froze, her eyes wide and wary in the dim light.

"What if I said I don't want to just be friends?" he asked, his voice raspy with sleep.

She stared down at him, emotions flickering across her face so fast he couldn't identify any of them. "I would say that's probably not the smartest thing we could do, given the situation."

"And if I said I'm willing to take my chances?"

She took her sweet time thinking it over. "I need some time to…adjust my expectations."

He stroked the tender underside of her wrist with his thumb, watching as her lips parted on a swift intake of air. He might not know her mind, but he knew her body, and he remembered exactly how she liked to be touched. "How long?"

"I don't know. This thing with my parents..."

"Will you let me know when you're ready?"

She shook her head and his heart sank, but then she blew out a reluctant sigh. "Check back with me in a couple of weeks."

"The middle of February?" he asked, unable to leave it alone.

She gave a half-hearted shrug, her gaze tracking to the door, though she still didn't pull away from his touch. "Sure. Why not?"

He could think of a dozen reasons—things he'd done and she'd done and all the ways they could hurt each other all over again—but he stroked her wrist one more time before sitting up to free her jacket. She pulled it on, tugged the zipper clear to her chin, and stuffed her hands in the pockets.

"You realize I'm a lousy emotional bet."

"Unlike me."

She gave a low, short laugh. "Think of the magic we could make together."

He didn't have to imagine. He had a perfectly good memory. As if reading his mind, she said, "I'm not that girl, Delon."

"You're a lot tougher."

She smiled slightly at her own words. "I'm also a lot more...difficult."

No kidding. But he needed to borrow some of that

toughness, from someone who'd gone through the worst and was emerging from the other side, singed around the edges but not destroyed. Tori understood the snarl of anger and guilt in his gut because it wasn't so different from what she felt about how Willy died.

"I'd like to get to know this you," he said softly.

"I might not be ready to decide who I am yet."

"*Decide?*" He laughed, incredulous. "You just get to make it up for yourself?"

"Why not? Didn't you decide who you wanted to be?"

His fists clenched in the plush throw. "We don't all have the luxury of reinventing our lives."

She gave him a long, level stare. His eyes dropped first. Her voice was low and surprisingly gentle. "Try it, Delon. You might be less likely to feel like punching strangers in bars."

She brushed a fingertip as light as a kiss across his cheek and left him to sleep on it.

━━━━━━━

When Tori pulled into her driveway, the cat was perched on a fence post, a disapproving sneer on her mottled gray face.

Tori stuck her tongue out at the hell beast. "Sorry, not the walk of shame."

But she was getting closer. Her heart kerthumped like a bass drum every time she recalled the stroke of

Delon's thumb across her skin, the husky timbre of his voice. *What if I don't want to just be friends?*

She shivered, huddling deeper into her jacket. Her body was a jittering mass of nerves, every one of them craving his touch. She could be smart about it, though. They'd both be crystal clear on what they expected. If those expectations didn't match, she would walk away.

And this time, she wouldn't leave her heart behind.

Chapter 24

SOMETIME JUST AFTER SUNUP, DELON LEVERED HIM-self off the couch and did a Frankenstein shuffle into the bathroom, leaving the door open and the light off. He wasn't ready to face his morning-after self in the mirror. But instead of sinking, his mood bobbed like a duck on a pond. For the first time in weeks, he felt a tiny ray of hope that his knee might come around. And he'd sort of asked Tori out, and she'd sort of said yes.

He worked through a set of gentle stretches, bending his knee a little farther every time. He might not be kicking himself in the ass anytime soon—literally, at least—but he was a damn sight closer than he had been. When he finished, he stuffed his feet into running shoes, grabbed the gel pack from the freezer, and headed downstairs, intending to poke around on the internet. Maybe even check out some rodeo results. The shop was quiet, the hard edges of tools and machinery softened by hazy morning sunlight angling through the narrow windows in the truck bay doors. The sight gave him the usual glow of pride, cut through with a twinge of frustration. Was Tori right? Could he just *decide* to claim his place at Sanchez Trucking?

He was surprised to hear music when he opened the office door. Charley Pride was not on Gil's playlist. Delon's dad stuck his head out of the open door of the dispatcher's office. He smiled, but it was wrapped in a question mark. "Hey, Delon. How're you doing this morning?"

Of course he'd heard. Probably from half a dozen different people. "A little sore, but no damage done."

"Well, good. That's real good."

If his dad wondered why Delon had been drunk and punching redneck pricks on Beni's birthday, he didn't ask. Not that he didn't care. Merle Sanchez was just more comfortable with the whats than the whys. He'd tended to their scrapes and bruises, cheered them on through flag football and junior rodeos and the National Finals, but he kept his feelings buried deep under that laid-back, cheerful surface and preferred everyone else to do the same. *The Sanchez way.*

"What are you doing in the office on a Sunday morning?" Delon asked.

"Jimmy's back haul from Tuscaloosa got canceled. I'm trying to find him a load by tomorrow night, or he'll be deadheading home."

Burning up hundreds of dollars' worth of fuel for zero return. Delon tilted his head toward Gil's bank of computer screens. "You know how to operate that thing?"

"Nope. I'm doing it the old-fashioned way." His dad waved the cordless phone. Then he heaved an aggravated sigh. "And not having a damn bit of luck."

The main door banged open behind Delon, and Gil stomped in, snarling. "This is the fourth time those fuckers have left us with our ass hanging in the breeze. I don't care if they offer double our usual rate, we don't ever schedule another load out of that warehouse."

"It's your call." Their dad shot out of the chair, slapping the phone into Gil's hand. "I gotta run. I've got a… ah…thing this morning."

And he was gone. Delon trailed Gil into the office. "Has he taken up religion?"

"A woman." Gil plopped down in his chair and swiveled to face his computer screens. "Dottie, Dolly—whoever his latest sweet young thing is. They had a sleepover. Seems like there was a lot of that going on last night."

"You took my keys and left me." Delon's mouth was speaking, but his brain was still processing *latest sweet young thing.* "Dad has a lot of…sleepovers?"

Computer keys clattered as Gil took his irritation out on the keyboard. "What are you, ten years old? You didn't think the old man got laid once in a while?"

"But he and Mom are still married. I thought…"

"He was pining away?" Gil snorted. "He just uses Ma to keep the Dollys and Dotties from getting ideas."

Delon braced one hand against the doorframe as his world tilted to accommodate Merle Sanchez, player. Of course he'd known his dad hadn't strapped on a chastity belt when his mother left. Truthfully, he'd avoided thinking about his dad's love life because, well, shit. Who wanted that in their head? But now…

"How young?"

Gil let loose a string of curses and pounded more keys. "He's not cruising the high school for chicks, but you might recognize some of 'em from back in your college days."

The earth shuddered beneath Delon's feet. "I really should have stayed upstairs."

"Fuck that. Why should I be the only one who suffers?" *Clack, clack, clack, clack*—Gil jabbed the same key repeatedly. "Hah! There you are, you sneaky little bastard."

Delon leaned closer, curious. The screen on the left showed a map of the Tuscaloosa region. The screen on the right was covered in lines of text he couldn't read from a distance.

Gil shot him a sour look. "Are you just gonna stand there or sit your ass down and learn something?"

"I can't…I mean, I didn't…" Think Gil would ever let him touch the dispatch system. With good reason. "I'm not very good at computer stuff."

"You're about to get better." Gil slapped the seat of the second chair. "Sit, Junior."

Delon sat, staring at a spreadsheet of distributors and warehouses in Alabama. Each name appeared to be a clickable link. "Is that a database?"

"Yeah. I didn't like any of the prepackaged stuff so I built my own." Gil's fingers danced over the keys to a beat only he could hear. "You can filter based on the distance from a certain zip code, type of load, and my personal rating system. Are they on schedule, how they treat our drivers, how they pay, that kind of shit. Today we start by looking at five-star joints within a hundred miles of Tuscaloosa that ship refrigerated loads."

Delon settled the gel pack onto his knee and watched Gil perform what looked like magic. Screens popped up, then disappeared, with Gil providing a running commentary as he clicked, scrolled, typed, and cursed. The longer Delon watched, the more patterns began to emerge from the chaos.

"It's like a scavenger hunt," he said.

Gil flashed a savage grin. "The whole thing is a big game, racing other dispatchers to get the best loads, pushing the schedule to keep our guys on time but not sitting on their asses waiting. You watch the maps, the weather, traffic and construction reports, try to route our drivers through and around as fast as possible. At the end of the week, the dispatcher with the most paid miles per truck is the champ." Gil jabbed a key for emphasis, then pumped his fist. "And we have a winner. A load of fresh peaches headed for Oklahoma, scheduled pickup canceled due to a break-down. Now we've just gotta grab it before anyone else."

Delon's heartbeat had picked up, his system oozing adrenaline. Leave it to Gil to turn dispatching into a battlefield.

Gil reached for the phone but paused before dialing. "Speaking of missing out, I wish you'd get over this shit with Violet. I'd give my left nut for one of Miz Iris's cinnamon rolls right now, and Dad's so deep in withdrawal he's hitting on women his own age just because they can make a decent meat loaf."

Delon gaped at him. What was he talking about? Gil always dropped by Iris's kitchen for coffee and baked goods when Jacobs Livestock wasn't on the road, and their dad wandered through around dinner time at least once a week. *I miss my boys,* Iris had said. Delon had assumed she'd meant him and Beni. He'd had no idea his dad and Gil hadn't been making their usual rounds.

"I'm not stopping either of you."

Gil shot him an impatient glare. "That's not how it works, D."

Because they were his family. And they'd had his back all these months without saying a word. Delon had to swallow a few times before he could speak without sounding all choked up. "Is that why you tried to hook me up with Tori? To distract me so you could get back on the cookie wagon?"

Gil hitched a shoulder, his gaze glued to the computer screen. "Worth a try. I might be willing to give my left nut for a cinnamon roll, but I'd rather sacrifice yours."

"Gee, thanks."

"You're welcome." Gil shoved his chair back and motioned Delon forward. "We need a load out of Denver next Thursday. The details are on that sticky note. Try not to fuck anything up before I get off the phone."

Chapter 25

TORI AVOIDED THINKING ABOUT ANYTHING ON Sunday afternoon by roping with Shawnee, but eventually even that had to come to an end. As Shawnee heaved her rope bag into the back of her truck, she asked, "You plannin' to go to the roping in Lubbock next weekend?"

"I don't have a partner." And it wasn't a draw pot like the one in Canyon.

"Yeah, well, turns out I've got a spot on my dance card."

Tori froze in the midst of buckling Fudge's halter. "You want me to rope with you?"

"Whaddya think we've been doing? Quilting club?" Shawnee screwed up her face in disgust. "My regular partner got herself knocked up and her husband's being a dick, whining about how she shouldn't be riding in her third trimester. Everybody else is already partnered up."

Tori stared at her. "You said your granny could've roped that last steer faster."

"Hey, Gran could fling some string in her day. So... you in?"

Tori stared at her some more, until Fudge rubbed his head on her shoulder and knocked her back a step. She shoved him away. "Fine. But I don't care where I rope the steer, you'd better be there when I turn the corner."

Shawnee just grinned. "As long as we're on the subject, you might not've noticed, but I could use a new pickup."

"How is that on the subject?"

Shawnee folded her arms and leaned back against the rust bucket. "They give pickups to the winners at the Turn 'Em and Burn 'Em roping in Abilene in March. That gives us six weeks to get you up to speed."

Tori stared at her, gobsmacked. The Turn 'Em and Burn 'Em was the biggest roping event in Texas short of the George Strait Invitational, but unlike George's roping, it was handicapped like a Pro/Am golf tournament—anyone had a chance to win the big prizes if they had their best day. But there would be hundreds of teams. Shawnee expected her to turn five steers fast enough to beat them all?

Tori swallowed hard. "Okay."

"Okay."

Tori hesitated, delaying the moment when she had to be alone. Her mother was home, and her dad had broken the news hours ago. The knowledge was like standing under a ton of boulders in a fraying net. She could practically hear the *ping, ping, ping* as fibers snapped.

"I suppose now that we're partners, I have to offer you a beer," she said, because yeah, she was that desperate.

"I've got a six pack of Shiner and last year's *World Series of Team Roping* on DVD."

Shawnee shot her a look, as if she thought Tori might be kidding, then shrugged. "I gotta be home before midnight or my royal carriage turns into a rusty old piece of shit."

When the horses were unsaddled, Tori led the way inside. She dragged out chips and salsa and they settled in, beers in hand, Shawnee in the recliner and Tori on the couch.

"These walls are the color of baby calf shit," Shawnee said.

"I know." Tori dug through couch cushions for the remote. "I hate painting."

"There are people who will do that crap if you part with a few bucks from the ol' trust fund."

"Too bad my family doesn't believe in them."

Shawnee did a double take. "You're kidding."

"Nope." Tori gave up on the cushions and started shaking out blankets. "The family corporation owns the ranch, the horses, the businesses, everything. Daddy is the CEO and gets a salary. We can live at the ranch and use the family stuff—with permission—but it doesn't belong to any of us. Every kid gets tuition at the college of our choice and five years max to graduate. It's assumed that we will excel to the point of being offered financial assistance for advanced degrees. Other than that, we're on our own."

"That's...not exactly how I figured."

"You and the rest of the world." The remote fell out of the blankets and thudded onto the floor. Tori bent to pick it up. "Blame my great-great-granddad. After he got filthy rich, he decreed that there would be no deadbeats living off his hard-earned bucks, and subsequent generations have continued the tradition."

"So this place..." Shawnee circled a hand in the air.

"Is mine. I made the down payment with Willy's life insurance, but I've got a mortgage like everybody else."

For once, Shawnee didn't have a smart-ass comeback. Tori turned on the television, still tuned to the news channel she'd had on earlier, keeping an ear out for any mention of her parents. Now her father's face filled the screen. The blood drained from Tori's head when she recognized the interviewer. Richard Patterson was a guest on the number one conservative political talk show in the country, with millions of viewers hanging on his every word.

"...been the poster boy for family values for your party," the talking head was saying. "How do you think your constituents are going to feel about your divorce?"

The senator considered the question, his expression regretful but resolute. "I don't want to imply that I don't care about the people who put me in the Senate. I do. Deeply. I've put the needs of my constituents ahead of everything, including my family. I allowed my marriage to degenerate past the point of no return, then instead of trying to fix it, I turned elsewhere for, um, companionship. I wasn't there for my younger daughter after her husband died, and I've encouraged my older daughter to keep her relationship with a wonderful woman under wraps for fear of damaging my career. In every possible way, I've failed at being a father and a husband."

Tori heard Shawnee suck in air. Well. At least one of them could breathe.

For once, the talking head didn't have to manufacture his shock. "You're saying...I mean, you're confessing...well, I don't know where to start."

"I know how you feel," the senator said with a grim smile.

The interviewer visibly collected himself. "Are you considering stepping down from office?"

"If that's what the voters want. Otherwise, I will serve out my term."

"And then? Your name has been mentioned in terms of a presidential bid."

The senator shook his head. "I would prefer to make a reasonably graceful exit, then figure out what's next for me. And spend more time with my girls."

"Well. That's very..." The interviewer trailed off, staring at the senator with the look of a man who'd just witnessed a disaster of epic proportions and couldn't find words to describe it. He tapped two fingers on the table and turned to face the camera. "You heard it here first, folks. Senator Richard Patterson of Texas—"

Tori cut him off and turned on the DVD. She stared at the FBI piracy warning on the screen, streamers of ice water trickling through her body as she imagined her mother and her sister, both watching what she'd just watched. Elizabeth must have known. He never would've outed her on national television without her approval. But their mother...

"What the hell?" Shawnee's voice had an odd, stunned pitch.

"I believe you'd call that a preemptive strike." Tori had to give the man credit. He'd most likely demolished his political future, but he'd also robbed her mother of any and all ammunition, at least as far as Tori could see.

"Did you know?"

"Most of it." She took a very long, deep breath, then let it out slowly. "I only guessed about the other women."

"Well...shit," Shawnee said.

"Yep."

"You wanna talk about it?"

"Nope."

"Thank the fucking stars. Fire up that video. Let's watch some ropin'."

They drank beer and shoveled in chips and salsa until the bag and the bowl were empty, watching team after team until they blurred together in Tori's head. Shawnee provided color commentary and criticism of every single run. She seemed to know half of the contestants and sprinkled her monologue with stories about the horses they rode, who was sleeping with whom, and that time her dad got caught out back in a horse trailer with Barney's wife and it's a damn good thing that pistol under the pickup seat wasn't loaded.

Tori wasn't required to do anything but listen, nod, and let her thoughts spin out into oblivion. It was so much like hanging out with Willy it felt like coming home and, simultaneously, like a black hole opening up inside her chest.

After Shawnee left and the beer bottles were gathered up and stuffed in the trash, Tori showered, pulled on her sweatpants and one of Willy's T-shirts. As she curled up on the couch, her phone rang. She snatched it off the coffee table.

"Daddy. Are you okay?"

"Tired and a little overwhelmed, but I'm more concerned about you."

"Me? Why?"

He made an angry, frustrated noise. "Elizabeth was more than happy to take whatever heat comes her way. Pratimi is thrilled to have a national platform to advance gay rights. Between that and digging up the dirt on my past indiscretions, I assumed the press would be too busy to bother you. But I had to go and mention Willy's death…"

Oh. Hell.

Tori's heart hit bottom with an audible thud. She should have anticipated this from the moment her father told her about the divorce. Of course the reporters would comb through every detail of their lives, looking for anything they could plaster on pages and screens. And Willy's story was irresistible.

Her father growled out a rare curse. "I'm so sorry, sugar. I should have waited—"

"No!" She didn't have to try to sound adamant. "You've waited too long already. I can deal with this."

He sighed. "I wish you didn't have to, especially on my account. I'll do everything I can to help."

"That's all I ask. I'll be fine. *We'll* be fine. I promise."

When he spoke again, he sounded exhausted, but she could hear a shadow of a smile in his voice. "You know what I regret most?"

"What?"

"That I've been gone so much I can't even take credit for the amazing women my daughters have turned out to be."

Tori drew a shaky breath and let it out on a choked laugh. "Okay, now you're just sucking up."

He laughed too. But after they hung up, Tori slumped back on the couch, crossed her arms over her face, and let loose every swear word she'd held back while he could hear.

So much for her all-too-brief trip to Normal Land.

Chapter 26

TORI WOKE MONDAY MORNING TO A WHITE Panhandle Security SUV guarding her driveway. A second car fell in behind her when she turned onto the highway and kept pace even when they were swallowed up by the snarl of morning traffic in Amarillo. At the medical complex, her shadow parked near the front driveway where he could see every car that came and went. Tori assumed there was another stationed in the back lot.

Beth made wide eyes at Tori and followed her into the therapists' office. "Okay, first, of all the things you just blurt on out, *my daddy is Senator Patterson* might've been a good one. And second, why didn't you call in sick today? It's going to be insane."

"It's as easy to deal with here as anywhere." And the sooner they got it out of their systems and moved on to the next ten-day wonder, the better. Tori dumped her jacket and bag in a heap on her chair. "Delon will be here any minute. He had an…incident over the weekend. I told him to come in for a quick evaluation." Tori's cell phone rang, setting her nerves jangling. Beth left as Tori checked the number and blinked in surprise. "Elizabeth?"

"Of course. I assume you're just getting to work, but we need to talk as soon as possible and establish a strategy for dealing with our darling mother. Do you have time this evening?"

Tori couldn't help a smile at her sister's brisk tone and made hers sugar sweet in contrast. "And good morning to you too, sister dear. How've you been?"

"Oh. Fine. Damn. I always forget that part." Her voice faded out slightly, as if she was speaking to someone else on her end. "Yeah, yeah, I know. You don't have to give me that look." Then her attention was back on Tori. "While we're talking, I want you to know I had nothing to do with that phone call from the dean of our School of Medicine. That was all Claire, trying to play the *but you'd get to spend time with your sister* angle."

"Only if I rented an adjacent stool in your lab."

Elizabeth grunted. "You'd be surprised. Pratimi is determined to expose me to at least twenty hours of natural light a week."

"Wow. That much? Do I need to lecture you about sunscreen?"

They both laughed, given that Elizabeth had done her dissertation on the occurrence rates of skin cancer in various ethnic groups.

"Have you heard from her yet?" Tori asked.

"Just the same email she sent you." Because yes, their mother had cc'd Tori, too efficient even in crisis to waste time writing two separate letters. "She's devastated and shocked, can't believe Daddy would do this to us, et cetera, et cetera. Sowing the seeds of resentment for later harvest. We've got a few days, I think. She'll start by trying to talk some sense into him. If that fails, she'll come after you."

"Why me?" Tori demanded, her voice jumping in alarm.

"You're alone and vulnerable. She'll think that makes you an easier target." Elizabeth didn't sound worried. But then, she wasn't the potential target. "Pratimi and I spent some time with a psychologist friend today, working out Claire's most likely angles of attack. I'm going to tell you exactly what to say to her."

Normally, Tori would have bridled at being ordered around. Today, she was grateful. She glanced at the clock. "I've got a patient. Call me tonight whenever you get home. We'll plan our defense."

When she hung up, she checked her computer screen. Delon's name was highlighted in green on the schedule. Her heart did a quick two-step when she opened the door to the waiting room. He stood at the desk wearing a black leather jacket with the Sanchez Trucking logo stitched above his heart. With his black hair tousled by the wind and those dark eyes gleaming with amusement at whatever Beth was saying, he looked hell-bent on trouble—a flyboy, a biker…or a trucker primed to sweep a woman up and away in his steel beast. Tori paused to let the shiver race across her skin and play itself out. Then

Delon looked over and saw her. His smile hit her like a blast of August sunshine, warming every inch of her body and turning the shiver into a quake.

"Hey." His voice was low and a little rough, like he'd just rolled out of bed, layered with promises Tori knew damn well his body could keep. "I've been thinking about you."

Beth's eyebrows shot up into her bangs. The heat gathered low in Tori's belly and billowed upward like steam to turn her face a shiny red. Even the old lady in the waiting room was a little slack-jawed.

Tori cleared her throat. "You should probably dial that down a few notches before all us girls burst into simultaneous orgasm."

Beth busted out in shocked laughter. The old lady gave a scandalized *hmmphf!*—as if those eighteen grandkids she liked to brag about were the result of immaculate conception. Delon stuffed his hands into the pockets of his coat and flipped off that overt sexuality like a switch, leaving a nice guy with a sheepish smile.

"I meant I wondered how you were doing, with your dad and all," he clarified.

"Right." *Down, girl.* "I'm coping, thanks."

She held the door as he walked in, his stride cautious but not a full-out limp. Tori followed him to the third treatment room and closed the door behind them. Funny, she'd never noticed how small these rooms were. Short of cowering in a corner, she couldn't move outside Delon's magnetic field.

"Should I take my pants off?"

"No!"

Then she realized he meant so she could examine his knee, not fulfill her fantasies, which hadn't been at the front of her mind until this precise moment. But now she was never going to be able to look at one of those padded treatment tables quite the same way. She closed her eyes and took a deep breath. Bad move. In the confined space, she inhaled him, all leather and man soap with a hint of eighteen-wheeler. She opened her eyes to find him watching her, amusement gleaming wickedly in his eyes.

"Yes," she said. "I mean, assuming you have something on underneath."

Which had not always been the case, back in the best of the good old days. His grin flashed as if he knew exactly what she was remembering, and the sparks shot through her like the crackle of embers in a campfire, leaving tracers of heat and smoke behind.

Then his jaw tightened. "I saw the security car in the parking lot. Is someone bothering you?"

Only you. But hot and bothered wasn't the same as harassed. "Not yet."

"But they will. After your dad's announcement, the press will be all over all of you again."

"No doubt, but I'm savoring my last few moments of denial, so take off those sweats, and let's see what you can do."

He grinned.

"With your knee, Delon." But damned if she didn't smile back.

Not good. Not here, at the clinic. She had to keep a firm line drawn between business and pleasure. And besides, this sudden shift into flirtation felt...off. As if the bar fight on Saturday night had broken something free inside him and he couldn't figure out what to do with the pieces. She could relate. He'd rattled her cage too. Her wrist still tingled where his fingers had caressed her skin. Plus she'd watched three years' worth of National Finals Rodeo telecasts after Shawnee left, all forty-five of his rides, studying his mechanics and making notes on what they might tweak. Necessary viewing, but she couldn't help noticing he had really, really nice...form.

He stripped off the nylon sweats and slid onto the table, and she tried to pretend putting her hands on his bare, muscled thigh didn't arouse interests that were everything but clinical. *Dammit, Tori, focus.* She forced herself to picture the structures beneath his skin — ligaments, tendons, bones—and tried to concentrate on examining only his knee.

"Well?" he asked after she measured how far it would bend.

She lowered the goniometer. "You gained almost fifteen degrees of flexion, and there's no sign of damage to the repair."

He blew out a breath that sounded as if he'd been holding it since Saturday. "Should I have an MRI, just to be sure?"

"If it would make you more comfortable."

He considered, then shook his head. "I trust you."

A different kind of warmth bloomed in her chest. Pride. Vindication. She had earned that trust…at least as a therapist.

"Now what?" he asked.

So many possible answers, but only one that applied to his rehab. "I don't need to see you again until next Monday, unless it starts to feel worse. In fact, from this point on, I suggest you switch over to working out at the club in Dumas and just check in with me once a week to adjust your routine. Ease into your basic exercises this week. You can push through the soreness, but avoid anything that causes real pain. Lots of ice. Lots of stretching."

"And then?"

"When the swelling is gone, we start figuring out how to make the most of what you've gained. I've been studying bareback riders." Which was better than admitting she'd been studying him. Closely. "With some changes in upper body position and hip rotation, we can make it work. I need to be able to put you through the motions, though, as realistically as possible. I'll rig something up."

"Or we could use my spur board." At the jerk of her head, he added, "If you don't mind coming out to the shop."

Mind? No. Her pulse jumped at the thought of more alone time with Delon, which didn't bode well for her vow to take this new phase slow.

"Violet is at the Fort Worth Stock Show until the end of next week," he added. "Beni is with me."

Her hormones sighed and took a back seat, foiled again. "Okay. Call me when you're ready."

One corner of his mouth curled, and his voice dropped to a quiet rumble. "I've been ready for a long time. But I'll let you know when my knee is up to it."

———

When Tori parked in front of the shop a week later, Beni Sanchez was down the stairs and beside her car before she could open the door, his video game clutched in both hands, talking fast. "I got the ice bombs and the fireproof armor, but I can't get past the Reef of Doom. Can you—"

"Beni! What did I tell you?"

Beni glanced up to Delon on the landing outside their apartment, then turned pleading eyes on Tori. "He said I shouldn't bug you, but it's not bugging if you like to play, right?"

Tori felt an unexpected flash of sympathy for Joe Cassidy. This kid must have had him tied up in knots before he even saw the rope. Tori, on the other hand, had been schooled by Willy's horde of nieces and nephews.

"Did you finish your dinner?" she asked, taking a cue from the dish towel in Delon's hand and the scent of meat loaf that had wafted down the stairs with Beni. Her pulse gave a little blip. What woman wasn't a sucker for a man who knew his way around a kitchen? She supposed Delon had to cook. He was a single father, raised by a single father, brother to a single father, and Earnest didn't have a whole lot of takeout options. Hell, Gil probably baked homemade cookies while wearing a *World's Best Dad* apron.

Beni's grin went flat. "I don't like broccoli."

"You don't like anything green that doesn't come in a cereal box," Delon said. "But you have to eat it anyway. Then you can ask Tori *nicely* if she'll help you with your game."

Wow. He sounded so…fatherly. Like a real dad. Which of course he was, but seeing it in action did odd, melty things to her insides.

"Get up here, Beni." Delon's black T-shirt stretched tight across his biceps as he flipped the dish towel over his shoulder and propped his forearms on the railing. His gaze drilled holes through Beni until the boy heaved a powerful sigh and started up the stairs. Delon gave her security shadow—parked out by the gate—a brief glance, then focused on Tori. "Sorry. I planned to be done with dinner earlier, but I got held up in the office. Are you hungry?"

"No." But now she felt vaguely guilty that she hadn't eaten her greens.

"Give me a minute. I'll meet you down there." He pointed to a door at the back corner of the shop. As Beni reached the landing, he ruffled the boy's hair, the gesture so natural and affectionate it warmed her a few more degrees.

Enough with the melting. Tonight was business. She went to the door Delon had indicated. Inside, fly-specked fluorescents illuminated a long, narrow space. The back corner had been cleared to form a tiny gym with rubber mats on the floor and racks of dumbbells against the wall, next to a weight bench. The spur board held the position of honor in the middle of the room. Everything was well-worn, scuffed, testimony to the hours he'd spent here, honing his body and his technique. She reached up to the shelf above the workbench and turned on the ancient CD player. AC/DC's "Stiff Upper Lip" boomed from speakers in all four corners of the room, the bass cranked high enough to make small wrenches on the workbench dance.

The door to Delon's apartment flew open, and he started down the stairs, shouting to be heard. "Sorry. I can change—"

Tori turned the volume down, amused. So this was what he played in those earbuds while he worked out at the clinic. She examined the stack of CDs next to the player. Nothing but hard rock and heavy metal. This playlist belonged to the Delon she'd met on that crazy New Year's Eve. Bold. Shameless. The accelerator mashed to the floor with the music cranked up loud.

"You can switch over to the radio if you want," Delon said.

No way. She liked this side of him. "This is fine."

He angled past her to dump his gear bag on the weight bench. "I need to stretch out first."

"Take your time." *Please.*

Delon's warm-up routine was a slow, graceful dance to the beat of the song playing on the stereo, muscles bunching, then uncoiling as he moved from one position to the next. Her fingers itched to stroke the length of his leg, his arm, across his shoulders, down the curve of his back…

Damn. She was staring. Not that it mattered. Delon was used to warming up in front of an audience. Blocking out distractions was part of his pregame routine, the familiar movements centering his mind and body like yoga or tai chi. She should try it. Maybe she could learn to block out Shawnee.

Then she shook her head. As aggravating as the woman could be, she was making Tori better. The more obnoxious Shawnee got, the harder Tori worked to prove her wrong. It felt good to throw herself into something, heart and soul. Her nerves jittered as she thought about the coming weekend. The roping in Lubbock would be the first test of her newfound aggressiveness. Could she really push that hard, take those chances in competition? Risk making a fool of herself?

Yep. Or Shawnee would humiliate her instead.

Delon finished his warm-up and strapped the rigging onto the spur board. The initials *DS* were stamped into the heavy leather, blocky and unadorned. The rigid handhold—constructed of multiple layers of rawhide—was black with rosin, the body nicked and gouged. Before his injury, Delon had routinely dragged his spurs over that rigging, right up to his butt.

Her job was to figure out how to make it happen again. His left-handed grip would make it more difficult. Simple biomechanics decreed that the leg opposite his grip had more strength and freedom of motion. If he'd injured his right leg…but he hadn't, so they would deal with what they had.

He pulled on his glove, then clenched one end of a leather lace in his teeth while he wrapped the other around his wrist and tied it off, ensuring that his hand and the glove would not part company in the middle of a ride. Then he glanced at Tori. "Ready?"

"If you are."

He replied by slinging a leg over the spur board and settling in. She strolled around to the front. Rosin creaked as he worked the glove into the handhold, using his other fist to pound his fingers tight, then scooted his hips up flush against the rigging. She turned on the tablet she'd brought along and activated the camera. "I'll video from the front and both sides, then we'll watch it together."

He cocked his free arm back and started to spur. *Thump!* His heels hit the neck of the spur board. *Scrape!* His heels dragged up toward the rigging. Then *thump!* His legs snapped straight and his heels hit the board again, so fast the movement was a blur. *Scrape-thump, scrape-thump, scrape-thump,* rapid-fire as a machine gun. Tori could feel herself goggling. She'd always known he had quick feet, but she'd never appreciated just how fast until she saw it close up. Even through the camera, though, she could see a noticeable deficit in the length of the stroke on the left side compared to the right side.

Delon finished off with two more strokes and then stopped. Tori paused the camera. Delon let his feet drop and waited, hand still in the rigging, while Tori moved around to the front of the spur board and focused the camera.

"Ready?" he asked.

She nodded. The muscles of his riding arm bunched as he leaned back and repeated the routine—*scrape-thump, scrape-thump*—with the same results. When he'd finished the third bout, he pried the glove out and braced his hands on his thighs, winded. His bare arms shone, the pumped muscles standing out in relief. Tori's pulse fluttered at the memory of tracing the shape of those muscles as they quivered under sweat-damp skin.

She cued up the videos and handed him the tablet, stepping around so she could watch over his shoulder. Halfway through the third video, Delon muttered a savage curse and jabbed the pause button. So they agreed. Excellent. Now—if he would trust her—they could buckle down and get to work.

Chapter 27

DELON WANTED TO GRAB THE TABLET AND FLING IT at the wall, as if that would obliterate the ugly reality. He was better. But he wasn't close to good enough. Tori didn't say a word, just leaned over his shoulder with her mouth pursed and a pucker between her eyebrows, mentally dissecting the video. Her loose hair swung forward to tickle his neck. He caught a whiff of her shampoo. No flowers, no spice. Just clean.

"You don't wear perfume anymore."

She gave a distracted shake of her head as she reached around him to drag her finger across the tablet, rewinding the video. "Too many patients have allergies."

Practical to the bone. But *this* Tori had somehow always been there, under the sparkle and lace. He even remembered the first time he'd seen her. He'd stumbled into Tori's apartment late one evening, worn to the bone from a mad scramble through California— Hawley, Ramona, and Redding—then pushing straight through on the drive home so he could have a few extra hours with her. He'd barely noticed what she was wearing, just stripped her naked and lost himself in the feel and the taste and the warmth of her. God, he'd missed that warmth. At four in the morning, he rolled over and found the bed empty. Pulling on his jeans, he wandered out to find Tori hunched over a mug of coffee wearing flannel pajama bottoms and a faded Tulane sweatshirt, hair wadded into a knot at her neck, books and notes scattered across the kitchen island.

When she saw him, she reached up as if to hide the dark-rimmed glasses he'd never seen her wear. Then her hand dropped and she gave him a tired smile. "You're awake."

"So are you. Why?"

"Cramming. I have a differential diagnosis final tomorrow—" She glanced at the clock. "Well, I guess that would be today."

And he was interrupting. The same way he'd interrupted the night before, without stopping to think that it was Monday of finals week. They stared at each other for a long, silent moment. He wanted to walk over, rub her shoulders, kiss her neck, offer to make more coffee, but this bookish intellectual was a stranger to him.

He crossed his arms over his bare chest and wished he'd buttoned his jeans. "I should go."

Her gaze flicked from him to her books, then back again. She shifted in her chair as if to rise, and he thought she might come to him, kiss him, insist he stay. She gave an almost imperceptible sigh instead and picked up a highlighter. "Sleep here for a few more hours if you want."

Alone. In her bed, while she was studying for something he'd never heard of. *Out of your league,* that persistent voice whispered in his ear. "I'm already up. I'll go on home, stop distracting you."

Something passed over her face. Disappointment? She'd ducked her head before he could be sure it wasn't just wishful thinking on his part and set down her books long enough to walk him to the door, but her smile had been only a reflex. Just tired, he'd told himself, but the whole dark, cold drive home to Earnest, he'd kept thinking how her kiss had tasted like strong black coffee and goodbye.

"What's our goal?" she asked.

He started at her voice so close to his ear, jerking him back to the present. "I want to ride again."

Her breath puffed against his cheek, impatient. "You don't just want to ride. You want to win. At a very high level. What, exactly, does your body have to be able to do for that to happen?" She circled the spur board, eyes narrowed. "I would describe your riding style as compact. Shoulders farther forward, knees closer together than most bareback riders. You gain points for control, but on average, your heel strike is lower on the horse's shoulder than the other top ten cowboys, which costs you."

He couldn't help bristling at her blunt assessment. "Well, that's helpful."

"It's our baseline. Your current style requires a lot of knee flexion to do this." She brushed her fingertips over the gouges his spurs had made on the front of his rigging. Then she tapped the shoulder of the spur board. "Put your feet here and your hand in the rigging."

He did.

She grabbed his left ankle and wrapped her other hand around the inside of his left knee. "Try to go limp and let me move you."

Any time, darlin'. But she was so focused, she missed his smirk. She played his leg like a puppet's— bending, straightening, rotating out at the hip, bending again, testing angle after angle until she found one she liked. He tried to stay loose, but her hand kept sliding up and down the inside of his thigh, every stroke heating his blood until *limp* was no longer a part of his vocabulary. The air got sideways in his lungs as she moved her hand even higher. *Think cold. Ice cubes. North Dakota in January.* He sucked in a breath through clenched teeth as her hand moved again. A couple more inches and she'd find out for herself just how not limp he was.

She gave his leg a shake. "Relax!"

"Tori."

She paused, looked up at his face, then followed his gaze to where her little finger was a hair shy of rubbing up against his balls.

"Oh." She didn't snatch her hand away, just moved it down to midthigh. "Sorry. But look."

He looked—straight down the front of her shirt, which had gaped open as she leaned over him. Her bra was plain beige, not a scrap of lace, but who the hell cared because…boobs. *Right there.*

She jiggled his foot. "Do you see?"

Oh yeah. He saw. If he leaned forward a little more, he could… He reeled in his tongue and looked down at his foot. Whoa. While he'd been distracted, she'd maneuvered his leg so the heel of his boot touched the front of his rigging.

"Try it on your own," she ordered and, sadly, straightened, ruining his view but improving his concentration by three hundred percent.

He went through the spurring motion while she kept pressure on his thigh so he had to stay in the groove she'd found. He strained, grunted, and finally forced his heel to touch the rigging. Great…assuming the horse would give him a minute or two between jumps.

"Good. Humor me?"

He gave her a cautious look. "Maybe."

"Switch hands," she said.

His feet thumped to the floor. "I can't."

"You've tried?"

"Yeah." He glanced around to be sure Gil hadn't snuck in. "When I was first learning, I insisted on riding right-handed just like my brother. I sucked. Bad. Until one day, Violet's dad gave me a left-handed glove and rigging and made me use it. Everything just clicked."

Tori contemplated him for a long, thoughtful moment. Then she said, "So we'd have to change over completely."

"Change what?"

"You." She circled a hand in the air to indicate his entire body. "We'd have to make you left-handed."

His stare turned incredulous. "You can't just decide to change."

"No? How do you figure amputees manage after losing their dominant hand?"

"I..."

She raised her eyebrows as if to say *point made*. "Give it a try."

"Right now?"

"Yes. Hold on with your right hand, and try the same motion we just practiced."

He scowled at her, then down at the rigging, then pried his glove out and grabbed the handle with his bare right hand. It was awkward, with the handhold angled for a left-handed grip, but he could hang on well enough for this slow-motion crap. He planted his heel in the shoulder, then dragged it up to the rigging. It still didn't touch.

"And now..." Tori kept her left hand on his thigh and gripped his right shoulder, tipping him back a few inches. "Again."

He tried again. Still not quite there. She leaned in, tipping him back a little more. "Again."

This time, the heel of his boot tapped the front edge of the rigging. The whole thing felt weird and off balance and maybe—just maybe—possible.

"Yes!" Tori's fingers dug in, holding him in that exact position. "This is it."

Her eyes shone with triumph as she smiled at him. Then, slowly, the smile faded as she became aware of her position, their bodies all but pressed together, their faces so close he could feel the air move when she sucked in a breath. His gaze settled on her mouth. So, so close...

"Whatcha doin', Daddy?"

Tori flinched but didn't jump back. Instead, she straightened, hands still on Delon's thigh and shoulder. Something flickered behind her eyes, a rapid calculation, before she looked up at Beni and smiled. "We're working on his new moves."

"He's gonna use his other hand?" Beni asked, peering through the railing at the top of the stairs.

"If that's what it takes." Tori's gaze met Delon's in a direct challenge. "Right?"

Damn her. Her mother wasn't the only bulldozer in the family. Tori had just shamelessly used his own kid against him. After all those talks about how a winner never quits, he couldn't look Beni in the eye and say, nope, he wasn't even gonna try.

"Right," he muttered.

"Can I help?" Beni asked.

Tori's smile widened. "Sure. You can be his coach. And if you're quiet and listen real close during his appointment on Monday, afterward I'll show you how to get through the Reef of Doom."

"Seriously?"

"Seriously."

Beni frowned, doing some calculations of his own. "You said you were gonna show me tonight."

"Actually, I didn't," Tori said. "I have to get home and do my chores."

"But—"

"Beni," Delon warned.

"But I ate my dinner!"

"Beni," Delon said again, sharper. "If I come up there, am I gonna find your broccoli in the couch cushions again?"

"No!"

"Or under the bathroom sink?"

"No." But Beni's gaze flicked guiltily toward the apartment door and he sidled in that direction. "Fine. I'll wait until Monday."

"What do you say, Beni?" Delon called after him.

Beni paused to bless Tori with a smile so much like Gil's it made the hair on the back of Delon's neck stand up. "Thank you, Miz Tori."

"You're welcome, Beni."

As the door thumped shut behind him, Delon swung his leg over the spur board and stood, only inches from Tori. She might have taken round one, but they weren't done yet. Not even close. He reached up, cupped her face, and planted a long, slow kiss on her mouth, taking the time to trace her bottom lip with the tip of his tongue. She didn't move—not into him, not away—but when he lifted his head, her eyes were the hot, hazy blue of a late summer sky.

"I thought we agreed to wait a couple of weeks," she said, her voice breathy.

Delon cocked an eyebrow. "I'm sorry. Do you feel rushed? Like I'm pushing you, and you're not sure if that's the direction you want to go?"

"Yes."

"Good. Then we're even." He dropped his hands and stepped back.

She blinked, then shook her head with a wry laugh. "Monday."

"Monday," he agreed.

He watched until the door closed behind her. Then he packed away his gear and went upstairs to hunt the elusive broccoli before it rotted and stunk up the whole apartment.

Chapter 28

TORI GOT THE DREADED PHONE CALL ON FRIDAY evening.

"I'm at the ranch, darling," her mother said. "I'd like to see you tomorrow."

Tori took a deep, bracing breath as Elizabeth's script raced through her head. *Game on.* "Sorry. I'll be in Lubbock at a team roping."

"Victoria. *This* is important." Only a touch of her impatience leaked through. "And I have to fly out tomorrow evening. I'm assisting with a trauma case at Cedars Sinai early Sunday morning."

Tori grabbed the notes she'd made while talking to Elizabeth and settled onto the couch. "I can talk now."

It was easier to defy Claire than she'd expected. Tori's give-a-shit-meter was bottomed out from ten days of awkward, abrupt silences when she entered rooms and unwelcome sympathy from both coworkers and patients. And worst of all, the pat on the arm and "But you must have been so proud of him."

Oh yes. Proud. So proud that Willy had tossed his life away without a second thought. But she just smiled and nodded, dousing the sizzle of anger and ignoring the inevitable trickle of guilt. Of course she didn't wish the children had been killed instead. And of course Willy hadn't meant to die. And neither of those things made him any less dead.

She had placated most of the media hounds by releasing a brief statement regarding the loss of her husband and what a comfort it was to be home in the Panhandle with her family, but she still had her security tail.

And she still had that kiss from Delon, bumping around inside her head and kicking the dust off feelings she thought she'd packed away for good.

Claire made a small, irritated noise, but her voice was butter-smooth. "I wanted to see for myself how you're holding up. You've always been so protective of your privacy, and now your father's impetuous announcement has stirred up all this attention, just when you were finally moving past your grief."

Wow. Motherly concern wrapped around a slick jab at her father. Tori was tempted to do a slow clap. "He doesn't see it that way."

"It's been a difficult term, with all the infighting." Her sigh was artfully sympathetic, with a touch of exasperation. *Those damn politicians.* "Richard is the man they count on to pull them together. He's exhausted and disillusioned, but he is exactly what this country needs."

"What about what he needs?"

In the beat of silence, Tori could feel the force of her mother's will even from a distance, attempting to rearrange her very molecules. "Your *father* has always understood that sacrifices are necessary for the greater good."

Unlike Tori. She felt the heat gathering in her gut but kept her voice cool. "He has sacrificed his entire adult life. I think he's paid his dues."

"You would." For an instant, the shell cracked, and anger leached out. "He seems determined to follow your example. Become a *normal guy*. Toss all his potential aside for *love*, since it's brought such joy into your life."

Tori's hand jerked up, physically lashing out in return. She closed her fingers into a fist and dropped it to her side. Her mother had lost her iron control. And that meant Tori was winning. As the wave of blind fury ebbed, it was replaced by a backwash of pity. Poor Claire. Her logical, calculated world had dissolved into a churning sea of emotion—and she didn't have the first clue how to swim.

"Be reasonable, Mother," Tori said, turning Claire's favorite weapon on her. "If you have to resort to asking *me* for help, you've already lost."

Her voice went icy. "I will not stand back—"

"You have no choice. The White House is already off the table."

"People have short memories, Victoria, especially in Texas. If we give this the right spin, present a united family front…"

Oh, they were united, just not in the way their mother wanted.

Tori gentled her voice, adding a note of conciliation. "His mind is made up. I couldn't change it if I tried. Let him go while there's a chance we can still be a family once this has all blown over."

Tori held her breath. In the extended silence, she could practically hear the keys clicking as Claire entered the information into her brain and crunched the data. Would she take Elizabeth's bait?

"I will do whatever is best for the family, of course." Claire's voice was stiff with offended dignity. "I had hoped you would do the same."

"This is my best, Mother."

"Nonsense. You are capable of so much more—"

"I'm doing work that is important to me and to my patients. Someday, I hope you'll be able to accept that as enough. Until then, I suggest you stop wasting your time and influence by calling in favors from people who have much better things to do than make me offers I won't accept."

Once again, her mother began to speak, then stopped. Even Claire didn't have an unlimited supply of influence. To waste it was impractical. Finally, she gave an embattled sigh. "If you're certain."

"I am."

"But if you change your mind," she couldn't help adding. "Find yourself in need of a challenge…"

"You'll be the first to know," Tori promised. And said goodbye while she momentarily had the upper hand.

Chapter 29

MONDAY MORNING, DELON SAT ON A TREATMENT table while Beni spun in circles on a stool, waiting for Tori. She walked in carrying a sheaf of papers and what looked like a wrist brace. Their eyes caught, and for a moment, that kiss at the shop shimmered in the air between them. Then she glanced away.

"How was your weekend?" she asked.

"Uncle Gil said he's gonna have to beat the dispatch stuff into Daddy's head with a keyboard," Beni chirped. "Then Daddy said—"

"You weren't supposed to be listening," Delon cut in before Beni could repeat his response word for word. *Note to self—noise-canceling headphones are not foolproof.* Delon gave Tori a wry smile. "My brother is not the soul of patience."

"Consider me shocked," she drawled.

Delon laughed. "How about you? Good weekend?"

"Had a visit with my mother. Won third at a roping in Lubbock with Shawnee. And there's now a Facebook page called *Keeping Up with the Pattersons,* in case you'd like to know what brand of tampons I prefer."

His face went hot. "I…uh…"

"What are tampons?" Beni asked.

"Girl stuff." The corner of Tori's mouth curled, sharp as a fish hook. "Ask your mother. In the meantime… ready to get started?"

"Yes!" Beni bumped a grubby fist against the one she held out.

Honestly. It was like dirt jumped up and followed the kid. Delon could've sworn he'd been clean when they left the house. And he was still flummoxed at how effortlessly Tori managed his child. More than just being comfortable with kids, the two of them seemed to be on the same wavelength, the way she anticipated every duck and dodge of that cunning little mind.

"The first thing you need is this, Coach." The devil danced in Tori's eyes as she pulled out a whistle and slipped the lanyard over Beni's head. It was heavy duty, real metal, the official kind used by referees and lifeguards.

Delon's ears wept at the sight of it. "You are a cruel woman."

"Who? Me?" She pressed a hand to her chest with a smile that sparkled with mischief. He blinked. The light was back, and he couldn't say whether it had flipped on all at once or slowly brightened like the sky before sunrise. Not her old, superficial gloss—this glow seemed to emanate from her soul. God, what he'd give to warm up next to that fire. Or jump right in.

She handed him the top two sheets of paper. "Look at these."

He did. One was a photocopy of the first page of an article from something called the *Journal of Clinical Oncology*. The title was an indecipherable string of words like *immunostimulatory* and *allogeneic*, dry enough to make his fingertips crack where they touched the paper. He switched to the second sheet. The words were handwritten in purple calligraphy on cream-colored parchment. The title was "Lost," and the language was so flowery and convoluted he had no more idea what it meant than the journal article.

A headache began to brew behind his eyes. Was this another test? If so, he was going to fail miserably. Again. He let a small, defeated sigh slip.

"Yeah," Tori said. "I don't have a clue what they mean either."

He lowered the papers. "So your point is?"

"My sister wrote both of them. The first is one of her research papers. The second is a poem she sent me after Willy died."

Delon looked from one page to the other again, then back at Tori. "Really?"

"Yes. And this is the good part." Tori took the papers and held them side by side for comparison. "She can't write poetry on a computer. She uses them constantly at work, and she says the minute her fingers touch the keyboard, those are the only kinds of words she has. But if she picks up a pen and writes in calligraphy, her mind automatically switches gears and she gets poetry."

Interesting. Sort of. But he still didn't understand...

"Think about it. She makes a physical change, and it causes a mental shift." Tori waved the papers in front of him. "This is what we're going to do with you. By forcing you to use your left hand for all your daily activities, I'm hoping to flip that switch in your brain. Turn off your old mechanics and turn on the new."

"Cool," Beni said. And damned if he didn't look like he knew exactly what she meant.

Delon gave her a dubious look. "You honestly think this will work?"

She folded her arms, so determined it was a tiny bit scary, like his knee had become one of those hurdles in her path and she was gonna get over it come hell or high water...and drag him along by the collar if necessary. "We proved you're physically capable. We just have to teach you to do it consistently—on a real live bucking horse."

"What the hell is that?" Gil demanded when Delon walked into the dispatcher's office.

He resisted the urge to hide his right arm behind his back. "Part of Tori's new plan."

"She's gonna fix your knee by making it so you can't wipe your ass?"

"Something like that." He joined Gil in frowning at the brace that curved all the way up the palm and fingers of his hand, leaving only his thumb free. "She's got this theory about how if we rewire my brain by forcing me to do everything left-handed, I'll ride better with my right. She says it'll change my center of balance."

Gil went still for a beat, then slouched back in his chair. "You're gonna try switching hands."

"Yeah." Delon made sure his voice was equally nonchalant. "I could use some help, if you're interested." *If you don't still hate that I can do this and you can't.*

Gil took a long, deep breath and let it stream out slowly. "Look, D, it was never about you specifically. For a couple of years, I hated anyone who could walk without a limp. But what I've really hated is watching you treat this thing like a nine-to-five job. Show up, put in your time, settle for whatever they decide to pay you."

"But I did get paid," Delon flashed back. "More often than any other bareback rider over the past five years, even if it wasn't the big check. I can live with that. I'm not like you."

"You're better." Gil jacked forward in his chair, his expression fierce. "That's what really pisses me off. You're so goddamn talented and you don't have a clue."

Delon gaped at him, stunned. "You're the one who racked up the arena records."

"Or got thrown on my head." Gil flicked a dismissive hand. "You're stronger. Faster. And so fucking controlled. If we could morph the two of us together, we'd have Kaycee Feild's bastard brother."

Kaycee, who had dominated bareback riding for years. And the best of Delon and Gil, mashed together, equaled the new style Tori had created.

Gil's expression didn't change as he leafed through the pages of exercises Tori had printed out, but Delon could feel the energy beginning to build around him. "This could be brilliant."

"Or a total waste of time."

"So what if it is? You got something better to do?" Gil gave him a heavy-lidded stare. "Rodeo is a fickle, jealous bitch. If you want a gold buckle, you gotta give her your whole heart, even though you know she'll stomp on it more days than not."

And Delon was asking to be destroyed twice over, putting his personal and professional future in the hands of a woman who had said outright she didn't want to be here and hadn't so much as knocked down the weeds around that crappy little house of hers. What was to stop her from disappearing again, especially now that the press was gnawing over every detail of her life like a pack of starving coyotes?

"Well?" Gil asked. "You up for it or not?"

Delon shook his head slowly. "I'll give it a shot, but realistically—"

"Fuck reality," Gil snarled. "That's what's left when you've used up all your dreams."

Or chased them so hard you crashed and burned. Delon couldn't take that risk. He'd do everything exactly as Tori instructed. He'd even follow Gil's lead—up to a point. But he wouldn't—couldn't—throw all caution to the wind.

Screw that little voice saying he couldn't ride a bucking horse with one foot on the ground.

The computer monitor behind Gil lit up with three consecutive messages from drivers. One was stuck in LaGrande, Oregon, because Deadman Pass had just been closed due to a winter storm. Another was nine hours late getting loaded out of Tulsa. The third was hunkered in a motel in El Paso, sure he'd contracted food poisoning from the shithole café where he'd had dinner the night before.

Gil gave Delon's wrist brace the stink eye. "Can you type while you're wearing that thing?"

"I can't type when I'm not."

"Good point. I'll put out the fires." Gil shoved the second keyboard toward him. "Check the status on the rest of the loads we've got moving. Use your dick if you have to. It's probably faster than those other ten peckers of yours."

The main office door banged open, followed by the long, air-shredding blast of a whistle.

"What the hell?" Gil demanded, whirling around.

Beni bounded through the door, grinning. "I'm Daddy's coach. Tori said I gotta have a real coach's whistle."

Gil turned his glare on Delon, who shrugged.

"Figures," Gil said sourly, spinning to face his keyboard. "Just when you start to trust a woman."

Chapter 30

On the afternoon of February 14, Delon stood in the Super Shopper store in Dumas and stared down an entire aisle stacked with boxes and bows in every possible shade of red and pink. He'd tried to hustle Beni past, but the kid had locked up his brakes.

"You always buy Mommy a valentine," Beni insisted.

"I know, but..." What? She's on a diet? She developed a sudden allergy to chocolate? She's sleeping with Joe now, so it's his job to buy her a cheesy cardboard heart? "You know, Beni, now that you're six years old, I think you should give Mommy her valentine."

Beni paused to consider, eyes narrowing in a way that indicated deep thought or plans for large-scale destruction. "Do I have to pay for it out of my allowance?"

"Nah. I'll front you the money."

Beni's face cleared. "Cool."

He scampered down the aisle, dodging shoppers. It was a measure of how much Delon's knee had improved that he could keep up. In the past two weeks, he'd done everything Tori had asked and then some, thanks to Beni and Gil throwing everything from Frisbees to medicine balls at him to improve his left-handed coordination. Even his dad had joined in, showing up last Sunday morning with a pair of left-handed clubs and dragging Gil, Delon, and Beni out for a round of golf. Merle played surprisingly well. Gil played as if the ball had insulted his manhood. Beni claimed he beat Delon by three strokes, but for a kid who was a whiz at math, the numbers on his scorecard didn't quite add up.

"This one!" Beni declared, standing on tiptoe to fetch down a god-awful neon pink and gold heart.

"Wow. That's really...big."

"And it's bee-oo-tiful." Beni clutched his prize and tromped back to their shopping cart.

Delon hesitated, then grabbed another—left-handed because, yes, he was still stuck in the damn brace—just to see Tori's face when he gave it to her.

"Who's that for?" Beni demanded when Delon dropped the second box in the cart.

"Miz Tori. For helping me get better."

Beni hopped up to hang on the side of the cart as a man squeezed past, loaded down with enough valentines for an entire office staff or a whole passel of special someones. "Do you sleep at her house now?"

Delon choked, coughed, and fielded a raised eyebrow from the guy with the armload of chocolate. Like he had any room to talk. "No. Why would I?"

"You don't sleep at Mommy's house anymore. And I saw you kissing Miz Tori."

Damn. He should have known Beni would spy on

them. "I only stayed at Mommy's house when I got in late from rodeos and wanted to see you first thing in the morning or if I had to drop you off then leave real early the next day. Now I'm not traveling, so I don't need to sleep over."

"And you don't want to sleep over at Tori's house either?" Beni persisted.

Oh yeah. He definitely wanted. It was pathetic how much he looked forward to their weekly appointments. The way his heart skipped when she called with her latest tweak to his program or to share some research she'd dug up. How he craved her smile, her approval, the too-brief, too-professional touch of her hands.

"Tori and I are friends," he said.

"Regular friends or friends with benefits?" Beni asked.

Delon choked on his own spit again. "What do you know about benefits?"

"My friend Avonlea says that's what babies are made of, and you and Mommy used to have benefits but now you don't 'cuz she's friends with Joe instead of you. Are they going to make a baby?"

So many questions and not one single coherent answer to be found. Delon could feel the sweat springing up in his armpits. Where did he start? Nowhere near that part about Violet and Joe and babies, that was for damn sure.

"Mommy and I are still friends." Sort of.

Beni fingered the neon pink bow on the box of candy, his expression uncharacteristically somber. "Avonlea said her mommy says I was a mistake."

Double damn. Call him selfish, but Delon had always hoped Violet would be the one who got stuck with this conversation. He crouched and put his hands on Beni's shoulders so they were eye to eye.

"You were a surprise, that's for sure. The best surprise in the whole world." After the panic wore off and Delon had been sure Steve Jacobs wasn't going to haul him down to the corral and castrate him like a fence-jumping bull. He squeezed Beni's shoulders. "And you know what? Uncle Gil and I were surprises too. And your cousin Quint. So you're just like all the Sanchez men."

Beni puffed up a little at being called a man. "Really?"

"Yep."

Beni cocked his head and thought about it for a minute. "That's cool."

Then he scampered off to check out a purple teddy bear with a red heart that lit up when you squeezed its paw. Delon dragged Beni away as it warbled *You light up my life*, insisting that no, Grandma Iris would not love to have one for Beni to squeeze over and over and over until Cole ripped its head off. They got in line at the checkout, an elderly couple in front of them, a trio of slouchy teenagers behind, and a prune-faced checker who, as far as Delon could remember, had been installed right along with the register when the store was built.

Delon blew out a sigh of relief. All in all, he hadn't handled that so bad.

Then Beni looked up and asked in a clear,

penetrating voice, "Daddy? Does anyone in our family get born on purpose?"

Delon had never been so glad to park in front of Violet's house. He'd distracted Beni from the talk of benefits and babies by handing over his smartphone, a rare treat since the last one had died of accidental root beer poisoning. Also, there was no chance of bumping into Joe. Joe had been on the road since the birthday party and for one reason or another had only been able to make time for one short visit in three weeks. Possibly the first sign he was starting to chafe at the bit.

Beni grabbed his box of chocolates and shot out of the car. Delon followed more slowly, schooling his expression. Violet was likely to be feeling lonely and let down, and he didn't want to rub it in by letting slip that he was eager to get on with his evening. But he couldn't be overly nice either. Any hint of sympathy could get him throttled because she would read it—rightly—as doubt on his part. Damn Joe Cassidy.

"Mommy!" Beni yelled, thundering through the front door and into the kitchen. "Hey, Mommy, we got you—" He stopped dead as Violet stepped out of her bedroom. "Whoa. Who's getting married?"

"Married?" Violet's face went pink as she twitched a skirt that didn't quite reach her knees. Delon could feel his eyes popping. The dress was very red and very clingy, especially the top, and there was a lot of Violet to cling to up there. "Does it look okay?"

"You look beautiful. Here." Beni shoved his box of chocolates into her hands with so much enthusiasm he nearly knocked her off her heels. Delon hadn't realized she owned a pair.

"Hurry up and open them," Beni demanded, dancing around. "I'm starving."

"The chocolate is for your mother. And it looks like she has plans." Big plans she hadn't bothered to share with Delon.

"I just found out a couple of hours ago." She set the chocolates on the table and picked at the cellophane. "Wyatt is flying Joe over from Fort Worth for the evening. We're going to the Lone Steer for dinner."

Because of course Wyatt had his own plane and flew it himself, so he could drop Joe practically at Violet's front door.

Beni brightened. "Hey! While you and Joe have dinner and stuff, maybe Wyatt could take me—"

"No," Delon and Violet said in unison. On that, at least, they still agreed. Wyatt Darrington was not taking Beni off barnstorming, or God knew what, in his shiny little Cessna.

Beni pooched out his bottom lip. "How come you and Daddy get to do something fun for Valentine's Day and not me?"

Violet's gaze shot to Delon. "You're going out?"

"I…sort of."

"You better take Tori her valentine tonight, else

you'll eat it all like you did my Halloween candy. And the Christmas fudge Grandma Iris sent," Beni said with an accusing glare.

Tattletale. "I left you the peanut brittle."

"Only 'cuz you don't like it."

Violet's eyebrows arched in amusement but flattened when she considered the rest of what Beni had said. "You bought Tori a valentine?"

Delon couldn't stop from ducking his head like an embarrassed eighth-grader. "To, um, thank her. For helping me out with my knee and all."

"I see. Delon, are you sure—" Then Violet stuck a hand up, stopping herself. "Never mind. I'm staying out of it. And, Beni, Grandma made Valentine's cookies for you to decorate."

"Are there sprinkles?"

"Loads."

"Well, I guess." He heaved a put-upon sigh, but he was already sidling for the door. "I'll just go to Grandma's now."

Delon edged after him, working up a smile. "Have a good night."

Violet's return smile was equally ambivalent. "You too."

———

His nerves jittered and danced all the way to Dumas. He turned the MP3 player over and over in his hand, mentally reviewing the playlist he'd been working on for days. Probably too schmaltzy, but too late to fix it now. He breathed a sigh of relief when he saw the lights glowing in Tori's windows and her car parked out front. He'd been afraid she might be out with her dad or something. Tucking the gaudy candy box under his arm, he took a deep breath and marched up to the front door to jab the bell before he lost his nerve.

Silence.

He shifted the box to his other arm. Brushed a Snickers peanut crumb from the sleeve of his coat. Counted to thirty. Damn. He hadn't considered that this might be a terrible night for Tori. What if she was huddled in there crying over her wedding pictures? He counted to sixty, cursing his dopey plan. He didn't want to force her to come to the door with red, puffy eyes, but he'd made his presence known, so it would be weird to just leave. He shifted the box to the other arm again. He could write a note and leave it on her doorstep with the box of chocolates, if he had a pen and paper and any idea what to say.

Sorry I missed you? Geezus. That sounded like a package delivery service. He searched his mind, but he seemed to be fresh out of witty messages for a former lover turned therapist turned— The door was yanked open so suddenly he jumped back, tripped, and nearly ass-planted on the front walk.

"Hello, Delon. Fancy you showing up all unexpected," Tori said sweetly. Too sweetly. And she sure as hell hadn't been crying. That smile of hers looked a little mean, and he could've sworn he heard a muffled f-bomb from around the corner behind her.

Her smile widened. "Where's your wrist brace?"

"I took it off, just for tonight."

She was in dusty jeans again, with her hair yanked back in a straggly ponytail. His gaze dropped to the floor. She'd kicked her boots off in the foyer. His stomach did a sick clench when he saw a second pair beside them. Fuck. There was a man in her house. Who? And when had she—

Tori grabbed the box of candy from under his arm. "Aw. Are these for me? That's so sweet."

"Uh…" Humiliation burned like acid injected straight into his arteries. "I'm sorry. I didn't realize… didn't think…I should've called first."

"Yes. You should have." Her false humor dropped away, leaving only cool reproach. "We're not doing this again, Delon. If you want to see me, you pick up the phone and make a date, preferably at least twenty-four hours in advance." Her smile was a lethal weapon, slicing clear to the bone. "But thanks for the chocolate. And the thought."

Then she closed the door in his face.

Chapter 31

"THAT WAS HARSH," SHAWNEE SAID AS TORI STROLLED back into the living room and tossed the candy box onto the cluttered coffee table.

Tori just wiggled her fingers in a give-it-to-me gesture. Shawnee cursed but dug out a crumpled twenty-dollar bill and slapped it into Tori's hand. As much as she'd hoped for better this time around, Tori had been willing to put money on Delon showing up unannounced on Valentine's Day, since it coincided with her dating deadline.

Damn, though, when she'd opened that door and seen him standing there, all hard body and melted chocolate eyes, with that hopeful smile...the déjà lust had blasted through her good intentions like a nuclear meltdown. If Shawnee hadn't been there, Tori would've been slamming that door behind him as she dragged his extremely fine butt inside. Which was exactly why she'd invited Shawnee in for a post-practice beer.

She sidled around to peek out the front window. His car still sat in the driveway, as if he was trying to figure out what had just happened. Good. She intended to lay out some very clear ground rules this time, and if he wasn't willing to play by them…well, better this sharp jab in the region of her heart than being gutted again.

Shawnee came to peer over her shoulder. "I never pegged him as a booty call guy."

"You have sex with someone on a barstool two hours after you meet, it tends to warp his expectations."

Shawnee choked on her beer. "You…him…on a—Jesus Christ, woman! You admit that to everyone?"

"Only if it comes up. No pun intended."

Shawnee sputtered, spraying beer on the back of Tori's neck. "Stop! I'll have that fucking picture—and I do mean fucking in every sense of the word—stuck in my head until my dying day."

"So sorry." Tori's voice was mocking, but her fingers clenched around the twenty-dollar bill as Delon's headlights came on. He made an L-turn to pull onto the road and away, the taillights two lonely pinpoints of red in the darkness. Her heart twisted, recalling the stunned look on his face. She *had* been too harsh. Once she'd made her point, she should have at least invited him in. Should have…

Down at the end of the lane, Delon's brake lights flared at the stop sign, but instead of turning onto the highway, the twin red beacons continued to glow like a pair of devil's eyes, as if he was just sitting there…what?

Her phone rang, startling her. Shawnee stuck an elbow in her ribs, shoving her aside to snatch it from the counter. "Well, lookee who's calling." She turned away, nailing Tori with another elbow to hold her off. "Hey, Delon. This is Shawnee. Tough night. Shot yer ass right outta the sky, didn't she?"

"Shawnee!" Tori made another grab for the phone and got straight-armed against the wall. Geezus. The woman was an animal.

"I gotta say, D, you really let me down," Shawnee said, oblivious to Tori's flailing. "And you cost me twenty bucks. But as long as you're in the neighborhood and you brought that ugly-ass box of chocolates, you might as well come on back. Our little princess has made her point. And if she doesn't want you, I'll be happy to lick your wounded pride."

Tori tried to bite the arm that pinned her to the wall.

"Gotta go. She's gettin' kinda testy. See you in a few." Shawnee poked the End button and tossed the phone.

Tori scrabbled for it as it hit her in the chest. "You are a lunatic."

Shawnee sauntered over and flopped into the recliner.

Tori stared at her. "You're staying?"

"Oh, hell yeah. I ain't missing the rest of this show." She wiggled deeper into the chair and fixed an expectant gaze on the door like a kid waiting for a birthday clown to pop out.

"God, you suck." Tori stomped over, grabbed her beer, and gulped down half of it.

The doorbell rang. Tori jolted like it was a shotgun blast and stood there, mentally flailing, until

Shawnee hefted a foot and kicked her in the butt. "I ain't got all night."

Tori dragged reluctant feet toward the door. When she opened it, Delon stood on her front steps looking equally gobsmacked.

"Hi...again," she said.

"Hi."

Neither of them moved. Neither of them spoke.

"Oh, for Christ's sake," Shawnee said. "Come in and sit down."

Delon's eyebrows rose in question. Tori stood aside, then closed the door as he walked into her living room, step by careful step, like a man expecting a snare to yank his feet out from under him.

"Sit," Shawnee ordered, pointing at one end of the couch. She gestured Tori to the other end. "You—sit there."

They sat.

Shawnee sat up, folded her hands in her lap and lifted her chin. "Now, let's see if we can't straighten this out."

"*Excuse* me?" Tori said. "What the hell—"

"Just call me Doctor Pickett." Shawnee gave them a smarmy television shrink smile. "I am here to be sure you don't screw this up every way to Sunday. Plus, I'm dying to know—did you really do her on a barstool?"

Delon shot a stunned glare at Tori. "You *told* her?"

"I warned you..." Tori waved a hand in front of her mouth.

Shawnee gave a gleeful snort. "Way to go, D. I didn't think you had it in you."

His face darkened to a shade Tori couldn't describe but was pretty sure had something to do with dangerously high blood pressure.

"Never mind," Shawnee said. "From what I understand, rocking the barstool wasn't the problem. It's what y'all did next."

"What we…" Delon trailed off, his eyes glazing over from shock. "Did you tell her everything?"

"No!" Now Tori's face burned like road rash. Or should she say rug burn? But she definitely had not said a word about the floor in front of the fireplace. Or the shower. Or…

"Holy shit. That good?" Shawnee snorted a laugh, then morphed back into the imperturbable Doctor Pickett. "As much as I'd *love* to explore the details of your physical relationship, I was actually referring to the part where you, Delon, left the next morning and didn't call for almost a month and then only when you were passing through and hoped for another roll in the hay. A pattern of behavior that Tori claims persisted throughout your relationship. Can you explain?"

Delon's expression suggested he'd prefer to give his opinion of the question. Or jump up and run for his life. His gaze dropped to the floor, and he mumbled something.

"A little louder please," Shawnee prompted.

He drew a breath big enough to lift his shoulders and blurted, "I didn't think she wanted me to call."

"*What?*" Tori turned on him, sputtering. "You

thought I *liked* having no idea when or even if you would show up again? Checking injury reports and rodeo results on the internet so I knew you hadn't broken your neck or run your car off into a river somewhere?"

He blinked at her. "You worried about me?"

Oh, that did it. She was gonna have to punch him. "Of course I worried, you dumbass. The miles you were putting in, driving day and night, all those rides…what did you think you were, a dildo with a pulse?"

Shawnee hooted, then tried to regain her faux professional demeanor but couldn't quite squash her grin. "Delon?"

"She was…I thought…I mean, after Violet told me…"

Fury reared up like a devil horse inside Tori, redeyed and snorting flames. She grabbed her pillow off the back of the couch and choked it so she didn't go for Delon's throat instead. "Do *not* even talk to me about Violet."

"I sense some serious hostility here," Shawnee interjected. "What did Violet say that made you change your mind?"

Delon stared down at his boots in stony silence.

"I assume she suggested he should avoid repeating his brother's mistakes," Tori said flatly.

Shawnee narrowed her eyes at Delon. "Is she right?"

He jerked a shoulder, refusing to answer. Still protecting Violet. But hey, mother of his child and all that. Then he turned his glare on Tori. "If you wanted more, why didn't you say so?"

"I…"

She got stuck, the ball of anger in her chest congealing into the familiar old lump of hurt and frustration. If she plastered the pillow over her face, would it all just go away? But no. She'd tried that, night after sleepless night, while every molecule in her body strained for the sound of the phone. A knock at the door. Incrementally less able with each passing hour to settle for whatever scraps of time Delon tossed to her but afraid to lose him altogether.

She blew out a long, hissing breath. "You were just hitting your stride. The last thing you needed was a girl hanging on your leg every time you left town, whining about when she would see you again."

If anything, that seemed to make Delon more furious. "So you acted like you couldn't care less if I came back?"

"If I'd done more to show you how much I enjoyed your company, I would've been arrested for public indecency! Why would you think…*shit*." She thumped the pillow down on her knees and buried her face in it to muffle her scream of frustration.

"You never said a word," he insisted, sounding bullish.

"Neither did you!"

The silence crackled with static built of regret, sexual awareness, and the echoes of old pain. Shawnee's voice cut through it, suddenly matter-of-fact. "So Delon *assumed* the Panhandle Princess was just kicking up her heels with one of the peasants, and Tori *assumed* you were happy to just take what you could as long as it was offered, and neither of you had the balls to tell the other what you wanted. Did I miss anything?"

Tori pushed up onto her elbows, raking her fingernails over her scalp as she shook her head. Delon followed suit.

"Excellent," Shawnee declared. "Since we've agreed you were both fence-post stupid, my professional advice is to shake hands, agree to leave all that crap in the past, and start clean. Think you can manage?"

Tori angled Delon a doubtful glance. He met her gaze head on, his eyes full of that dogged intent. He stuck out his hand. Tori hesitated, then reached out to take it. A wave of heat rolled up her arm and rippled through her body at the familiar scrape of his palm against hers. The calluses were on his right hand now. Because he trusted her. Believed her when she said she could give him back his career. God, she hoped he was right.

Shawnee's phone buzzed. She read the message and frowned before turning her attention back to Delon. "One last thing—you're over that little fantasy about settling down with Violet to make a proper family for your boy, right?"

"Yes." He spat the word out like a rotten sunflower seed.

"Good. That's real good." Shawnee held up the phone. "'Cuz according to my sources, Joe Cassidy just got down on one knee in the middle of the dance floor at the Lone Steer and asked her to marry him."

Tori pushed the door shut behind Shawnee and sagged against it. "Dear mother of God. That woman is barely housebroke." She shoved away from the door and strode to the refrigerator. "Do you want a beer? Because I'm having another. Maybe two. Hell, I might just clean up the six-pack."

If Delon hadn't been driving, he would have helped her. He slumped deep into the couch, closed his eyes, and concentrated on breathing. Slow. Steady. He should know how to keep his shit together, even when his heart was racing, his muscles quivering as if he stood on the back of chutes, feeling like his whole body would be blown apart by adrenaline. Control was always the key.

Tori set a chilled bottle in his hand. "If I'd had any idea what she had in mind, I would've screamed at you to run like the wind."

The couch jolted when she plunked down on her end. Delon stuck the beer bottle between his knees and laced his fingers behind his head so that on the off chance his skull actually did explode, his brains wouldn't splatter on the walls—although it might be an improvement. To the walls, not his brain. He opened his eyes. It looked like someone'd painted the place with a broom and a vat of mustard, then slapped down a dingy gray industrial carpet remnant. But the coffee table was cool, made of an old iron wagon wheel with legs welded on and a glass top. In the pie-shaped, felt-lined slots between the spokes, trophy buckles gleamed in the feeble glow of the dusty overhead light. The pair closest to Delon were both from a roping in Sheridan, Wyoming: one for champion header, the other champion heeler. Tori and Willy, roping together.

Delon dodged that thought, letting his gaze wander the rest of the room. Other than a miniature grandfather clock, the shelves of the entertainment center held a stack of DVDs, a couple of pictures, and a few books propped up at one end by one of those fancy glass candy dishes people give for wedding presents—probably priceless crystal, if it came from her side of the family. It doubled as a depository for spare keys and crumpled receipts. The bowl on the other end was made from an old rodeo rope coiled around and around.

The only other decor was a ridiculous metal armadillo dressed up as a cowboy, with a Shiner Bock bottle cradled in his horseshoe arms. What the hell...?

Delon shook his head but couldn't help a grin, which faded as he continued to take in the lack of much of anything that would make the place feel like a home. Just the big leather couch, the recliner, the coffee table, and those few random objects on the shelves, as if she'd opened one box, unpacked the contents, then lost interest. Or figured what was the point, when she was just gonna pack it all up again sooner or later?

Tori rolled her head to look at him, the movement weary and boneless, and he was struck by a fervent wish that the couch wasn't quite so big. She was too far away to loop an arm around her shoulders and pull her up snug against him. Just to talk. Share body heat. Maybe one kiss. Or two…

She tipped her face away, breaking eye contact. "That is one ugly box of candy."

"Beni picked it out. He always goes for the biggest and brightest."

Tori shot him a startled look. "Beni picked out my valentine?"

"Uh, sort of. He had to get one for Violet, so I figured as long as we were at it…"

"Wow. A secondhand valentine. You are a true romantic." Her voice was dry enough to dehydrate prunes.

"I thought it would make you laugh." But like everything else about this evening, he'd misjudged it. Badly.

"Sorry. I was too busy making a point to get the joke." She set her beer aside, hoisted one hip to pull out a pocketknife—yeah, this Tori packed a knife, and why was that so sexy?—and sliced open the cellophane. "So. Joe proposed."

"Apparently." But he preferred to shove that in a very tiny box in the darkest corner of his head so it didn't ruin whatever chance he had to salvage this night.

Tori lifted the top off the box and took her time picking out a chocolate. He braced himself for *How do you feel about that, Delon?* Then he would either have no answer or say something totally wrong, and either option would put Violet as squarely between them as if she'd plopped down on the couch.

Tori finally chose a chocolate, settled back, and, bless her heart, left it alone. "Beni was pretty pumped about golfing with the Sanchez men. First time?"

"Yeah. We've never…" He fumbled for a good reason and shrugged. "We've just been too busy, I guess."

"Easy to let that stuff slide." She held up the chocolate between two fingers, examining it as if trying to determine the filling before biting in. "My sister and I have talked more since the divorce went public than in the last ten years. I like her. I want to know her better. We've missed a lot, but I'm going to make sure it doesn't happen again."

Ah. Not a change of subject after all. "And you think I should do likewise?"

She nibbled a corner of the chocolate, taking time to choose her words. "I think you and I have underestimated our families, and it's not all bad that circumstances have forced us to take a closer look."

He couldn't argue. It felt good to say "the Sanchez men" and know it meant more than an accidental collection of humans who shared the same genetics. He and Gil might never get back to what they had once been, but that might not be all bad either. They were men now, eye to eye and working side by side, rather than Delon forever being the little brother, looking up.

"I read your mother's press release," he said.

She lifted her beer in a mocking toast. "An exquisite blend of sorrow, self-reproach, and a sprinkling of martyrdom, without a single passive-aggressive cheap shot. Bravo, Claire. And pray to God it gets the media off our backs."

Delon wasn't optimistic. Texans had latched on to Tori with an obsession that would turn any Hollywood publicity whore green with envy. She was the mystery girl, the prodigal daughter, the tragic widow, and people couldn't get enough of speculating. Spying. And flat out making shit up. In the past week, the *Keeping Up with the Pattersons* page had linked Tori with the governor's son, a country music star, and a married surgeon at Panhandle Medical Center. A clairvoyant had claimed to act as intermediary for her conversations with her deceased husband.

"This isn't a trick…your mother is really throwing in the towel?" he asked.

"The lawyers are divvying up their personal possessions as we speak. Shouldn't take long, since she's not contesting the prenup."

"You don't seem surprised."

She nibbled another corner off the chocolate. "We had a nice mommy-daughter chat over the weekend. I was cautiously optimistic that she recognized her options were limited. Plus that ever so gracious statement left the door wide open for a reconciliation."

Reconcil… "Is she delusional?"

"Claire is the most lucid human being you'll ever meet. It's the worst thing about her." Tori took a sip of her beer, made a face, and set down the chocolate. Her priorities were clear. "She sat down and calculated the odds of a man of his age, social, and financial status finding his soulmate while fighting off swarms of gold diggers and decided they were in her favor. She practically said so." Tori's voice went silky smooth. "*It will be so difficult to move on alone after all these years. I only wish we could turn back the clock.* And my favorite part— *Richard and I are the best of friends. He knows I'll always be here for him.*"

Dear Lord. She was right. "Do you think he'd go back?"

"Depends on how many times he gets kicked in the nuts when he gets out there." She circled a hand in the air to indicate the world in general. "Hopefully freedom turns out to be everything he dreamed of. Dating is hard enough for normal people."

Dating. Right. Delon had started this evening with a purpose, which had been derailed the moment he knocked on Tori's door. "Do you still like barbecue?"

"Was I born in Texas?" she asked dryly, then gave him a speculative look. "What do you have in mind?"

"Someplace quiet. You don't even have to change clothes."

Their eyes met, got tangled up for a few breathless heartbeats, and then she smiled. "Give me a minute to knock the worst of the dirt off."

She disappeared down the hall. Delon sank back into the couch, dragging in what felt like his first real breath in hours. Okay. Not quite how he'd planned it, but phase one, complete. Now if he could just pull off the rest.

Chapter 32

Tori tossed her dusty sweatshirt on the laundry pile in the corner of the bedroom and pulled on a clean one, simultaneously exhausted and wired. For two weeks, her dreams had been a jumble of Willy and Delon, their faces fading in and out, their bodies morphing, one into the other, as her hands moved over them. She woke every morning with guilt curdling in her gut, aching, body and soul. It had to end. She had to move forward. Beginning tonight.

She splashed water on her face, ran a comb through her hair, then pulled open the vanity drawer and considered the unopened box of condoms inside. She'd bought them the day after he'd kissed her, before the press frenzy got so bad she couldn't set foot in a drugstore without someone taking a photo and plastering it all over the internet. Even then, she'd known it was inevitable. The delay she'd insisted on was only so her mind could catch up with her body. Adjust to the idea of being with a man who wasn't Willy. She wasn't sure if she was there yet, but why take chances? She tore open the box and stuffed a condom in the pocket of her jeans.

Then a second, because yeah, she did remember, and one might not cut it.

When she walked into the living room, Delon sidled away from the entertainment center, pretending he hadn't been checking out the pictures of her with Willy. Delon looked out of place in her faded living room, buffed and glossy as a life-size cutout of one of his sponsor ads. When she breathed deep, she could smell whatever spicy stuff he'd slapped on after his shower. She wanted to wrap herself around him. Bury her face in the curve of his neck and sink her teeth in.

He shoved his hands into his jacket pockets, pulling black leather snug across shoulders that were broader now, the strength more than muscle. Those shoulders carried the weight of maturity. Of fatherhood. Her fingers itched to peel away the layers, get down to that warm, dark skin. Find out if it still tasted sweet and salty and gave her system the same kick as a triple-shot latte.

Something of what she was thinking must have shown in her face because his gaze shifted to the couch, clung there for a moment, then slid slowly back to her. "Ready to go?"

She considered the many interpretations of that question. Was she ready to cross this line? Presentable enough for whatever he had in mind? Did she want to leave the house? Or just say damn the consequences and throw him down on the couch?

Her common sense gave her hormones a slap upside the head. She only wished it was that simple. This final step away from Willy was like teetering on the edge of the dock while everybody tried to tell you the water was fine, but you were pretty sure they were full of shit, and finally you just had to jump in and hold your breath through those first shocking moments. Except if Delon made her shiver, it wouldn't be from cold.

"Let's get out of here," she said and broke for the door before she decided to close her eyes and yell *Banzai!* instead.

―――――

A cowbell jangled as Delon pushed the door of the Smoke Shack open, then held it for her to go in ahead of him. A pair of boys in their late teens slouched at one of the dinky tables along the wall, dressed in the standard uniform of Carhartt coats, boots, and ball caps. A mountain of stained, crumpled napkins filled the tray between them. Their gazes skimmed past her without much interest until they spotted Delon. Then they bounced back to her, baffled, as if they'd never seen Delon with a girl before. At least not a girl who wasn't Violet.

The leaner, darker of the two eyed her with open, avid curiosity. "Hey, Delon."

A pained expression flickered across Delon's face. "Hank. Thought you were in San Antonio."

"Dad said if I wasn't getting paid to fight bulls, I could just as soon stay home and make myself useful." Hank made a disgusted noise, then grinned. "I'm flyin' back with

Joe and Wyatt to work the Extreme Bulls event this weekend, assumin' we can get Joe on the plane, since he—"

"Yeah, I know," Delon cut in before Hank could pry open the lid of that little box of TNT.

Hank scowled, clearly annoyed that he hadn't been the one to break the news. Then he gave Delon a sly smile, his gaze slithering to Tori. "Guess you've been busy too."

"Don't be a dipshit," Delon said and turned his back to look at the menu.

Another teenager waited behind the counter, eyes bright as a sparrow. "What y'all want, Delon? Ma's got a Valentine's special, the works for two. Like anybody's gonna bring a date here." He wrinkled his nose, then registered the significance of Tori's presence with a visible double take and stammered, "I mean, this ain't so bad, but most people are into all the romantic shit, so they go, you know, other places—"

"We'll take the special," Delon interrupted. "With sweet tea for me."

"Same here," Tori said.

"Stayin' or goin'?"

"Going," Delon said.

"It'll be up in a couple of minutes," the kid said, passing over their drinks.

"Thanks, Korby." Delon took one, passed the other to Tori, and they stood awkwardly, not sure where to put themselves to wait. Another of those little rhythms they'd never established. "Sit?"

"Sure."

They settled in at the only other table. Tori glanced over and caught Hank checking her out, a glimmer of almost recognition in his eyes. She gathered up every crystal of ice in her soul and put it in her eyes, then flicked it at him like a dagger, tossing in a contemptuous lift of her eyebrows for good measure. A real Claire number. *Who the hell are* you *to stare at* me? Hank blinked, then his face reddened and he dropped his chin, suddenly fascinated by the screen of his smartphone.

Tori let the ice melt away as her gaze drifted over the faded walls, the worn linoleum floor, and the handwritten menu on the chalkboard over the counter. "Places like this are always the best."

Delon missed a beat, staring at her with a wary expression. "The food is pretty decent."

"Smells amazing." She inhaled, drawing the aroma of smoke and spices and meat clear down into her pores. "I'm starving."

"Me too."

Well. That exhausted her supply of small talk. The boys were sucking up every word, so no discussing the state of Delon's knee. Anything concerning the senator was off-limits. The weather hadn't even been worth bitching about—a stretch of bland, fifty-degree days with no change in sight. The boys hunched over their phones, risking occasional furtive glances across the room while Tori and Delon pretended fascination with the ice cubes in their tea. Finally, Korby plunked a brown bag onto the counter. Tori and Delon bolted from their chairs. While Delon paid the tab, Tori snatched the bag and her drink. Excited voices broke out before the door slapped shut behind them.

Delon slammed his car door and hissed out a curse. "Sorry. Should've done the drive-through."

"No big deal." If the aromas wafting from the warm bag in her lap were any indication, it was worth it.

He drove a sturdy, economical four-door much like hers, except his had multicolored crumbs in the creases of the seats, unidentified sludge hardened in the cup holders, and a scatter of chocolate bar wrappers on the floor. Delon turned on the stereo, his usual hard rock drowning out the hum of nerves that filled the car. Tori crimped and uncrimped the edge of the takeout bag as he headed in a familiar direction.

"We're going to your place?" she asked.

"Only for a minute. I need to pick something up."

She didn't ask for details because what if he'd decided he'd better grab some condoms too? Awkward.

He parked in his usual spot and got out, then totally baffled Tori by walking around to her side and opening the door. "Bring the food."

"I thought you were just…"

Her voice trailed off as he pulled a second set of keys out of his pocket and jingled the Freightliner key fob in front of her like a carrot. "Wanna go for a drive?"

She gazed at the sleek black truck, whispering its

siren call into the still night air, and laughed in surprise and delight. "I thought you'd never ask."

———

Tori ran her hands up and down the armrests, practically bouncing. "These seats are awesome. But it's so quiet. I expected it to sound...tougher."

Delon grinned at her unapologetic giddiness. "It's a truck, not a Harley. Quiet is good when you're living in your truck."

"I suppose so." She twisted around to examine the sleeper. "You can walk around in here like a motor home."

"They're not all this fancy. This is the first brand-new, top-of-the-line truck we've ever bought."

She arched her brows. "Business is good, then?"

He hesitated a fraction too long. "Getting better all the time."

"And that's a problem because..."

"Not a problem. Just..." He shrugged, then ran a hand across the top of the steering wheel. "I haven't been around enough the last few years to take any credit."

"Ah. That does take some of the fun out of it."

Damn her, seeing straight through him. Again. "Here, I'll show you how the onboard navigation system works."

She let him change the subject, content to fiddle with the touch screen, testing the maps, driving directions, and the forward camera system. Yes, he was showing off, but it was worth it to see her awed reaction. And wasn't that just a kick in the ass. All the times he'd told himself a Patterson couldn't possibly be interested in a glorified truck driver and here she was, happy as a kid at a carnival.

He turned south at Dumas to roll past arrays of blinking red lights atop ghost-white windmills and between jagged, shadowy arroyos. At the highest point between Dumas and Amarillo, he steered into a pull-out, put the truck in park, and turned off the lights. Ahead and to the north, small towns sparkled like star clusters in a sea of black, while the lights of Amarillo blared to the south. They ate barbecue, listened to the radio, and talked about music and trucks and whether the Rangers would have a decent closer out of the bull-pen this year.

She licked her fingers and gave a deeply satisfied sigh. "Damn, I missed this. Doesn't matter how hard they try, barbecue never tastes the same anywhere else."

"Is that all you missed?" he asked, then wanted to swallow his tongue because it sounded like he was fish-ing. "I mean, you mostly grew up here. Didn't you ever get homesick?"

She took a sip of her sweet tea, then twiddled with the straw, looking thoughtful. Finally, she said, "Pecans. There are big ol' trees at the ranch, and when the nuts dropped, the cook would send me out to gather them. She made the most awesome pralines and pie. Plus the nuts were fresher or something."

Delon understood. Food harvested with your own hands always tasted best. "Miz Iris used to pay us a dollar a bucket to pick apples off her trees, and Steve would make hand-cranked ice cream to go with whatever she baked with them."

"Mmmm." Tori tilted her head back against the seat, her expression dreamy. "Now I want pie and ice cream—but only if it's handpicked and homemade, so I guess I'll have to settle for a cookie."

Delon laughed at her tragic sigh. Their gazes caught as she handed him his cookie, and he felt the click of a new kind of connection. He'd spent so much time focusing on all the ways they were different, and yet at the heart of it, the memories they cherished were very much the same. Unlike him, though, the good times hadn't been enough to keep her in the Panhandle.

He brushed the cookie crumbs off his jacket and fired up the truck, heading in the direction of Earnest. A few miles out of town, he turned off the local highway onto a narrow gravel road and stopped.

"Your turn."

Tori's eyes went wide. "I'm not licensed to drive a truck."

"This is a private road. The ranch belongs to friends." He slid out of the driver's seat and stood. "So if you want to give it a try..."

"Bet yer ass." She popped up and angled past him in a flash, wiggling her butt into the driver's seat and placing both hands on the wheel. "All right, master. School me."

He had an intense pang of…envy? She was so gung-ho. Unguarded. He'd never been able to drop all his defenses that way and just let go. Except with her. As long as he'd kept her separate from the rest of his life, for those few months, those amazing hours, he could be different. Daring. Shameless. Exciting. In other words, not himself. But if the fake Delon was the man she wanted, they were both out of luck.

They bumped down a two-mile stretch and back again, no problem. She'd driven enough manual transmissions to easily handle the truck's lower gears. The washboards and potholes in the gravel road didn't allow for anything above third, which left Delon free to watch her face, as intent in the glow of the dash lights as if she was bringing the space shuttle in for a landing. When they had completed the round trip, she slowed to a stop and cast a wistful look at the highway. "I bet it's amazing out on the interstate, sitting way up here, looking down at the little people."

"I dunno. I'm still debating whether sunroofs are the work of angels or the devil. The things I've seen…" He gave a mock shudder.

She laughed. Then she traced a finger all the way around the steering wheel. "I wouldn't mind running away for a few days. Just drive and drive…"

"Is that what you've decided to be?" he teased. "A tough truckin' mama?"

"Tempting, but since I don't want to actually be the death of my own mother…" She caressed the steering wheel with both hands and gazed out the windshield, her chin lifting as if she'd come to a conclusion. "This is *how* I want to be, though. The way I feel sitting here. Bold. Powerful."

"Fearless."

"Everyone is scared. The people we call fearless are just the ones who don't let it stop them." Her eyes sparked with humor. "Or psychopaths incapable of emotion." She gave the steering wheel another pat. "I guess the word I'm looking for is unstoppable."

He opened his mouth to tell her that some days, trucking was all about sitting in one place—road construction, traffic, loading docks, mandatory rest breaks—but he didn't want to extinguish any part of that fire in her eyes. Instead, he yearned to hit the highway with her. See it from her perspective—always searching for openings, seeing only detours where he saw roadblocks. Besides... he grinned, imagining how Tori would react when Gil tried to tell her where she should stop to pee. That alone would be worth the price of admission.

"Now what?" she asked.

"Make another U-turn, then take that road to the right."

Road was a generous description. The ungraded track angled off to skirt the edge of a bluff above the Canadian River, worn by the tires of generations of local teenagers who'd used the place they called the Notch as their lovers' lane and party spot. Like most everything else, the lawyers had ruined it for the current

generation, the threat of liability forcing the landown-
ers to put out the word that they'd prosecute anyone
they caught trespassing there. Which meant even on
Valentine's night, it was deserted.

Tori pulled up where Delon indicated, put the truck
in neutral, and set the parking brake. Before them, the
river breaks were a shadowy, silver-edged maze in the
moonlight.

Tori gave an appreciative sigh. "Nice."

"Come on. We'll take a better look."

Before climbing down, he doused the headlights,
plugged in his MP3 player, and rolled down the windows. When he stepped outside, the effect was exactly
as he'd hoped. The lights along the front bumper, the
top of the cab, and the running boards created a pool of
amber. The first song began to play, soft, romantic, with
just the right touch of Texas twang. A guy couldn't ask
for a better wingman than George Strait, with Stoney
LaRue and Randy Rogers for backup.

Tori turned from where she'd gone to stand at the
edge of the bluff, staring out over the breaks. Her hair
spilled loose around her face, and she looked younger,
softer, more like the girl than the woman. She didn't
speak, only cocked her head in question.

"I never took you dancing. And now, with all the
publicity...this'll have to do." He held out his hand.
"Dance with me?"

Her smile bloomed, slow and full. "Again...I thought
you'd never ask."

She slid into his arms, her body melting against his as they swayed together on their own private dance floor, lit by the moon, the stars, and the glow of the truck lights.

Chapter 33

SHE'D DONE IT AGAIN—COMPLETELY MISJUDGED him. She'd accused him of dropping in without a thought, when in truth he must have been planning this for days. Maybe weeks. He'd remembered how she'd rather order in barbecue than pizza. Noticed her fascination with the truck even when he was half-drunk and hurting. Found a way to take her dancing without all the looky-loos ruining the mood. Thank God for Shawnee—and wasn't that just a kick in the ass—or Tori would've missed it all.

Her heart spasmed, opening like a flower bud, the tightly curled petals unfurling with the sharp ache of an atrophied muscle. *This. This is everything I wanted from you.* She pressed her cheek into the curve of his shoulder because words would break the spell of the music, the night, his body so strange and familiar against hers. So alive.

She swallowed against the rush of sorrow that welled in her throat. It had to happen. *Had to.* She couldn't exist without the heat and torture of need, the ecstasy of release, those quiet moments of simply *being*.

If someone had patted her shoulder and said, *Willy would want you to be happy,* she would've kicked them. Because…no. Willy would want to be the one here right now, though she wasn't absolutely sure whether he'd be more jealous of Delon for having her or that totally kick-ass truck. But he'd left her no choice except to scrape up the pieces and move on.

A part of her—the small, scared, guilty part—clamored at her to pull away. Run home to her safe little nest of blankets and the cold comfort of isolation. The rest of her clamored in a whole different way, her body straining at the leash, reveling in Delon's closeness and frustrated by the layers of cotton and leather that separated them. The tug-of-war raged inside her—a push and pull of conflicting emotions. If she was going to do this, she had to do it fast. Rip off the proverbial bandage before the cowardly part of her won.

A Staind song began, low and slow, the lyrics raw yearning set to music. They wound down into her soul and pricked the edge of a truth buried so deep, the barest glimpse of it made her shy away. No. She wasn't ready to examine just how tangled up she was in Delon.

Enough thinking. She tugged her fingers free from where they were laced between Delon's and slid her hand inside the open front of his jacket. Her fingertips found the slight ripple of his abs, without a hint of fat to hide them. So not like Willy—

No! She pulled her mind back from the comparison and concentrated on pure sensation. On leather and spice, warm skin, and eau de truck. A mixture so potent, so utterly Delon that simply inhaling sent pulses of heat through her. She burrowed in closer and his arms came around her, his hands stroking the curve of her back. Her hips tilted in response, bringing them snug against his, a signal he couldn't misinterpret. He pulled back slightly to gaze down into her face. In the dim light, his eyes were unfathomable. She skimmed her thumb across his chin, then higher, across the full curve of his lower lip. Back and forth. He stared at her, mesmerized, as she tilted onto her toes and replaced her thumb with her mouth, her tongue tracing that same path. She felt a shudder ripple through his body.

"I thought you wanted to take this slow," he said, his voice rough.

"I took the time I needed." She touched the tip of her tongue to the crease at the center of his upper lip. "Now we can move on to what's next."

His feet slowed, losing the rhythm of the music. "I wasn't planning…I'm not…ready."

"I am." She reached into her pocket and pulled out the condoms.

He didn't reach for them. She shoved the condoms into the pocket of her sweatshirt and moved in close again, sliding her hands up and over the glorious contours of his chest. "It's going to happen sooner or later. We might as well get it over with."

His body stiffened under her touch. "Get it over with?"

"I didn't mean…it's just that I haven't…" For someone who'd turned into the poster child for too much information, she found the words surprisingly difficult to say.

"Since Willy," he said flatly.

She nodded, misgiving prickling the back of her neck at his grim expression.

"I'm sorry. It's hard, you know? But it's time."

He slid his fingers into her hair and lifted it away from her face to study the effect as the ends trickled free. "Are you sure?"

She picked these ever-so-important words with care. "I trust you. I always have. Even when I didn't know if I'd ever see you again, I never worried that what happened between us would end up as a crude joke you told all your buddies behind the bucking chutes. You just…wouldn't."

"I wanted to call," he said abruptly. "A hundred times. From Denver, Tucson, Red Bluff. All the nights in between. I was afraid if I pushed, it would change everything, and you wouldn't…we wouldn't…" He trailed off, then lifted his hands to cup her face, his gaze boring into hers. "Every time you agreed to see me, it was a miracle. I kept hoping you'd ask…anything. When I'd be back. How long I could stay. If you could come watch me ride somewhere…"

"I did. Watch, I mean."

He blinked in surprise. "Where?"

"Houston. San Antonio. Fort Worth. Any place

I could squeeze in around school and nab tickets through my father."

"You never said. Never came down…"

"To hang out with the rest of the groupies?" She shook her head. "I didn't know where I stood, and I didn't want to see that look in your eyes. Embarrassed. Awkward. Or worse. I mean, if there was another girl."

"Never. Not while we were…together. There was only you."

"Oh." Wow. She'd hoped, of course. Dreamed. But never assumed or demanded. How much difference would it have made if she had? "You too."

He smiled, the kind of wide-open, no-holds-barred smile she hadn't seen since she'd been back. She lifted her arms to lace her fingers behind his neck, their lips only a breath apart.

"Can I at least get a proper kiss?"

He laughed softly. "I thought you'd never ask."

And then he kissed her, but it wasn't the explosive, mind-blowing collision of the past. This kiss started easy and heated up slowly, very deliberate, very thorough but restrained, as if he was alert for any hint that they were moving too fast. But she wanted speed. Heat. Passion faster than her churning thoughts. She wanted to dig her fingers into his flesh, drag him to her and set off the powder keg that had once sizzled between them. Blast away her ability to remember. Compare. Regret.

Their bodies swayed as one to the music that went on and on, each song more perfect than the next. He must've spent hours putting together this playlist. Picking this song, discarding that one, creating a soundtrack just for this night. Lord. He was destroying her, one thoughtful gesture, one song, one kiss at a time. She could've gone on forever, just kissing, stroking, being stroked, but her leg bumped against the running board of the truck, and she realized he'd danced her up to the door.

"It's getting cold." He laid the backs of his fingers against her chilled face.

As if his words had conjured it, a shiver pebbled her skin. She leaned her cheek into his touch. "This was… special. Thank you." She hesitated, then inched out onto the limb. Asked for more. "Maybe we can do it again sometime, when it's warmer."

"It might be tough to get my hands on this truck."

She leaned in and kissed the spot where his jaw met his earlobe, letting her breath whisper over his skin. "I'll settle for getting my hands on you."

"That, I can arrange." He stepped up to open the door, then handed her in like a lady into a carriage. "Scoot on over."

"I don't get to drive home?" She paused, standing between the seats, to give him a mock pout.

He climbed in behind her, shut the windows, and cranked up the heat. "Over my badly beaten body, if either Gil or my dad found out."

"Well, we can't have that." She couldn't resist. She feathered her fingertips down his chest. "I prefer your body just how it is."

For an instant, he was utterly still. Then in one swift move, he whipped the seat around and stood, his grip hard on her shoulders, his eyes hot. "Are you sure you're ready for this?"

"I…uh…yes." The intensity of his gaze, the tightly leashed desire in his voice was like a flash fire across her nerves. "Yes," she said again. Louder. More certain.

He closed his eyes, his eyelashes a dark smudge against his cheeks. Then he nodded slightly, as if agreeing with a voice inside his head. When his eyes opened, his gaze was softer, and his grip loosened. He edged her into the sleeper and pulled the curtain, plunging them into darkness. "If you change your mind…"

He would stop. No matter what it cost him. And that, she realized, was why she could say yes. Because she *did* trust him. A weird conundrum. He'd unleashed her wild side before because she'd sensed she was safe with him. Well, that and he looked like Zorro and made love like…well, hell, she had nothing to compare. Not even Willy. Sex with him had been rambunctious and fun, occasionally tender, but it wasn't like…

She jerked her mind back again. *This man. This moment.* But her vision wavered, images of past and present flickering like an old filmstrip behind her eyes, and she couldn't find the *off* switch for the projector. Willy, laughing. Teasing. The feel of his big, bearlike body engulfing her, even as her hands pushed the jacket off Delon's shoulders and reacquainted themselves with the fantasyland of skin and muscle beneath. Smooth, taut, nearly hairless, where Willy had been furry. Navajo blood. Hadn't she heard Native Americans tended to have less body hair?

Stop. Thinking. Dammit. She stepped back to yank her sweatshirt over her head, and her elbow made solid contact with some part of Delon's anatomy. He swore.

"Sorry." She reached to touch his face and nearly poked him in the eye. "Shit. Sorry again."

"I'll get the light—"

"No." She made a blind grab and managed to catch his arm. "The dark is…good."

For this night, when she couldn't hide the visions wheeling behind her eyes. *Get it over with. Move on.*

"Okay."

She heard uncertainty in his voice. Retreat. *No time to think.* For either of them. She found his waist and tugged at his shirt while her mouth sought and found his. *Don't think. Just do.* Like Shawnee said about roping. Oh God. Shawnee. Leering at her. As if her head wasn't full to bursting already. The kiss turned frantic, trying to drive everything out but the taste of him.

He cupped her face, his thumbs caressing her cheeks. "Shhhh," he whispered against her mouth.

She was trembling, tiny earthquakes deep in the fibers of her muscles. Could he feel them? He took command and changed their tempo to match his caress, deep and drugging kisses that first calmed, then stirred her. Her body relaxed, became fluid and malleable, flowing into him. He kept kissing, kept stroking, pushing away his clothes and hers and drawing her down onto the narrow bed. His body was hard and urgent, but his touch was distilled tenderness. The truck was toasty warm, Delon a wonder of taut skin and heat against her nakedness. So long. It had been so very, very long since she'd been touched. Held. Treasured.

More memories flickered, of a time when this man had owned her body. Her soul. Delon's hands explored her, those same slow, bone-melting strokes over her ribs, her belly, her thighs, lingering to cup her breasts as if measuring, calculating the changes in her body. The air caught in her chest at the faint rasp of calluses against her skin.

Not the same. Not at all. This was now, and these calluses were on his right hand, because of *her*. This wasn't the old Delon. And it sure as hell wasn't some random body she could use to get anything *over with*. He deserved better.

They both did.

"Turn on the light," she said. Too loud. Too abrupt.

Delon froze for a heartbeat. Then he clicked on a small lamp at the head of the bed. Tori sucked in a breath.

God, he was beautiful.

His skin glowed in the soft light, his body a bronzed study in male perfection. He was still, watchful as she reached out to trace his muscles with her fingertips, mesmerized by the contrast of satin over steel. *Trapezius, pectoralis, serratus, latissimus*—the names were a seductive whisper in her head as she explored each in turn. Then she moved on to that perennial favorite, *rectus abdominis*, giving each ripple its due as she worked her way down.

And speaking of erect…

His stomach twitched in anticipation, but she veered to the side, following the clearly defined curve of his obliques. "These are new."

"Thanks to you." His voice was a low rasp, his touch featherlight as he drew one finger along her forehead to skim back a lock of hair that had fallen across her face. "All those damn medicine ball routines of yours."

Her hand stilled as if fused to his skin. Like the calluses on his right hand, she had helped build this small part of him—and she felt a rush of intense possessiveness. This muscle, these fibers were hers, as surely as if they'd been grafted from her body to his. She leaned down and replaced her hand with her mouth, drawing a line of slow kisses, on the verge of love bites, over the curve of his hip to his navel.

"Geezus!" The air exploded out of him when her cheek brushed his erection. He hitched his hands under her armpits to drag her up, an electric slide of skin against skin. He twisted, pinning her under him as his mouth took hers. Deep. Greedy. All semblance of patience gone.

She responded in kind, driving her fingers through his hair and arching into him, craving the weight and the heat and the hardness of him. Those quick, magical fingers played over her skin, setting her blood to pulsing like one of his favorite songs—the beat heavy, relentless, demanding. She slid one hand down the sleek curve of his back to close around his butt—sweet heaven on earth, he had an amazing butt—while the other hand reached down and fumbled in the pocket of her sweatshirt on the floor. Delon plucked the condom out of her fingers and ripped it open with his teeth.

Oh dear Lord…

And then he moved over her. Into her. Sure and swift, making her gasp with the exquisite shock of it.

He paused, pulsing inside her, his eyes dark and intense. "Okay?"

In answer, she wrapped her legs around his hips and drew him even closer. He made a noise low in his throat—half groan, half curse—and began to move. She matched him, their bodies finding perfect unison in this primal dance. He reared back onto his knees, his fingers digging into her hips as he lifted her to drive even deeper. Harder. His thumb finding and stroking that certain spot that electrified her, an explosion of white-hot sparks that sizzled down every nerve. Through the waves of crackling sensation, she heard him give a harsh, guttural groan and felt his body jerk with his release.

Boneless, mindless, she sprawled on the bed, making a small *mmm* of protest as he eased away. Before the stars stopped pulsing behind her eyelids, he was back, nudging her over so he could stretch out beside her on the bunk. He switched off the light and gathered her up, spooning around her, a living wall between her and the world.

"Okay?" he whispered again.

"Fantastic," she said.

But as her body cooled and her mind cleared, the enormity of the moment struck, a blow no less painful for being expected. That last tenuous connection broke, the frayed ends slipping through her fingers as she finally—finally—let go.

Tears slid, fast and silent, down her cheeks and into her hair. If Delon felt or saw, he didn't let on, but his arm tightened around her.

And then she slept. The dense, dreamless sleep that had evaded her for so long.

The place, the night, Delon—came back to her in layers as she surfaced, then floated, feeling an odd lightness, as if she'd shed a burden. She waited for it to crash down on her again. Guilt. Regret. Shame. Instead, there was only acceptance. That final stage of grief she'd described to Delon as if she knew what it meant. Now it flowed through her like a sip of strong whiskey that both burned and warmed as it smoothed away the last ragged edges of pain. She hugged the blanket around her and sighed from pure, blessed relief.

"Are you awake?"

His voice was pitched low and came from too far away. She scrubbed her palm across heavy eyelids. At some point, he'd left, replacing his warmth with a soft cotton comforter. She forced her eyes to open and focus. He was in the driver's seat, swiveled to face her, arms folded across his chest and earbuds dangling, fully dressed. She pushed up on one elbow, clutching the blanket to her chest. How long had he been sitting there, watching her? She glanced at the illuminated clock on the radio and jerked upright.

"Four thirty! I've been asleep for…" She shook her head but was unable to make even that simple calculation. Hours. How long had it been since she'd slept for hours? She raked her hair away from her face. "I'm sorry. I just…crashed, I guess."

"It's been a long couple of weeks," he said, voice noncommittal.

She couldn't decipher his expression. She looked past him, out the windshield. They were parked in front of her barn. "You brought me home?"

"You have work. I figured I'd let you sleep until around five thirty. Wasn't sure how long it takes to do your chores and get to the clinic."

Everything he said was so calm. So thoughtful. And so damn polite it was like a kick in the stomach. She willed him to get up, come to her, kiss her, but he just sat, the only sound in the cab the barely audible rumble of the truck's engine and the faint screech of music from his earbuds, which sounded suspiciously like "Highway to Hell." She hoped it was a coincidence and not his opinion of where their relationship was headed. Her skin prickled with unease. He seemed so…grim.

Or he was reacting like any normal man faced with

a potentially weepy woman. Not much chance she'd hidden her tears. Plus, Violet was getting married. Giving Beni a stepfather. Serious brooding material there.

She swung her legs over the side of the bed and faced him. "That was classy, having my way with you, then rolling off and falling asleep. Was I drooling on your shoulder?"

That got a hint of a smile and a shake of his head. "My knee starts to ache if I stay in one position too long."

So he'd snuck out to sit for hours, waiting, watching over her. Crap. There was that damn lump in her throat again and the heat behind her eyes, because the whole night had been so…so…everything. She needed a moment, so she reached for her jeans, found her underwear tucked inside, and pulled both on behind the blanket. Then she dug a breath mint out of her pocket and popped it in her mouth.

Cinching the blanket around her like a toga, she stood and leaned over Delon, bracing one hand on the steering wheel for balance. "You are somethin' else, you know that?"

He blinked, wary. "How do you mean?"

"I haven't decided yet." She cocked her head and let her gaze sweep over him, slow and deliberate. "I still wouldn't call you a nice guy, but you are a very good man."

She kissed him. A deep, leisurely, morning-after kind of kiss. When she pulled away, his mouth no longer had that grim set, but he looked tired, and no wonder. He probably hadn't slept at all. She turned, let the blanket fall to pull on her T-shirt and sweatshirt, stuffed her bra in a pocket, then dropped another quick kiss on his cheek and climbed down from the cab. He gave her a single, crisp wave as he backed the truck around and drove away.

Tori shivered in the early morning chill. She turned and found the cat glaring her disapproval from the top of the same fence post. Tori held both hands up in surrender. "Yeah, fine. Walk of shame. And you might as well get used to it. He's gonna be back, and he'd better not leave here bleeding again or you're out on your ass."

The cat narrowed her eyes, as if considering the ultimatum. Then she gave one long, slow blink that either meant agreement or *go fuck yourself*.

Delon *would* be back. Tori wasn't fooling around, playing emotional tag this time. Digging out her phone, she typed in a text message and hit Send before she could reconsider. When am I going to see you again? Let him say she was pushy and overeager. He would not be able to say he didn't think she cared if he came back. She tucked the phone away and headed for the barn. It was early to feed but too late to go back to sleep, so she might as well do her chores before she went inside to take a shower.

As Tori climbed up the ladder to the hayloft, she heard the scrabble of claws on wood. The cat landed a few feet away and stood, tail twitching. Tori froze. The cat stretched, an indolent ripple from head to tail, then strolled over and sideswiped Tori's leg with a slow press of her body before hopping up to the top of the stack of bales. Tori let her breath go on a quiet laugh, her heart taking a ridiculous, joyful bound. The cat's eyes narrowed in warning.

"Don't worry. I won't tell anyone you're going soft."

The cat sneered at her and disappeared into the haystack.

Tori hummed softly as she walked across the yard, still feeling that odd, weightless sensation. As she let herself into the house, she realized it was a Stoney LaRue song. And no, her feet didn't quite feel as if they were touching the ground.

Chapter 34

PLEASE, GOD, LET THERE BE COFFEE. DELON SHUFFLED down the back stairs and toward the mechanics' break room, mug in hand. His head pounded, as if every thought was a boulder slamming around inside his skull, and his body ached like he'd been run over by the Freightliner. He pushed open the back door and sent up a heartfelt *hallelujah* at the scent of fresh brew. He didn't bother making his own when there were drivers who swore they stayed at Sanchez Trucking solely for the premium, high-octane fuel Merle brewed in the battered, olive-green, twenty-cup percolator.

He was lifting his mug for the first life-altering sip when Gil stuck his head in the door. "What was my new truck doing parked out at the Notch last night?"

Hell. The GPS. Delon was in no mood to explain himself, so he took his time getting a slug of coffee into his system before he answered. "Last time I checked the sign, there was no *Gilbert* in front of Sanchez Trucking."

Instead of snapping back, Gil leaned against the doorframe and crossed his arms with a faint smile. "Took you long enough to say so."

Delon glared at him for a full count of five. He was so not up to this today. He dropped his chin to his chest, winced when it made the boulders rattle and smash inside his skull, and breathed out a heartfelt f-bomb.

"You aren't even worth picking a fight with this morning." Gil scuffed over to refill his half-gallon insulated coffee tanker. "Guess you heard about Violet."

"Yeah." Another boulder smashed into his cranium. Violet. Joe. Married. He and Tori...what? Even after all the hours he'd sat, swapping between watching Tori sleep and staring out the windshield, he couldn't fathom how to make all those pieces fit together. His head told him people did it all the time. His heart cracked at the realization that he would never again wake up in Violet's spare room and roust Beni from bed to share a lazy Sunday breakfast, just the three of them, until Cole or Steve popped in for a cup of coffee or Iris with fresh-baked cinnamon rolls. His imaginary family had evaporated, like the mirage it had always been. And just to drive the point clear through him, Joe had proposed at the Lone Steer, where it had all begun.

"You've been there," he told Gil. "Got any advice?"

Gil watched the coffee trickle into his mug for a long moment. Then he turned bleak eyes toward Delon. "Don't let yourself get fucked over."

"How do you mean?"

"You and Violet don't even have a formal visitation schedule. And Joe's mother is married to some billionaire in Idaho. What happens when she insists they all spend Christmas break at her ski lodge in Sun Valley? Or Joe and Violet decide to surprise Beni with a birthday trip to Disneyland next year without bothering to ask how you feel about it first?"

Delon's skin went cold. "She wouldn't..."

Gil raised skeptical eyebrows. "I'd like to say you're right, but as much as I respect Violet, I wouldn't bet my kid on it."

In his head, Delon heard the echo of Iris's words as they watched Violet and Joe together. *This is our family now...*

"But I'm a cynic, for obvious reasons, so you might want to take my opinion with a grain of salt." Gil snapped the top onto his cup. "Now, about my truck..."

Delon dragged his thoughts back from the edge of the cliff his brother had so kindly pointed out. "I think I've at least earned the right to go for a drive without your permission."

"You think so?" Gil prodded the single stale donut from the box Merle had picked up the day before, testing its edibility. The unfrosted ones were always the last to go.

"Yeah." The muscles in Delon's shoulders drew up tight, braced for combat.

Gil broke the donut in half, grimaced, and tossed both pieces in the trash before giving a nonchalant shrug. "I suppose, since either directly or indirectly, you account for about a third of our current business."

Delon damn near dropped his coffee. "How the... I've barely been here."

"Don't need your body. Just that pretty face and spot in the top fifteen in the world standings." Gil grinned at him, every angle of his face sharp as honed steel. "You think that load of asswipes is the first time I ever whored you out? Think about it, D. What's the first load you always get when you're home?"

Sagebrush Feeders. Every damn time. Not that Delon minded the haul from the feedlot to the processing plant, but he'd never once snuck a load out without the loud-mouthed owner, Jimmy Ray Towler, catching him and insisting they have breakfast or lunch or a cup of coffee to "catch up." Delon could hardly refuse when the contract was every trucking company's dream—a steady supply of short, local hauls.

"You *asshole*. You tell him when I'm coming."

Gil laughed. "Hell, yeah. How do you think we got the contract in the first place?"

Delon felt his aching eyes bug out. "Just so Jimmy Ray can take me to lunch?"

"Your name got our foot in the door. I took care of the rest." Gil's mouth curved. "Promised him the best service he'd ever get, short of that whorehouse he pops by on the way home to the little wife."

"Geezus shit. You actually said that to him?"

"Pretty much. Which is why I can't be the one sucking up to guys like Jimmy Ray. And Dad ain't got a bullshit bone in his body. But you—" Gil waved the coffee tanker in Delon's direction. "You've got that crap down pat. Smile and nod, Jimmy Ray gets to brag how

Delon Sanchez never makes a trip home without stopping in for a visit, and we get twenty loads a week out of Sagebrush, guaranteed money—which is how we paid for that new Freightliner."

Whoa. Delon had to lean against the table to catch his balance.

"But you're worth twice as much to us when you're gone, so get your ass back out there and ride, Poster Boy. Speaking of which…" A gleam came into Gil's eyes that made Delon distinctly nervous. "I called your therapist this morning."

Delon snapped upright. "Tori? Why? What did you say to her?"

"Chill. I didn't ask if she enjoyed gettin' physical in the Freightliner. Although I gotta say, she sounded a hell of a lot more chipper than you look. Problem there, D?"

Delon gave his head a shake. He only succeeded in rearranging the boulders. "It was fine."

Amazing. Unbelievable. And scary as hell, how much he wanted her again, knowing full well there had never been such a thing as enough when it came to Tori.

"Fine?" Gil snorted. "What happened to the *blew my brain to Mars* look you used to have when she got done with you?"

"We grew up!" he snapped.

Gil looked insulted. "Why the hell would you do that?"

Delon hissed out an aggravated breath. "Since you've

gotta be a nosy prick, it was her first time since Willy died. She was…" He shrugged, unable to find words to describe the instant when that first tear dripped onto his shoulder.

Gil studied him for a long, uncomfortable moment. Then he sighed. "You're gonna screw this up again."

"I'm not—"

"Bullshit. I bet you barely got your clothes on before you were dreaming up reasons it won't work, starting with how she's just using you to get over her dead husband."

Delon managed not to flinch at the direct hit. Barely. He stared down into his cup. "It wasn't supposed to…I didn't plan it to happen this way."

"And while you were busy planning, she decided to do. You. Again." Gil made a show of scratching his head. "Call me stupid, but damned if that doesn't make me think she might actually like you."

Or figured he was a known quantity. What better place to start getting over Willy than where she left off when she put the Panhandle in her rearview mirror? He'd given her what she wanted. Heat, speed, oblivion. *Get it over with.* Now he'd give her space, time to shed whatever tears she had left. Time for him to patch up the hole those tears had drilled in his defenses. Tough, capable Tori might turn him on, but those silent teardrops had taken him out at the knees, and that was no position to be in when a man had to guard his heart.

"'Course, she could be thinking the same thing," Gil said.

"What?"

Gil arched his brows. "Gotta make a girl wonder, you all of the sudden gettin' romantic on the night Violet got engaged."

"That had nothing to do with it!" Delon shook off the spurt of anger and rerouted the conversation. "Why did you call Tori?"

"To ask when you can ride some real horses."

Bam! There went the air, right out of him. He had to drag it back in to make words. "What did she say?"

Gil scowled. "Bunch of bullshit about patient privacy. Said she'd text you the answer. Guess she hasn't got around to it."

Or Delon hadn't got around to turning on the phone he'd shut down during his date with Tori. It started bleating text alerts as soon as he turned it on, one after another after another. Christ. How many people were convinced it was their God-given duty to tell him about Joe's proposal? Some even attached pictures, for hell's sake. He scrolled through until he saw Tori's number. Two messages. The first only a few minutes after he'd left her house this morning.

He opened the message and *bam*! There went his air again. When am I going to see you again?

Just like that. No games. No second-guessing. He should be thrilled. He was thrilled, damn it, even if it did feel an awful lot like that moment at the top of the roller coaster when you wondered what you were thinking, strapping yourself onto this ride, and your good sense was hollering at you to bail out, but it was already too late. He gave his head an impatient jerk that slammed another boulder into his temple and scrolled down to her second message.

> Pepper says three weeks. But you can start riding a live-action bucking machine now, if you have one.

Gil had angled closer to read over his shoulder. "We still got ol' Tin Lizzy."

Delon barely had time to consider what it might take to resurrect their homemade bucking horse when his phone went nuts again with texts beeping in. Honest to God. The people in this town seriously needed to get a life. Then he read the subject line on one of the texts and stopped cold. Heart pounding in rhythm with his head, he opened the internet link that had been so helpfully included.

"Holy shit. Almost a thousand comments." Gil slapped him on the back. "Congrats, D. You're viral. And it ain't even the kind that'll make your dick fall off."

Delon cursed, stringing together every foul word he knew in every possible combination, ending with, "I'm going to kill Hank."

The front office door banged open, and long, swift footsteps came down the hall toward them. Gil and

Delon barely had time to exchange a questioning glance when Violet appeared in the doorway. She jerked a nod at Gil, then narrowed her eyes at Delon. "We need to talk."

Delon returned her gaze without flinching. "Yes, we do."

They stomped silently up the stairs to Delon's apartment. Violet waited until the door closed behind them before turning on him.

"You're out early," he said, taking the preemptive strike. "I figured you'd be wallowing in pre-wedded bliss."

Violet flushed but didn't back down. "Actually, I was, until my mother called, all in a tizzy. Seems she let Beni use her laptop to play *Candy Crush* on your Facebook account while she made breakfast, and he wanted to know why everybody was posting pictures of your new Freightliner at someplace called the Notch, and what do they mean, 'When this truck is rockin', don't come knockin''?"

Fuck. Forget Hank. Tori was going to kill *him*. Just what she didn't need, on top of all the other media and internet attention. And her father...Delon shuddered, imagining the senator's reaction when he saw those posts. Delon was gonna have some serious explaining to do. But first, he had to deal with the woman standing in front of him.

"Thank God you've never done anything to embarrass the family," he drawled, heavy on the sarcasm. "Or are you pissed because you consider the Notch one of your and Joe's special places, since it's where you got caught naked together?"

Color blazed hotter in her cheeks. "I'm not saying I've never done anything stupid. It just seems pretty convenient that you pulled that stunt last night, of all nights."

"You think I had sex with Tori and got Hank to plaster it all over the internet just to steal your thunder?" He was so stunned, it took a few seconds for his anger to catch up. "Sort of like the way Joe made his big proposal at the Lone Steer, of all places?"

Her hands fisted, and her eyes sparked with fury. "News flash, Delon. Not everything is about you. Joe picked the Lone Steer because we have history of our own there."

"And it obviously never occurred to him to discuss it with me first."

"Discuss it—" She threw up her hands. "He doesn't need to ask *you* for my hand in marriage."

"And Beni's."

She gaped at him. "What?"

"He didn't just propose to be your husband. He's going to be the stepfather of my son. I think I deserved at least a heads-up."

Her mouth snapped shut. The anger drained from her face by degrees, leaving it stiff and cold. "I'm sorry for that. Joe wanted to surprise me. He didn't think…"

"Yeah. Joe does a lot of that—not thinking. Seems to me that's how he ended up in Texas to begin with."

She sucked in a breath that broke at the end. Delon folded his arms over a pang in his chest at the sight of the tears beginning to glisten in her eyes. How had they come to this? Since childhood, he'd admired and cherished and, yes, even loved her in his own way. They had endured pregnancy and childbirth and six years of parenting together, and he'd sworn to protect her and Beni with his life, if necessary.

This should have been one of the happiest days of her life, and he was ruining it. He kicked aside the guilt. She and Joe had ruined a whole lot of days for him too. And could do worse if good ol' Delon sat back and let them.

"What else is Joe gonna do without checking with me?" he asked. "Persuade Beni to go out for soccer next year instead of baseball, because that's what Joe played? Convince him that being a bullfighter is way cooler than riding bucking horses like his old man? Buy him his first beer or box of condoms?"

Violet's mouth worked, as if the words were piling up so fast they were getting jammed in her throat. "Joe would never—"

"Right. Because he's so responsible. He wouldn't make a big spectacle instead of proposing to you in a nice, quiet place so we could all sit down and discuss the best way to break the news to *my* son."

"Our son!" She jabbed a finger at him. "And in case you forgot, Joe did try to talk to you. And we all know how that turned out."

"At least I didn't get cuffed and hauled away by the

cops," he shot back, feeling sick and mean even as he said it.

She hissed at the reminder of the worst of her dating disasters, then drew a deep, deliberate breath in a visible attempt to calm herself. When she spoke, her voice had only a slight tremor. "I am gonna marry him. I love him, and I believe he's good for Beni. I'm sorry you don't feel the same way. I will talk to Joe and make sure we don't spring any more surprises on you. What more do you want from me, Delon?"

"A formal custody agreement," he blurted.

She jerked back as if he'd taken a swing at her. Her eyes were dark and hurt as she stared at him. "Okay," she said finally. "If you want to hand over Beni's college tuition to a pack of lawyers, just fucking dandy. Have yours give me a call. From what I hear on the news, your girlfriend should be able to recommend a great attorney—assuming she hasn't cut and run before you see her again."

"Don't even start—"

"I didn't," she spat. "You picked this fight. But you can be damn sure I'll finish it."

She left Delon with the slam of the door ringing in his ears.

Chapter 35

Beth cornered Tori midmorning and held out her phone. "You're famous. Well, more famous."

Tori swore. Right at the top of that stupid *Keeping Up with the Pattersons* page was a picture of her and Delon at the Smoke House and another of the truck parked out at the Notch, lit up like a neon billboard. The contributor had helpfully included a title. *The mysterious Miz Patterson doing a little sleeper creeping with local rodeo star Delon Sanchez. Does this mean they're picking up where they left off in college?*

If it had been hers, Tori might have thrown the phone across the room. As if on cue, her cell buzzed with an incoming text. Delon, finally replying. Her heart stumbled, part thrill, part fear that he'd decided to haul another load to Duluth and not come back for, say, six months.

You'll see me after work, if you still want to. Your place?

Tori let go of the breath she'd been holding. Yes. You okay?

There was an interminable pause before he replied.

Hey, I snagged a princess. I'm the coolest guy in the Panhandle right now.

Yeah, right, and she was Roy Rogers, but at least he was coming to see her tonight. She tossed her phone down on the desk a little harder than was good for its health. Nosy goddamn assholes. They wanted to talk? Fine. She'd feed the gossips until they choked.

———————

When she got home from work, Panhandle Security had added a second vehicle on the dirt road behind her property—*thanks for that, Daddy, but please don't read the comments*—and a black Dodge Charger was parked in front of her house. Delon leaned against the hood, arms crossed over his equally black T-shirt, looking like an advertisement for trouble, the kind a woman would jump into—or just jump—without a second thought. The wrist brace was back, and he radiated a kind of reckless tension that made her hesitate a few steps away.

"Lookin' pretty badass today," she said.

He brushed his fingers over the Charger's silver racing stripe. "Gil's."

"It suits you better."

Delon looked startled. "It's not my style."

"It's exactly you. All-American muscle—strong and fast but with room for a car seat."

He shook his head, but she got the impression that he was pleased.

"Why do you have Gil's car?"

Delon's eyes glinted. "He put on a cowboy hat and my jacket and took my car and a couple of reporters for a drive to the sleaziest titty bar in Amarillo."

Tori laughed, half in delight, half in relief. By the time she'd left work, she'd convinced herself Delon was only stopping by to call it quits. Who needed this kind of crap? Instead, he was giving the gossips a metaphorical stiff middle finger too.

"It wasn't my idea. Well, it was, but I was just shooting off my mouth. I wouldn't have actually gone." He angled her an unreadable look. "You're not upset?"

"About which part?"

The question seemed to stymie him for a beat. "Take your pick."

Well, that opened up some interesting possibilities. Should she rank them chronologically or by perceived order of importance? "I'm not sorry we had sex. And the internet stuff...that's on me, not you."

"Uh, not exactly." He ducked his head. "You remember Hank?"

"From the Smoke House?"

"Yeah. That private road we were on...it's his parents' ranch. I should've remembered he'd go home that way."

"Oh." So it was Hank who'd taken and posted the pictures. She cataloged that information for future retribution. "Not the smartest move on your part."

Delon grimaced in answer.

Tori took stock of her reaction and decided her low-banked anger was directed solely at Hank and the rest of the life-sucking internet leeches. "I can live with it, but I've got to warn you, it's only gonna get worse. I took a long lunch and did some shopping at my local adult toy store…with witnesses." She dangled the bag temptingly from one finger. "Wanna come in and play?"

His gaze jumped past her, as if looking for an escape route. "*Now?*"

Ouch. Surprise—even shock—was understandable, but outright horror was a little tough on the ol' pride. Her cheeks stung as she dropped the bag to her side. Her only option was to bluster on through. "You're right. Probably better to have dinner first. Strenuous stuff, what with the whips and—"

"Why are you gonna whip my daddy?" a voice asked from the vicinity of the barn.

Tori froze. Oh. Dear. Lord. Beni.

"She meant she's gonna whip me into shape." Delon barely hesitated, even if his face had gone a dusky color. "And I thought I told you to stay out of the barn. There's a cat—"

"I know!" Beni waddled out into the light, his arms latched around the cat's armpits, her front legs pinned to her ears and her hind feet dragging in the dust. "Look, Daddy! It's big as a lion!"

Tori and Delon simultaneously sucked in air. Delon managed to incorporate a curse, but not loud enough to startle the cat. Her eyes were slits, her teeth bared, but she hung limp, as if stunned that someone dared manhandle her. Any second now, she would regain her senses and explode into a ball of claws and teeth.

"Uh, Beni?" Delon spoke slowly, with extreme calm, as if addressing a person standing on a land mine. "Remember how I said you should always ask before you touch a strange animal?"

"Oh. I forgot." Beni spun around to face Tori, the cat swinging in his arms. "What's its name, Miz Tori? Can I pet it?"

Only if you want to lose an arm. "Um…she doesn't really have a name, and maybe you should put her down *very carefully* and then ask her if she wants to be petted?"

Beni plunked the cat onto her butt. She sprang to her feet, paused long enough for one full-body shudder and a death glare, then stalked into the barn, fur rumpled and tail rigid with indignation. Tori sagged, knees gone to jelly.

Beni gazed after the cat, crestfallen. "I guess that means no."

"Guess so." Delon's jaw was tight with the suppressed fury of a parent recently scared shitless and trying not to come undone.

Tori finally regained function of her peripheral nervous system, and though she would've rather asked how in the *hell* Beni had managed to get his hands on the devil cat, she plastered on a smile and said, "This is a surprise. I thought you were staying with your mother for a few days."

"She went back to San Antonio with Joe 'cuz they got 'gaged."

"Ah. Yes. I heard." *Shut up, Tori. It's none of your business.* "Are you happy about that?"

Beni stuck his lip out. "No. I wanted to go with them, but Grandma said I better stay home 'cuz Daddy needs help with his workouts."

Not exactly the answer she was looking for. "Do you know what engaged means?"

Beni brightened. "Joe's gonna be my stepdaddy, so now he has to buy me birthday and Christmas presents. And he says we can still be buddies and do cool stuff, but Mommy said he better buck up 'cuz her and Daddy aren't gonna be the ones making me clean my room and do my homework while he has all the fun. And Uncle Cole says it means Joe can quit pretending to sleep in the bunkhouse." He scooted closer, whispering loud enough to be heard in the next county. "I asked Joe if he plays video games under the covers too when he's pretendin' to sleep. He said yeah, something like that."

Tori choked off a laugh, checking to see how Delon was taking all this. His jaw was clenched so hard she was surprised she didn't hear teeth cracking. So. No chatting about the engagement.

"I sure wish I could pet the cat some more." Beni sighed, then turned hopeful eyes on Tori. "Since Daddy doesn't want to play with your new toys, can I?"

Tori goggled like a beached carp.

"They aren't the kind of toys kids like," Delon said, impressively calm.

"Oh." Beni made a face. "Like those video games in Vegas that just take your money and don't have ninjas or dragons or anything cool."

"Yeah. Like those. How about we take a drive to Dairy Queen instead?" Delon raised an eyebrow at Tori with a gleam in his eyes that made a little heat wave shimmer over her skin. "Miz Tori likes things with big engines."

Yes, she did, and they weren't just talking about the car.

"Yay!" Beni pumped his fist. "Can I get a chocolate-dipped cone if I promise not to let it drip all over again?"

"Sure."

Tori had to squelch a laugh. Dear God. After Willy's family, she'd thought she knew kids, but Beni Sanchez was way out of their league.

"We can sneak through the drive-up lane," Delon said, misreading her hesitation.

"Sounds like a plan." Tori scooped up her bags, tossed them in her car, and locked it for good measure.

Beni clambered into the Charger. "Hey, Daddy, I thought Uncle Gil said there was no sticky crap allowed in his ride."

"Uncle Gil should've thought of that sooner." Delon tossed the keys to Tori.

She snatched them out of the air. "I didn't ask—"

"You wanted to," he said and slid into the passenger seat.

Chapter 36

By Friday afternoon, Tori's spurt of rebellion had faded. She refused to skulk around in disguise, but if one more freak asked her to take a selfie while standing in line for coffee, there would be widespread annihilation.

She slouched at her desk, scooping one weary hand through her hair while she propped her cell phone against her ear with the other. "I'm sorry about the roping tomorrow. If I have to interact with any more humans this week, I can't be held accountable."

"I'd like to call you a wuss," Shawnee said. "But there are some seriously whacked-out people in the world. I hope you haven't been reading that crap."

"God, no. I endured enough of the wrath of the righteous in Wyoming, up to and including the waitress who called me a home-wrecking whore because Willy's oldest brother took me out to lunch."

"Jesus Christ. How's Delon taking it?"

"Better than I expected."

It didn't hurt that suddenly everyone remembered how her daddy had insisted Delon sit with them at the

Buckaroo Ball. Plus—big surprise—an anonymous source close to the senator had leaked that he was pleased to see his daughter moving past her grief with a man he liked and respected. Delon had the official Patterson stamp of approval. In the Panhandle, that was as good as being blessed by the pope or picked for Oprah's book club, only without the depressing ending. Or so one could hope.

"I gotta go," Shawnee said. "Want to borrow my shotgun for pest control?"

"Nah. I'll just quit putting out cat food."

When they'd hung up, Tori propped her feet on the desk, feeling marginally better. Shawnee had a way of cutting through the bullshit that made it seem irrelevant, and the office was blissfully quiet and empty of other humans at a quarter past five. Maybe she'd just sit here for an hour. Or three.

Beth poked her head around the door. "I'm bustin' loose from this chain gang. You should do the same. There's something outside you need to see." At Tori's groan, she laughed. Bless her heart, unlike most everyone else, Beth's attitude hadn't changed one iota despite having to field calls from reporters and various other morons trying to get through to Tori. "You're gonna like this one, I guarantee."

Curiosity pushed Tori to her feet. She stepped outside the front door, scanning the immediate area until her gaze caught on the truck parked across the street, hitched to a refrigerated trailer. Not the sleek black Freightliner but a boxy, vintage-looking white Peterbilt.

Sanchez Trucking was stamped on the door in plain block letters. As Tori started across the parking lot, Delon opened the door and climbed down. She paused on the sidewalk, across the narrow street.

He stood, one hand braced on the door, the sunlight picking out the blue-black glints in his hair. "I know it's not twenty-four hours' notice, but we got a last minute load to Pueblo, with a back haul from Colorado Springs. Wanna come?"

Her heart leapt like a rabbit at the sight of an open cage. "Right now?"

"You said you wanted to run away." He waggled the door in invitation. "I figured this was as good a time as any, considering."

Go. Just hit the highway. And Pueblo sounded fantastic. Then reality stuck its cold nose on her arm. "I can't. I've got Fudge, and the steers—"

"One of our mechanics lives in Dumas. He said he'd run over and feed them. Just tell him when, what, and how much."

There it was again. The unfailing attention to detail that got him what he wanted because he made it so easy to say yes. Of course, the same could be said of her mother, but Delon had used his powers only for good where Tori was concerned. Making her feel special. Cared for. And damn, it was nice to just close her eyes for once and go along for the ride.

She waved a hand at her work uniform of khakis and blouse. "These are the only clothes I have with me."

"I'll pull in at the first big truck stop along the way. We'll get you a do-rag and a *Stay Loaded* T-shirt, make a real trucker chick out of you." He grinned, the devil dancing in his eyes. "So, you in?"

And just like that, she was. All in. All done. Again. Her heart tumbling off the ledge she'd been so determined to cling to this time, at least until she knew there was a soft place to fall. She took a deep, grounding breath. Too late now. Consequences be damned. She wasn't passing up a chance to hit the road.

She grinned back at him. "Take me away, cowboy."

He held the door for her. She burst out laughing when she stepped up into the truck. "Somebody got a leather fetish?"

It was everywhere—on the insides of the doors, the ceiling, and lining the entire sleeper, which was only a few inches taller than the cab. Diamond-quilted red leather. The effect was like a rolling bordello.

Delon grinned. "What can I say? It was built in the seventies."

He claimed the best part about the Peterbilt was the lack of an onboard computer, but since Gil couldn't track every turn of the wheel, he compensated by peppering them with texts.

Delon handed her his phone. "Ignore everything except delivery instructions or load information."

"Hmm." She scrolled through the texts. "He hopes you did a really good pre-inspection—there's an asshole on a witch hunt working at the weigh station south of Trinidad today. And the Wally World is off Highway 45 on Northern Avenue in Pueblo if you need to load up on half-priced Valentine's candy."

Delon muttered a curse. Then he tilted his head thoughtfully. "We could stop there to get you some clothes and stuff."

"Your call," she said, stifling a grin.

North of Trinidad, as the sun sank behind the mountains, the country opened up into rugged, inhospitable high desert.

"Have you ever been to Navajo country?" Delon asked out of the blue.

"No." She wasn't sure how to proceed. He'd never voluntarily mentioned anything to do with his mother before. "The pictures look amazing."

"It's…harsh. And beautiful, I guess, but where my mother lives…" He shifted to check the rearview mirror, angling his face away from her. "I'm never comfortable there. When I was little, I refused to even look outside on moonless nights. Something about not being able to see a single light anywhere…I was sure I wouldn't last ten minutes out in all that nothing. Like it knew I didn't belong."

Is that why…? Don't you ever wish…?

He didn't say anything more. She let the questions fizzle out. He'd already told her everything she needed to know about his relationship with his Navajo homeland.

Like it knew I didn't belong.

She had never shopped for clothes at Walmart. Yet another way in which she had experienced life a step apart from the majority of the world. She made a beeline for the underwear department while Delon hit the deli for fried chicken and the fixin's so they could eat dinner while they waited to unload. She also grabbed jeans, a T-shirt and sweatshirt, and a pair of flannel pajama bottoms. Then, inspired, she made a quick swing through the grocery department before checking out.

When they reached the distribution center, the line of trucks waiting to unload stretched half a mile. Delon grimaced as he steered the Peterbilt into place at the end. "This is the not so fun part."

"It's fine. Great, actually." With him. Exactly as she'd fantasized, back in the day.

Delon shook his head. "Give it another few thousand miles. You might change your mind."

Her breath caught, and she quickly turned her face toward the window before he saw the effect of his casual words. *A few thousand miles.* Literally going the distance. Together. But he'd only been speaking rhetorically, and she was racing way too far ahead. A real future with Delon meant tying herself to the Panhandle. He would never leave Beni or Sanchez Trucking. Could she stand to stay, give up any chance at normal—if the alternative was walking away from Delon again?

Too soon, too soon...

Delon crawled into the sleeper and napped, leaving her to keep them moving up the line and wake him when they got close to the front. It was very late—or very early, depending on your definition—when they pulled into a truck stop on the edge of town and found an open parking space. Delon shut the truck down and leaned back, hands still propped on the wheel. "Want to grab a shower or anything?"

"Maybe in a bit. I was thinking about dessert right now."

He stretched, arms overhead, arching his back, his T-shirt hitching up just high enough for a glimpse at *her* muscles. "They probably have pie and ice cream in the café."

"Actually, I brought my own." She reached into the Walmart bag beside her seat and pulled out a jar of Nutella.

Delon's eyes lit up. "Did you grab graham crackers or vanilla wafers too?"

"No. I thought we could do some…home cookin.'"

Delon blinked. Then smiled, slow and wicked, as he took the jar from her hand. "I believe I can come up with a recipe or two."

As she'd suspected, Delon was a very, *very* good cook.

———————

They loaded out in Colorado Springs at nine the next morning. Tori alternately read and dozed as they rolled south toward home. Delon tapped his fingers along to the heavy beat of the music on the cassette player his father had refused to let him swap out. Their sparse conversation centered around the traffic, the scenery, and what each of them had on their agendas for the coming week. Simple. Easy. Comfortable. Other than the insatiable itch to take her turn behind the wheel. If she and Delon ever—

She ruthlessly chopped off the thought. Too much. *Way* too soon. For both of them.

A cold front had rolled in overnight, pushing clouds heavy with the threat of rain. A few drops smacked the sidewalk at the rest stop outside Raton, New Mexico, as Tori walked out of the bathroom and around a corner to hear Delon say, "I know, but it just won't work out this time. Tell him he can ride along on Wednesday instead, when I go to Sagebrush Feeders."

Tori paused, then took a step back, out of sight but not hearing.

"Oh, right. I forgot. Well, next week, then." His voice was tight, his tone defensive. "Tell him I'm sorry."

She waited until she was sure he'd disconnected, then strolled out. He stood, phone in hand, looking wretched.

"Something wrong?" she asked.

His head jerked up. "No. I just…by the time we dump this load in Amarillo, I'm going to be late picking Beni up. I had to let Violet know."

"We're taking 285 right through Dumas. Can't we swing by her place? It's not far out of the way."

Delon turned his back, shoulders tense. "I don't want to be late on the delivery."

But—

Tori choked back her protest, letting him stride ahead of her toward the truck so she didn't have to school her expression. Habit had her analyzing his gait, looking for a deficit. There was none. But based on the evidence, the same might not be true of their relationship. Beni obviously wanted to ride along in the truck with his dad into Amarillo and back. Barring unforeseen delays, they could make a quick stop at the Jacobs ranch and still have an hour to spare.

Since Delon hadn't hesitated to bring Beni along to her house, she assumed he wasn't concerned about Tori's influence on his son. Which left her with one painful conclusion—

He would rather disappoint Beni than take her anywhere near the rest of the people who mattered most to him.

The dark clouds pressed down, turning late afternoon to dusk, and the rain had settled into a steady, bone-chilling drizzle by the time Delon parked the old Peterbilt beside the shop. He shut the truck down and tapped out a quick text to Violet.

I'm home.

She had texted earlier to tell him that Cole had to run into town to the feed store so he'd bring Beni along, saving Delon the drive out to the ranch—and avoiding an opportunity for Beni to notice the anger simmering between them. Fine by him. He hadn't got around to finding a lawyer. Just thinking about it made him queasy. But he'd heard—been forced to hear repeatedly—that Joe and Violet were planning a fall wedding, so he had plenty of time.

He grabbed his logbook, stuffed a folder full of paperwork inside, and tucked both into the front of his jacket for the dash to the front office door. He could actually dash, even after hours in the truck. Thank the stars and Tori, when it came to day-to-day life, his knee felt almost back to normal. And during the last few workouts on ol' Tin Lizzy, he'd finally started to settle into that elusive new groove, thanks in large part to Gil watching like a hawk and barking curses at him every time he lapsed into his old style.

Gil was worse than their junior high football coach. "Pick your feet up and move that lazy ass!"

Delon left the logbook on the front desk to deal with later. The door to his dad's office was open, the lights out. Gil's door was closed, but the murmur of voices was audible. Another video call, most likely, and Delon wasn't in the mood to make nice. He needed a shower. A shave. And time to process the fact that he'd dropped

Tori off less than twenty minutes earlier, and he already missed her so much it was all he could do not to call just to hear the sound of her voice.

He headed for the shower instead, but she stayed with him as surely as if her soap-slick body was pressed up against his. Damn, he needed to get her into a shower, first chance he got. Tori—naked, wet, and wrapped around him—had been one of the toughest memories to shake after she'd left for Wyoming. Delon had intended to make this shower a quick one since Cole and Beni could arrive any minute, but what the hell, the door was open. They could let themselves in. He cranked up the hot water and let his mind wander to all the sweet, hot places he'd avoided for so long.

The water abruptly turned cold, startling him back to reality. He scrambled out and grabbed a towel. Damn. How long had he been in there? He opened the door a crack, but the apartment was still empty. Hitching a towel around his waist, he hustled out to find his phone, sitting dark and silent on the kitchen counter. No reply to his text. No message. He checked the time. Forty-five minutes since he'd parked the truck. The drive in from the ranch took no more than ten, even in this crappy weather.

His temper flared. So now Violet was going to play games, keep him waiting, just to prove she could? Not fucking likely. He punched in her number and glared at the rain spattering against the window as he listened to it ring.

"Delon?" She sounded surprised, as if she hadn't expected him to call her on this bullshit.

"Don't screw with me, Violet."

"What are you talking about?" She seemed honestly surprised.

"You ignored my text. It's only half an hour until the feed store closes. How long were you figuring on waiting before you told Cole to go ahead and bring Beni in?"

A few beats of utter silence passed on her end of the line. "I got a call from Kirsten Vold. We were hammering out details of what stock we'd be bringing to Casper when I got your text. And one of the yearling colts got into the barbed wire. Cole had to take it to the vet in Amarillo." She hesitated, then rushed on. "I sent Beni with Joe. Straight to your place. They left the minute I got your message."

Delon's anger dissolved at the tremor in her voice. His pulse began to thump heavily against his eardrums. Shit. *Shit.* Over thirty minutes late, on a ten-mile drive? No. He would not jump straight to worst-case scenario. Would. Not. He pushed away images of mangled metal and blood oozing onto wet pavement. It could be as simple as a flat tire or...

Violet cursed, and Delon heard scuffling on her end of the line, as if she was pulling on a coat. "Joe's cell phone is going straight to voicemail. I'm gonna grab Daddy and head toward town."

Delon had already dropped his towel and grabbed for a pair of sweatpants from the laundry basket on the couch. "I'm leaving here right now."

He yanked on a sweatshirt, shoved his bare feet into boots, and snatched his car keys as he ran out the door. His heart slapped against his ribs in time to the windshield wipers as he gunned out of the lot, around the edge of town, and onto the rural route. Three miles out, he saw the amber flash of emergency lights on the edge of the road. Violet's car. Upright. Undamaged. But the dome light glowed, and the rear passenger's side door hung open.

As Delon screeched to a stop on the opposite side of the road and jumped out, Beni's head popped up over the roof. He flashed a wide grin, with a noticeable gap. "Look, Daddy! I lost my first tooth!"

"I...wow, that's...great." Delon had to brace both hands against the roof of Violet's car and breathe deeply, waiting for his heart to stop fibrillating. "Why are you stopped here?"

Joe appeared beside Beni, rising as if he'd been crouched beside the car. His hair was plastered in straggly strands to his face and neck, his expression wary, apologetic, with a touch of exasperation. "He literally *lost* his tooth. He pulled it out and then dropped it in the back of the car. I stopped to help him find it. And then he did and tried to show it to me and dropped it again—in the dirt." Joe glared at the ground below him. "Do you have any idea how small those things are and how many little rocks on the side of the road look just like a baby tooth?"

Delon drew a deep, shuddering breath, on the verge

of hysterical laughter. A tooth. He'd just had the life scared damn near out of him over a stupid tooth.

Joe lifted a clenched fist. "I found it. Just now, when you pulled up. Your headlights—"

"Yay!" Beni made a grab for Joe's hand.

He jerked it away. "Uh-uh. I'm holding on to this thing until your mother—" He cut off, knocked the fist on the side of his head, then extended it toward Delon. "I'll give it to your daddy. It's his job to deal with the tooth fairy."

Delon didn't reach out immediately, just stared at Joe as he stood, his sweatshirt soaked through, rain dripping from his hair and off the end of his nose.

"I'm sorry I couldn't call." Joe's teeth chattered and he hunched his shoulders against a shiver. "Beni was playing with my cell phone, and I didn't realize he'd run the battery down."

So he'd let them all panic when he could've just told Beni, "Tough shit, kid. Take better care next time." Or promised to write a note to the tooth fairy to put under Beni's pillow in lieu of the actual tooth, the way Delon's dad had done once with Gil. But no. Joe would rather freeze his ass off crawling around in the rain and mud, picking through roadside gravel piece by piece, than disappoint Delon's son.

And this was the man who thought he deserved to be Beni's stepfather.

Delon extended his palm over the roof of the car. Joe lowered his fist. His icy fingers pressed into Delon's palm, their gazes locked, as the tiny, cherished bit of Beni's childhood passed carefully from one to the other.

A pickup roared up behind them and lurched to a stop. Violet and her father burst out and came running.

"Oh my God. You're safe." Violet flung herself at Joe, simultaneously reaching for Beni. "Are you okay?"

Joe looked at Delon. Their gazes locked again as Delon shoved his hand, tooth and all, deep into his pocket. "They're fine," he said. "We're all gonna be just fine."

Chapter 37

By the second week of March, Delon could sign his name with his left hand almost as well as his right. He could also throw a decent Wiffle Ball pitch and catch a Frisbee—Beni's favorite of Tori's unending list of exercises—plus hold his own in a game of pool and hit the occasional bull's-eye on a dartboard—Gil's idea of agility training. He'd become so accustomed to doing everything backward that just that morning, he'd flipped Gil the bird left-handed without even thinking.

But he could not tear a piece of athletic tape, and when you were fixin' to wedge your hand into a rigging strapped to a half ton of bucking horse, you'd best give your body any help you could. With his shirt stripped off the right half of his body, he held his bare arm crooked, attempting to run the tape in a figure eight around his forearm and biceps, crossing at the bend of his elbow to keep the horse from jerking his arm straight. He spooled the tape out long enough to tear with his teeth, then cursed when it folded in half and stuck to itself.

When Gil shouldered through the gate from the arena, the sight of him sent Delon spinning into a time warp. All the years. All the rides. If anyone ever committed murder in this spot, the CSI team would find Sanchez DNA in the dirt. Sweat. Spit. Blood. And once, after being kicked in the gut during a spectacular buckoff, everything Gil had eaten since breakfast.

Gil eyed the mangled tape job. "Shoulda brought your personal trainer along."

"She's a therapist. Taping isn't her thing."

Plus he'd sort of failed to mention this little practice session to Tori. He'd meant to, from the moment he'd gathered up his nerve and called Steve Jacobs to ask if he could come out and get on a few, but every time he tried, his tongue balked and his brain peppered him with reasons to keep it to himself. Things were better between him and Violet, but the truce was fragile enough that Delon didn't want to risk stirring things up. He hadn't told Tori about the fight because it made him—rightly—look like a selfish, insecure prick. And because Tori had a tendency to foam at the mouth when she heard Violet's name.

He fumbled the tape again. Geezus. He was so nervous, his fingers were numb. Having Tori here would have been that much more pressure. She had worked so hard, constantly digging up new research, tweaking his training plan, testing his balance and reaction time. She'd even put him through a two-hour brain function screening so that if he should ever suffer a concussion, she'd have baseline measurements.

Relentless. Delon wasn't rock-stupid enough to

openly compare Tori to her mother, but she could be a little overwhelming. It'd be better to quietly get these first horses out of the way—see how it went—then bring her along next time, when his stomach wasn't already a wreck.

Gil set down the tablet he'd brought along to video Delon's rides and snatched the roll of tape out of his hand. Delon flexed his biceps while Gil expertly wound the tape around his arm, flicking a glance at his bare torso. "Nice six-pack for a guy who's single-handedly keeping Hershey in business."

"Stress. The phone and the computer are driving me nuts." Thank God. It had helped block the worst-case scenarios that kept popping into his head, leading up to this moment.

"Tough deal, having more loads than we can handle." Gil tore off the last strip of tape and smoothed it flat, then stepped back and tossed the roll to Delon. "Next time business is slow, you and your girlfriend can take the Love Machine and go park in some public place. My favorite kind of advertising. Free."

And crazy effective. All of the sudden, everybody wanted a truck with the Sanchez logo backed up to their loading dock. Some even asked for the black Freightliner specifically—sick bastards. But *your girlfriend?* Delon winced, though he couldn't come up with a better description. He and Tori had spent plenty of time together over the past three weeks, and he'd enjoyed the hell out of having her as a copilot, but being with her was like sitting behind these chutes. Familiar but turned on its side. He wasn't quite sure how he fit into the picture, especially when the frame was totally out of whack, with all the internet bullshit. He couldn't even take her out to lunch.

Luckily, she was happy with pizza and a video game marathon with Beni on a rainy Saturday afternoon. As he'd watched them, sprawled on the floor exchanging trash talk and fist bumps, it had hit him like a ton of bricks that he wanted this to be his future. Wanted it so hard it made him suck in a sharp breath.

Tori had glanced over at the sound with a smile that promised he'd have her undivided attention...later. His blood had risen, instant and hot, and he understood why Violet had insisted on dancing on the edge of emotional disaster, time after time. This was what had been missing between them. What she'd found with Joe. Which was why he had to be so very, very careful not to let go completely. No matter how Tori and his own raging desire tried to nudge him over the edge into the old insanity, he couldn't give in. Not yet. She hadn't mentioned leaving again, but other than buying a bed, she hadn't done anything to make that house of hers look like a place she wanted to stay either.

God, he hated that house.

"You're pathetic." Gil gave a pitying shake of his head. "It's like watching Beni eat dinner. How long do you figure you can keep it all on your plate without letting anything touch?"

Delon just shot him a dark look and shrugged into his shirt. *Focus on now. Deal with the rest later.* Male voices rumbled and the thud of hooves sounded out back, Steve and Cole bringing up the horses they'd picked from the practice herd for Delon. Rather than easing his nerves, the quiet behind the chutes only amplified his anxiety. There should be half a dozen other cowboys jostling and joking around him. And if it was weird for him, what must it be like for Gil, who hadn't set foot here since his own accident?

"Hey, Dream Boy! You gonna be ready any time today?"

Delon made a rude gesture at his brother, then strapped on his spurs and zipped his Kevlar vest. They molded to his body, armor he'd carried into so many battles it conformed to his shape. He did a couple of final warm-up squats, then climbed up onto the back of the first chute as two horses came snorting and blowing up the lane. At the sight of the sorrel mare in the front, his jaw dropped.

"Riata Rose?"

"Colts are too unpredictable," Cole said gruffly.

He slid the gate shut behind the best horse in their herd, vaulted over the fence—a slick move for a guy his size—and untied his horse. Again, not a backup but Cole's number one mount. As Cole strapped on his heavy, padded chaps, the arena gate swung open. Violet stood, reins in hand. Like Cole, she'd left her second string at the barn and saddled Cadillac, her bulletproof brown gelding.

"I, uh, thought I'd give y'all a hand," she said, eyes and voice uncertain. "Unless you'd rather have Daddy."

She was asking his permission, at her arena. Violet, who'd pulled him off at least a hundred broncs. Who'd damn near gotten herself killed trying to save his neck. Yeah, she'd run him down in the process, through no fault of hers. Delon had told her so—everyone had told her so—but obviously he wasn't the only one with a few demons to slay today.

"I trust you." And he realized he meant it in every way possible.

He caught a flash of her bright, relieved smile before she turned to grab the chaps looped over her saddle horn. His throat knotted, an embarrassing heat gathering behind his eyes. He crouched and bowed his head on the pretense of stretching as he fought the wave of emotion. All the months he'd avoided these people, slapped away their compassion, and the first time he gave them an opportunity to help, they responded by giving him their absolute best.

Gil thumped him on the back, rattling his teeth. "Come on, numb nuts. Let's ride."

Delon thought he was ready, but when the gate swung open and the full force of Riata Rose's first jump hit him, his right arm went *Huh?* and his head snapped back and hit her rump. Then she made her signature leap into the air, and the hang time gave him a chance to catch up. Each progressive stroke was a little stronger, his balance a little more sure, but his shoulders were forward one jump, back the next, his heels not quite finding that new groove.

A whistle shrilled—Beni, perched next to Iris on a beer cooler outside the fence, acting as official timer. Violet moved in to trip the release on the flank strap while Cole rode up along the opposite side where Delon could throw an arm around his waist and pull free from the mare. Delon dropped to his feet in the dirt and took three steps before he realized he'd been so focused on his mechanics he hadn't thought about his knee once since he called for the gate.

Score one for Tori. She'd done exactly what she'd promised—moved his focus off his injury. The guilt pricked at him again, but he shook it off. He wasn't excluding her. With both Gil and Iris taking videos, she could study his rides from every angle and analyze her heart out. He walked to the stripping chute, where Riata Rose stood calm as a show pony while Steve uncinched the rigging.

"Not bad, considering," the big man said.

Pretty high praise from Steve Jacobs. Delon nodded his thanks, draped the rigging over his arm, and gathered up the cinches so they wouldn't drag in the dirt. Cole slammed the sliding rear gate shut behind the next horse. Delon's muscles clenched in a combination of anticipation and dread as he eyed the dun horse they'd run in, a gelding they called Stoneboat because when his front end dropped, it felt like a two-ton boulder strapped to the end of your arm. Delon had better nut up and prepare to take the fight to the horse or Stoneboat would thrash him.

From the instant the gate swung wide, it was a matter of pure survival. He forgot all about mechanics and just scrambled to stay hooked. His spur strokes were about six inches long, and Stoneboat still managed to jerk the rigging away from him, so that the last five jumps yanked him to the end of his arm, then slammed his crotch into the back side of the rigging. God bless Violet for being right there to snag him before his balls were hammered up into his guts, despite his athletic cup. She circled around and dropped him a few paces from the bucking chutes. He stumbled over to sag against the nearest gate while he caught his breath. Geezus. What was wrong with him that he did this for fun?

Gil clambered down the chute next to him. "Lookin' good, D."

Delon shot him a *the fuck you say* look.

"Seriously." Gil held out the tablet. "I mean, yeah, you spurred like you're tryin' to pinch a raisin between your ass cheeks, but you stayed square, never got rocked into your hand. Now you've just gotta be more aggressive with your feet."

Delon could barely stand to watch. Ugh. He looked like a high school rookie, scared to pull his feet out of the horse's neck. His balls throbbed in time with every jump Stoneboat took on the screen. He grunted in disgust, then cleared his head and replayed both videos, this time dissecting each ride, part by part, as if it wasn't him on the screen. No, it wasn't all bad. He had stayed centered, used his free arm like he should, and kept his chin tucked, except for the last few jumps when Stoneboat got him really strung out. As Tori would say, they had a good foundation to build on.

Another pang of guilt, this one with serious claws, but then Violet rode up and handed him a bottle of Gatorade, passed to her from Iris's cooler, and Steve strode over to take a look at the video. Violet and Cole leaned down from their horses to watch, and they all added their two cents, which totaled up to what Gil had already told him. He'd climbed on those two horses with the sole purpose of proving his knee could take the punishment. Mission accomplished.

"You up for one more?" Steve asked.

Delon took stock. He was sweating more from adrenaline than exertion. Thanks to Tori, he was in the best shape of his life, but come morning, he was still gonna feel like he'd been booted down a staircase. One more ride wouldn't make it any worse. Then an unmistakable blue roan came snorting into the chute, and the red dirt trembled under his feet. Blue Duck. The bronc he'd been on the night of his wreck. Steve Jacobs was gonna force him to get back on that horse and ride in the most literal way possible.

While Gil and Steve set the rigging and the flank strap,

Delon took a few steps down the back of the chutes and crouched, head bowed, taking deep, cleansing breaths. *Nothing to get worked up about.* The wreck had been due to wet equipment and a muddy arena. Blue Duck was better than average, strong but not dangerous. But as Delon stood above the horse, a foot braced on either side of the chute, his mind was full of the smell of rain and wet horseflesh, arena lights glistening on a near solid sheet of water where there should've been dirt.

Instead of fighting the flood of memories, he opened his mind and let them come, drowning his senses. The rodeo announcer's patter over the blare of music. The rising buzz of adrenaline in his blood and the slow thud of his heartbeat in his ears. His rosined glove creaked against rawhide as he ran his hand all the way into the rigging, then backed it out a tad to make the leather pucker at the base of his fingers, forming the bind. Once again, Blue Duck cocked his head and watched from under a tangle of black mane as Delon pounded his fingers closed around the handle.

He scooted his hips up snug against the rigging and planted his feet in the gelding's shoulders. Tucking his chin into his chest, Delon focused on the initials burned into the leather. *G.A.S.* His pulse gave a single, hard thump. *Gas it.* Delon cocked his free arm back and nodded his head.

Blue Duck exploded from the chute like a steel spring, straight into the air. Delon held his feet rock-steady until Blue Duck's front hooves hit the ground.

Then he jerked his knees, his spurs singing and his shoulder blades bouncing off the horse's rump as his rowels clicked the front edge of the rigging. Then *snap!* Heels planted back in Blue Duck's neck before the horse's front feet hit the ground again. Two jumps, three, his body falling into that perfect groove. Delon's heart soared, higher and higher, as if it could fly right off into the blue Texas sky.

Then his hand popped out of the rigging and he *was* airborne, flailing in the nothingness, an instant of sick anticipation before he slammed into the dirt hard enough to drive every molecule of oxygen out of his body. He tried to inhale, but his body refused. Panic coiled through him, his mind flashing back to those horrible moments after his lung had collapsed. His muscles convulsed, fighting, fighting...*please, God, don't let me die!* He was so consumed by the memory that he was stunned when a hand touched his arm and he opened his eyes to find not an EMT but Iris, her round face pinched with worry.

"Are you hurt?"

Her touch and her voice broke through the panic. He forced himself to feel for the quality of the pain. Nothing sharp or stabbing, just a standard issue body slam and the wind knocked out of him. His diaphragm relaxed fractionally. Delon held up a hand in a *give me a minute* gesture. Slowly, painfully, the spasm receded and he could take a shallow breath. Then another.

Beni's face popped into view. "Wow, Daddy, that's the first time I ever saw you catch air."

"That's why he sucks at the landings," Gil said. He hooked a hand under Delon's armpit and pulled him into a seated position, grinning like a loon. "That was awesome!"

Delon pried off his hat and knocked the dirt from the smashed brim. "Especially the part where I didn't make the whistle."

Gil waved that off like a pesky fly. "New glove, different rigging. We just need to adjust your bind. But geezus, D, look!"

Gil shoved the tablet under his nose and hit Play. Delon's breath caught in a whole different way as he watched. The chaps, the hat, the vest were all him, but the ride…God, it was like watching an old video of Gil, only better. Snappier. For a few miraculous seconds, he had found that sweet spot between control and reckless abandon. Adrenaline pulsed through him in waves as Gil and Steve hoisted him to his feet and Iris dusted him off. Delon clutched the tablet like it was the Holy Grail. Just wait until Tori saw…

His joy bubble deflated some but didn't burst. Sure, she'd be bent out of shape that he hadn't told her about today, but once she saw the payoff for all their hard work, she would be so thrilled she'd get over it, and then they could celebrate. He could think of a *lot* of ways to show his appreciation.

"It is so good to have you both back." Iris threw an arm around each of them, squeezing hard. Then she nudged Delon. "Next time, you bring your new friend along. After all her hard work, I bet it's killin' her to not be here."

Because, yes, Tori was infinitely more than his therapist. And she had rebuilt him—mentally, physically, emotionally. Refused to let him doubt that they would succeed. And in return—

All the air emptied out of his lungs again as the miserable truth he'd been dodging slammed into him. Possibly the most important moment of his entire rehab, and he had excluded her. But—

But *nothing*. All the excuses—the tension between Violet and Tori, the awkward introductions that might have interfered with his precious focus—none of that was Tori's fault. He'd known this day was coming, and he'd had three weeks and endless opportunities to get it over with. Once again, he'd failed the test. Bombed it. A big fat zero.

And being left out might not kill *her*, but it could be fatal for him.

Chapter 38

TORI WAS ROPING BETTER EVERY DAY. THREE strides from the chute, her loop cracked around the steer's horns. She ripped out the slack and dallied up, Fudge already moving left as the rope came tight around the saddle horn. The steer had barely changed directions when Shawnee scooped both hind feet out of the dirt. Fudge hit the end of the rope and pivoted to face up. *Yes!*

An appreciative clap sounded from the arena gate. "That'll win you a check in anybody's roping."

Tori was so startled to see Violet she released her dally, paying no mind as the steer dragged her brand-new Rattler rope to the stripping chute. She shot a questioning look at Shawnee. *What is she doing here?*

Shawnee gave a *beats the hell out of me* shrug and rode straight up to Violet. "Let's see the glitter."

Instead of holding out her hand, Violet pulled a silver chain from under her shirt. "Joe says it's too dangerous to wear a ring working stock, but mostly he's such a cheapskate it'd kill him if I broke it or lost the stone."

Shawnee leaned down closer to examine a silver

pendant that glinted with diamonds. "Aw. A heart. Ain't that sweet?"

Violet flipped it around. "Read the back."

"'For bail money, contact Joe Cassidy.'" Shawnee hooted a laugh. "It's even got his phone number."

"He has a warped sense of humor." Her voice was dry but laced with such affection, such suppressed joy that Tori had to make a pretense of smoothing Fudge's mane while she fought down the lump in her throat.

There were moments with Delon—a glance, a smile—when she knew they were sharing a thought. A memory. When his eyes went warm and sweet as melted chocolate and she wanted to lick him up one side and down the other, and she could read the response in the crook of his mouth. *When I get you alone...*

And then he would throw up the *Not so fast!* sign so deliberately she could hear the rattle of jake brakes, like a truck decelerating down a long incline. Delon was thoughtful and sweet and knew exactly how to touch her—body and soul. But he somehow stayed just out of reach. He'd taken her to dinner. He'd taken her to the movies. But he hadn't taken her anywhere near Miz Iris or the Jacobs ranch. The heart of his world. So why had Violet come to her?

"Sorry to interrupt." Violet's voice held a shimmer of nerves along with the apology. "I had to run into Dumas for groceries and I thought...um, hoped we could talk."

She stood beside Roy, one hand resting on the horse's neck, tall and strong and intrinsically right in her jeans and boots. Tori felt as if she'd dropped through a wormhole and they were back at rodeo team practice, Shawnee and Violet on one side, her on the other.

Shawnee picked up her reins, spun the buckskin on his hocks, and rode over to the heeling box. "Me 'n' Roy'll be over here out of the line of fire."

Left alone in the middle of the arena, Violet braced her shoulders as she met Tori's gaze. "This was the third weekend Beni insisted on staying with his dad instead of with me, even though Joe was home. He says he has to be there to coach Delon."

Yeah. Tori knew. It was one of the excuses Delon used to avoid spending time at her place. She let her voice cool to just above freezing. "So…what? You want me to fire him?"

"No." Violet took a deep breath. "I wanted to thank you."

Tori felt her jaw sag and hoisted it up again.

"Kids that age are self-absorbed little bastards." Violet's mouth twisted into a grimace. "Those first months after Delon's injury were hell. Beni couldn't see why he should have to hang out with Delon when they couldn't do anything fun. Why couldn't he play with Joe instead? If I made Beni go, he pouted the whole time and made Delon miserable. If I let him stay with me, Delon pouted and made me miserable. And Joe…"

She drew another breath and puffed it out. "Joe's got no experience at being part of a family, and he's sure he's gonna screw it up. The worse things got with Delon and

Beni, the more Joe was convinced it was his fault. The fight at the Lone Steer was the last straw. Joe started finding excuses not to come home between rodeos, and I was afraid…"

Violet's voice wavered. She cleared her throat. "When Beni got all excited about helping with Delon's rehab and insisted on spending all his time with his dad, Joe finally understood it was never about him." She hooked a finger under the silver chain. "That's when he bought this."

Tori blinked, stunned. She'd been braced for Violet to warn her away from Delon. From her son. "You aren't upset about all the stuff online?"

"I may not have taken it well right off." Then Violet snorted a laugh. "But come and talk to me when one of you ends up in handcuffs."

"We don't…" Tori's face went hot. "I mean, we haven't since—"

"Not that kind of handcuffs, perv," Shawnee said.

Violet's eyes widened. Then she snapped her mouth shut and shook her head. "I do *not* want to know."

"I do, but the selfish wench won't spill the details," Shawnee grumbled.

Violet's face had flushed almost as red as Tori's. "Seriously. *Way* too much information. But if it helps any, Joe tossed Hank's phone out the window of Wyatt's plane on the way back to San Antonio and told him he was going with it next time he did something idiotic."

Tori almost smiled.

Violet almost smiled back, the gleam of it in her eyes. "I'll let y'all get back to your roping. But thanks again. For everything. It's amazing what you've done with Delon's rehab. The way he rode today—"

"He *what?*" The words were out before Tori could stop them. As she absorbed the full ramifications of what Violet had said, her body went cold, layer by layer. Skin, muscle, bone, marrow—the chill sank clear to her soul, where it froze into razor-edged shards of ice.

Violet looked stricken, her voice dropping to a guilty stutter. "He, um, rode. Some horses. Out at our place. I...we, ah, assumed...he didn't *tell* you?"

Tori could only stare, words washed from her mind by wave after wave of hurt. He hadn't told her what he had planned. Hadn't invited her to be with him at one of the most pivotal moments of his recovery. Hadn't even come straight to her from what had apparently been a successful practice session to share his triumph. As his therapist, she felt slighted. As his...his...what the hell was she exactly? She'd thought she'd known. Or at least had an idea. But now...

Violet was looking at her, anxious and apologetic, and damn it to hell, if that was pity, Tori was gonna have to punch something. Or someone.

"Well, fuck," Shawnee said. "Just when I thought he was gettin' a clue."

Violet's forehead creased into a puzzled frown. "I swear, lately it's like he's possessed. He's always been such a nice—"

"Bullshit." Tori loaded the single word with every ounce of her gathering fury.

Violet blinked, taken aback, then narrowed her eyes. "You haven't known him since…forever."

"You've been acquainted with him. You don't know him at all if you think he's *nice*." Tori hissed it like a curse.

Violet's expression went mulish. "We have experienced childbirth together. Stayed up all night taking turns rocking a colicky baby. I *know* Delon better than anyone!"

"Really? And yet you've never noticed that not once in his whole damn life has he gotten what he wanted most—and he's pissed as hell about it."

Violet shook her head so violently a strand of dark hair caught at the corner of her mouth. "Delon hasn't been himself lately, but normally he's the most easygoing—"

"It's an act," Tori said flatly. "He just moseys along, playing the part, never sticking his neck out because that's a good way to get your head ripped off."

Violet snorted her disdain. "And you're the expert because…"

"I grew up eyeball deep in politicians. I know spin when I see it."

"But you're still attracted to him," Shawnee drawled. "Lookin' for a man just like dear old daddy?"

Tori recoiled instinctively. "No!"

The twinge in her gut said it was true, though…up to a point. Delon could be an awful lot like her father: gorgeous, charming, thoughtful in a way that made a girl feel like she was the only thing in the world that mattered. Impossible to pin down if he didn't want to be. She swung off her horse and yanked at the latigos with hands almost too unsteady to loosen the cinches, using Fudge's big body to hide the emotions that pummeled her heart.

Maybe that was why she could see behind Delon's mask. She'd watched her father put on the senator along with his suit and tie, donning the face the public wanted to see. The difference was Delon didn't trust anyone enough to shed his protective layers, even in private. She'd had most of him once, in those first few exquisite hours after they'd met, before he'd decided she was someone he had to guard against. And she'd had most of him even after that. It was as if he'd realized it was too late to hide the passionate, reckless streak he caged up deep inside him. These past weeks, she'd kept hoping it would break loose. After today, after this, she suspected he'd strangle it to death first.

"I'm sorry," Violet said. "I shouldn't have…he's probably got a perfectly good reason, if you'll give him a chance to explain."

Make excuses. More fucking spin. Tori gathered up every ounce of her self-control and used it to tamp the hurt and anger down, out of sight. When she turned to confront them, her expression was blank. "He doesn't need to explain. I understand perfectly."

And of all the damn things, her eyes chose that moment to fill. He'd cut her out. Coldly. Intentionally. Well, to hell with all of them. She spun around and walked away, Fudge trailing meekly behind without even a parting nicker at Roy, as if he knew she was at the end of her leash and God only knew what might happen if it snapped. Dammit, dammit, *dammit*. She'd barely finished crying for one man and here she was, dripping all over her sweatshirt because of another one.

No way would she let Shawnee and Violet see her brush the tears away. At the end of the arena, she retrieved her rope and released the steer from the stripping chute, then kept going. Out the back door, across the pasture to where she could kick inanimate objects, probably break her foot, and howl her pain into the darkening void of the evening sky.

Chapter 39

Delon had timed his arrival almost perfectly. As he pulled into Tori's driveway, Shawnee was loading her buckskin in her trailer. Delon intended to smile, wave, and skedaddle past without stopping to chat. Shawnee cut him off and drove two stiff fingers into his solar plexus hard enough to make him yelp like a kicked puppy. Geezus. Why did women keep doing that to him?

"*You* are a total piece of shit." She turned on her heel and stomped to her pickup. As she climbed in she added, "She's in the barn. Take your phone. You'll need 911 to come and gather up the bloody scraps."

Delon sank back to brace himself against the car, reeling. Son of a bitch. Tori knew. How? His stomach rolled into a queasy ball. He'd planned to start off with the surprise he had tucked in his pocket, then once she was softened up a bit, throw himself on her mercy while she might have some. He rubbed a fist over the throbbing bruise on his sternum. Too late for that now.

He pushed away from the car and started toward the barn, step by dreaded step. Inside, only the light in the tack room was on, spilling a rectangle of illumination across the dirt floor. His heart thumped like his grandfather's old Navajo drum as he crossed the threshold, squinting into the shadows.

"I didn't realize you planned to stop by tonight."

Delon jumped at the voice that seemed to come from nowhere. Then he saw her shadow in Fudge's stall. She pulled the saddle and blanket off the horse and shouldered open the stall door to carry them across to the tack room, her cap pulled low over her face. He could read absolutely nothing in her body language as she set the saddle on the rack and hung the blanket over a bar mounted on the wall above it.

"I…forgot to call."

She made a noise that could have meant anything from *No big deal* to *Fuck off*. He dared a couple more steps while she scooped sweet feed from a metal can into a bucket. Her movements were brisk and efficient as usual, but it seemed to him that she deliberately kept her face in shadows.

"It was an asshole thing to do," he said.

"Won't get any argument from me." She went back into the stall, clipped the bucket to a strap on the fence, then stood fingering Fudge's mane as he ate, obviously waiting for Delon to either go on or drop dead.

"I'm sorry. It was just…" He grasped at a random straw. "I was nervous."

"And having me there would make it worse?"

Her voice was still so damn neutral. How was he

supposed to know how to play this? Claws scritched on wood overhead. Delon took an abrupt step back as the cat shimmied down a pole from the hayloft, prowled along the top rail of the stall until she reached a post directly between Delon and Tori, and settled down to regard him with unblinking contempt.

He kept a wary eye on the cat, lowering his voice. "I was afraid this first time would be ugly, and I didn't want to disappoint you, after all the work…"

"Don't." Tori whirled fast enough to make Fudge jerk his head up, scattering drool-soaked oats. Her body was rigid as a quivering arrow, her face a pale blur in the dark stall. "At least we've never lied to each other. Don't start now."

"What do you want me to say?"

She laughed, a sound brittle enough to make the cat's upper lip peel back. "You really should run for office. You're a natural. Just find the right words, smile the right smile, and let the people think you gave them what they wanted."

"I'm not blowing smoke." Anger fingered in between the strands of panic tugging at his heart. "I'm trying to explain."

"No need. I get it."

"Get what?"

"You." She brushed at the slimy grain Fudge had drooled on her leg, the motion dismissive. "Everything in its place, right? Me over here, them over there. Wouldn't want anyone thinking I was important to you."

The razor-edged words sliced open his gut, letting every dark, slithering secret fall out. He recoiled, anger the only weapon he had left. "All I did was get on a few bucking horses."

"At the Jacobs ranch." She cocked her head, her voice mocking. "Was everyone present and accounted for? Miz Iris. Steve. Beni. Violet's cousin…what's his name? Maybe I'd remember if I'd ever been introduced." This laugh was razor-sharp. "And Violet was there, of course. Your whole happy family. Imagine if you'd told me ahead of time. I might have insisted on coming along and meeting them." She gave an exaggerated shudder. "The horror."

"You and I have only been together for a few weeks."

"Together?" She snorted. "Funny. It feels more like I'm sitting in one place again while you circle around, making sure you never get close enough to get burned."

The fingers of anger clenched into a red-hot fist in his gut. "Oh. Right. You want me to just bail in and assume you're going to stick this time, based on…what?" He flung an arm toward the house. "Most of your stuff is still in boxes. You could back your trailer up to the front door and be gone tomorrow. You haven't even named that damn cat."

The cat bared its teeth and made a low, yowling noise that puckered Delon's skin.

Tori ignored it. "What does my cat matter?"

"Nothing, apparently, just like your house and your yard. Show me one thing that proves you give a damn about anyone or anything around here."

She went very still. Then she took four steps forward, until the light from the tack room fell across her face and he saw her eyes, red and swollen from tears that had left tracks in the dust on her cheeks. Worse, so much worse, was the look in her eyes. Utter devastation, and she put it right out there for him to see. She couldn't have knocked the stuffing out of him faster if she'd hauled back and punched him.

"Take a good look," she said. "And for the record, it's nowhere near the first time on your account."

Son of a bitch. He wanted to hold her, kiss away the evidence of her pain, promise never to do it again. He wanted to shake her. With all she'd suffered after losing Willy, how could she let anyone do this to her? Why couldn't they just have something comfortable and safe?

"What do you want from me?" he asked again, desperation leaking into his voice.

"Everything."

He didn't…he couldn't…he turned his palms out and lifted them away from his sides. "This is it."

"It's not enough."

He let his hands fall limp and gave a bitter laugh. "What's new? But it's all I've got."

"Bullshit." She folded her arms, everything about her posture screaming a challenge. "I had all of you for one night. One morning. Before you chickened out."

"*Chickened*—" He stepped toward her, outraged, but the cat hissed a warning that stopped him dead.

"That's what I want," Tori said. "What we had the very first night. I won't take anything less."

Delon shook his head. "Well, you're shit out of luck, because that man was not me."

"You're wrong."

"So you say. But hey, you're your mother's daughter—you'll find a way to be right, and to hell with anyone else." He turned, then paused, pulling the card out of his pocket and tossing it into the empty wheelbarrow beside the door. "Consider that a token of appreciation for being a great therapist, even though it doesn't look like you intend to be around long enough to enjoy it."

She didn't try to stop him from leaving. He didn't look back.

Chapter 40

THAT SON OF A BITCH. COMPARING HER TO HER *mother*. And what was that bullshit about her house? And her cat, for Christ's sake? As if he had any room to talk, living above a damn shop. When he came back…

Tori drew a deep, shaky breath, unclenching her fists. He would come back. He had to. That was the way fights worked. You blew up and said things you didn't really mean. Things like "You are just like your mother!" Then somebody stomped off, and after you'd both had time to cool down, someone said they were sorry and the other said "Me too," and then you talked it out and had crazy-good makeup sex.

She waited an hour. Then two. A whole day. Then another. As the sun set on the second day, she sat on the fence with the cat perched on a post on one side of her and Fudge rubbing his head against her shoulder on the other and stared down the empty driveway, her heart slowly disintegrating. Obviously, Delon had meant every word. Tears welled up and she slapped at them with an angry hand. Yeah, she'd pushed him. For his own good. Made him better, forced him through to the other side when he didn't believe it could happen.

And he'd compared her to Claire. Cold. Calculating. Unfeeling. It was like dozens of her mother's scalpels, slicing into her flesh. A thousand stab wounds to her soul. She'd poured everything into healing him, loving him, trying to show him what he could be—what they could be. Let him inside her head and shown him the person she'd been and the person she hoped to be. *Bold, powerful, unstoppable,* she'd said. And he'd seen an overbearing bitch who wouldn't take no for an answer.

On the third day, she wiped away the last tear she was gonna shed for that man and went to clean Fudge's stall. The first pitchfork full of manure landed on the card Delon had tossed into the wheelbarrow. She fished it out by one corner, stared at it for a long moment, then flung it as hard as she could, sailing it into the back corner of the tack room where it hit the wall and slid down behind the saddle rack while she went back to shoveling shit.

On the fourth day after the fight, Delon was staring blankly at a computer screen—again—when Gil walked into the dispatcher's office and shoved a piece of paper under his nose with a list of scribbled dates and times.

"What's this?" Delon asked.

"I entered you in Beaumont and Nacogdoches next weekend so you can work the kinks out before Austin."

Delon snatched the paper out of Gil's hand, adrenaline and terror cartwheeling through his gut. The first two rodeos were small town deals, he could slide in and out without much notice, but everybody who was anybody would be at Austin—and they'd all be waiting to see if Delon Sanchez had come back a champ or a chump.

He mashed the paper in his fist. "What if I'm not ready?"

Gil hitched an indifferent shoulder. "You can either go to the rodeos or drive over to Dumas and fix whatever mess you made with Tori. Either way, I want your mopey ass out of here."

For a brief, wild moment, Delon considered crawling back to Tori. Telling her he hadn't meant what he said—not the way it sounded. But then what? Even if she'd give him another chance, he wasn't the man she wanted, and she couldn't have the normal, anonymous life she craved here in the Panhandle. He could hardly blame her for wanting out, considering some of that crap on the internet—especially since the gossip about the two of them had spread to Wyoming. Geezus. He'd never seen anything so cruel. Regardless of how he was riding, Delon might have to think twice about entering Cheyenne this year. The people there were downright scary.

So there was no point in making that drive over to Dumas. He couldn't fix anything with Tori. Not permanently. At best, he'd give them time to do more damage.

She hadn't even acknowledged the gift inside the card he'd given—okay, sort of thrown at—her. If nothing else, he'd expected to have it dumped in his driveway. But nope. Not a word. Humiliation scorched through him, imagining her opening that card, rolling her eyes at his attempt at a grand romantic gesture. So lame.

He smoothed out Gil's paper, studied the dates, and felt the rodeos rushing at him like the reflector posts on an icy curve. His body was ready, but his mind… he wouldn't truly know until he climbed down into the chute. Odds were he'd crash, but so what? Most likely he'd only injure his pride, and that was already shredded. At least he would be able to tell Beni he'd tried. And if he could find the magic he'd captured for those few brief seconds on Blue Duck, he'd show Tori—

Dammit. He curled his hands into fists and thumped the arms of his chair. Every thought circled back to her. Whether his career lasted a week or another ten years, she'd be a part of every ride, ingrained in every single spur stroke. He couldn't climb into the Peterbilt or the Freightliner without picturing her in the passenger's seat. And the sleeper. He would never be free of her again.

Hell, let's be honest. He never had been.

"There's a practice session tomorrow night at the ranch," Gil said. "We still need to do some fine-tuning on your bind."

Delon jumped up, his chair slamming into the wall. "I'll go get the rigging."

Chapter 41

TORI LATCHED FUDGE'S STALL AND LEANED HER forehead against the gate. "Sorry, buddy. Couldn't seem to get my head into it tonight."

"Any chance you'll snap out of this before we get to Abilene?" Shawnee asked from the barn door.

Tori blew out a weary breath. "Sure. It's not like it's the worst thing that ever happened."

"I guess not." Shawnee was quiet for a few respectful beats, then she shrugged. "Probably for the best. Delon is planted here for life, and it's not like you were planning on sticking around long."

Tori lifted her head, manufacturing a snarl. "Why do people keep saying that?"

"It's obvious. You're basically camping in that shitbox of a house and you don't even own a lawn mower. You might as well have a moving van parked in the front yard."

You could back your trailer up to the front door and be gone tomorrow.

"Just because I haven't had the time or inclination to slap on paint and plant daisies—"

The sound of a truck pulling into the driveway cut her off. Shawnee turned around, squinted, then glanced back at Tori. "Then what is *that* doing here?"

Tori went to peer over Shawnee's shoulder. What the hell? "They must be lost."

The pickup had a *Johnson's Nursery* logo on the door and a flatbed trailer loaded with two fifteen-foot, fully leafed trees, their roots packed in big burlap bags, and a yellow tractor with a huge circular spade on the front for planting the things. The driver stood beside the truck, looking around dubiously.

Tori strode out to meet him. "Can I help you?"

"I sure hope so." He shoved an invoice at her. "Guy came in, wouldn't give his name or a phone number, just this address. Paid cash and said someone would make arrangements for delivery, but that was over a week ago and nobody has called, so the boss said just haul 'em out here."

"Daddy." She sighed. He couldn't resist trying to fix her.

The nursery man frowned. "The guy who came in didn't look like he could be your daddy. Too young. And real dark."

Tori's heart bumped, and she shot a look at Shawnee. "Delon? But he never said…"

Then she spun around and ran back into the barn. Behind her, she heard Shawnee drawl, "Don't mind her. She's a little high-strung…if you know what I mean."

Tori dropped to the floor and crawled underneath

the saddle rack, shoving cinches and stirrups and cobwebs aside until she found the manure-stained envelope. Kneeling on the dusty concrete, she tore at the flap and fumbled out the single sheet of blue construction paper, spreading it on her thigh. Glossy magazine pictures were pasted on it to form a collage—huge, spreading pecan trees shading an emerald green lawn with a pair of Adirondack chairs set beneath. Piles of raw pecans, chocolate chip pecan cookies, and pralines. By the pecan pie, he'd written *I'll make the ice cream*. And next to the gooey brownies, he'd drawn an arrow and a note that said *I kept the recipe for this one, just in case you bake too*, punctuated by a smiley face.

Of course he'd picked the chocolate. She choked on one of those stupid, sobby laughs. Sinking back on her heels, she let her hands fall limp, picturing Delon examining every tree at the nursery to find just the right ones, refusing to give either of their names or phone numbers so news of his purchase wouldn't show up online before he got out of the parking lot. How much time had he spent standing in front of the magazine rack at whatever store, shuffling through one after another until he found the perfect pictures? Then cutting and pasting and scribbling those notes…

Shawnee reached down and plucked the paper out of her hands. After a long moment, she said, "The guy says those trees won't produce for at least another couple of years."

Tori nodded mechanically. *I'll make the ice cream,*

he'd written. Did he even realize the commitment those pictures and words painted?

"Ya know," Shawnee drawled, "even Dr. Pickett can see the boy is asking you to put down some roots."

What do you want from me? he'd asked.

Everything, she'd said, then steamrolled right over him before he could hand it to her.

"Am I cold and manipulative?" she blurted.

Shawnee cocked her head. "Do you want the truth or something that'll make you feel better?"

"As if you'd lie to save my feelings."

"In a heartbeat, if it'll make you rope better." Shawnee settled more comfortably against the doorframe. "You can get a little frosty. Manipulative? Nah. Sneaky ain't your style. You prefer blunt force, but you mean well, and you're not afraid to say you're wrong. Why?"

Tori clenched and unclenched her hands against her thighs. "Delon said I'm like my mother."

Shawnee gagged. "And he walked out of here under his own power?"

"He caught me flat-footed. And…well, he might be right. Sort of."

She'd been so focused on fixing *him,* she hadn't considered what her home said—hell, screamed—about her. She hadn't even been able to commit to a shade of paint for her living room or decent curtains for the kitchen windows, and she'd expected him to believe she wasn't just using him to scratch an itch? And she definitely had used him as an excuse to avoid a decision that had to be hers alone.

She frowned up at Shawnee. "What if I can't stand to live here? The web pages, the gossip, people judging every move I make…I couldn't hack it in Cheyenne."

"You take zero crap off me, but you'd let a bunch of pinhead strangers run you out of town?" Shawnee curled her lip in contempt. "You don't even have to play nice anymore on your daddy's account. Why do you give a puckered-up rat's ass what anyone thinks?"

"I…" *Don't.* The realization stunned her. She really couldn't care less what they thought of her, personally. Her father, Elizabeth, Delon—none of the people who might be hurt gave a damn. All the leeches had done was generate a ton of new business for Sanchez Trucking. Even Willy's family had reached out to let her know they understood and wished her only the best.

She rocked back onto her heels and looked around. This was her place. Not just this barn, this acreage, that damn house. Texas. The Panhandle. Bone, muscle, and blood—she'd grown from the red dirt just like those pecan trees at the ranch, and if she let herself, she could feel the solid tug of the roots she'd never quite been able to sever.

Shawnee made a rudely impatient noise. "Geezus, you smart people make things difficult. Let me simplify. You can have your precious privacy, or you can have Delon. What'll it be?"

Well. When you put it like that, it was a no-brainer. Tori picked up the nursery card and rubbed her thumb across the embossed tree on the front. Delon had given her a present that represented the best of both the past and the future. Pasted his heart onto a piece of paper—and she'd told him it wasn't enough. She closed her eyes against the searing stab of guilt. How could she possibly convince him to give her another chance? It would take more than a phone call or a text. The boy who'd been abandoned too many times needed irrefutable, concrete proof that she was here to stay.

"I need help," she told Shawnee.

"No shit."

"Not that kind." She scrambled to her feet. "I'm talking actual physical labor."

Tori talked fast, explaining what she had in mind as she brushed off her jeans and headed out to chat with a man about some trees.

"We have to leave for Abilene by ten o'clock Friday morning," Shawnee reminded her.

"I'm calling in sick tomorrow. And you're gonna pitch in."

"Oh goody. What about the senator? He's in town. And he has minions."

Tori started to shake her head, then set her jaw. For one day, the American people would have to step aside. She was repossessing her father—and a few things from the attic at the ranch. "I'm recruiting him too."

Shawnee's scowl deepened with every step. "Can't you just drive over to Earnest, jump Delon's bones, then hire somebody to do the rest of this shit?"

"He's not there. He rode in Beaumont on Sunday and Nacogdoches last night."

"And you know this because..."

"They won't let me *not* know." Patients, coworkers, total strangers at the In and Out Burger, all determined to share their opinions. People had lined the fences to take videos of the official start of Delon's comeback, and then they posted them all online. Yes, she'd watched every one of them. Repeatedly. Especially the close-up parts.

"How'd he do?"

Tori made a face. "It wasn't pretty."

The scores or the rides. The first horse hadn't given him much to work with, squealing and kicking at its belly the whole eight seconds, but the second could have been decent if Delon hadn't tightened up and tried to ride the old way. Frustration had boiled inside her, but she couldn't call, couldn't text, couldn't do a damn thing to help him.

"He's in Austin this weekend," Tori said. "The horse he drew has a lot of power, huge moves. If Delon isn't aggressive, it'll be ugly, but if he really goes after her..."

"He'll be ninety or nothin'."

Tori stopped dead. "That's it."

"What?"

Tori took off again, her mind hustling faster than her feet. "First I have to deal with these trees and call Daddy." She smiled grimly. "Then I need to have a chat with the devil's sidekick."

And pray he didn't tell her to go to hell.

Chapter 42

IF LIFE WERE LIKE THE MOVIES, DELON WOULD either be dead or riding high. It was always one or the other when the hero made his big comeback. Triumph or tragedy...not half-assed with a side of mediocre. He flopped down on the bed in yet another hotel room, popped a chocolate Kiss into his mouth, rolled the foil into a tiny ball between his fingers, and tossed it at the wastebasket. And missed.

He checked the time again. Four o'clock. All the afternoon's interviews and autograph sessions were done, and he didn't have a traveling partner to shoot the bull with or play a few hands of pitch. It was too early to go to the arena, too late to take a nap, too much anticipation humming through his system to relax anyway. Nothing to do but spin the tread off his mental tires.

Delon had decided—yeah, he could see Tori smiling her *told you* smile—as long as he was on the road with time to kill between rodeos, he might as well become the official PR department for Sanchez Trucking. Gil had packed his schedule with meetings in every town along the way—current clients, potential clients, appearances at western stores and ranch supply stores for his various sponsors. What Delon used to consider a necessary grind had become a passion, and he *was* damn good at it. By the time he and Gil were done, there would be more than enough business to keep them both hopping.

He took out his phone and poked through the screens. No messages. No one to call. He'd played enough solitaire to rot his brain, he'd already talked to Beni this morning, Gil had analyzed his first two rides to death yesterday, and he wasn't enough of a masochist to go anywhere near a social media site.

He'd been prepared for some hoopla when he showed up at the first rodeos. He hadn't expected the winks and nudges, the sly smiles. "Looks like you been making good use of your downtime. S'pose your girl-friend will let you borrow the family jet over the big Fourth of July run?"

Delon just shook his head and kept his mouth shut. He wasn't going to break the news that Tori wouldn't lend him a bicycle. His index finger tapped the side of the phone, twitching to hit speed dial. Right about now, Tori and Shawnee would be pulling into Abilene for the Turn 'Em and Burn 'Em. Tori had been wound up since they'd entered, so he could imagine how wired she was now. He felt the hum across the miles as if they shared a high frequency bandwidth. Did she feel it too? Or could she use that bulletproof concentration to block him? If only he could call, they could talk each other down…

Not enough.

The words ground like broken glass in his spleen. Never enough. He should be used to it by now. Delon Sanchez—perennial runner-up and nice guy, favorite of fans, sponsors, and fellow cowboys. He'd had everyone fooled. Except Gil. And Tori.

They saw straight through him in a way that was both unnerving and an incredible relief. They didn't hide their warts or scars, so he didn't have to either. His hands clenched around the phone. God, he wanted to talk to her. Soak up some of that unsinkable will. Let her convince him he could be what she was determined to see in him. Plus, this was the biggest competition of her life. If she expected too much from him, she demanded ten times as much from herself. He wanted to reassure her, encourage her, wish her luck.

The phone buzzed in his hands as if he'd willed it to happen. His heart lurched, then sank. It was from Gil.

A friend from Wyoming sent me this song, said it sounded like you. I agree.

Wyoming? Delon's heart lurched again. Had to be a coincidence. Gil knew people all over the country. Besides, Gil and Tori might've been united in their determination to push him beyond all limits, but Delon still wouldn't call them friends. He clicked on the attached file and saw the title of the song. "Ninety or Nothin'," by a singer named Jared Rogerson.

He gave a disgruntled sigh and texted back: Is that all you've got, Coach?

It's all you need, if you decide to be this guy.

Delon's lungs seized up. *Decide.* Coincidence? Or an indirect message from Tori? He hit Play, and the opening chords strummed his hypersensitive nerves, sure as his brother's fingers on the guitar strings. The words felt as if they were plucked straight from his soul. He listened all the way through. Then he grabbed his earbuds, plugged them in, and settled back on the bed to listen again.

––––––––––

Tori slung her rope bag over the saddle horn, untied Fudge from the horse trailer, then pulled out her phone. She'd check one last time to see if Delon had—

"Uh-uh." Shawnee snatched the phone from her hand and shoved it into a pocket on the side of her rope bag. Tori made a grab for it, but Shawnee blocked her with a forearm to the chest. "Don't think I won't knock you on your ass. We have a deal. You can't check your texts, your email, your voicemail, or the rodeo results from Austin until we're done roping."

Tori stopped, drew a deep breath, and stepped back. "Thanks."

"You're welcome. Want me to slap you around a little, or are you good?"

"I'm good."

And she meant it. She flipped the reins over Fudge's head and swung aboard, her pulse revving up to competition speed. She'd done what little she could to help Delon. For the next few hours, the only thing she could control was what happened inside her own arena. Austin was up to him.

Chapter 43

DELON RAN A GAUNTLET OF BACKSLAPS, HAND-shakes, and good-to-see-yous as he made his way behind the chutes to dump his gear bag. It was marquee night in the bareback riding. He couldn't turn around without tripping over a world champion—Kaycee Feild, Bobby Mote, Will Lowe, Steven Peebles.

Not ready. Not ready. He angrily squashed the little worm of doubt that kept slithering into his subconscious. He'd done the work. His knee felt fine. It was his head that'd tripped him up at Nacogdoches. If he could get his mind right...

His phone buzzed. Gil again.

Quit fighting your head and let your wild hair loose.

Delon shook his head and typed, What wild hair?

It's there. But until you find it, borrow mine. Don't have much use for it tonight.

The familiar pain tugged in Delon's chest. Gil should be standing beside him. He'd be one of those gold buckle boys by now if only...

I'm watching live online, so ride like you give a fuck.

Yes, boss.

Delon tucked the phone away with a little itch between his shoulder blades as if he could feel Gil's gaze. Pressure built inside him, a swelling, whirling supercell of energy and emotion. He tried to push it aside, breathe through to his usual calm, but voices and phrases and memories rumbled through his mind like thunder.

Gil, eyes dark and intense. *Rodeo is a jealous bitch. You gotta give her your whole heart.* Tori's hand on his thigh, pushing him past his comfort zone. Tori's body, long and lean and naked, moving under him. The way she'd looked at him as he leaned against Gil's car and said, "It suits you…strong and fast…"

He wasn't Gil or the guy in that song, laying it all on the line for one big score. *Ninety or nothing.* But… his pulse kicked into a new, unfamiliar gear. He had the horse to do it. The first few jumps were doozies, but if he set his feet and picked her up, she'd go straight into the air, kicking over her head and giving him a chance to show off—assuming she didn't blow him out the back end before they got that far.

You could stick your heels in her shoulders and hold 'em through the tough part, the devil whispered in his ear. *Be safe and get into the short round.*

And give away at least five points. He shook off the buzzing thoughts and started warming up to his usual playlist, but the harsh guitar riffs grated on his nerves. Halfway through, he switched to the new song and put it on repeat. His heart thumped along with the heavy beat. *He pulls into the bright lights, time to lay it on the line…*

Boots, chaps, vest, spurs…he donned his gear piece by piece, his elbow already taped by the sports medicine crew. He bent to wrap and tie the long leather straps around the tops of his boots, the energy level around him rising as contractors and crew yelled orders.

The chute boss strode past and called down, "You're in number three, Delon."

Outside the main gate, the flag bearers' horses shuffled impatiently, waiting to burst into the arena for the grand entry. The broncs banged and snorted up the alley and into the chutes, gates ramming shut behind each in turn. Delon's horse tossed her head and blew out a loud, challenging huff. He braced a foot on either side of the chute to straddle the piebald mare. As he settled the rigging into place, the song continued to echo in his head. *Feels the leather, hears the rosin burnin'*…

The lights of the coliseum dimmed, and everything paused at the opening strains of the national anthem. Delon straightened and took off his hat, but instead of bowing his head, he let his gaze run across the packed house. His already overstimulated senses opened up, drinking in every sight and smell, all the faces, the buzz of expectation. He took a deep breath and sucked their energy into his lungs, felt it burn through his veins like a shot of whiskey. *Rising adrenaline puts his heart in perfect time*…

The grand entry thundered out, and the announcer's voice crackled with excitement. "Coming out of chute number one…"

The mare shifted restlessly beneath him as a chute gate banged open and the crowd roared its approval of the first ride. The buzzer sounded and the pickup men closed in, setting the cowboy safely on the ground. Overhead, the big screen replayed the ride, and Delon dimly registered a score in the high seventies. Good. Not great. As the gate man moved to the next horse out, the chute boss yelled, "On deck, Delon!"

He drew another long, deep breath, fighting for his usual control, but it was nowhere to be found. The thunderheads inside him roiled and crackled, lighting up every neuron, flooding every muscle fiber with adrenaline. *Branded brave or just insane, to him it's really all the same…*

Why not be that guy? He had nothing left to lose. Steady, reliable Delon Sanchez had been stomped into the mud—stripped down to nothing and reassembled from the scraps by a woman who attacked every setback like a personal insult, a brother who roared through life with the accelerator jammed to the floorboard, and a son who would idolize him no matter what happened in the next eight seconds. All they asked of him was one thing.

Ninety or nothin'.

He glanced down the back of the chutes and saw Kaycee Feild standing, feet braced, arms crossed, eyes fierce as he waited his turn. Not a hint of uncertainty there. He was human, just like Delon. Not any stronger. Not any faster. If Delon's body was up to the challenge, what was to stop him from rocking this arena?

Nothing but himself.

"You're next, Delon!"

Settling onto the mare's back, he felt the twitch of her muscles, winding up to explode. He ran his hand in deep and worked it back and forth until the bind felt just right, then pounded his fingers tight around the grip with his other fist. As he waited for the arena to clear from the previous ride, Delon bowed his head over his rigging and stared at the initials burned into the leather. *G.A.S.* He slid his hips up snug against the rigging and, without thinking, pressed two fingers to the initials, then to his heart. Screw careful. He cocked his free arm back, nodded for the gate, and let the storm break.

He held his body tight through that first powerful lunge, chin tucked, heels planted in her shoulders. The instant he felt the jolt of the mare's front hooves hitting the ground, he fell back and let loose, as if his brother truly had taken possession of his body. His spurs sang, then snapped back to her neck with Delon's speed and precision, a beat ahead of the slam of her hooves into the dirt. Each successive jump was higher, the hang time longer, until it felt as if they would take flight, the flapping of his chaps like beating wings. His heart soared, the blood pounding so loud in his ears he barely heard the eight-second whistle.

The crowd had gone insane, the screams deafening. Delon pried his hand free and latched an arm around the pickup man to let himself be dragged off the horse and dropped on his feet in the middle of the arena. His boots barely hit the ground before he bounded straight in the air, punching a fist over his head, then spun around and did it again for good measure. The hell with humble. He'd just made the ride of the night—the ride of his *life*—and every person in the arena knew it.

But not Tori, who deserved to be in this moment more than all the thousands of spectators combined. And that's when it finally hit him. *This.* Complete surrender to the moment. To her. That was all she was asking.

What do you want from me?

Everything.

He could do that—if she'd still let him. As he strode back to the chutes, applause raining down on him, he was already trying to figure out how to persuade her to give him another chance.

───────

Dust haloed the arena lights above the Abilene arena, and the night had turned chilly by the time Tori tracked their second steer to the stripping chute to retrieve her rope.

"Well, it could've been worse," Shawnee said as they rode out of the arena. "With any luck, we've drawn our quota of shitty steers for the weekend."

Tori grunted in agreement as she stepped off Fudge and loosened the cinches, her whole body limp with exhaustion and relief. So far, this roping felt like a western version of *Survivor*. Their first steer had run like a striped-ass ape and been even wilder on the end of the rope when Tori turned him. It was a miracle Shawnee had managed to snag two feet. The second steer had ducked left under Fudge's neck, tripping the horse up so he'd almost gone to his knees. They'd gotten the steer roped, but it hadn't been pretty. Or fast.

"We're clean on two and we get to come back tomorrow," Shawnee said. "That's better than three-fourths of the teams."

True. Everybody got to run their first two steers, but only the top forty in the aggregate progressed to the second day, like making the cut at a golf tournament. Tori was happy they were still in the hunt, but she'd prefer to be in the top half of the qualifiers instead of the bottom.

Shawnee dismounted and gave Roy an *attaboy* rub between the ears. "You did a hell of a job staying cool, especially when Fudge was skidding along on his nose."

"Thanks. You too."

Shawnee shrugged like that was only to be expected and fished Tori's cell phone out of her rope bag. "It's after ten o'clock. You can check the results from Austin now."

Tori stared at the phone without reaching for it, a churning wave of hope and dread rolling through her. If Delon had wasted another good horse in Austin, he'd be so disappointed in himself. And in her. She'd sworn she could make him good as new. One more broken promise, to a man who'd been dealt a lifetime of them.

Tori spun around and crouched to pull off Fudge's front splint boots. "You look."

Shawnee made a disgusted noise but tapped the screen. Tori moved to Fudge's other leg, sneaking peeks at Shawnee under his belly. Her face remained impassive as she stared at the phone. Then she tapped the screen and stared some more. Tori's stomach sank further with every passing second. Finally, she couldn't stand it anymore.

"Was it terrible?"

"Depends on how you look at it." Shawnee turned the phone around and stuck it under Tori's nose. "Sure sucked for everybody else, as bad as he kicked their asses."

Tori snatched the phone, her heart hammering. *Sanchez Lights Up Austin* the headline shouted. She clicked to play the video, and her body twitched with every jump as if she was riding right with him.

"Oh my God," she breathed, light-headed from forgetting to inhale while she watched. "He did it."

She was dialing his number before she consciously made the decision to call. It went straight to his mailbox. The instant she heard his voice telling her to leave a message, she panicked and hung up. What had she planned to say? *Congratulations, here's a gold star for my prize patient! Oh yeah, and sorry I was such a bitch.*

Or *I love you, and I am so damn proud.*

And she would be just one more of the horde jumping on the *Welcome Back, Delon* bandwagon. She had a
flash of how many of that crowd would be single, female,
and more than willing to help him celebrate, and her
stomach twisted. She tucked the phone into her pocket.
Better to stick to the plan. After they got the horses put
up, she'd send him the text messages she'd so carefully
composed, along with the photos she'd taken back
home. He'd have until nine o'clock tomorrow morning
to answer before Shawnee confiscated her phone again.
If he didn't delete them on sight.

But still, it was all she could do not to break out into
an impromptu victory dance. They'd done it. Delon
was back.

Chapter 44

DELON STAGGERED INTO THE HOTEL COFFEE SHOP AT a little after ten on Saturday morning. So many people had pounded his back, punched his arm, and slapped his hand in congratulations he felt as if he'd been beaten with broomsticks. Dozens more had offered him a beer, a shot, and in one particularly persistent case, the key card to her hotel room. His phone had been flooded with calls and texts—Gil practically yelling, he was so pumped, Violet and Beni both jabbering with excitement, even his dad, sounding downright giddy.

Plus every other person who knew his number, until the battery died before the rodeo performance was halfway through. Over and over again, he was peppered with the same question. "Where did *that* come from?"

He had only one answer: Tori. Sure, Gil had inspired him. But Tori, day after day, with every challenge she accepted, had shown him how to not only survive but thrive. She refused to let anyone or anything define or diminish her. She amazed him. Humbled him. Owned him, body and soul.

As corny as it sounded, in all his life, only Tori had

possessed the magic key that could set him truly free. Which was why he needed to get his damn phone charged. Last night, he'd stuffed it in his gear bag and let himself be swept away on a celebratory wave, to the beer stand first, then on to the hotel bar, not stumbling up to his room until closing time—alone, despite all efforts to the contrary—and falling face-first into exhausted sleep.

This morning, though, as soon as his brain cells and his phone had returned to the land of the living, he would call her. Explain that standing out there in the middle of that arena, he'd finally grasped the difference between just showing up and really living—and loving. He'd only felt that unbridled euphoria, the sense of endless possibilities, once before. He would not fail her again. He would go after her this time and would keep going after her until she realized she didn't have to leave. She was already right where she belonged.

But first, coffee. Triumph still pulsed in tiny bursts under his skin, but it was no match for his adrenaline hangover. The aftermath of his visit to the Lone Steer had been fresh enough in his mind to keep him sipping his drinks instead of gulping, but dear God, if he didn't get caffeine soon...

"Table for one and I'll double your tip if you grab the coffeepot on the way," he told the hostess. He held up his phone and the charger. "Got an outlet?"

"Just that one." She pointed at a booth a few feet away, already occupied. "If y'all don't mind sharing."

No damn way. But before Delon could say so, Wyatt Darrington vaporized the hostess's brain with a lazy smile and drawled, "Who doesn't want to hang out with the champ?"

Delon hesitated long enough to reel off a string of silent curses, then stepped around the puddle of dumb-struck females and slid into the booth to see what game Wyatt was playing today. But first he plugged in the phone, then added enough cream and sugar to his coffee to make it cool enough to guzzle. Ah. Yeah. He closed his eyes, tilted his head back against the padded seat, and waited for the magic beans to work their voodoo.

"If you're looking for the results from the roping in Abilene, they're not posted online," Wyatt said.

Damn. He didn't bother to ask how Wyatt knew he hadn't been talking to Tori. Violet to Joe to Wyatt, with Shawnee mixed in. Easy trail to follow.

"Tori and Shawnee made the cut," Wyatt said. "They were in thirty-second place after last night. They roped their first steer of the semifinals this morning in eight point six seconds, which moved them to nineteenth, with all the other teams that tripped up. They should be roping their second one any time now."

Delon opened his eyes and stared in disbelief.

Wyatt gave one of those cryptic smiles as he tapped his phone with one finger. "I keep an eye on things that interest me."

"And Tori is one of them?" Delon's temper flared, fueled by a spurt of jealousy and, yeah, insecurity. Wyatt was practically a clone of Richard Patterson. He'd slide into their world without a ripple.

Wyatt shook his head. "She and I are too much alike. Put us together, we both revert to exactly what we ran away from."

"So why—" Delon gestured at the cell phone.

"I knew you'd want to know, and after seeing you at the bar last night, I assumed you wouldn't be leaving the hotel for breakfast, so…" Wyatt made a gesture that included the booth.

Delon blinked. Then blinked again. But no, Wyatt wasn't a hallucination bred of overstimulation and lack of sleep. "What do you *want*?"

"For Joe and Violet to be happy. That's a lot more likely if you're not stirring up trouble." Wyatt leaned back and folded his arms, narrowing those intense blue eyes. "There's not much I won't do for my friends."

Including getting Delon out of the way by whatever means necessary. The skin prickled at the back of his neck, and he was suddenly reminded of the rumors that had run rampant for a while, about how Wyatt's family back east had mob connections. Before he could compose a response, Wyatt's phone chimed. He checked the message.

"Eight seconds flat on their fourth steer, and a bunch of miscues by the teams ahead of them in the aggregate. They're through to the finals."

Delon's heart gave an exuberant leap that had nothing to do with the coffee. Tori must be thrilled. And nervous as all get out. Which meant…

He sighed in frustration as his phone vibrated, indicating sufficient battery to power up. He was too late. The last thing she needed now was a call from him to mess with her concentration. He turned on the phone and it began to chime, more congratulatory texts and voicemails. He flicked his finger across the screen, speed-scrolling through the names and numbers so fast he almost missed the most important one. Wait. Make that four?

His pulse thumped in his ears, and he could feel the weight of Wyatt's unapologetic stare as he opened the first message. Instead of the congratulations he expected, it only said thank you. The attached picture was of Tori's front lawn, complete with two newly planted pecan trees, their leaves a fresh, vibrant green against the drab little house. Two white Adirondack chairs were set between them, just like in the picture he'd given her. Then he looked closer and saw there were also new wooden planters on either side of the front door, spilling over with flowers. His fingers felt fat and clumsy as he scrolled to the next message.

I decided I should settle in.

Whoa. What? He peered closer at the next photo. If it hadn't been for the couch, her living room would've been unrecognizable—walls painted dark brown with turquoise accents to match the curtains and area rug. That same high oak café table and chairs and above it, the Buck Taylor original that was still Delon's favorite. And next to the kitchen pass-through, a familiar pair of wrought-iron barstools.

His heart was racing so fast his ears rang from the blood singing through his arteries. He scrolled down to the third message. One word. Followed by a picture of the cat, ears pinned, fangs bared.

Delon grinned so big it hurt his face. "She named the cat."

Wyatt snagged the phone and grimaced. "Muella? It goes out and skins puppies?"

"I wouldn't doubt it."

Wyatt shamelessly read the last text. "This one says, 'Shawnee here. I have her phone. She's not getting it back until the roping is over. Then you get one text. Three words. They'd better be the right ones because if I have to listen to her snivel all the way home, I'm coming after your ass.'"

Delon choked out another laugh. Dammit. He should be there to either congratulate or console her, depending on how it went.

"I checked the schedule for the roping," Wyatt said. "They're taking a break for a barbecue lunch and the Calcutta auction. The finals don't start until three o'clock."

Four hours. Abilene was a little over two hundred miles away. Taking traffic into consideration, there was no way Delon could drive it fast enough, but if he had a plane…

He leaned back and narrowed his gaze on Wyatt. "You said you'd do damn near anything."

Wyatt nodded. "I can get you there, but I can't hang around to bring you back here in time to ride tonight."

Delon considered it for about ten seconds. Then he scooted out of the booth. "Let's gas it."

———

Tori's mind was a sieve as they waited behind the chutes to rope their last steer. Thoughts flowed over and through her, occasionally catching for a moment, then slipping on by. Fifth place. In the two semifinal rounds, they'd jumped all the way from thirty-second place to fifth. She'd just kept nodding her head, throwing her rope when she got her shot, and letting Shawnee clean up behind her, while around them, team after team fell apart.

So here they were. Fifth place paid over ten thousand dollars, and so far none of the teams behind them in the aggregate had made anything better than average runs. All she had to do was be consistent. Take a good solid shot and make sure they got a time…

Shawnee rode up, knee-to-knee, face-to-face, and glared at her. "Don't you dare back off on me now, Peaches. We didn't come here just to get a check, and we've got the best steer in the pen."

"But we're three seconds off the lead—"

"Then you'd better rope quick and make the rest of 'em worry about beating us."

Tori nodded dumbly. Shawnee needed the money a damn sight more than she did. If she wanted to go for broke, so be it.

The announcer called their names, and everything clicked into brilliant focus. The flags snapping in the breeze above the crow's nest. The radiant blue of the afternoon sky. The beer bottle that dangled from a cowboy's hand when she rode past him into the arena. She took a deep breath, cleared her head, then turned Fudge around to back him into the corner. Her gaze locked on the buckle of the steer's horn wrap, centered at the back of his head. She didn't glance over before she nodded. Shawnee would be ready.

The gate banged open, and it all unfolded precisely as she'd imagined a thousand times. Three swings and launch, her loop cracking around the horns. Yank the slack, one quick dally around the saddle horn, go left. She barely had time to look back over her shoulder before Shawnee scooped both hind feet up. As the ropes came tight, Fudge pivoted to face up.

Oh. My. God. They'd done it! The breath she'd been holding blasted out of her lungs. The run seemed as if it had lasted forever and no time at all.

"Five point eight seconds!" the announcer hollered. "Fast time of the day and puts them way out in the lead."

Tori gulped, feeling as if she was fighting her way to the surface of a very deep well. As she let her dally go and reined Fudge to follow the steer to the catch pen, Shawnee loped up alongside and punched her in the arm so hard she dropped the end of the rope. "What in the ever-loving *hell* was that?"

Tori blinked at her. "You told me to go fast."

"Which is not the same as crazy." Shawnee flapped a hand over her heart. "Do you have any idea how far you threw that thing? Me and Roy were so shocked we damn near missed the turn."

Tori rubbed her arm, mind staggering back from the zone. "I just did what you said."

Shawnee let loose one of her big, bawdy laughs. "Remind me never to suggest that we rob a bank, or you'll whip out an Uzi."

"Sawed-off shotgun," Tori corrected automatically. "My father has consistently advocated bans on fully automatic weapons, and I support his position."

Shawnee stared at her. Then she laughed again, shaking her head. "Well, we do want to be politically correct."

Then came the worst part. Waiting. Watching the four teams that had come into the finals with faster aggregate times. As if Tori had thrown down a gauntlet, the next header also took a long shot and missed. Then the next. The third clutched and missed the start and had to run the steer too far down the arena.

Shawnee grinned at her. "We blew their minds, Peaches."

One team to go. "This pair will have to be faster than eight point eight seconds to move ahead of Hancock and Pickett," the announcer declared. "And they've got a steer that'll test 'em."

At the bang of the gate, the steer launched like a sleek black missile. The header kicked hard but didn't catch up until halfway down the arena. Tori sucked in her breath and held it as he roped the horns and turned off. The heeler cut around the corner, took one more swing, and snatched up two feet. The entire crowd was motionless, waiting for the time.

"Nine seconds flat!" the announcer shouted. "Ladies and gentlemen, your Turn 'Em and Burn 'Em champions and winners of two brand-new Ford pickups are Tori Hancock and Shawnee Pickett!"

Tori swiveled her head to stare at Shawnee. Shawnee stared back at her. Then slowly, a wide grin split her face. "Honest to God, woman, if you weren't already spoken for, I'd kiss you."

The next half an hour was a blur of congratulations and fist bumps, photos and handshakes, and a key slapped into her hand. A pickup. *Her* pickup. *Oh my God*. She'd won an actual *pickup*. And a really big check to keep the fuel tank full. As the final handshakes were exchanged and photos taken, Tori emerged from the haze of shock and wonder.

"Oh shit! I have to go." She took off toward the arena gate, tugging at the reins to urge Fudge to keep up.

Shawnee broke into a jog to catch her, holding Tori's phone. "Don't you want to check your messages first?"

"I'm going no matter what." So maybe it was better if she didn't know how Delon had responded.

"Then you don't care what this text says." Shawnee made as if to tuck the phone in her shirt pocket.

Tori snatched it out of her hand and read the message. Then checked the number to be sure it was Delon's and read it again. "'It's about time'?" she echoed, her voice perilously close to a screech. Those were his three words? "What the hell is that supposed to mean?"

"It's about time we got this right," a voice said behind her. She spun around and found Delon standing, hands jammed in the pockets of his unzipped black and red NFR jacket. He rocked back on his heels and grinned at her. "Hey, Champ."

She stared at him for a beat, then checked the time on her phone. Five o'clock. "What are you doing here?" she snapped.

He raised his eyebrows, but the grin didn't falter. "Not exactly the welcome I was hoping for."

"You have to ride in *two hours.*" She stepped closer, fuming. "You've got the bareback horse of the year drawn in the short round at *Austin.* What kind of idiot blows that off to watch a team roping?"

"An idiot who's stupid about you?"

Tori's mouth dropped open. He just stood there, buff and beautiful in a snug black T-shirt, energy crackling around him and that gleam in his eyes that promised... *oh.* Heat flooded through her, scalp to toes.

Shawnee pried Fudge's reins from her fist. "Y'all might want to take this to the trailer, unless you want to watch the replay online."

Tori glanced around. Sure enough, some of the

stragglers had lingered to rubberneck. She grabbed Delon's wrist. "Come with me."

The heat in his smile shot fire through her veins. "I thought you'd never ask."

Chapter 45

HE LET HER DRAG HIM INSIDE THE TRAILER BEFORE pulling free to prowl the living quarters, tossing his hat on the table while his gaze lingered on the king-size bed up in the nose. She kicked a stray bra into the corner.

"Nice trailer," he said.

"Thanks." She crossed her arms, glaring at him. "Of all the boneheaded stunts…"

Delon swung around to face her. "You should lock that door."

Her eyes widened as she read the intent in his gaze. "I…okay."

He closed in as she fumbled with the dead bolt, backing her up against the door with a hand on either side of her head. His system was revving even hotter than it had been when the whistle blew at the end of his ride, and he could see the same triumphant glow in her eyes.

"I know we need to talk, but I swear, watching you rope was the biggest damn turn-on."

His mouth closed over hers, hungry and demanding. She stiffened for a beat from the blast of his pure, unadulterated desire, then gave an actual growl, her hands tugging at his T-shirt in search of bare skin. He broke away from her mouth to trail kisses and bites along her jaw and down her neck and grinned when he found the first button on her blouse.

"Pearl snaps." He grabbed both sides and yanked, ripping them open in a series of emphatic pops.

"Delon, we—*ah, shit, that feels so*—listen…we have to…"

"We will. In a minute." Or twenty. The front hook on her bra went next, and then his hands were on her. She moaned at the scrape of his calluses over her nipples as he molded and caressed, all gentleness forgotten. Her body jolted and the need roared through him like a tsunami, drowning every thought except *now*.

"I'm sorry I didn't tell you about the practice session," he muttered as his tongue explored the hollow below her collarbone while his hands jerked at her buckle and shoved her jeans down.

She managed to kick off one boot and free herself from one leg of her jeans while getting her hands into his Wranglers. "I'm sorry I was too hardheaded to let you explain. You'll have to get used to that if you plan to stick around."

"Just try and shake me loose." He groaned as she shoved at his jeans. "Unless you want me to nail you against this door, you should find a better spot while I suit up. Where do you keep your condoms?"

Her hands froze. "My…what?"

He pulled back to look into her flushed face. "Condoms. You always…"

"Not in this trailer."

He was still for a beat, then whispered a curse and let his forehead fall against her shoulder.

"You didn't bring any," she said flatly.

He rolled his head back and forth without lifting it. *Stupid, stupid, stupid.* "I was too worried about getting here on time."

She echoed his curse. Then she dragged in a deep breath. "Okay." She sucked in more air, let it out, as if trying to blow off pent-up steam. "Okay," she repeated, but her hands were still glued to his ass, and she was still pressed into him, her body vibrating with desire and frustration.

No, dammit. Not okay. This was their big moment. The time for all the truths he'd denied her for too long, words he'd rehearsed over and over on the flight from Austin. Playing out in his head, it had been flawless, but before he could even start, he'd ruined it all.

Unless…

His immediate, visceral reaction was to pull away. Too risky. Too…naked. But his heart and his head overruled his gut. This was Tori. From the night they'd met, he'd trusted her with more of himself than anyone else in his life—even if he'd been too scared to let her know. And this was the first test of his newly minted vow to hold nothing back.

"Do you want me to stop?" he asked.

She twisted her head around to look at his face. "What?"

"I know you're on the pill. And even though I've always been careful, as soon as I realized you and I might end up together again, I got tested. I'm clean." He injected his gaze with every ounce of sincerity he could muster. "You'll have to take my word for it. But I hope you know I'd never hurt you. Not intentionally."

She stared at him for a breath. Then another. Then, "God, I love you," she blurted.

Just like that, she destroyed him. The last shred of his control blown to smithereens.

"I'm taking that as a yes," he breathed and pushed between her legs.

Oh God. So hot. So…so…

She braced one hand on his shoulder and used the other to guide him home. He drove inside her, then froze, hissing a curse.

"What? Is there something—"

His chest heaved, his breath coming in strained gasps. "I've never… I didn't know it would feel this… oh, *geezus*."

It was so much more…everything. His body spasmed, bucking against her. He gritted his teeth, fighting for control, but it was too much. She wrapped her bare leg around his waist, and he was just *gone*, his thrusts hard and frantic. She'd barely caught up when he cursed again as the climax rolled over him, pulse after mind-altering pulse.

For a few long, shaken moments, he held her there. Then he groaned and let her slide to the floor, burying his face in her neck. "Well. That was humiliating."

Her fingers skimmed down his back, the caress more thoughtful than soothing. "You've never had sex without a condom? Ever?"

"No. I didn't expect... Well, obviously." He dragged in a deep lungful of air. What he needed here was a nice change of subject. "I lost track. Did I mention I love you too?"

Her fingers dug into his flesh for an instant, but her voice was amused. "No, but I got the picture."

He breathed some more until his head cleared enough to remind him he still had work to do. He slid his hands down her sides, thumbs tracing the creases of her thighs, where he knew she was particularly sensitive. There were a dozen ways he could pleasure her without leaving this door. "Now it's your turn."

She gently pushed his hands away. "Not right now. *Later*."

A little bubble of panic wound up through his chest. He had to make this right. "I need to finish what I started."

"I'm sure you do." She patted his butt. "But my orgasms—or lack thereof—aren't really about what *you* need."

He pushed away to examine her face. The gleam in her eyes. The smug smile. "Are you...gloating?"

"You bet your exceptionally fine ass." She stretched

her arms out and arched her back, smile widening at his indrawn breath. "I'm your first commando sex. It's almost like I took your virginity."

He groaned again, ducking his head at the reminder of his juvenile fumbling. "You're not going to let me forget this."

"Oh, hell no."

He gripped her hips, a strange sort of desperation clawing at him. If he let her down now... "Please. Just let me. I had this all planned. I wanted it to be perfect for you."

"Exactly." She grabbed his wrists and dragged his hands up to clasp between hers. "*This* is how real love works, Delon. It's hardly ever perfect, and it doesn't give a shit about your plans, and in the end, none of that matters. I know you would give me an amazing orgasm. But I want *you*. The guy who doesn't always get it right. Because damned if I'm gonna put up with some asshole who insists on perfection. It's a lot of work, and it's boring, and I suck at it."

"But..." He had no words. She'd sliced him open, seen all the twisted, ugly parts, and declared him...*not* perfect. Just real. And *hers*.

The idea, the unconditional acceptance, was staggering. And incredibly arousing. He kissed each of her knuckles. "If you give me a minute or two—"

"Nope. You're gonna have to live with not making the eight-second whistle on this one." She punched him in the arm. "And besides—you're supposed to be in Austin. All our hard work, and you're just tossing it down the drain—"

He cut her off with a kiss. "I needed to be here. For you. With you. There will be another rodeo next week, and the week after that, but I might only have this one chance to prove that you mean more to me than any championship in the world. And if that means we have to live somewhere else..." He squared his shoulders, determined. "We'll work it out. It's not that far to Santa Fe or Albuquerque or southern Colorado, and people there wouldn't be so—"

She gaped at him for a beat. Then she punched him again. "Don't be stupid. I just got my house fixed up. Why would I leave now?"

He scowled at her, confused. "You said you didn't want to come home."

"I think I might have lied." She breathed out a soft, incredulous laugh. "I think I actually came back hoping to find you."

And just when he thought his feelings couldn't get any more intense, she blew him away all over again. He flashed a crooked smile. "Then it's a good thing I waited for you."

Her laugh was soggy, the tears brimming in her eyes. He brushed them away with his knuckles. "I wish I could say this is the last time I'll make you cry."

"That's okay. I like a good fight. The makeup sex is totally worth it."

He laughed and folded her into his arms, rocking her

against him. "I'll fight every damn day to keep you, if that counts."

She melted into him—filling the space he'd been saving just for her—and drew a careful breath. "Even though I'm my mother's daughter?"

"That was a cheap shot." His arms tightened and he pressed a kiss to her temple. "Yes, you are relentless, but in a good way. I just pray I'm always on your side, because truthfully? You can be a little scary."

She snorted. "You're as pigheaded as I am—you just smother it in honey and watch people eat it up."

He laughed with the pure joy of being so *known*. Then he kissed her, long and sweet.

Finally she shoved him away, trying to scowl but not quite getting there. "After the rodeo, you can make me scream until someone calls hotel security. But first we have to get you to Austin."

"It's too late. Even if I had a plane, getting from the airport to the coliseum takes too long."

"You forget who you're talking to." She fumbled to clasp her bra and snap her shirt. "Button up, cowboy. Daddy's waiting out back with the helicopter."

―――――――――

If Senator Patterson insisted on flying in at the last minute, the Austin rodeo committee was determined to milk every possible drop of publicity out of it. They cleared an area for a landing pad in full view of the throng of spectators entering the building and made sure everyone knew why. When Delon bailed out, he was met with a roar of applause almost as loud as the screaming turbine of the helicopter.

Tori planted a quick, hard kiss on his mouth, then slapped him on the butt. "Go get 'em."

Even as he hustled inside to gear up, he knew in his bones how the ride would end. When a man made an entrance like that, he damn well better kick ass.

Epilogue

On the first day of December, Cole Jacobs rolled down the rear door of the cattle hauler to secure it behind the last bucking horse. Then he ambled along the side of the trailer, peering through the vent holes to be sure each of the occupants was settled in its compartment.

"Still seems like a waste when we could haul six horses to the Finals with the pickup and stock trailer," he told Delon.

"But then *we* wouldn't get the advertising." He jerked his thumb over his shoulder at the black Freightliner. The sleeper now featured a life-size action shot of Delon with *Sanchez Trucking* emblazoned below in foot-high letters. "And you wouldn't get to drive that."

That being Delon's brand-new bloodred Charger, his present to himself after winning the hundred-thousand-dollar bonus round at Calgary. Streaks of splattered black paint ran down each side, condensing into a silhouette of a bareback rider on the rear fender. Delon's signature graced the back side of the rear spoiler. And yeah, there was a booster seat in the back.

Shawnee had snorted and declared, "You're the only man I know who turned into a badass *after* he got shackled down."

Cole only glanced at the car and grunted, but he hadn't argued real hard when the swap had been suggested. Of course, that was when he thought Delon would be driving the semi. Now he peered doubtfully at the cab, where Tori was perched behind the wheel, watching them in the rearview mirror. "You're sure she's ready for this?"

"She's been hauling her own horses for years, she scored a hundred percent on her CDL exam, and we've hauled three loads of cattle for Sagebrush Feeders so she could get used to this trailer." And dazzle the pants off Jimmy Ray Towler. The man would never hire anything but Sanchez trucks for the rest of his life. "She's ready."

Cole didn't look satisfied, but he never did when it came to his precious livestock. Especially these six horses, the first Jacobs Livestock had ever sent to the National Finals. "You'll take over before you get into Las Vegas?"

"Cross my heart." Even if it meant a battle with Tori. Especially if. Delon grinned. He might be a latecomer to the concept, but he had gained a deep appreciation for makeup sex. He waved Cole off and swung up into the passenger's seat.

Tori tried to look blasé, but her eyes were dancing. "We're off?"

"Gas it, baby."

She grinned, shifting the Freightliner into gear. Delon tipped back in his seat, ripped open a Snickers, and prepared to enjoy every minute of the drive to the City of Sin, with scheduled rest breaks for the horses that would give them plenty of time for some sinning of their own. He'd been doing a lot more of that in the past nine months—not just the sinning but kicking back and letting go. As a result, his season had been unlike anything he'd ever experienced. He'd never won so many first-place checks, and he'd never heard so many eight-second whistles blow while he was flat on his back, knocking dirt out of his ears. Boom or bust. Between the two, he'd ended up in his usual spot entering the Finals—right in the middle of the pack.

The difference was now he knew he could take on anyone in any round and come out on top. And bit by bit, he was settling into his new groove and getting more consistent. If he could put it all together in Las Vegas, there was no telling how things might shake out. Lord knew the last few months had proven damn near anything was possible.

The internet storm had raged for weeks, taking a bizarre turn when the Texans got all up in arms because the Wyomingites were talking shit about their girl. Tori and Delon had practically been forgotten as the two sides screamed cyber insults at each other's states. They'd been on the verge of declaring war and forming volunteer armies when sites related to the whole mess started to crash. Every time a new social media page sprang up, it would be shut down within days, if not hours. Site administrators swore they had nothing to do with it and scrambled to patch up the holes in their security. Everyone had assumed the senator must be pulling strings, but when Tori said so to her sister, Elizabeth had laughed.

"Daddy's in the government. He doesn't know people who have those kinds of mad hacker skills," said the woman who was engaged to sweet-faced, unflappable Pratimi, who could probably hijack the entire internet if she set her mind to it. Further proof it wasn't wise to mess with any of the Patterson women or what they considered theirs. Which, thankfully, included Delon.

And speaking of…

"Your mother does understand that we are not sending Beni to a boarding school for gifted kids just because she's offering to pay?"

"No, but you might be able to put her off for a couple of years." Tori shot him a wicked smile. "Besides, I'd give it a week, max, before Beni educated them to the point that they were begging to send him home."

Delon shuddered, imagining the damage his child could do in that amount of time. Ever since Claire had informed them Beni was an actual genius, he'd been campaigning to skip kindergarten *and* first grade. "Does she test every kid who comes to dinner?"

"Only the ones she considers family."

Delon let that sink in and decided he would be pleased—for now. Claire was still one scary lady. And they'd always known Beni was smart, but it was a tad bit frightening to know he was literally capable of anything.

Or he could turn out to be the world's smartest truck driver, barring Tori. She wove flawlessly through the traffic in Amarillo, then merged onto the four-lane headed west. Beni had rejected both the Freightliner and the Charger in favor of flying in Wyatt's plane along with Violet and Joe. The thought made Delon a lot less nervous since his firsthand experience with Wyatt's skill as a pilot.

How all the bits and pieces of his life had come together into this big, jumbled whole was beyond him. He might never get accustomed to the sight of Senator Patterson sipping sweet tea on Miz Iris's deck, arguing farm subsidies with Steve. Even Shawnee had gotten sucked in, her presence for Thanksgiving declared mandatory when Miz Iris learned she wouldn't be spending it with family. Not a dull moment around that table, with her on one side and Gil on the other.

He'd thought he loved Tori the first time around. And he had, as much as either of them had been capable of at that point in their lives. Now, though, they were both so much…more. The depth and breadth of his feelings still terrified him sometimes, but at least he knew he wasn't in it alone.

The phone rang. Tori punched a button on the steering wheel, and Gil's voice came through the speakers.

"There's construction forty miles west of Albuquerque, but if you take a long lunch break, you'll get there after they knock off at five. And don't scratch my paint, Blondie."

Tori flipped him the bird without taking her eyes off the road.

"*Our* paint," Delon said. "Same goes for you and Cole with my car. I made him promise, scout's honor, to keep you away from the titty bars and whorehouses. My name is all over that thing."

Gil gave an evil chuckle. Then he said, "Speaking of putting your name on things, we're all gonna be in Vegas. Why don't you two tie the knot while we're there? Save a lot of hassle."

The suggestion sent Delon's heart tumbling end over end. He'd intended to propose, but he'd planned to wait until after the Finals, when he could work out the perfect time and place. Not rolling down Interstate 40 with his brother putting the words in his mouth.

"Thank you, Mr. Romance," Tori said. "If this dispatcher gig ever falls through, you have a bright future as a matchmaker."

Gil laughed and hung up. The truck hummed along in complete silence for almost five miles. Then Tori angled a look at him and raised her eyebrows. "Well?"

His heart hammered in triple time. "I... You want to?"

"Yeah. I do."

"Oh. Okay then."

She extended her hand and they sealed the

proposal not with a kiss but a fist bump. "I'll let my family know. Daddy intends to be there the whole ten days, and Elizabeth and Pratimi are flying in for the last three rounds."

"What about your mother?"

Tori shrugged. "I'll invite her, but she just got back from her own honeymoon. I doubt she can clear her schedule again this soon."

Of all the shocks, that one might've been the biggest. Once she'd accepted that Richard Patterson was truly done with politics, Claire had abruptly married the owner of a medical equipment company with whom she'd been *working closely for years*. The senator seemed stunned and even a little hurt. His dating life had been much more cautious, at least partially due to his daughters' mandate that all candidates be screened by them, and none could be more than fifteen years younger than him.

So he'd bought a horse instead, boarded it at Tori's, and started roping with her and Shawnee whenever he was in town. Fudge, especially, was ecstatic. He finally had a full-time friend. The cat was not amused.

Tori sighed happily. "We'll have the whole drive home for our first honeymoon."

"First?" Delon echoed.

"Please." She did a patented debutante eye roll. "We have a private jet, and my father will want to foot the bill. There will be a beach. Maybe our own island. Do you prefer the Mediterranean or the Caribbean?"

Delon gave a disbelieving laugh. "I will never get used to this."

"Sure you will." She reached over and patted his arm. "You've got the rest of your life."

He took another bite of his Snickers bar and smiled. From where he was sitting, it looked like it was gonna be one hell of a ride.

*Keep reading for a sneak peek of the next
book in the Texas Rodeo series*

TOUGHER *in* TEXAS

Chapter 1

ALL OF COLE'S PROBLEMS WOULD BE SOLVED IF HE just found a wife.

The thought popped into his head at the exact instant that a ton of bovine suddenly bellowed and kicked, slamming into the steel gate Cole was holding and knocking him flat on his ass. If Cole hadn't stood six foot six, he probably would've lost some teeth. The gate caught him in the chest instead and sent him sprawling in the dirt. His red heeler, Katie, barked once and launched herself at the bull to protect him, but Carrot Top just trotted off down the alley, more interested in checking the empty pens for leftover hay.

Cole scrambled to his feet and snarled as his gaze zeroed in on the bright-yellow cattle prod in the hand of one of the men who rushed to his aid. "What the *fuck* are you doing with that thing?"

The cowboy took a hasty step back, then another when Cole stalked toward him. "Just hurryin' things along."

"My stock moves just fine without a hotshot." Cole made sure of it, training them from birth to handle easily. The rodeo season was a cross-country marathon of long miles and strange places. Less stress equaled better performance, and even though the low-current buzz of the cattle prod was more startling than painful, Cole wanted his stock as relaxed as possible until the moment they exploded from the bucking chute. Carrot Top was an old pro. He'd earned the right to inspect the loading chute before setting hoof on the steep ramp.

And to come unglued when some asshole zapped him.

The cowboy ran out of room and backed up against the fence. Cole snatched the hotshot, busted it over his knee, and then tossed it back, the ends dangling by the wires that ran down the long shaft. "Pack that and the rest of your shit and get out of here."

The cowboy clutched the broken prod to his chest, jaw dropping. "But I'm your pickup man."

"Not anymore."

Cole turned his back and strode down the alley to

retrieve Carrot Top. As far as he was concerned, the conversation was over.

Half an hour later, his cell phone buzzed. He was tempted to ignore it, but she would only keep calling until he answered. There was a strong undercurrent of stubborn in the Jacobs gene pool. He heaved a deep sigh and put some distance between himself and the rest of the crew before he accepted the call, holding the phone three inches from his ear in anticipation of his cousin's displeasure.

"What the hell is wrong with you?" Violet yelled.

"He used a hotshot on Carrot Top."

"So ban him from the stock pens. Hell, ban him from the whole rodeo grounds except when he's working the performances, but did you have to fire him?"

"He used a hotshot on Carrot Top," Cole repeated, slower this time.

"I understand. It was stupid. But what do you suggest we do next weekend when you're the only pickup man in the arena?"

Cole hadn't thought about that at the time. He'd been thinking about it since, but hiring contract personnel was Violet's job. If she was here like normal, he wouldn't have had to put up with a stranger. He wouldn't have to put up with any of this crap. He could go back to just taking care of his stock and leaving all the *people* bullshit to Violet. He couldn't say that, though, and as usual, his brain collapsed under pressure and offered up only the one sentence in his defense. "He used a hotshot on *Carrot Top*."

Violet huffed out a breath so exasperated he swore he felt the breeze on his end of the line. "You do realize the doctor sentenced me to bed rest because my blood pressure is through the roof, right?"

Cole ducked his head, crushing a dirt clod with the toe of his boot. He wasn't trying to aggravate anyone, especially Violet. She was command central for Jacobs Livestock. The hell she'd been going through had thrown all of them for a loop, Violet most of all. She hadn't been sick a day in her first pregnancy, though Beni had decided to make an appearance six weeks early. She'd been prepared to be cautious and watchful. She had *not* expected to be sick as a dog practically from the moment she and Joe had seen the telltale line on the home pregnancy test.

Besides, Cole was almost as excited about the baby as its parents. He loved being Uncle Cole, and now a little girl? He grinned at the thought of a future full of ponies and pink cowboy boots—assuming his family didn't string him up for driving Violet into another premature labor.

Cole huffed out a breath, leaning a shoulder against the back of the infield bleachers. Around him, the empty rodeo grounds looked like a hangover—garbage cans overflowed with empty bottles, corners of banners drooped along the fences, spilled popcorn and a smashed glob of cotton candy littered the ground. Katie nosed around under the bleachers and came out packing a half-eaten hot dog. It all looked ill-used and abandoned—sort of like Cole felt.

Yes, he had put them in a tight spot, but there were some things he wouldn't tolerate when it came to his stock. Okay, many things. *Obsessive-compulsive prick* was another way of putting it, though only Joe dared say that to his face. He was family. Plus, he was a lot faster than Cole.

"Don't try to say I didn't warn you," Violet said, her voice laced with grim amusement.

Cole froze. She couldn't mean... "I thought you were kidding."

"No, I was not, any more than I was kidding when I told you to make this one work or *else*."

Panic churned Cole's gut. "Violet, you can't. There must be somebody else—"

"I refuse to even ask. This makes three perfectly good pickup men you've chased off. If you can't force yourself to get along, I'll send someone you can't fire."

"Don't. Please." He didn't hesitate to beg. If she followed through on her threat, he'd either be insane or under arrest by season's end in September. "Just one more. I promise—"

"Nope. I'm done. If you can find a replacement before tomorrow morning, I'll hire him. Otherwise..." He could hear her smirking, dammit. "Your new partner will meet you at Cuero."

"Violet, come on—"

The phone had gone dead. If he called back, it would go straight to voicemail. When Violet said she was done, she meant it.

He jammed the phone in his pocket and stomped

over to his rig, his stomach rumbling right along with the big diesel engines of the stock trucks that sat idling, waiting for him to lead the procession to the next rodeo. Yet another reason he needed to get on that wife thing. He'd never realized how much food it took to keep this big ol' body of his fueled until he'd had to start rustling it up for himself. Living with his aunt Iris, there'd never been any need to learn how to cook. But she was with his uncle Steve in Salinas, California, at one of the most venerable rodeos in the country, always held the third week of July. They did the subcontracting, hauling the very best of the Jacobs string to elite shows too big for any single producer to handle.

Leaving Cole to handle all of the rodeos where Jacobs Livestock was the lead contractor. And starve.

He scowled into the fridge in his trailer—cold cuts, store-bought rolls, and plastic deli tubs of gooey macaroni and potato salad. He slapped together three sandwiches, grabbed a Coke, and kicked aside a pair of jeans that had spilled out of the overstuffed laundry hamper. His socks were turning gray and there wasn't a crumb left from the last batch of cookies Miz Iris had mailed to him. He hadn't had a homemade dinner roll since the Fourth of July.

"This is no way to live, Katie girl."

The dog gave a little whine of agreement.

He slammed into the cab of his pickup and tossed one of the sandwiches to Katie in the passenger's seat. She ignored it. Even the dog was sick of cold cuts. At his growl of frustration, she cocked her head, the brown patches above her eyes creasing in concern.

He rubbed a hand over her head. "First, we call everybody we know and try to find a new pickup man. Then we're gonna figure out how to get us a wife."

Katie shot him a dubious look, then sighed and began to pick at her sandwich.

Chapter 2

As FAR AS SHAWNEE PICKETT WAS CONCERNED, WHEN most women went out to get a Brazilian, they were doing it all wrong.

Yawning, she stretched, then rolled over to admire the long, lean body sprawled beside hers. She trailed her finger down the dark bronze arm slung over the pillow and paused to wrap her hand around his biceps on the off chance she might be able to absorb some of the brilliance humming under his skin. That arm was property of the hottest young team roper to explode onto the pro rodeo scene in years. Maybe decades.

Some people might not be thrilled about the Brazilian invasion of a sport they liked to think belonged to North America, but Shawnee sure wasn't complaining.

Her phone buzzed on the nightstand, then began to dance to the tune of Garth's "Friends in Low Places." Tori. Shawnee let it play a few bars, then peeled herself away from all that tempting bare skin and picked up. "Yes, Mother?"

"I slept in, had breakfast, and drank two cups of

coffee. Then I read the Sunday *Dallas Morning News* front to back, so thanks to you, I've lost what little faith I had left in humanity." Damn. Tori always made sarcasm sound so classy. "You've been holed up in that room for almost twelve hours. Don't you think you've had enough?"

"Says the woman who was just whinin' about not gettin' to wrap her hands around Delon's hot little ass for another week."

At the sound of Shawnee's voice, Joao Pedro Azeveda—alias J.P. because most people were too lazy to learn to pronounce his name—stirred. Without opening his eyes, he reached out and hauled Shawnee over to where he could nestle his face in her bare cleavage. She sighed.

"I heard that," Tori said. "I'm loading the horses right now. If you're not standing out in the parking lot when I swing by the motel, I will keep going and let you hitchhike home."

Now J.P.'s hands were getting in on the action, despite the fact that he'd only slept for four hours. Lord. Twenty-two was a beautiful thing. Shawnee stifled a moan. Maybe a quickie...

"Don't even," Tori warned. In the background, Shawnee heard the sound of hooves thudding on the floor of the trailer as the horses hopped in. "If that boy is too weak to swing a rope at Bandera tonight, his partner will wring your neck."

Aw, hell. Shawnee caught J.P.'s wrist before either of

them could get too heated up. He lifted his head and cocked it, questioning. Shawnee shook her head, pointing to the phone, then the door. He flashed her a coaxing grin as he slid his palm down her side and along her hip, pulling her against him so she could feel what she was missing. Her body responded in kind. She breathed a silent curse and shook her head again. He did one of those shrugs that was worth a thousand words, rolled over, and buried his face in the pillow.

"Ten minutes," Tori said.

"You know you suck, right?"

Tori gave an evil laugh and hung up. She didn't judge, bless her heart, but she also didn't make idle threats.

Nine minutes later, Shawnee hopped around muttering curses while she tried to tug jeans on over shower-damp skin. Might help if she had slightly less butt to stuff into them. As she dragged a comb through her wet mop of brown curls, she gave J.P.'s gangly body one last, lingering glance. Asleep, he looked even younger. Suddenly she felt every one of the eleven years between them, and for an instant, she wished…

She shook off the weird little ache, grabbed her wallet, and headed for the door. This was how she rolled—keeping it loose and easy with guys who didn't expect her to be there when they woke up.

And yeah, she was aware that *loose* and *easy* were the most polite of the words tossed around behind her back. Well, fuck those sanctimonious assholes and the donkeys they rode in on. This was the life that had chosen her, and she was bound and determined to live it to the hilt. She didn't hear J.P. or any of his predecessors complaining.

She spared a glance in the mirror and winced. Without makeup, her face was a doughy blob with a couple of finger holes poked in it for eyes. Oh well. She could slap on a little something in the pickup.

J.P. didn't twitch when she opened the door. She didn't wake him to say goodbye. Spanish she could handle. So far, Portuguese had eluded her, and JP had only mastered the bare bones of English, which wasn't all bad. When their paths did cross, they never wasted time on chitchat, though she wouldn't have minded hearing him explain how he'd learned to snatch up both hind feet on wild, ass-slinging steers.

As she stepped outside, a pickup and horse trailer rolled around the corner, right on schedule. After the cool dimness of the motel room, the midmorning sunlight slapped Shawnee in the face like a hot, damp towel. Still, her heart did a little happy dance at the sight of the rig. All hers. *Turn 'Em and Burn 'Em Champion Heeler*, the bold letters scrawled across the double-cab declared. Three years, and she still got a thrill every time she looked at it. Or its twin, which was parked in Tori's driveway.

The icing on the cake had been the monster prize money that came along with the pickups. Enough for Shawnee to finally get rid of her granddad's rickety old stock trailer and buy herself a decent used gooseneck with a small but adequate living quarters in the front section. Sure as hell beat camping in the back of her old rust-bucket pickup.

The rig barely rolled to a stop to let Shawnee hop in before Tori swung back out on the street and hit the gas. Shawnee dug her sunglasses out of the center console, jammed them on her face, then squinted through the blessedly dark lenses. Tori Patterson Hancock Sanchez didn't look like the daughter of Texas's version of royalty. Her caramel-brown hair was yanked through the loop of her baseball cap, and she wasn't wearing a scrap of makeup. Her jeans were smudged with dirt from the previous evening's roping, though her sky-blue tank top was clean. She filled it out better than when they'd first met. Either Delon's chocolate habit was contagious or being disgustingly well loved gave her an appetite.

Speaking of which…

"Can we swing past a hamburger stand? I'm starving." At Tori's impatient grunt, Shawnee scowled. "What, you're in such a rush to get out of town you can't spare three minutes to feed me? You got something against this place?"

Tori threw her a dark look. "My memories aren't quite as pleasant as yours."

In other words, she'd spent the last eight hours brooding because she'd missed their last steer and a shot at winning third place and a couple thousand dollars. Tori was good at many, many things, but failure was not one of them, which made her an excellent partner and an occasional pain in the ass. She took pity, though, and pulled over at the Dairy Queen on the edge of town. Shawnee had just dug into her one fast food fix of the week when her phone rang again, this time to the tune of Joe Diffie's "Pickup Man."

Shawnee's pulse kicked up its heels. "Hey, Violet. Fancy hearing from you on a Sunday morning. Does this mean what I think it does?"

Violet made a growling noise. "Can you be in Cuero by Wednesday at noon?"

Shawnee's pulse did another jig. She'd been both anticipating and dreading this call since Violet had asked her to be on standby. On the downside, keeping her promise meant no serious team roping for two months. Shawnee hadn't gone more than a few days without roping since back when...

She flicked that thought aside and concentrated on the here and now, something she'd been doing so long it was second nature.

She'd agreed to Violet's proposal because she was ready for a change. Her life had settled into a groove the last couple of years—rope with Tori, work at the cattle auction, train some horses, hang out at the Jacobs ranch when they weren't on the road—but a comfortable rut was still a rut. Time to shake things up. Or in this case, some*one*.

"I'll be there," she said, grinning as she hung up.

"Sounds like I'm losing a partner for the rest of the summer."

"Yep." Shawnee tipped back her seat and got comfortable, munching fries and mentally making lists of everything that needed doing before she could pack up and leave. "You'll have your weekends free to chase your pretty husband around the country."

After ten years on the rodeo trail, Delon finally had his gold buckle—*World Champion Bareback Rider*—and was well on his way to defending the title. Tori certainly wouldn't mind missing a few ropings to spend more time with him. Delon was a sight to see even when he wasn't spurring a bronc, and given how long it'd taken the two of them to get their shit together, they were bound and determined not to let it get scattered again.

Shawnee jabbed a french fry into the ketchup so hard it broke in half. All her cronies were pairing off, turning into husbands and wives, daddies and mommies. She had accepted that it would happen eventually. She wouldn't pretend it didn't bother her at all, but she'd learned to accept it—most of the time. It was like being born knowing you were allergic to ice cream. Just looking at it might be enough to make your mouth water, but as long as you'd never tasted it, you didn't really know what you were missing.

"You should take my trailer," Tori said. "I won't be using it while you're gone, and yours is too small to live in for that long."

Shawnee debated for all of ten seconds. The living quarters in Tori's trailer were like a top-of-the-line

RV—four times the size of Shawnee's, with actual appliances and satellite TV. "That'd be great. Thanks."

Tori shot her a curious look. "Are you nervous?"

"Nah. Violet and her dad put me through the wringer at all those practices and dragged me along to a couple of high school rodeos." Her grin widened. "Besides, it's a dream job. After all these years of just doing it for fun, I'm gonna get paid to irritate Cole Jacobs."

Acknowledgments

A huge thank-you to Jared Rogerson, who allowed me to use his song in this book and whose experience as a professional bareback rider shines through in all his music. You can find him and "Ninety or Nothin'" at JaredRogerson.com.

To my amazing editor, Mary Altman, who gently but firmly reins in my infatuations with subplots and minor characters, delightful as they may be, and the art department at Sourcebooks Casablanca for allowing me to indulge my pathological need for authenticity with this cover. And to my fabulous agent, Holly Root, without whom I would never have gotten to work with this wonderful team.

Thank you to Richard and Dale Bird and Three Forks Saddlery (via my sister Lola) for lending us equipment for the photo shoot, and to Beau Michael for providing both the chaps and the inspiration for the scene in *Reckless in Texas* in which Violet and Joe meet for the first time. For Beau and everyone else who is or has been a rodeo kid—Beni Sanchez is all of us.

A big pat on the back to my invaluable readers, Janet

and June, for their brutal honesty but also for being there to tell me that no, the book doesn't suck. Just these few parts.

To Tanya Hancock, who, over a few beers at a rodeo, shared her experiences as a young widow, the final pieces that brought Tori into focus for me.

And as always, kudos to my husband, my son, and my parents for giving me the time and space to work when I need to and tolerating my frequent bouts of writer brain, during which I have forgotten everything from the tractor parts I was supposed to pick up in town to the fact that I have a child, let alone that he requires feeding on a semi-regular basis.

And finally, here's to all the women like me and Shawnee and Tori who are proud to say that they Rope Like a Girl. May you do the same, in all aspects of your life.

About the Author

In memory of Kari Lynn Dell; your
books will always bring us joy.

———————

Kari Lynn Dell was a ranch-raised Montana cowgirl who
attended her first rodeo at two weeks old and existed in
a state of horse-induced poverty her entire life. She lived
on the Blackfeet Reservation in her parents' bunkhouse
along with her husband, her son, and Max the Cowdog.
There was a tepee on her lawn, Glacier National Park
on her doorstep, and Canada within spitting distance.

TOUGHER IN TEXAS

He's got five rules, and she's aiming
to break them all.

Rodeo producer Cole Jacobs has his hands full running Jacobs
Livestock. He can't afford to lose a single cowboy, so when Cousin
Violet offers to send a more-than-capable replacement, he's got no
choice but to accept. He expects a grizzled Texas good ol' boy. He
gets Shawnee Pickett.

Wild and outspoken, Shawnee's not looking for anything but a
good time. It doesn't matter how quickly the tall, dark, and intense
cowboy gets under her skin—Cole deserves something real, and
Shawnee can't promise him forever. Too bad Cole's not the type to
give up when the going gets tough…

"A fun, wild ride! You need to pick
up a Kari Lynn Dell."
—B.J. Daniels, *New York Times* bestselling author

For more info about Sourcebooks's books and authors, visit:
sourcebooks.com

FEARLESS IN TEXAS

He'd step in front of a bull to save a life, but even
he's no match for a girl this Texas tough.

Rodeo bullfighter Wyatt Darrington's got it all figured out. He may be
on the fast track to the Hall of Fame, but he knows he'll always be an outsider to people like Melanie Brookman. Texas-born and bred, with the
arena in her blood, Melanie's come to see Wyatt as her personal enemy,
and that suits him just fine—this way, she'll never realize the truth.

He's been in love with her for years.

Melanie's always been a fighter. But now her infamous temper's
got her on the ropes, and there's nowhere left to run but toward the
man she swore she'd never trust...and this time, there's no denying
just how hot he makes her *burn*.

**"When it comes to sexy rodeo cowboys,
look no further than Kari Lynn Dell."**
—B.J. Daniels for *Fearless in Texas*

For more info about Sourcebooks's books and authors, visit:
sourcebooks.com

LAST CHANCE RODEO

He came to Blackfeet Nation looking for his missing horse.
Instead he found the heart he'd lost along the way.

Four years ago, one thoughtless moment cost David Parsons everything. Now he's finally tracked his lost horse to the Blackfeet Reservation and is ready to reclaim his pride. But the troubled young boy who's riding Muddy now has had more than his fair share of hard knocks, and his fierce guardian Mary Steele will do whatever it takes to make sure this isn't the blow that levels him. Soon David is faced with a soul-wrenching dilemma: take his lost shot at rodeo glory...or claim what could be his last chance to make his shattered heart whole?

"Dell takes you on a fun, wild ride!"
—B.J Daniels, *New York Times* bestselling author

For more info about Sourcebooks's books and authors, visit:
sourcebooks.com